THE ALEXANDER INHERITANCE

ERIC FLINT
GORG HUFF
PAULA GOODLETT

A Baen Book

Baen Publishing Enterprises
P.O. Box 1403
Riverdale, NY 10471
www.baen.com

ISBN: 978-1-4814-8248-6

Cover art by Patrick Turner
Maps by Michael Knopp

First Baen printing, July 2017

Distributed by Simon & Schuster
1230 Avenue of the Americas
New York, NY 10020

10 9 8 7 6 5 4 3 2 1

Pages by Joy Freeman (www.pagesbyjoy.com)
Printed in the United States of America

CONTENTS

Maps   vi

The Alexander Inheritance   1

Cast of Characters   389

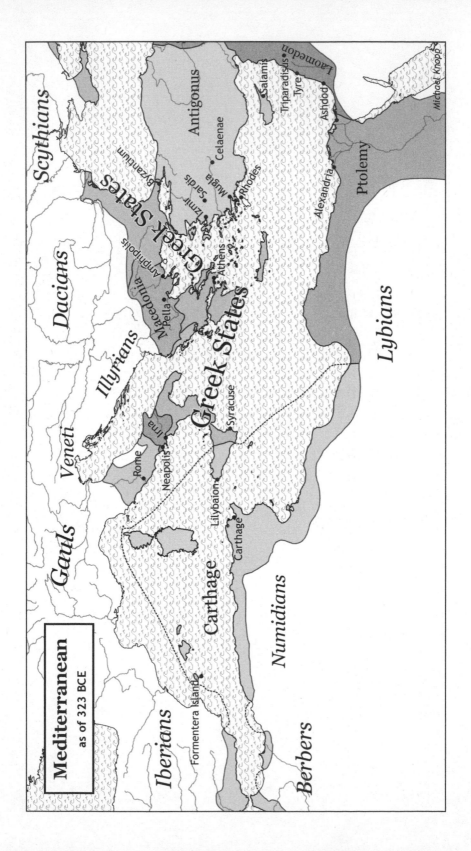

Mediterranean
as of 323 BCE

Michael Knopp

Scythians

Gauls

Dacians

Veneti

Illyrians

Iberians

Formentera Island

Rome

Neapolis

Etna

Numidians

Berbers

Carthage

Carthage

Lilybaion

Syracuse

Greek States

Macedonia

Pella

Amphipolis

Byzantium

Athens

Izmir

Sardis

Celaenae

Antigonus

Salamis

Tripardisus

Tyre

Ashdod

Laomedon

Mus̆a

Rhodes

Alexandria

Ptolemy

Lybians

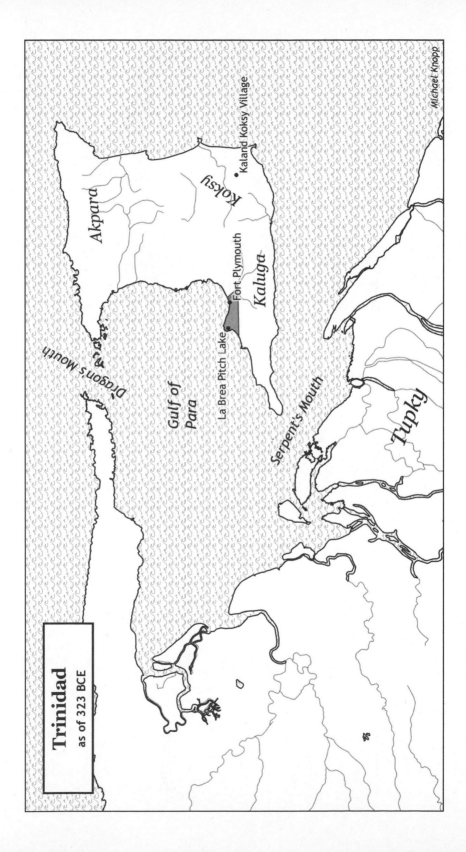

Trinidad
as of 323 BCE

Akpara

Koksy

Kaland Koksy Village

Fort Plymouth

Kaluga

Dragon's Mouth

La Brea Pitch Lake

Gulf of
Para

Serpent's Mouth

Tupky

Michael Knopp

PROLOGUE

"Eurydice." Roxane bowed slightly in acknowledgement, but was careful not to bow too deeply. She couldn't afford to let the fiery sixteen-year-old think she was in any way superior. Roxane was twenty-two and the mother of Alexander the Great's heir. Her beauty had captivated Alexander, but without Alexander as protector, Roxane's beauty was as much a danger as an asset. Tall, with rich, lustrous black hair and eyes, a lush figure and a dancer's grace, Roxane was a temptress whether she wanted to be or not. But she wasn't Macedonian like Eurydice or Alexander's sister Cleopatra. The generals wouldn't be competing to marry Alexander's beautiful widow...just to use her.

Eurydice, on the other hand, wasn't beautiful at all. The teenager had a beak of a nose and an almost mannish face, full of sharp edges and hard features. But she had a presence that was potentially dangerous to both Roxane and her son. Eurydice was a powerful speaker and a member of the dynasty, Philip II's niece. Roxane was noble, but not Macedonian.

Eurydice had the bloodlines and knew it. She barely nodded in returning Roxane's bow. "Will you support me against Antipater when he gets here to Triparadisus?" she asked bluntly.

"Why should I risk such a thing?" Roxane looked at Eurydice, ignoring the lamps that had been lit as the sun got low in the sky, paying no more attention to the polished wooden floor of the hunting lodge, the rich draperies that hung from the walls or the expensive rugs. She pointed to the figure watching them from the corner of the room, a little boy with black hair and eyes and the features of Alexander the Great already beginning to show in his face. "Will my son be safer with you as regent than Antipater?"

"I am the wife of Philip III Arrhidaeus, half-brother of Alexander."

"He's an idiot."

"No, he's not. He just thinks differently."

"Drawing curving lines and numbers on paper doesn't make him any less an idiot." Roxane forced herself to stop. She didn't actually dislike Philip. She resented that he was co-king with her son, who already understood things that Philip never would. And she was afraid of Eurydice, who, it seemed likely, would have Roxane and her son killed to pave her way to power.

"Never mind," she said. "Whether he 'just thinks differently' or not, having you as regent is not something that fills my heart with peace."

"And Antipater does?"

"Antipater is seventy-six years old and not long for this world. Also, my son doesn't stand between him and the throne."

"I wouldn't count on that if I were you," Eurydice insisted. "He has sons, after all. Think, Roxane. If we are allied, the army will listen to us."

Eurydice tried to put on a wheedling tone, but Roxane didn't believe it. Eurydice was good at commanding, and her speeches could move an army. Had, in fact, over the weeks that they had been traveling from the disastrous battle on the Nile. But the teenage firebrand didn't wheedle well, especially women. In this case, she had focused on the short-term goal of stopping Antipater and assumed that Roxane would fail to see the danger she represented.

"And how long will our alliance last? You are as much a pawn of the generals as I, but were I to help you to become a queen, I would be sacrificed in an instant, and my son with me."

"You're a fool. Perdiccas is as dead as Alexander. The generals are all out for themselves. The empire is coming apart and bleeding its honor onto the ground as Alexander's soldiers kill each other."

"Eumenes maintains his loyalty to the Argead dynasty."

"Eumenes is a Greek, not a Macedonian, or he'd be rebelling

with the rest. And anyway, the army has already declared him outlaw. It will be made official once Antipater is regent. The generals won't have any choice. Eumenes isn't going to come riding out of the east to rescue you and little Alexander. Nor me and Philip. We'll have to rescue ourselves."

It would have been a good argument, Roxane thought, *if I could trust Eurydice as far as I could throw her. And Eurydice is the wrestler, not me.*

Life in the household of Alexander the Great had been a mixture of terror and exultation from the beginning. Terror because Alexander's generals weren't happy that he married a Bactrian. Exultation because Alexander was truly a great man, frightening and tempestuous, but a man of great and grand dreams. A man who, if his life hadn't been cut short, might have melded all the peoples of the world into one people. A man who saw past the surface, who could even see civilization, or at least the potential for it, in a blond Gaul or a Roman.

But that dream was as dead as Alexander now, and the generals had turned into jackals.

And Eurydice was a hungry tigress, swishing her tail and ready to pounce.

CHAPTER 1

Port Berry, Royal Cay, Bahamas
6:15 AM

At dawn, the *Reliance* was alongside and the fuel lines were being attached. Dag Jakobsen watched through his camera feed. There were three flat-screen monitors set into the wall next to his desk. One was showing the fuel line hookup, the second would show the fuel flow and fuel levels in the form of a bar graph as soon as fueling started. *And there it goes*, Dag thought. The third was his computer monitor, which had a form that Dag would be filling out as the fueling proceeded. There was a leak in the fuel line coming from *Barge 14*, but it seemed to be very minor. Dag zoomed in on the connection and saw that it was only a few drops. He made a note on the form.

The *Reliance* and *Barge 14* together made up an ATB, articulated tug barge. While attached they were one ship, but the *Reliance* could detach from *Barge 14* in a few minutes to perform other functions while *Barge 14* was being loaded or unloaded.

Dag was lucky to get this slot on the *Queen of the Sea*. The newest ship of Royal Cruise Line had flex fuel engines and was larger than any other in the line. This was a load of fuel oil, just as a matter of price. They had gotten a bargain on the oil, while the methanol was still pricey. The great thing about flex fuel engines was they could burn anything: fuel oil, ethanol, methanol, even gasoline or crude oil. If it was liquid and would burn, they could use it for fuel.

Then the power went out. Dag lost his video feeds and heard a *boom*. The *boom* was followed by a crunching sound, and the ship shook.

That was bad. This was a four-thousand-passenger cruise ship. It didn't shake. Not unless there was very, very heavy weather or a tidal wave. Dag was already out of his chair, running for the fuel-loading area, when the emergency power came on.

Arriving at the forward fuel loading station, Dag heard a welter of shouted arguments. The room was a large one with pipes painted in bright colors to indicate the type of liquid they carried, but even on a new ship and with a good crew this was a working area. Dirt, smudges of oil, and the other natural byproducts of work being done were present and so was a bucket with a mop in a corner, ready to fight the never-ending battle against the oil and grime. Sunlight poured into the space from an opened porthole the size of a garage door. Four fifteen-centimeter-wide fuel lines went from the red pipes out the porthole.

"What was that?" Bayani Pascual asked.

"Dammit, Bayani. The *Princess* is gone, and so is that bar on the point. Hell, the *point* is gone. Will you stop asking what it was?"

"But what was it?" Bayani almost whined.

And suddenly Dag was afraid. Because while Bayani wasn't the brightest crewman on the refueling detail, he was perhaps the most phlegmatic. Bayani was nearly two meters tall and weighed upwards of a hundred kilos. He was the biggest Filipino Dag had ever met, and as calm and unflappable as you could hope for. Besides, Romi Clarke was sounding belligerent, and the little Jamaican was not someone Dag would want to meet in a dark alley.

"Then tell me, Romi. What happened?" Dag shouted over the hubbub.

Romi spun, and then visibly got himself under control. His dark skin was gray under the normal color, and he pointed out the port. "The *Princess of the Sea* is gone, Mr. Jakobsen. Just gone. Like it was never there. There was a flash, like lightning way too close and a clap like thunder right on it. Then everything was different. And something's happened dockside." Dockside was the other side of the ship. The *Reliance* had pulled up along seaside, as was standard practice. "And the Point Bar is gone. Hell, Mr. Jakobsen, the *point* is gone."

Dag almost called Romi a liar, but by then he'd reached the port and could see for himself. To avoid panicking, he focused on his job. He checked the fuel lines. They were still attached. He leaned out the port and looked at the *Reliance*. Tug and barge were still locked to one another and still tied up to the *Queen*, but *Barge 14*'s cylindrical fenders were compressing like marshmallows, as *Barge 14* bounced against the hull of the *Queen of the Sea*. The fenders were big, heavy, rubber cylinders which meant that Romi was probably right about that, as well. Something was disturbing the water and that almost had to be something on shore. There was a shore line visible ahead of the ship, but it wasn't the shore that should be there. And, sure enough, their sister ship was gone. A vessel weighing almost 150,000 tons had just . . . vanished.

Dag headed to the wall and pushed the intercom button. "Bridge, what's going on? Should we stop refueling?"

"We don't know, Dag," Apprentice Deck Officer Douglas Warren said. "I'm looking out at a town that ain't there anymore. I don't mean it's wrecked, except the part right next to the docks. I mean it's gone. As though it had never been built. Even the land is different."

"Right, Doug. The point is gone. We can see that from here."

"It's not the point. It's *us*. Us and the docks, and maybe half a block of the port. We're not where we were anymore. Hell, Dag, the *sun's* not where it was a minute ago. Look, no one knows what's going on yet, but it's a safe bet we are going to need full fuel tanks. Captain says to top them up."

"We'll do that, Doug." Dag turned away from the ship's intercom. "You heard, people. We continue refueling."

It was then that the regular lights came back on.

Dag got on the radio and called Joe Kugan, the captain for the *Reliance*. The *Reliance*, with *Barge 14* attached, had roughly one hundred fifty thousand barrels of fuel bunkerage, a crew of seven and a top speed of twelve knots.

Captain Joe Kugan was in the pilot house when whatever it was happened. He was looking at the *Queen*, not at the shore, so he was only momentarily blinded by the flash, but nearly lost his footing as not just the *Reliance* but also *Barge 14* rocked violently.

When he regained his balance, he looked around and saw that the world had been replaced by a new and different place. Instead of the flat landscape typical of islands in the Bahamas, he was looking at an island that didn't have much in the way of elevation but had more than he'd been looking at a short time before. The vegetation looked wrong, too, although he couldn't have said exactly why. Kugan's knowledge of botany was abysmal and his interest even lower.

For a moment, he felt a strong desire to panic or beat the crap out of someone. By the time he was back under control, the radio call from Dag was coming in. Given the circumstances, Joe was tempted to tell Dag to screw himself and stop the pumping till they knew what was going on. But he didn't. There were contracts involved and if he refused to finish the refueling, he would be in a lot of trouble. The *Reliance* or *Barge 14* was still bouncing against the *Queen*, but most of the wave front was gone on out to sea. The waves had stirred up the water, and what had been fairly pristine Caribbean ocean was now a lot cloudier.

Off an unknown island
Late afternoon

Lars Floden, the captain of the *Queen of the Sea*, looked down the table at the assembled staff. The conference room on the bridge deck was full. It was on the port side, just aft of the bridge and had one wall of smart glass windows. Right now the windows were set to opaque white. The opposite wall had cabinets and a countertop to hold whatever was needed from snacks to papers. Also a projector, so that the smart windows could be used as large display screens if needed.

Jane Carruthers was doing a really good stiff upper lip. He wasn't surprised, as she was very British, even for a Brit. A thin woman, with a ready smile that hid her thoughts admirably. The hotel manager was not in the chain of command, but was—in a sense—second only to Lars in real authority, and in some circumstances, she might hold even more.

Not these circumstances, though. "How are the passengers doing, Jane?" he asked.

"Congressman Wiley is threatening to have our whole company barred from operating out of the United States." Carruthers twitched a half smile for a moment. "I'm fairly sure that he's playing for the camera phones, though, since he's not stupid and knows perfectly well that isn't going to happen."

Her smile died. "There was one heart attack—not fatal, thankfully—and quite a few panicked passengers, and some falls."

Jane turned to Dr. Laura Miles, the head of the ship's medical department. Miles had two doctors, five nurse practitioners, and five registered nurses as well as nurse's aides, in her department. It wasn't exactly a hospital aboard ship, but it was a decent emergency room.

"The heart attack is stable and only one of the falls resulted in a broken bone," said Miles. "So far we haven't lost anyone on board. The docks didn't fare so well. It was too early for the shore activities, but a lot of the shops were getting ready. We had over fifty injuries over there and four deaths when the buildings came down. The fatalities included Anne O'Hare, who apparently had an arm cut off when whatever it was happened. She was in the back of a shop and the building collapsed on her, making it impossible for her to do anything or for anyone to reach her in time. At least it was probably quick. She would have bled out in minutes and lost consciousness even faster."

She looked at Floden. "Captain, that many injuries put a major strain on our supplies. We need resupply and we need them soon."

Staff Captain Anders Dahl cut in. "We have all the shore side personnel on board for now. It's unsafe on the docks and worse in the shops behind them." Anders paused for a beat. "Captain, should I have people going through the ruins for salvage?"

Lars Floden looked back at his number two. Staff captain was the same rank on a cruise ship that executive officer would be on a warship. The cruise lines did it that way so they could have two captains, and thus two captain's tables. Regardless of the titles, the staff captain had much the same job as a warship XO, including bringing questions to the captain that the captain would rather avoid.

Questions like this one. They didn't have a clue what had happened. It was possible that they were going to need everything in those buildings, down to the toilet seats. But the buildings over there were half-collapsed, and Lars wasn't prepared to send his sailors into a situation like that if he didn't have to.

"No, at least not yet, Anders," he said. "I doubt there's anything over there worth risking our people's lives for."

"The Cabana Drugstore," said Dr. Miles. "Unless we can get medical supplies, we are going to start losing people to chronic conditions that are treated with drugs." She looked at Lars. "And one of the losses is going to be me. Our supply of warfarin is very limited, and my prescription won't last forever. We can use aspirin and it will help, but people like me who have heart issues are going to be in real trouble if we can't get back in touch with civilization, Captain. Most of our passengers aren't nursing home ready, or at least they weren't before this. But a lot of them *were* assisted living ready."

"Sorry, Doc," Anders said. "I was over there just after the event. The part of the Cabana that held the drugs was on the other side of the—" He paused, apparently looking for the right word. "—line of demarcation. Whatever brought us here left the drugs in the Cabana Drugstore behind. There was some of the over-the-counter stuff on this side of the line." Anders looked over at Captain Floden.

"Sure, Anders. Grab anything that's out in the open. Just don't risk our people digging through stuff."

"Captain, where are we?" Daniel Lang, the chief security officer, blurted.

The sun hadn't set, though it had shifted in the moment of transition from early morning to midafternoon, east to west. Time of year was harder to say. It depended on where on Earth they were. There were people on the island they were next to, but they were staying out of sight, at least for now. The sun was farther south than it should be even in midwinter in the Caribbean. If the compass readings were right, they were in the northern temperate zone, not the tropics.

They had lost satellite communications. Both radio and GPS were gone. So were all the familiar works of man, aside from the *Queen of the Sea*, the *Reliance*, the dock and about a block of Port Berry, the little town on the company's private island. The dock and the block or so of town weren't in great shape. They had ended up partly over water instead of land and had tilted. Most of the buildings had collapsed.

Lars couldn't help feeling that whatever had happened had to be the work of someone or something, because it didn't make sense that any sort of natural occurrence would pick up his ship and the fuel barge and not chop them into little pieces. The lozenge-shaped zone of transference had to be just the right size and shape and had to have just the right orientation. To have that happen by accident was like having an avalanche build the Taj Mahal. Well, not really. But it sure wasn't the sort of thing that happened by chance.

He'd read a magazine article a couple of years ago analyzing the Grantville and Alexander disasters, which had included speculation by some scientists that whatever caused the catastrophes didn't seem to be simply random cosmic accidents. But he couldn't remember any of the details. When he had time, he'd have to see if he could find copies of the article—or, better yet, find a passenger who had some real expertise on the subject. The odds that such a passenger was aboard the ship were actually not bad. People who went on cruises tended to be better educated than average and included a fair percentage of scientists and academics.

All of that had been circulating through Lars' mind since the event, bouncing off his assumptions and being modified as more information was added. The ship's sonar was working just fine and the bottom of the ocean was different in an oval-shaped patch below the ship. Or, more accurately, the bottom of the ocean was different outside that oval-shaped patch just under the ship, taking into account the chunk of dock and shore that had come with them.

Lars looked back at Daniel. "I don't know. I don't even know what universe we're in. It appears we're at least on an analog of Earth, but we clearly aren't in the same place we were"—Lars looked at the clock on the wall—"three hours ago. For all I..." He took a breath and reined in his speculation. "We may know more after the sun goes down and we get a look at the night sky. In the meantime, we need to keep the passengers and the crew as calm as we can and avoid useless speculation."

Lars turned to Staff Captain Anders Dahl. "Anders, where are we on food?"

"We have seven days' worth without rationing. We can stretch that a day or two by just limiting the servings in the all-you-can-eat buffets, and with real rationing we can double it. With severe rationing, starting right now, we might last a month. That would be pushing things a lot. We're going to need resupply of food probably sooner than drugs."

The meeting continued and not much new was discovered.

However, things that were minor before had suddenly gained much greater significance.

Congressman Allen "Al" Wiley, Fourth District, Utah, sat in his stateroom and fumed. He was here because his daughter Charlene was marrying that moron, Dick Gibson, and wanted to be married by a ship's captain. Romantic, she called it. Al called it crap, though never in public. They could have made a lot of political capital out of this wedding if they had just stayed in Provo and done it there.

But Charlene had wanted "romantic," and her mother agreed with her. Darn Doris, with all her silly romance novels. And now some sort of disaster had happened. They were stuck out here on the company's island and he wasn't being allowed to make a call back to Washington to get some help. Wiley didn't believe for one minute that the ship's communications with the rest of the world were out. Any sort of disaster that would cause that would have wrecked the ship entirely. The lights were working. Hell, his phone had bars, all five bars, and if his phone was working, the only reason he wasn't getting through to Washington was that damn Norwegian captain was blocking his calls. That had to be it.

Al's mind cycled back around. Maybe it was a conspiracy. Royal Cruise Lines had screwed the pooch somehow and were trying to cover it up. He called Amanda, his aide. "Amanda, you get me a meeting with that captain. Not the hotel manager, the captain."

"Yes, sir," Amanda Miller agreed.

Amanda stopped pacing when her cell rang with the congressman's ringtone. After he finished, she sat down on the bed in her stateroom and called Jane Carruthers. She made the request as tactfully as she could. "I know that this is an emergency situation, Ms. Carruthers, but the congressman is on several committees that have oversight over corporations like Royal Cruise Lines. So, if you could free up a few minutes for the congressman to make sure he and the captain are reading from the same playbook... Believe me, it will save us all trouble in the long run."

"I'm sure you're right, Miss Miller. And under other cir-cumstances, the captain would be happy to make time for the congressman. But we are still trying to figure out what's going on." She sighed audibly—and intentionally, Amanda was sure.

"There isn't anything that the captain could tell him that hasn't been part of the announcements already made."

Amanda bit her lip. There had been announcements, one almost immediately after the event, explaining that the ship was in no immediate danger, but that something out of the ordinary had happened and for the moment the crew asked that people stay inside and off the Promenade Deck. Fifteen minutes later, the prohibition against going on the Promenade Deck had been removed, but shore excursions were still off limits. Amanda had immediately gone up to the Promenade Deck and looked out on a disaster. The dock was tilted, actually *tilted*, and the block or so of buildings behind it were in ruins. The crew was running around doing rescue work, trying to save the people who had lived and worked in those buildings. She reported to the congressman, and Al immediately tried to call Washington to get some help. It was the fact that he couldn't get through that made the congressman so angry. He wanted to help, and they weren't letting him.

By now, Amanda was convinced that the satellite receiver on the ship was down for some reason. And it was clear that something drastic had happened to Royal Cay Island. "You need to get the captain to tell the congressman what the problem is with the phones."

"We don't know what's wrong with the phones," Jane said. "Whatever it is, it's not on the ship. Everything on the ship is working just fine. The problem is... Amanda, I honestly think the problem is with the satellites."

"That's impossible. Nothing could take out the satellites, not even a nuclear war. So unless we've been invaded by Martians, it can't be the satellites."

"Amanda, the *sun* moved," Jane said. "Look at your watch. It's supposed to be 10:00 AM in December in the Caribbean. The sun should be to our southeast—but it's west of us, and obviously a lot closer to sunset than sunrise. It's also farther south than it should be, by a considerable margin. Like fall in Maryland or Spain."

Amanda did look. She knew where the sun should be and she saw where it was. "Thanks, Jane. For telling me." She hadn't noticed till Jane mentioned it, too focused on the broken buildings and injured people. Now she did notice and became truly frightened.

Then, perhaps for the very first time since she had gotten her job with Congressman Wiley, Amanda put herself before the congressman. She turned off her phone, went to the bar, and got plastered.

Off Formentera Island
After nightfall
September 15, 321 BCE

The sun had gone down. Elise Beaulieu, the first officer for navigation, adjusted the sextant with careful fingers. Instruments from fifty years ago were being brought into play and combined with ship's computers. So far they had found that the North Star, Polaris, was not in the right place. Even in the two hours since sunset, they had been able to detect motion in Polaris. That was enough to tell them that they were before the birth of Christ, or at least not that long after it.

The planets were giving more precise data, and as soon as Mars came up they ought to be able to get a year....

And there it was, just on the horizon. Elise plugged the numbers into the slate's program and got a date. According to the computer, they were in the year 321 Before the Common Era. That was using the standard calendar of the twenty-first century and counting backward, using modern knowledge and technology.

She tapped another icon and called the captain. "Captain, we're in 321 BCE. From the moon, September fifteenth."

Lars Floden nodded. "Thanks, Elise." He tapped off the phone. "Did you get that, Jane?"

Jane Carruthers pulled up the date from the encyclopedia. "The experts aren't in agreement about how the dates line up with the events of this time. It's a safe bet that Alexander the Great was—is—dead, but whether he's been dead for six months or six years is less certain."

The *Queen of the Sea*, in order to save bandwidth, updated the most popular—read, most accessed—web locations every time they hit the Port of Miami. It saved the satellite link for things like email and instant messages. They had a complete and up-to-date mirror of Wikipedia, Encyclopedia Britannica, online *New York Times* website, and even Google Earth, all stored on a set of computers in the IT section of the ship and accessible instantly through the ship's wifi or any of the half-dozen internet cafes on board. "Alexander the Great is two years dead. Rome is a republic, but what they meant by republic isn't what we mean by it. Besides, Carthage is the big dog in the Mediterranean."

"What about the rest of the world, Jane?" the captain asked.

Jane clicked the mouse, then read for a moment. "China is a bunch of warring nations. Qin Shi Huang won't be born for a couple of hundred years." She looked up from the computer. "In the Americas, the Olmec have collapsed and, according to Wikipedia, it was because something happened to the land so it wouldn't support farming."

That doesn't sound like good news, Lars thought, *because we are going to need farmers. We have almost five thousand people to support, and we can't feed them on nothing except fish.*

"Any idea where we are?"

"Best guess, Captain, somewhere in the Med," Anders said. Then he got a distracted look. "Give me a second." He called up a camera view. "I know where we are, Captain. We're on the south end of Formentera Island, about seventy miles off the coast of Spain. My wife and I vacationed on the island of Formentera for our second honeymoon. About two years ago. Nothing else is the same, but the coastline is."

"So what's happening in Spain in 321 BCE?"

"Nothing we want any part of, Captain," Jane Carruthers said. "I think the Carthaginians owned it at this time in history, and if I recall my third form history, they sacrificed babies to their gods."

"Is there any place in this time where they didn't?"

"I'm not sure, Captain. But we can't just sit here forever."

"All right. I'll talk to Joe Kugan and we'll get some sea room. Meanwhile, find me someone who knows something about this time."

"Also, Captain, we need to tell the passengers and crew what we have found out."

"I don't want a panic, Jane."

"Better one now than one later. One later that is laced with mistrust because we were hiding things. Panics wear themselves out, sir. If nothing drastic happens, then people get back to business."

CHAPTER 2

Off Formentera Island
9:00 PM, September 15, 321 BCE

The voice over the loudspeakers was calm and matter-of-fact, as if the ship's officer was simply reporting on the weather:

"Ladies and gentlemen, using astronomic instruments, we have determined the date. It is the year 321 Before the Common Era, and it is September fifteenth by our calendar. Also, we believe we are in the Mediterranean Sea, off the coast of Spain. We have no idea how this has happened, but the captain has decided that for all our safety, we need some sea room. We will be moving away from the docks to insure that boarding by the locals is more difficult."

All around the ship everyone reacted individually, as their natures dictated. There were cases of panic, but more often than panic was disbelief. There was consternation and curiosity. The phones of passengers all over the ship were turned on and 321 BCE was looked up. Other people shrugged and went on with their gambling, shopping, dining, or other entertainments.

Jason Jones pulled out his cell phone and tried to call his mother. He got a "no signal" message. Then he tried to call his father, who was just five feet away, sitting on his bed with his laptop opened. Dad's phone rang with the *Lone Ranger* theme and he looked over at Jason.

"I can't get Mom," Jason explained.

Dad's face got a pinched look on it and Jason got even more scared. Almost in desperation Jason asked, "Dad, if I can't get Mom, how come I can get you?"

"Good question!" Dad seemed relieved. "It could be that the phones are in range of each other. A cell phone is a small radio combined with a computer, and good ones like ours have the ability to talk directly back and forth if they are close enough. That's how we can share photos when our phones get close to each other. But it might be the ship. I think the cell providers have restrictions built in. Let's look it up."

That was Dad's answer to everything. "Let's look it up." Dad called up the ship specs and got a rate listing, a chart of how much cell calls, wifi, and internet cost per minute or megabyte. A couple of links below that was a description of how it worked. The *Queen of the Sea* was wired to a faretheewell, with hotspots and wired connections all through the ship. Those led to the ship's Communications and Data Center. That, along with mirror sites and catching, constituted the ship's cloud. All phone and internet access first went into the ship's cloud. A phone call from one cell phone on the ship to another never left the ship's cloud. But you still got charged for the call as though it were going through the satellite. That was even true on some of the ports, because the *Queen of the Sea* had its own cell tower, called a repeater. In fact, it had three. One forward, one amidships, and one near the stern. Each station had a satellite link, a cell repeater, and ship-to-ship and ship-to-shore radios. That gave the ship's cloud considerable range, so if you were on an island excursion and called someone on the ship, it usually went through the ship's cloud. The reason there were three was to ensure that there was adequate bandwidth, and as a safety feature, redundancy in case of accident. Finding all that out took time, and long before they finished, a history professor decided to take a hand.

In Stateroom 601, Marie Easley, a small woman with black hair and just a touch of gray, looked over at her daughter. Josette Easley was looking frightened. She was recently divorced and, as amicable as it had been, she needed to get away for a while. Marie got dragooned into accompanying Josette because she didn't want to go alone. And now it looked like the trip was going to be a lot more life-changing than either of them had thought. Not that Marie hadn't had enough life-changing since being widowed three years ago.

"Mom," Josette asked, "what was going on in 321 BCE before the common era?"

It was a perfectly reasonable question, since Marie had a doctorate in history with a specialization in Ptolemaic Egypt.

"Well, Alexander is dead, and so is Aristotle. A shame, that. I would have liked to meet the philosopher."

"Not Alexander?"

"Didn't you ever listen to our discussions around the dinner table, Josette?" Marie grinned. "Alexander the Great may well have been the greatest man of his time, but almost anyone who comes down in the history books with 'the Great' attached to their name has piled up a very impressive body count. Alexander was certainly no exception. He was anything but a good man by any modern standard of 'good.' He and his cronies make the characters in *Game of Thrones* seem positively benign."

She thought for a moment. "Well, Epicurus was alive—is alive—and I suspect I would like to meet him. Perhaps even more than Aristotle."

"Do you think the captain and crew can get us back home?"

Marie considered. It seemed highly unlikely on the face of it. And if the captain and crew were unlikely to be able to do so, how likely was it that anything would take them home? There was a tightness around Marie's abdomen as she considered the world they were now in and the possibility... *no, face it squarely, Marie*...the almost certainty that they were here permanently.

"No, dear, I don't. Wait here. I need to speak to someone in the crew about this. There is information they are going to need and they are going to need it sooner rather than later." Marie grabbed her laptop as she left the room and headed for the information desk.

The Help Desk was, unsurprisingly, swamped by people asking questions that the staff was in no position to answer. So Marie answered them. "No, Alexander the Great died two, possibly three, years ago in Babylon."

"What about the Romans?"

"Rome owns a strip of the west coast of Italy, but not much more." Marie stopped and thought. She wasn't nearly as familiar with Rome in this period as she was with Greece and Egypt but, yes, this was the middle of the second Samnite War. She wasn't sure, but she thought the battle of the Caudine Forks was either about to happen or was recent—

Never mind. "Rome is a republic of sorts, but it makes banana republics look good. Also, it doesn't control enough territory to be of much use."

A teenager was scrolling through his phone. "What about Carthage? Aren't they the great sea power of the age?"

"Very little of Carthage is known. But, honestly, young man, most of what is known isn't very complimentary. At this point, we are between the second and third of the Greek-Punic wars."

By now there was a crowd around Marie, and the clerk at the Help Desk called her over and asked about her credentials.

"Captain, we've found an expert," Jane Carruthers said. "Professor Marie Easley is a professor with a specialization in the history of Ptolemaic Egypt and we are in the time of the first Ptolemy."

"Fine, Jane. Get her up here. We need to decide what to do, and soon."

Jane knew that better than the captain did. Even though they were limiting portions now—which might cause resentment among the passengers and crew—they were going to run out of food in no more than a fortnight. They needed a supply base and they needed it now.

Jane escorted Marie toward the captain's conference room, explaining the situation, what they knew of it, and what they needed.

"We need to go to Egypt," Marie said, as soon as they'd entered the conference room. Everyone sitting at the table in the center looked at her.

"Please explain why," said the man at the head of the table. He had a Scandinavian accent but it wasn't pronounced. Marie wasn't quite sure of the meaning of the various insignia on his uniform, but she thought this was the ship's captain. Although she cautioned herself not to jump to conclusions. She might be influenced by the fact that he was distinguished looking and rather handsome, in a late middle-aged sort of way—the way a ship's captain was supposed to look.

"There are several reasons," she said, "but the most important are that Egypt is the richest province in the Macedonian empire and will be the richest in the Roman empire. It's the breadbasket of the Mediterranean, even more than Sicily. And Sicily is in conflict at the moment between the Greeks and the Carthaginians. Also, I don't speak Phoenician, but I may be able to get by in Macedonian Greek. Certainly, I can write in Greek, even if the spoken language has changed more than we think."

"We can be off the coast at Alexandria in two days, Captain," said the man sitting next to him, who was looking at his computer screen. There were coffee cups scattered across the table, and the internal lights made the windows night black. "Fuel isn't a problem. We were just loading up and the *Reliance* filled our tanks to capacity. Water isn't a problem, either. We can purify what we need as long as we have fuel, but food will become an issue."

The one he'd addressed as "Captain" nodded, then smiled at Marie and gestured toward an empty chair. "Please, Professor Easley, have a seat. Before we go any further, some introductions are in order. I am Lars Floden, the captain of this ship. This fellow"—he nodded toward the man who had just spoken—"is Staff Captain Anders Dahl. My executive officer, if this were a naval vessel. Next to him is our environmental compliance officer, Dag Jakobsen."

Now he nodded toward a woman seated at the far end of the table. "That is our chief purser, Eleanor Kinney. Who, judging from the way she is fidgeting, has something urgent on her mind."

He said that in the sort of relaxed, good-humored way that Marie recognized as the mark of a capable team leader. She relaxed a little and slid into the seat he'd indicated. Having an effective ship's captain would be critical in the situation they were in.

As soon as she sat down, Kinney spoke. Her accent was American—from somewhere on the east coast, Marie guessed. Not New York or Boston, though.

"That still leaves the question of how we're going to pay for it," the chief purser said. "It's not like we can pull out the ship's credit card and charge it to the company account."

"Good point, Eleanor," said Floden. "What do we have that we can afford to sell? We need an inventory of all goods owned by all the shops on the ship. Also ship's stores. Nothing irreplaceable if we can avoid it. What can we make in the machine shops?"

"We can probably restock the ship once, maybe twice, out of the jewelry onboard. But that's not a renewable resource," Eleanor said. "The same thing is true of the fabrics on the ship but, again, it's not a renewable resource."

"Maybe not, but the laundry is. We can wash local fabrics. I don't know how much of a market there will be for that, but it's something."

"Wait a moment, Captain," Marie said. "You are assuming that these are civilized people."

"Well, of course. I mean, Aristotle was Alexander's tutor."

Marie opened her mouth, then she closed it. Opened it again. "Alexander the Great truly was great for his time. He had a wide view of humanity, one that included not only his native tribe, but Persians and other Greeks as well. But Alexander was an *exception*. As much of an exception for his time as Martin Luther King, Junior, was for his. And Alexander would be tried for war crimes in our century. Murder, rapine, slavery, brutalization, theft by force of arms—all these things are considered perfectly acceptable, even honorable, behavior in this day and age. Failure to kill your enemies is considered insane weakness.

"In the years after Alexander's death, every single member of his family was murdered. Some of them quite brutally, and often killed by other members of the family. His mother Olympias killed his half-brother, Philip III, and forced Philip's teenage wife Eurydice to commit suicide. Well, will kill. It hasn't happened yet. Alexander's wife, Roxane, had his other two wives killed within a week of his death, and she was later murdered herself, along with his only legitimate son, Alexander IV. Of the roughly two dozen top military commanders who launched the decades-long civil war that followed Alexander's death, only three survived— Seleucus, Antigonus—not the first one, called 'the One-Eyed,' but his grandson—and Ptolemy. And Ptolemy, perhaps the sanest of his generals, founded a line of monarchs where incest was not just allowed, but required."

She looked around the table. "We have arrived in the historical period known as 'the Age of the Diadochi.' That's a Greek term that means 'successors.' Have any of you seen the TV series *Game of Thrones*?"

Anders shook his head; Floden and Kinney nodded.

"Well, you can think of the Age of the Diadochi as *Game of*

Thrones on steroids. Captain Floden, these are *not* civilized people we will be dealing with. I can say with a high degree of certainty that the only civilized people on the planet are on board this ship. And I am actually an admirer of Alexander and Ptolemy, if you take them within their context. Further, we are just at the beginning of the wars of the Diadochi. The political and military situation of the eastern Mediterranean and the Middle East is out of control right now, rudderless because Alexander was the rudder, the center that held everything together. As brutal and ruthless as the people of this era were in ordinary times, they will be even less civilized now."

She moved her finger in a circle, indicating her surroundings. "They will attempt to take this ship by force of arms and failing that, by treachery. Any other course would be rank insanity by the standards of the time."

Floden took a deep breath and let it out. "What do you recommend then, Professor Easley? Should we go back to the island? Should we head for America? Understand, we will be out of food by the time we get there, but we *can* get there."

"No. We will have to deal with Egypt. It's probably the most civilized place on Earth. But deal with them with guns out and armed, and with one hand on your wallet."

Floden made a face. "Professor Easley—"

"Call me Marie, please." She smiled. "You'll wear yourself out if you plant 'professor' in front of my name every time we talk."

He returned the smile. "Marie, then." He made no reciprocal offer but Marie wasn't offended. There were good reasons to keep calling a commander by his title in a situation like this. Her title just got in the way.

"This is not a warship, Marie. We have a total of twenty pistols locked in a safe," Floden said.

"Well, bring them out and have the security people start wearing them," Marie said. "And see if you can get them some swords and armor too. Something that the Greeks and Egyptians will recognize as weapons. Understand me, Captain, this ship is worth fighting a war for. Worth risking a thousand men in a foolish charge, if there is one chance in fifty of taking it."

"Come now, Prof—ah, Marie. I know that we are . . ." Anders Dahl's voice trailed off as he ran out of the right words to say what he wanted to convey.

Marie could make a good guess at what that was. However advanced their technology, they were only five thousand people and only one ship. Granted, it was the biggest and best ship in the world, but still only one. That had to put a hard limit on its value. She understood, and even sort of wished the staff captain was right. Instead, she shook her head.

"No, Staff Captain Dahl. If any king in this world could, he would trade his capital city for this ship without a moment's hesitation. Babylon, Memphis, Athens—all of them *together* don't represent so much wealth, in machines, in knowledge, even in direct ability to exert power. Pack them to the deck heads and you can put an army of twenty thousand men on any coast, anywhere in the world, in days or, at most, weeks."

"We'll run out of fuel," Anders started, unwilling, or perhaps unable, to give up his point.

"We have the new flex fuel engines, sir," Dag Jakobsen said. "They were designed to be environmentally friendly, but in our situation they mean we can burn just about anything liquid. Alcohol, crude oil . . . if it's liquid and it burns, we can use it.

"Our best bet is crude oil. It's not the most environmentally sensitive choice, but under the circumstances, it has the best combination of energy density and availability."

"Are you sure of that, Dag?" the captain asked. "I agree about energy density, but availability? Wouldn't it be easier to just use alcohol? The Egyptians have been brewing beer for centuries."

"Sure. But beer doesn't burn. That takes a much more concentrated form of alcohol. We would have to introduce large-scale distillation and that's effectively a new industry. I've been digging into the computers. Back in the eighteen fifties, they drilled a producing well in Trinidad that was something like two hundred fifty feet deep. And some in Wisconsin that were as little as fifty feet deep. I don't know where we're going to get it. They may even have it around here, but the cheapest way to get fuel is to drill a well. And, at least for the well in Trinidad, we have grid coordinates. We can fabricate a drilling rig in the ship's shops onboard a lot easier than we can fabricate a whole distilling industry. I looked at Google maps. We know pretty close to right where to dig in Trinidad."

"Write me up a report, Dag. Once we have stocked up on food, we might find it necessary to cross the Atlantic and set up things of Muhammad and Allah had had enough. So Yaseen had believed—no, *known*, with confidence and comfort in his certainty. That wasn't the problem. The problem was that the transfer of the Kaaba had happened at a certain very specific time. Seventeen months after Muhammad had taken his followers to Medina. During noon prayers on February 11, 624 of the Common Era. Nine hundred forty-two years from now.

The transfer of the Kaaba hadn't happened yet! Would not happen for almost a millennium, if the effect they were going to have on history didn't change it. Did he pray facing Kaaba in Mecca or the sanctuary in Jerusalem?

At this distance the difference was miniscule, but it was the intent that mattered. Did Allah placing him and the other modern followers of Islam in this time mean that the Jews were getting another chance, or that they were already lost?

Islam respected the people of the book. Even Jews. But now the only people of the book were on this ship, and they were mostly Christians. Only the Jews in this time were people of the book. That decided him. For now at least, he would pray facing the temple in Jerusalem. But the comfortable certainty of his faith was missing as he prayed to Allah to guide his steps in this strange world.

On Formentera Island
September 16

Mosicar looked out at the ocean where the giant ship had been and wondered. Mosicar was the owner of a village of fishermen that was only a few miles from where the giant ship had appeared. He had ordered a watch placed on it, and a little after the middle of the night, it had sailed away.

No. That was wrong.

There had been no sail involved, nor any oars. No means of propulsion that he could imagine, not that he could imagine anything other than the will of the gods that could move such a structure.

Yamm must favor their endeavors, and Mosicar didn't want such people angry at him. Still, he had obligations to the crown in Carthage, and there was—at least potentially—money to be made. The whole village was set to going through the ruins left when the dock arrived, to find anything of value.

some sort of a base. Meanwhile, for right now, I think
to take Professor Easley's advice. We'll head for Egypt."

Rabbi Benyamin Abrahamson sat on the loveseat in his
and prayed. He recited from the Torah under his breath
tried to wrap his mind around the news. God had sent t
back to this time. A time that some scholars insisted inclu
the next best thing to polytheism in Judaism. It wasn't the ti
of Moses, but Moses was closer to them in time than was t
modern world. Even Abraham was closer to them than the wor
they had left.

What did God want of him to put him here?

Lawrence Hewell, a Baptist minister, was having a similar
reaction, if one that was perhaps more emotionally confusing.
"Dear Lord! Father in Heaven, why have you sent me into this
wilderness? Not just among the heathen, but to a time when the
entire world was heathen! A time before our blessed savior had
come among us to offer himself in sacrifice."

Lawrence wasn't mumbling. It was closer to a wail of despair.
Close enough to a wail, in fact, that someone in the next cabin
banged on the wall and a woman's voice shouted, "Would you
mind holding off on your spiritual crisis till we've gone to dinner?"

*Even here on this ship, where at least at this moment the only
Christians in the world are!* Lawrence thought. *Even here, calling
on the Lord brings the wrath of the unrighteous! Is that why God
brought me here? To be John the Baptist? Three hundred years
early? To prepare the way?*

In his quarters below decks, Yaseen Ali prepared to pray and
stopped. Mecca was that way. He had an app on his phone that
used the ship's net to provide the direction and the app was
working again. The problem was that the Kaaba wasn't there yet,
or if it was, it was the altar to a pagan god. The focal point for
prayer had, for the first thirteen years of Islam, been the Noble
Sanctuary, the temple of Jews in Jerusalem. Allah had moved it
in the middle of prayers. Yaseen had always assumed that th
move was because Allah was angry with the Jews. Allah, no
Muhammad, later politics, or later mullahs. Allah. The Jew
had rejected the teachings of Christ and then they rejected t

What they found was strange beyond imagining. Aside from the lumber and odd daub-like stuff that made up the walls, there were pipes made of a white material. There were copper wires inside the walls, that were coated in a flexible covering like leather, but fitted around the wires like skin. There were scissors made of the best steel that Mosicar had ever seen. There were books and pamphlets with strange writing on them. Mosicar thought it might be like the Latin script, but he wasn't sure. It was almost as though they used occasional Latin letters mixed in with a different script.

None of it made sense, but parts almost did. There were images of people, of beaches and seas, and more of the giant ships—as though the whole world was filled with them and the people that occupied them. There were pools of water on the ships on the upper decks, and that was the strangest of things, for there seemed to be deck stacked upon deck upon deck upon deck, more than any ship could carry.

"No!" Mosicar shouted when one of the women started to throw away one of the sheets. "We throw away nothing. Collect everything and store it all in casks and amphoras. I will send a boat to Ibiza and hire a ship. This will all go to Carthage to sell at auction." He looked around as his villagers stared at him. "You will all get a share of the profits. But don't be too greedy. Hiring the ship will cost money."

For the next few days, the villagers focused on stripping the dock and ruins of anything of any possible value. Two people were injured in collapsing buildings, and one died, but they picked the ruins clean. In doing so, they learned a large amount and made some surprisingly good guesses. They found a battery-powered flashlight and realized that the copper carried the power that produced the light. That explained much of the use of the wires in the walls of the buildings. They realized that light bulbs were light bulbs, and even managed to hook up a light bulb from a ceiling to a battery, and got it to light dimly.

By then the boat sent to Ibiza had returned, escorted by a larger ship. Mosicar and his wife boarded the ship, along with the goods for the trip to Carthage. This was a major risk, and his wife was going along to make sure Mosicar didn't screw it up. As a rule in Carthage and its territories, the wife was in charge of dealing with the household gods. And, more generally, the household management.

Men were left in charge of politics and fighting.

Queen of the Sea, *en route to Egypt, approaching Carthage* September 17

The officer of the watch looked out at the galley off the starboard bow. It had come over the horizon from the direction of Tunis—or at least what would be Tunis in a couple of millennia—gotten one good look at the *Queen*, then turned tail and run for port.

Honestly, Second Officer Adrian Scott wasn't at all sure that he blamed them. He pulled up a camera, zoomed in, and took a quick snap. Eighteen oars on a side, a single sail that was not in use at the moment. They were making good time.

Adrian wondered if the rowers were slaves. He wasn't sure. He knew that some of the ancients used slaves as rowers and some used soldiers or sailors who got paid. And those were probably Carthaginians, and what Professor Easley had said last night was that very little was known about the Carthaginians, aside from the fact that the Greeks and the Romans didn't care for them.

It wasn't the first ship they had seen on this watch, and probably wouldn't be the last.

Lars Floden waved Al Wiley to the small table in the dining nook of his private cabin. "I'm sorry it took me so long to get back to you, Congressman, but the things I absolutely had to do took precedence." The captain was trying to be polite, but he wasn't trying all that hard. It wasn't as if the U.S. Congress was anything he had to worry about three hundred years before Christ was born.

"I understand that the...urgencies, let's call them...of command can make the long-term consequences of our actions seem to fade in importance." Al waved at the window. "I note that we are under power and the rumor is that we are headed for Egypt. Is that true?"

"Yes, Congressman." Floden nodded as Wiley took his seat at the table.

"Is that wise? Wouldn't it have been better to stay where we were in the hope that we might return to our own time? I only ask these things, Captain, because they are the questions that the passengers are asking me."

"We have looked into that question, Congressman, and the answer clearly seems to be that there is no chance we will be returned. Are you familiar with what is called the Minnesota Hypothesis concerning the mysterious disasters that befell the town of Grantville in West Virginia and Alexander Correctional Center in southern Illinois?"

Al shook his head. He knew about the disasters, of course. Everyone in America did—probably everyone in the world, outside of a few people in places like New Guinea. But he'd never studied the issue.

"Well, I just spent a fair amount of time with two passengers—both physicists—who have a great deal of knowledge of the matter. The Hypothesis argues that the records from the Alexander disaster are impossible to explain unless an element of deliberate purpose is included in the explanation. The term 'intelligent design' is not used, but that is clearly what is being suggested."

Al's expression must have looked skeptical because Floden shrugged his shoulders. "I have no opinion on that matter," the captain said. "But what is relevant to us is that everything we can determine about our situation is that we have suffered something very much like what seems to have happened to Grantville and Alexander prison."

He gestured toward the window. "Consider two things. First, we have definitely been moved in both time and space—more than two thousand years, in terms of time; almost five thousand miles, in terms of space. Second, the...let us call it the transposition, caused almost no damage to the ship and while it did damage the docks, it resulted in only one fatality. What are the chances of that happening if the disaster that befell us did *not* have elements of purpose? It would be like an explosion right next to someone that caused no damage except a ringing in the ears."

Al frowned. "But...*what* purpose?"

"I have no idea, Congressman. Neither did the authors of the Hypothesis. But it really doesn't matter, because what is uncontestable is the third feature of the Grantville and Alexander disaster."

"Which is?"

"Whatever happened, no one ever came back. There is no reason at all to think we would either. So, we have come to the conclusion that we have no choice but to assume that we will remain in this new universe we find ourselves in for...perpetuity, let's call it."

Al grunted. "As long as we can stay alive, you mean."

The captain smiled thinly. "Your words, Congressman. Not mine."

Tug Reliance, *in the Mediterranean*
September 17

Captain Joe Kugan muttered curses. He was still in radio contact with the *Queen*, but they were over the horizon from him now. The *Reliance* could only make twelve knots, not the twenty-two that was the *Queen*'s most efficient cruising speed, so the *Queen* had left them behind. Using the *Queen*'s charts and the inertial compass as well as the magnetic, they followed as they could, keeping farther out to sea just to be safe.

Meanwhile, Joe was cursing himself for a fool for having given away a full load of fuel to the *Queen*, based on a bill of lading that wouldn't be good for two millennia and more.

"Captain, sail off the port bow."

Joe looked up from his muttering and saw the monitor for the mast camera. What he saw was just the tip of a sail, and unless they had someone in the crow's nest, there was no way they had seen the *Reliance*. "Bring us a point to starboard." *And more delay.*

Queen of the Sea, *en route to Egypt*
September 17

Dag looked at the designs and wondered. It wasn't as though there was anything in the designs that the ship didn't either have or at least could make, but it seemed like a lot of work to fight off a bunch of primitives who couldn't even climb the hull without a lot of help or a lot of luck.

He was looking at a WikiHow article on how pneumatic cannons worked and could be built. All because Marie Easley was an anal-retentive paranoid. Professor Easley had convinced Jane Carruthers, and Jane had convinced Staff Captain Anders Dahl, that they needed real weapons.

Anders hadn't bothered to convince. He'd simply ordered.

"What do you think, Romi?"

"It looks fine, Mr. Jakobsen." Romi Clarke was grinning

broadly, displaying the gap in his teeth where he had lost some in a bar fight. Romi had a partial, but it was not something they could easily replace, so he wasn't wearing it.

"How long?"

"It depends. If I have first call on supplies and labor, only a couple of days. We have the piping in stores and the machine shop can turn out what we need. If it's as we have time, it'll take a couple of weeks."

"I'll check with the staff captain, but for now treat it as when you have time." Actually, Dag was pretty sure that the staff captain was going to want a higher priority than that, but Dag and the whole crew had a lot on their plates. They were preparing the ship for anchoring in Alexandria, Egypt, and converting the lifeboats to act as loading boats and transports while not losing their functionality as lifeboats. It was likely that this was going to be the fifth or sixth top priority on the list.

CHAPTER 3

Queen of the Sea, *off Alexandria*
September 18

Sixty-seven hours after the *Queen of the Sea* started the trip, the passengers and crew got their first view of Alexandria. Not that they could see much. It was a bit after 8:00 PM and there weren't any electric lights in this time. As well, the famed Lighthouse of Alexandria was yet to be built. It was a work very much in progress and it was being built by hand. Lots and lots of hands. It would be dawn on the 19th before they could see much of anything.

However, the reverse wasn't true. The citizens of Alexandria—from Dinocrates of Rhodes and Crates of Olynthus, all the way down to the slave workers who were building the outer wall of the bay—could see the mountain of light that had moved into view and sat the better part of a mile out to sea.

And it *was* a mountain of light, because the captain had made the decision that they would not try to hide the existence of their technology. Whether to hide the way it worked was another question, and one that was the subject of heated debate onboard the ship.

Dinocrates of Rhodes, a tall, good-looking man who normally possessed a dignified air, looked out at the device that made all his works and dreams seem little more than a child building sandcastles. Envy and awe warred in his heart, and the dignified air that he normally showed the world was notable by its absence.

It wasn't real anyway, just a mask he showed to the world. He was as much showman as architect, and compared to the people on that ship he was neither.

"I don't believe it," Crates said for the third time since they had been called from their dinners to the heptastadion, a seven-stadia-long mole that connected the island of Pharos to the mainland and created the harbor at Alexandria. Crates was in part responsible for the heptastadion. He was the hydraulic engineer who was in charge of designing the sewers for Alexandria, sewers made necessary by the fact that Alexandria was being built in a swamp. He was a scholar, and at the same time, practical in his works. Dinocrates had never seen him so bereft of sense as he seemed now.

"It is, Crates. Believe it or not, it's there."

"But it can't be. Don't you understand? Look at the length! Look at the height! It's not as tall as the Great Pyramid, but it's longer. You can't float something that big. No tree on earth is strong enough to take the stresses."

Dinocrates simply pointed.

"I know," Crates complained, "but it can't be."

"Fine, it can't be. But what are we going to do about it?"

Crates shrugged. "Send a message to Ptolemy at Memphis."

Dinocrates nodded. With the signal fires the news would reach Ptolemy by morning. The satrap of Egypt would probably be here in three days. "What do we do in the meantime?"

Crates looked at him, then back at the ship. "Whatever you do, don't piss them off."

Dinocrates laughed. "I agree, but I was asking about the rest of it. There are seventeen ships in the harbor and fifty or more boats. If we don't do something by tomorrow noon, half those ships and more than half the boats will be gone and the news is going to spread."

"I don't see that there is anything we can do about that," Crates said. "For myself, I am going to get my instruments and make some estimates of the size of that thing. But I'm not going out to it until I know more. And not in the middle of the night."

Not everyone in Alexandria was so cautious. Atum Edfu slammed his hand down on the table and glared at the oar captain of his family galley. "I told you to get the men to their oars." The room was dim, lit with oil lamps. This wasn't Atum's home, but his dock office. It had large unglazed windows. Atum didn't miss glazing. It would not be invented for another four hundred years. He and his clerks worked here most days with the shutters open to let in the sea air and the light, but the office wasn't designed for nighttime use. The dim lamps in nooks on walls filled the room with shadows, adding a spooky feel that Atum noticed no more than he noticed the lack of glazing.

"I know, sir, but the men are afraid."

"Afraid? Afraid! I'll give you afraid! Half their job is to be the family's bodyguards at sea! And they're afraid of a big boat?"

Atum was a grain seller of mixed ancestry who spoke Egyptian, Greek, Carthaginian, even the language of the barbarian Latins. He looked at the ship and saw profit. Such a ship would need to feed its rowers, for he saw no sails. He didn't see oars either, but something had to be pushing the ship, and if it wasn't the wind, whatever it was probably needed to eat. He had calculated that the first merchant to greet them would have the advantage. So, after his first good look at the ship, he had hurried to the docks and rousted out his crew.

Atum owned a large number of slaves that he used in loading and unloading boats in the harbor, and for farming and other jobs, but he didn't use slaves to man the oars on the family galley. For that he used hired rowers who were armed and could fend off pirates. Just at the moment, though, he was considering a change in policy. Slaves wouldn't be giving him back talk.

"Well, they will get aboard the galley and they will row me to that ship out there, or they will be looking for new jobs tomorrow morning."

It took him almost until midnight to get the crew on the galley, and another half an hour before he could reach the ship.

"Ahoy!" he offered in Egyptian. Then in Carthaginian. Then in Greek. He had gone through several more languages before he got an answer in what was probably the very worst Athenian accent he had ever heard. He introduced himself in Greek and explained that he was here to trade. By now, looking up the wall of what was starting to look like iron, and hearing the magnified voice out of the ship, he was beginning to wonder if his avarice hadn't gotten the better of his good sense. It wouldn't be the first time, after all.

A hole opened up in the iron wall of the ship, and a ramp was lowered to tie onto the galley. With trepidation starting to win out over greed, but pride now weighing in on greed's side, Atum made his way up the ramp and into the ship, and was probably more scared than he had ever been in his life. It wasn't because he was threatened. He wasn't. There wasn't a sword or a bow in sight, much less a spear. The men and women in strange clothing were apparently unarmed, though they wore on their belts a strange device that he thought from their gestures might be a weapon of some sort. But he only noticed those at all because his fear was making him more vigilant than usual.

What terrified him was the light. It wasn't coming from fires. Instead they had little bits of the sun locked into the ceiling of the room they were in. They led him through a door, then down a hallway to where a set of doors opened, sliding out of the way, and leading into a small room. One of the guards—he was almost sure they were guards—preceded him into the small room and the other gestured for him to enter.

Terror had given way to a curious fatalism, and Atum shrugged and went in. The guard pressed a finger against a circle with a character of some sort on it. As the dot was pressed, it lit up, and a moment later the doors closed. A moment after that, the room moved. Up, he thought. Atum stood still for just a moment, then he started to smile. He understood. He had been lifted up on a platform before. It had been an open platform, not a room like this one, but it had moved, powered by a slave in a wheel. It had been used to lift heavy loads gradually to higher places, so that they might be used in making walls. Somewhere on this massive ship, Atum was now convinced, was a slave in a wheel providing the motive power for the moving box. He would have one installed in his town house.

He looked where the guard was looking and saw symbols like the ones in the dots lighting up in order. Again, his quick mind figured it out. There was a light moving along behind the strip of symbols, lighting each in turn as they moved. He could almost see the gears. He was familiar with gears. They were all the rage in Athens for astrological calculating devices.

That lasted till the doors opened and he was led into a room with leather-covered seats, more like thrones than the sort of stool Atum was used to. There he was introduced to an older woman named Marie Easley and a younger woman called Eleanor Kinney. The older woman spoke something approaching passable Macedonian Greek. She didn't speak it well, and there was much too much of the Athenian about it to be proper Macedonian, but it was closer to understandable than the pidgin Greek he had heard up to now.

"Welcome. I am Marie Easley, a scholar of this time," the woman said.

"Explain, please. You study the present? Recent history, perhaps?"

"We are not of this time. We on this ship come from far in the future. We have learned a great deal and I am a historian, one who studies Ptolemaic Egypt."

Atum didn't believe her, but he couldn't say that. For now at least, he was in these people's power. So he leaned back in the seat and considered her words as though they were true. *Ptolemaic Egypt?* That would mean that Ptolemy would become pharaoh. Alexander's empire would collapse. Or would it? Would Ptolemy become the next king of Alexander's empire and move the capital to Egypt? That seemed possible, certainly. Even though Ptolemy protested his loyalty to Alexander's heirs in every second sentence. "What is Ptolemaic Egypt to be, then?"

The scholar pursed her lips and tilted her head slightly. "We aren't sure. The truth is, we don't know how it happened that we came here, or really even what happened. We have no record of a ship such as this arriving off Alexandria at this time. I assure you, there would be such a record. And there are causes and effects, so we must assume that history will take a different path in this time than it did in our history. If that is not too confusing."

"I think I understand, at least in a general way," Atum said. "What happened with Ptolemy and the generals in your history is not necessarily what will happen now."

"Yes, that's the conclusion we have at least tentatively drawn. But what brings you to brave this ship? You said something about trade?"

"Yes. I assume you will need food and provisions. If you have goods or money, we can deal. I am a wheat merchant, and I buy from the farmers up the Nile and sell to the construction crews. I can arrange for grain to feed your rowers."

"Rowers?" she asked.

Atum shrugged. "You must have something to propel your ship." Seeing the confusion on her face, he rephrased the question. "Something to push the ship through the water."

She turned to the young woman and spoke. The young woman wore her hair short, but not shaved with a wig as was sometimes done by women in Egypt. She had a heart-shaped face, with brown eyes and hair. The hair had blond streaks, bleached by the sun, Atum thought. The woman was attractive and the style made her more exotic than her features did. The woman spoke back to the scholar, and they turned to a young man who seemed to be the chief of their guards. He took a device from his pocket and touched it, held it to the side of his head with one end next to his ear and the other near his mouth, then spoke and apparently listened. He pocketed the device and spoke to the women, all while Atum looked on and tried to understand what was going on.

Atum didn't speak the language they were speaking, but he didn't need to. He was good at reading people. It was a large part of his business. It was clear that the women were in charge in this room, but that the young Gaul was high in their trust. He had been asked about something and Atum, after his earlier experiences, guessed that the device he had used was some sort of a speaking horn. And he wanted one. As he watched, it seemed to Atum that they at least believed their tale of traveling through time. Either that, or they were much better liars than they seemed to be.

"We needed to speak to the captain of the ship," the scholar explained. "The ship uses burning naphtha—or any liquid that will burn, for that matter—to push it through the water and to power many of our devices." She pointed at the lights in the ceiling and then at the slates, like the one the young Gaul had presumably used to talk to the captain. "But we do need grain and other foodstuffs. Sheep, goats, pigs, cattle, fruits and vegetables."

Then they got down to business. For the next hour, Atum dealt with Eleanor Kinney through the scholar. He guessed that Kinney was a skilled negotiator, and they had a series of goods brought in. Including account books, and a box of writing implements that the scribes in the royal palace would be lining up to buy at almost any price. Eleanor warned him that they would run out of ink eventually. It wouldn't be soon, months of use, perhaps as long as a year. That would lower the price, but the "pens" would still be valuable, as would the very fine papyrus they used, neatly formed and lined.

Ten minutes in, Atum knew he wasn't the only person in the room who could read people. The fact that the women were doing the dealing didn't upset Atum. He was half-Egyptian after all. But it did make it clear these people weren't Greeks. They appeared to be of every tribe imaginable—and some he had never imagined—but were all of one culture. Or seemed to be, at least.

He bought a backpack. *What a useful device that! How odd that people who could come up with such devices would accept barbarian Gauls into their ranks!* He sold, for a backpack full of pens and paper and five thousand "dollars" in ship's credit, a ship's boat full of wheat. This agreement was a bit of an experiment, both on his part and on theirs. It would take him a little time to find the resale price on the pens and paper, and they would need to examine the grain. It would give everyone a chance to judge the value of what they were buying and selling.

They showed him around the ship. He had a meal in one of the "restaurants," and he looked around the shops. Then they reached the "casino."

Atum didn't lose his head. He was careful. But he did, gradually, gambling till dawn, lose three thousand of the five thousand "dollars" credit. He would win some, lose some, win some more. It was great fun and very exciting, if a little overwhelming with the noise and the lights. He realized that the wrong person could lose a kingdom in a night in this room. Or, if the gods were smiling, win one.

Alexandria
September 19

The next morning, as the sun came up, an exhausted Atum boarded the boat he had promised to fill with grain. It was a small ship almost the size of his family's galley, and it escorted Atum's galley back to the docks. The small ship had no rowers, but it was obvious to Atum that it could have made circles around his galley if it had chosen to. Atum was on the small ship and found it comfortable, if noisy.

"How is it powered?" he asked in Greek and got no response other than pointing at ears and shaking heads. He pulled out the tablet and pencil he had bought at one of the great ship's "gift shops" and wrote in Greek.

He passed the tablet over to the young man in the white clothing and the peculiar hat that was called a "uniform," and watched as that man pulled out one of the magical "electronic devices" they had and tapped it with his fingers. Atum was almost getting used to that, and this Dag seemed a nice enough lad for a barbarian Gaul.

Dag pushed a final button and the device spoke. It was Greek of the horribly accented, almost unintelligible version Atum had heard on the great ship. It said almost what he had written. Almost, but not quite. He corrected the missed word and Dag tapped some more. Again that voice from the magic slate, and this time Atum nodded. He was getting used to the horrible Greek by now, or at least starting the process of getting used to it. Now the translation to that strange speech, and Dag tapped again. By this point Atum had almost forgotten the question, but the funny Greek answer brought it back.

Atum had learned quite a lot in the last ten hours. He was shocked and amazed by what he had seen, but he had tentative agreements with the travelers from the future who occupied the great ship. It was named *Queen of the Sea* and it could well rule all the world's oceans. And its coasts as well. Or it would have been able to if it were a warship, but it wasn't. It was filled with people who had boarded it for a pleasure cruise, not soldiers.

The slave, Abd Manaf, looked out at the big white ship sitting just outside of Alexandria harbor with his mouth agape. The overseer, also a slave but of higher status was gaping too, as were most of the rest of the slaves in the work crew. Partly it was just the size of the enormous ship, but partly it was the smaller ship that was moving toward shore with no oars or sails, as though being pulled along by an invisible team of horses. One of the brighter slaves got back to work and that got the attention of the overseer, who started shouting at the men in the work crew.

Abd Manaf wasn't the smartest slave in the crew. He was still staring when the overseer's eyes fell on him. The overseer hollered and laid into Abd Manaf with a reed whip. The whip, a piece of wood thin enough to bend in the swing and to leave welts or cuts, snapped against Abd Manaf's back, leaving a welt.

Not the first. There were a welter of them on Abd Manaf's back. And the backs of the other slaves, if not as crisscrossed by red as Abd Manaf's, were still marked. The cries of pain and the smell of blood added to the miasma of the port, along with the smell of dead fish and salt water.

Abd Manaf's back wasn't the only one laid open that morning. But, in spite of the whippings, there were a lot of people watching the strange boat approach the docks.

On reaching the docks, Atum climbed out and waved away the guards that the arrival of the magical boat had brought out. He spoke to Ahmose, one of his foremen, giving orders that the boat be filled with sacks of unthreshed wheat till the Gaul said it was enough. Then he went home to bed.

Dag watched as the Egyptian workers carried the bags of wheat to the boat. It was a lifeboat that had been modified to act as a tender for the *Queen*. It was limited in that it was restricted to fuel oil, not having the flex fuel engines that the *Queen* and the *Reliance* had.

Dag watched as naked men carried sacks of grain on their backs, up to the pier where the lifeboat was tied up. He was uncomfortable at first with the nudity, but that changed quickly. What bothered him more was the sacks on their backs. They seemed to weigh as much as the men themselves did. Wheelbarrows and dollies occurred to Dag as items of trade. He would have to talk to Romi about that. Still another first priority to add to the list.

For most of the day, they loaded grain onto the boat, and by the end of the day the ship had probably broken even on food. That is, they had added enough to equal what the passengers and crew had eaten. He was approached by people speaking to him in Egyptian and Greek and who knew what, but he couldn't understand more than a word or two, which he had to make clear with gestures. Luckily, Atum's guards were doing a pretty good job of keeping the riffraff back. Atum had given them instructions before he left.

By this time, Dag was pretty sure the men doing the loading were slaves and a part of him was ready to pull the pistol and make a point. At the same time, Dag had seen poverty before, and seen employment that was as close to outright slavery as made very little difference. Besides, this was likely the ship's only source of enough food to keep the passengers and crew going. He couldn't afford to do anything that might jeopardize that.

Around noon, two sources of lunch arrived. Another ship's boat brought sandwiches, and some women brought up a cart with bowls, soup, and flat bread. The soup was vegetable and pretty good, but the bread was tough and grainy. Dag really preferred the ship's bread to the Egyptian flat bread. He gave the chief guard a roast beef on rye with mustard and pickles. The guard tried it, and apparently found it good. The guard spoke Greek and yet another language that Dag didn't know, but it sounded sort of like what you heard among the Arabs on the ship, or what you might hear in a synagogue. The guy was wearing a long dress, and he had a sword at his side. He also had purple tassels on his "dress." Dag didn't know what to call the thing, and didn't think it represented anything effeminate, but it sure looked like a dress to him. He would learn later that the guard captain, Josephus, was a Jew, though a somewhat Hellenized one.

Atum got back to the pier about the time they were finished loading, and he had brought his wife, Lateef, who was a black-haired lady of middle years with a long nose and sharp features. She had a pleasant smile, though, and a friendly manner, and Dag liked her. Also with them were two Greeks, one called Crates of Olynthus, the other Dinocrates of Rhodes.

Dag got the impression that they were important people. Then he made the connection. He remembered from Wikipedia that Dinocrates of Rhodes was the one whom Alexander the Great appointed to design Alexandria. It piqued Dag's interest in the man. Dag was interested in how systems interacted. That was what had led him to his job as the Environmental Compliance Officer on the *Queen*. In spite of the job title sounding like a rulebook pain in the ass, it was actually about making sure that the ship worked and that it didn't screw up the ocean it was traveling through. There was a lot of practical engineering, knowing where you could cut corners and where you couldn't. Not that Dag was all that concerned about the environmental impact of a single cruise ship. Even if they dumped oil over the side by the ton, it wouldn't have any significant effect on the oceans of the world.

It was back in the future, where there were hundreds of cruise ships and thousands of cargo ships, that it had a cumulative effect. But the Greek guys were talking and Dag didn't have a clue what they were saying. He looked to Atum.

Atum pulled out his pad and wrote. Dag pulled his comp-pad from its case and typed in the characters. What he got back was: *they want to go to the ship.*

"Right," Dag said. "Let me call it in." He used the phone function on his pad and called the ship. He got Adrian Scott. "Hey, Scotty. We have Dinocrates of Rhodes here and he wants to come by for a visit, along with a guy named Crates."

"Who's Dino of Rhodes and why should I care?"

"Ask Marie Easley. In the meantime, tell the captain that we have important company coming."

CHAPTER 4

Royal Lounge, **Queen of the Sea**
September 19

Al Wiley had barely gotten invited to this little dinner in the Royal Lounge.

Every ship that belonged to Royal Cruise Lines had a Royal Lounge, and they were always reserved for private parties. This one was one deck up from the pool deck, and you could see the swimmers from the windows. The windows were massive picture windows that went from floor to ceiling. At the moment, they were transparent but Al knew that they could be opaqued with the flip of a switch. There was a well-stocked bar next to the main doors and both a large conference table and a set of smaller tables where people could eat, drink or chat. The chairs were white naugahyde, but of good quality. The tables were plastic, but heavy and colored to resemble teak or other dark woods.

Al was miffed about the trouble he'd had getting this invitation. The captain was being unreasonable.

But he pulled himself up short. This situation was upsetting him more than he wanted to admit. The captain was being the captain. And, technically, at least until things got a bit more organized, the captain had a point. He was the one with a legal obligation to care for the passengers and crew. Al stood up as the locals in linen robes came sauntering into the room like a bunch of tribal chieftains decked out in native attire. Which, Al guessed, was what they were.

They were escorted by one of the ship's officers...he thought it was Dan, no, something foreign...Dag, that was it. Right there on his nametag, Dag Jakobsen.

The guests were shown to seats and Captain Floden introduced everyone. Dinocrates of Rhodes was tall, a dignified-looking man, going a bit gray at the temples and around the beard. Crates was shorter, balding, with bad teeth. Al had seen the Egyptian, Atum, before, though he hadn't been introduced. The woman, Lateef, was apparently Atum's wife and Al wasn't sure why she was here.

The captain finished the introductions, and Marie Easley translated. At every name, the Greeks nodded their understanding till they got to Al. He listened carefully, but couldn't follow. Then she said, "tribune."

"What's the problem, Professor Easley?" Al asked.

"They don't have an equivalent title to congressman. The closest I was able to come was the Latin 'tribune.'"

Al nodded. It made sense. But it also brought some potential problems forward in his mind. Al was a Republican, and that wasn't just his party. He believed in representative government, not the right of kings. And these people, even the Romans, didn't get that. Not in the modern sense, anyway. That could produce errors in judgment among them, but there was a more insidious danger if they were stuck here permanently. Al had no desire to live in a world where the citizenry were lorded over by the kings and captains of antiquity.

For the rest of the meeting, while Al listened and even participated, that thought was bouncing around his mind. They might be stuck here, not just for a time, but forever.

They talked about resupply. They talked about fuel and its availability. They talked about taxes and duties. And it was mentioned that signal fires had been used to transmit word of their arrival to Memphis and Ptolemy. The satrap of Egypt would know that they were here by now.

Then Dinocrates of Rhodes asked a question, and Marie translated. "Who owns the ship?"

"Royal Cruise Li—" Captain Floden started to say, but Al interrupted.

"The people on board!"

"Congressman!" Captain Floden said.

Al said, "Wait, Captain, please. And listen. This is vital and it will affect all our dealings with these people. If the ship is owned by a company that will not exist for two thousand years, then it's owned by no one, and is open to seizure. It's in Egyptian territorial waters and, absent an owner, it is the property of the government of Egypt. Ptolemy. Don't give them that opening."

"He's right," Marie Easley said. "Captain, we can't leave it the property of a future company licensed by a nation that itself doesn't exist yet."

"That doesn't mean that it has become the property of everyone on board equally," Captain Floden said. Then his lips twitched in a sort of half smile. "I didn't expect such a communistic viewpoint coming from a Republican congressman."

Al felt a grin twitching his own lips and, without hesitation, let it show. "We aren't insane, whatever the liberal media has told you, Captain. And I didn't say it was equally owned by everyone, but who owns how much and how it's shared out is something for us to decide, not the locals."

Captain Floden nodded. Professor Easley spoke in Greek, was questioned, and then spoke again.

She turned to them. "Well, now they understand why Congressman Wiley is here. Or at least they think they do. He is here as a representative of the owners of the ship."

"That's not too far off," Al said.

"With all due respect, Congressman," said Staff Captain Dahl, "you represent your district in Utah, not the people on this ship, many of whom aren't even Americans and less than a hundred of whom are from Utah."

"This isn't the time, Staff Captain, but we need to have a meeting soon," Al said.

Then they got back to business until the Greeks were taken off on a tour of the ship by Professor Easley and Dag.

"All right, Congressman," Captain Floden asked after the Greeks had left the room, "what did you mean when you said you represented the passengers?"

"Yes," Staff Captain Dahl said. "Who elected you?"

Al took a sip of ice water and carefully put the glass back on the table before he answered. "Staff Captain, as to who elected me, the people of the United States did. The chain of command runs from the President to the Vice President to the speaker of the house and president pro tem of the Senate, and then through all the members of the cabinet starting with the secretary of state. If they're all dead—or gone missing—then it goes down the congressional chain of seniority, to me. As it happens, I am three hundred fifty-seventh in the House. It matters for things like committee seats, which is why I know. For this ship, in these circumstances, I am the next in line for the presidency of the United States of America. And if you find that notion something between obscene and ridiculous, believe me, I am no more fond of it than you. But it's true. There will need to be elections, but until they are held, I am the commander-in-chief of the citizens of the United States on this ship."

"But we aren't in the United States, Congressman. We weren't in the United States when The Event happened. We weren't even in her territorial waters."

Al shrugged. Captain Floden had a point. "I agree that it's a gray area, and I am not trying to usurp your authority, Captain. But, like it or not, it leaves me with a responsibility to the American citizens on this ship, and that's the majority of the people here."

"Does that make me the queen of England?" Jane Carruthers asked with a smile.

"I have no idea, Ms. Carruthers." Al laughed. "I don't know your relationship to the crown, or the relationship of the other British citizens on board."

"I can't let command of the *Queen* fall to an unqualified person or, especially, a group, just because they have the most votes," Captain Floden said. "And I can't run for election, either. I'd lose and that still wouldn't make me unqualified to command this ship."

"No, you're right about that, Captain. Command of this ship, at least in the immediate sense, must remain with you and your staff."

"In the immediate sense?" Dahl asked. "What other sense is there?"

"The long-term policy sense," Al said. "If we are truly stuck in this time and it's permanent, then we can't stay on this ship having shrimp cocktails and wieners on a stick forever. We have to do something. Something beyond getting more shrimp and bread. The planning for that something can't be the purview of one unelected man. It must represent the views of the majority of the people on the ship, passengers as well as crew."

"How would you go about that, Congressman Wiley?" asked Jane Carruthers. "I'm not objecting. In fact, I rather agree with you, at least in principle. I just want to know how you plan to hold elections and what level of... well, civilian oversight... you're looking to impose."

"I don't know yet, but we all need to be thinking about it."

"I wish to see the movers," Crates of Olynthus said yet again. Marie didn't even need to translate it because Crates had made the same request every time they had gone anywhere on the ship. So far they had been to the casino, two restaurants, a stateroom, the Royal Duty Free Shop, the Coach shop, where Dinocrates had bought a leather jacket, a backpack, and boots. They'd just finished the visit to Guess, where Dinocrates bought a pair of blue jeans and a silk shirt, putting the whole thing on Atum's ship account. Atum wasn't looking very pleased, but he had nodded acquiescence. If Dinocrates kept this up, they would be owed another boatload of wheat.

Dag said in English, "We can take him to see the engines if you want, but there won't be a lot to see. They are turbines and all the moving parts are covered."

"Show him what you can, Dag," Marie said. "Almost twenty-four hundred years later, this man's name is still remembered. He's the one who designed the sewer system for Alexandria."

So they went down many decks, and Dag took them into the crew section where the passengers weren't allowed, and showed them the engine rooms.

"But where are the machines you mentioned?" Crates asked.

"They are under the covers and behind the shields. Understand, we use great heat and spin the turbines very fast. So fast that even were there not shields, you couldn't see the blades."

"Well, what *can* I see?" The little balding man seemed pretty upset.

Dag thought about showing them the machine shop, and then remembered what Romi was doing in there. Instead, Dag took him to one of the monitors that could be used to see the props on the nacelles. The nacelles had cameras and lights. Looking at the monitors, you could see the props turning. As he showed

Crates the moving propeller, he wondered how Romi was doing with the steam-powered guns.

Romi cursed and sucked on a skinned knuckle. "What you think, Marcus? Will the arrester valve hold pressure?"

"It should, Romi. It's the rest of the rig that bothers me. It's going to take a lot of steam pressure to run this thing."

"We've *got* a lot of pressure. High pressure fire-fighting gear all over the ship. It takes a lot of pressure piping to run those, and we can use the spares to set up the feeds for the cannon."

"You really think anyone would try to take the ship?"

Romi considered. "No. They may be primitive, but I doubt they're idiots. They couldn't even reach the deck without help and they know it, or should. It's seventy-five feet from the sea to the Promenade Deck. Figure that even a tall ship for these people is maybe thirty feet up. That's another forty-five feet. They might be able to get a rope up to the Promenade Deck, but then they spend ten minutes climbing rope ladders while we drop flower pots on their heads. And when the survivors get here, they are so tired that a ten-year-old with a belaying pin could beat the bunch of 'em."

"So why are we..."

"Because officers are obsessive idiots in any century. At least, ours are."

Dag showed the party into another part of the engine room, and Panos Katsaros said something in Greek.

Once Panos had everyone's attention, he asked, "What about some shore leave, Mr. Jakobsen?" Then more Greek, apparently translating for the locals.

Panos was a Greek lower deck sailor, an able seaman, whose job was engine wiper. He had also been an ongoing discipline problem. Nothing serious, but the man liked to party.

The room held one of the emergency backup generators and it was receiving standard maintenance. Crates started talking in Greek and Panos held up his hands and made a downward pushing gesture. Crates slowed down, and Panos started pointing at the components of the generator, the coiled wires and the drive shaft. Just the sort of thing that any industrial worker would know about the machines he used and worked on.

While Panos was impressing one of the great minds of ancient

Greece with his knowledge, Atum spoke to Dag. "I can arrange something, Mr. Jakobsen. I know how to deal with sailors."

"I'll have to talk to the captain, but I think that Panos here may be the only Greek speaker we have in the crew."

"I'll make arrangements, and we can add the costs to my shipboard account."

Alexandria Royal Compound
September 19

Gorgias of Thrace looked out at the harbor and measured with a stick. It could be done. Not against a capable foe. Not against a Persian or even an Egyptian. But rumor had it that these were philosophers, mewling infants. Still, he was just drawing plans in the air, not doing anything real, not yet. But the prize . . . a ship like that, owned by real men, could rule the world. Gorgias was loyal to Ptolemy, but with a ship like that he could be king of Macedonia, Persia, even India or Carthage.

"Menes, what do you think?"

"It's a fool's quest, General. I'd rather go over the walls of Babylon by myself."

"You don't believe the rumors then?"

"That they are a bunch of western barbarians from the future?" Menes shrugged. "I don't know. But I don't believe that they can't fight. No one who can build something like that can't fight. Rather, no one who owns a ship like that can't fight. If they couldn't, someone else would have taken it from them by now."

"You lack imagination, Menes," Gorgias said. "It could be done."

Menes shook his head at the general's back and looked out at the ship.

Queen of the Sea, *Alexandria Harbor*
September 20

"Atum told me that Ptolemy is at Memphis?" Marie asked the locals. They were back in the Royal Lounge and taking a break from negotiations on resupply. Dag was present because his knowledge of environmental systems was turning out to be useful in terms of handling the unprocessed products of the environment—all the fungus and poisons and stuff that was in unprocessed fruits, grains and meats. Eleanor Kinney was in the room. She had done most of the negotiating on price and, as a demonstration, had arranged to have fresh loaves of brown bread served. Bread made from the local wheat and ship's yeast. This bread didn't have the ground rock from the milling in it, and it tasted a lot better.

The locals included Atum and Lateef, Dinocrates, Crates and two other merchants, along with Gorgias of Thrace, who was apparently in charge of the garrison of Alexandria. Marie listened to the Macedonian Greek pronunciation of the general's name and it sounded like Gorgeous, which she knew was an ancestor of the name George, which brought to mind the professional wrestler called Gorgeous George. And if ever she'd seen a man who looked less like the iconic wrestler, she couldn't remember it. This man had lank black hair and a heavy beard, a scar down one cheek and a nose that had been broken several times. He was also missing at least a couple of teeth and the ones he had were pretty ground down, and brown.

Dinocrates and Gorgeous George looked at Atum, who shrugged.

Then Gorgeous George nodded. "Yes. The battle with Perdiccas was over a month ago and things are getting back to normal in Memphis. We haven't gotten word from Satrap Ptolemy, but I would guess he will be coming this way. As to the others, by now Alexander's generals will be heading for the meeting at Triparadisus. From what we hear, the troops aren't happy with Peithon and Arrhidaeus."

Dinocrates smiled, then said, "Peithon and Arrhidaeus are apparently having difficulty holding the army together."

"And such troubles couldn't happen to a more deserving pair," Gorgeous George said. "Opportunists, the both of them, and disloyal as well. We got word a day before you arrived that Antipater was expected there soon."

"I wonder how they will react to news of us when it eventually reaches them," Dag said.

Dinocrates seemed confused, then offended, and said, "They will know of your arrival by tomorrow night. The signal fires will tell them. We even know how to read and write."

"I am truly sorry if I gave offense, sir," Dag said and Marie translated. Then she added, "I'm sorry, Dag. I should have edited that or just explained, myself. They had an extensive network of signal fires and pony express to get messages across the empire quickly. I knew that, but I was so distracted by what General Gorgias just said that it didn't really register. Within a week, two at the outside, they will know we have arrived, everywhere from Athens to the Persian Gulf."

"What did he say that distracted you?"

"Antipater isn't at Triparadisus yet."

Dag shook his head in confusion. "So?"

Marie ignored Dag's question to ask one of her own in Macedonian Greek. "Have Peithon and Arrhidaeus been forced to resign?"

"What? They will be forced to resign?" Dinocrates seemed shocked.

But Gorgeous George was wearing an expression of surmise. "No, not yet. When did that happen?"

"I don't know, neither in our calendar or yours. Shortly before Antipater got to Triparadisus, the tensions between Eurydice and those two got so intense that they were forced to resign as regents and send messages to Antipater to hurry up. Then, when..."

Marie stopped speaking. She had to think. She could change history now, assuming the timing was right. The question was: should she?

Eurydice might well have Roxane and Alexander IV murdered if she got solid control of the army that had mutinied and killed Perdiccas. It wouldn't be out of character for any of the players in this history to order or commit murder. Most historians agreed that Roxane had had Alexander's other wives murdered, or at least had been involved.

On the other hand, Marie could be sure from her study of this time that if Cassander, Antipater's son, got his hands on them, both queens and both kings would end up dead. And pretty horribly dead, at least in the case of Eurydice, although it was Alexander the Great's mother Olympias who had murdered Eurydice and Philip in the timeline Marie had come from.

But Cassander was a snake. Even Antipater so despised his son Cassander that he gave the power to others instead of Cassander, and Antipater was no great prize either. Nor Antigonus One-eye. It might turn out that Eurydice and Roxane wouldn't do any better. But could they do any worse?

Marie looked at the locals and realized that she, by herself, couldn't change history. It would take the signal fires. "Here is our best understanding of what happened in my history about this time. As Antipater approached, Peithon and Arrhidaeus were forced to resign. Antipater came into the camp and was, in turn, captured by the troops loyal to Eurydice and held separate from his army."

Dinocrates gave Marie a look, and Marie almost laughed. "Granted, that army probably wasn't loyal to anyone. Say rather, the troops who had listened to Eurydice—or been bribed by Attalus—got hold of Antipater. That situation held for a while, I don't know how long. Then Antigonus One-eye arrived, camped his army with Antipater's across the river from the—call them Eurydice's army—and Antigonus put on his fancy armor and fooled them. He crossed the bridge with just a few select cavalry-men, and gave a long rambling speech in support of Antipater, watching for the guards on Antipater to grow distracted. He was supported in his speech by Seleucus, who got the better part of the eastern empire for his bribe. Antigonus then rescued Antipater and somehow got him back to his side of the river and escaped himself. In exchange, Antigonus got possession of the kings and queens, and got assigned to go hunt down Eumenes. Which took him years, because Eumenes turned out to be a better general than anyone thought. I don't know how detailed your codes are for the signal fires, but if you can get a message to Eurydice with that information, it might make all the difference."

Gorgeous George was looking at her with disbelief clear on his face. Dinocrates pointed at one of the lights and the general's eyes followed his pointing finger. Then he looked back at Marie and nodded.

"What's going on?" Dag asked.

Marie explained. "We're in a position to affect the outcome of the next battle in the succession wars."

"Which adds a certain urgency to my question," Dag said. "How will the generals react to the news of our arrival? And when will they learn of it?"

Marie had given those people who were interested a quick rundown of the wars of the *Diadochi*, the generals, and clearly Dag had been looking stuff up on his own. Marie tried to explain what was going on.

"You should have talked to the captain before you said anything,

Professor Easley," Dag said. Eleanor Kinney was looking daggers at Marie too.

"Does Captain Floden have a doctorate in ancient history that I'm unaware of?" Marie asked.

"He's the captain," Dag insisted.

"His authority on board this ship is based on the law from two thousand and more years in the future, and his expertise. He knows how to make the ship go where we need it to go. I would never dream of questioning his decisions on things like when to drop anchor or how many points to port we should turn. But he is not an expert on this time. I am! This is a political decision, and even in the twenty-first century his authority would not extend to that."

"I'm going to have to report this," Dag said.

"Go right ahead, young man. It won't bother me at all." Marie smiled, then turned back to the locals while Dag made his phone call.

"General Gorgias, what do you plan on doing with the information that I gave you?"

"Professor, is it?" he asked and Marie nodded. "The answer is, I don't know. On a personal basis, I respect Antigonus One-eye as a brave commander. And as little use as I have for Peithon and Arrhidaeus, I have to respect that Antipater is the ranking officer in the Macedonian army. I think I will wait until Ptolemy gets here."

Marie noticed a look between Crates and Atum, but didn't ask about it. And Gorgeous George was still talking. "I was surprised to hear that the future thought so well of Alexander's scribe. He's won some battles, but I assumed it was mostly luck. He's not general material."

"History is quite favorably inclined to Eumenes," Marie said.

"History written by Greeks. Eumenes is a bookkeeper and the son of a wagoner," Gorgeous George said, and both Crates and Atum rolled their eyes.

House of Atum Edfu
September 20

"Who can you contact?" Crates asked.

"That's less the issue than what to say. I have friends among the merchants and an army is always in need of food."

"Then Attalus, I think. He's the one with the money, so he will be in touch with the merchants," Crates said.

"Fine. I will send a message to a merchant I know, and have him talk to Attalus. But what should we say? I don't like Antipater, and I am not all that enamored of One-eye either. But do we really want to put Perdiccas' family back in power?"

"No, but that's not what I think will happen."

Atum looked at Lateef, then back to Crates. "What do you think will happen then?"

"I think that it's all going to come apart, no matter what we do. That being the case, I think we should encourage it to come apart quickly so that Egypt doesn't get hit by the flailing parts of Alexander's empire again."

"So what message? Remember we are limited by the signal codes and the time it will take."

The signal fire network that used bronze mirrors in the daylight hours was owned by Alexander's empire and maintained in each province by the satrap of that province. So the messages of the government would go first, but after that the private merchants could use it by bribing the men manning the signal fires. All of which meant that if they wanted to send a message, they could, but it couldn't be too long, and there was a good chance that a copy of anything they sent would be sold to anyone willing to buy it. The merchants were used to the system, so they used codes. Unfortunately, the codes weren't robust and focused on matters of business, so sending something political would be more challenging.

Atum tried to explain. "It would be easy enough for me to tell Cleisthenes that a shipment of wheat flour would be delayed or arrive early, but telling them that Antigonus is going to steal Antipater away from the army with the help of Seleucus...that's going to be harder. Even with the signals, it will be two days before today's message gets there."

"I know," Crates agreed. "The message we sent when the ship arrived will probably be received in Triparadisus about now."

CHAPTER 5

Triparadisus
September 20

Eurydice sat on the couch, leaning against one arm and listening
to the soldier read out the report from the signal fires. She knew
that someone had gotten the size wrong. There was no way a ship
could be that big. It wasn't possible. Philip, though, was mumbling
and Eurydice slid over to listen. He was muttering numbers as
he often did. Philip wasn't stupid, whatever the others thought.
He just thought differently. He didn't understand the value of
a drachma and he never looked at people directly, but he read
everything he could get his hands on and was constantly doing
calculations. It was more than simple counting, what Philip did.
He understood the world through numbers, shapes and vectors.
So she listened carefully and began to wonder. Philip seemed to
think it was at least possible.

Once that was out of the way, Eurydice got up and moved
over to Roxane, who was sitting in state across the room. Philip
would be busy with his calculations for a time. "What do you
think?"

Roxane sniffed dismissively and Eurydice wanted to slap the
spoiled bitch, but managed to restrain herself. She waited, and
after a moment Roxane said, "With the army in the state it's in,
it could mean anything. Remember, Antipater is on his way, and
will be arriving in no more than a week."

"I'll deal with the old man," Eurydice said.

Roxane looked back at her. "Don't underestimate him. Your hold on the army is weak, and Antipater has the rank. These are soldiers, Eurydice. Unpaid and angry, but soldiers. They are conditioned to respect rank."

"They killed Perdiccas," Eurydice insisted.

"No. Peithon and Arrhidaeus killed Perdiccas, and the army let it stand. And that only after the idiot had lost a third of the army trying to march them across the Nile."

Eurydice didn't like Roxane, but had to admit that the woman was astute. She understood politics, even if she lacked the guts of a Macedonian. Now Eurydice considered what that would mean for herself. Roxane was probably right about the reverence that Antipater was held in by the common soldiers, especially since they hadn't had to deal with the old man for decades. Antipater wasn't fond of Eurydice, and Eurydice didn't trust him. She didn't trust any of them. But old man Antipater despised anything that wasn't Macedonian, and despised women even more than he did Greeks. Until now, Eurydice had been planning to continue her bid for the regency, or at least a real place on a regency council. But with Antipater running things, that seemed a lot less likely to succeed. She would need to push the sub-commanders so that the old man didn't get to use his rank. "Do you want to be left in Antipater's hands?"

"Do you think we have a choice?" Roxane hissed at her, her eyes slitted. "Disabuse yourself of the notion that we are queens, little girl. We are no more than bargaining chips in the game of power that the generals play now."

"Is that what you want?" Eurydice hissed back. "To be a playing piece?"

"It's—" Roxane started in what was almost a shout and suddenly everyone in the room was looking at them. Roxane looked back and they looked away, then she continued much more quietly. "It's not a matter of what we want or don't want. It's a matter of what is."

"But the ship," Eurydice insisted. "It changes things, doesn't it?"

"Maybe. If it's real, and not some plot. At this point, how it changes things is anyone's guess."

Eurydice turned away from Alexander's beauty and went back to Philip. The woman's perfume was giving her a headache.

Reliance, *Alexandria Harbor*
6:23 AM, *September 21*

Joe Kugan saw the bulk of the *Queen of the Sea* rise out of the horizon with a mixture of relief and resentment. He'd had plenty of time to think as he made his slow way across the Mediterranean Sea. Everything was left back in the future. His wife, his sons, the company . . . everything. Meanwhile, he and his crew had been left behind by the *Queen* as she rushed off to Alexandria. They could have gone slower. They could have waited, but they didn't. Well, fine. If they were going to be that way, so was he. The *Reliance* was his ship, and the fuel oil on her was his fuel oil. His and his crew's.

"Radio message, Captain," Michael Kimball said. "They want us to pull up on the starboard side of the *Queen* and prepare for fuel transfer."

"We'll go ahead and pull up to the side, but not a drop of our fuel oil is going to leave the barge till I have a few things settled with Captain Queeg over there."

"Fine by me, Captain," Michael said with a grin.

"The *Reliance* confirms that she will pull up alongside, but says that refueling will have to wait until a price and a medium of exchange are established."

"Fine." Lars Floden rubbed his eyes. He had been in meetings almost nonstop since they reached Alexandria. Meetings with the cooks and the engineering staff as they tried to come up with ways of separating the wheat from the chaff and grinding the wheat into flour suitable for making bread. Fortunately, there was yeast in the bakery. By using some of that, they had established a good colony of twenty-first century yeast, which they might be able to sell to the locals because clearly the *Queen*'s bakery turned out better bread than the locals. Then there were the meats, which often had tapeworms and other parasites. For right now, that was being handled by cooking everything well done. The vegetables were of indifferent quality and it was all expensive.

In spite of the amount of the provisioning problems Jane handled, a load of it had made its way to the captain's desk because people didn't like the answers Jane gave them. "Set up an appointment with Captain Kugan and the staff captain." Lars felt himself smile. "And include Congressman Wiley. If he wants to be involved so much, let him tell Joe Kugan that the oil in *Barge 14* is owned by all the passengers in common."

"Yes, sir." Doug smiled and pulled up the captain's schedule. It was—unsurprisingly—full. It would be the next afternoon before the captain, staff captain, and Congressman Wiley would all be free at the same time.

Royal Lounge, Queen of the Sea
September 21

"Not at all, Captain Kugan. I agree completely. You and your crew own the *Reliance* and the fuel on board her as well." Al Wiley smiled generally around the room and even snorted a laugh at the captain's expression. "You always knew I was a Republican, Captain Floden, not a communist. I am simply concerned that all the, er, found wealth be shared out in a reasonably equitable manner. The people on the *Reliance* own the *Reliance*. The people on the *Queen of the Sea* own the *Queen of the Sea*."

By now Kugan was looking smug, Floden was looking pissed, and Dahl was looking ready to chew nails and spit tacks. Which was pretty much what Al had been going for in all cases. "You and your crew have a valuable ship there, Captain Kugan, and a valuable cargo. However, it's a very limited cargo too."

"What do you mean?"

"You don't have machine shops on the *Reliance*. You can't fix anything that can't be fixed by hand. You don't have food, water or the means to get any of those things on your own. Perhaps most important of all, you don't have someone who can speak to the locals to allow you to negotiate with them directly. And even if you could, what makes you think they would negotiate in good faith?"

Royal Palace, Alexandria
September 21

"We need to learn their language," Dinocrates said. "I don't like the idea of everything we say going through that woman. There's something odd about her. For one thing, I'm sure she's much older than she looks."

Atum suppressed a grin when Ptolemy looked first at his hetaera, Thaïs, then back at Dinocrates.

"There are options, *Philos* Dinocrates," Atum said. *Philos* was a court title roughly on a par with the later "count," and had been given to Dinocrates by Alexander when he was given the job of overseeing the construction of Alexandria. Ptolemy reaffirmed the title when he was made satrap of Egypt by Perdiccas at Babylon, just after Alexander's death.

"What alternatives?" asked Ptolemy.

Atum bowed. "They have a sort of magic slate." He waved to Dinocrates and Crates, as well as Lateef. "We've all seen them." Atum was referring to the e-pads and phones with their gorilla glass fronts. Something that you really had to see to believe. "Please withhold your judgment on our sanity until you have had a chance to see them. In any case, there is a demon or ghost they call a *program* that can be placed in the slates, and it can translate, if not well. Its Greek is barely understandable, and it speaks no other tongue known in this time."

"I thought they knew Egyptian in that future," said Thaïs.

"So, apparently, did they," Lateef said. "The language of my home has changed even more in the intervening centuries than Greek has. What about Latin, Atum? Didn't Marie say something about the translation ghost having Latin?"

"I've heard it. It sounds a little like Latin, but it's hard to tell. Perhaps I should have said 'it speaks no other *civilized* tongue.' The point I was trying to make is that if we can get one of their magic slates, we can use it to learn their language."

"Will the slates work for us?" Ptolemy asked.

"I asked about that, and if I understood the answer, they will for a time, if we are given the spell to unlock them. But they run out of life force and must be fed their vibrant force. They call it 'e-lek-trik' I think, and it is made of the same stuff as lightning."

Dinocrates, Crates and Thaïs all nodded in support. Some of the Greek philosophers had experimented with the same power. No one in the room knew the distinctions involved. The experiments they had read about had been with static electricity, and to a lesser extent with bioelectrical sources, like the electric eel. Direct current and alternating current would be new to them, but not completely unfamiliar.

"Then we should see about gaining one or more of the magic slates and some means of providing them with the 'e-lek-trik,' you mentioned," Ptolemy told Atum, "and learn how they are fed.

I hope it can be done like the experiments discussed in works, and doesn't require sacrifices to their gods.

"What can you tell me about that other ship that arrived this morning?"

"I was on the *Queen* when it arrived," Atum said. "It is a fuel ship, loaded with the refined naphtha they use to power the larger ship. That's all I know, but I got the impression that Dag was less than pleased with the crew of the *Reliance* for some reason. He didn't say why, and I didn't want to ask."

"Yet another reason we need one of those magic slates."

"It won't be cheap, Satrap. I bought one of their 'flashlights,' and it cost a thousand pounds of wheat. The 'L-E-D flashlight' is a relatively simple device, so Dag explained to me, and I saw the same thing in their gift shop."

Ptolemy's expression went dark, and Atum lost any urge to smile in response. "I will send messages to Memphis for more grain and foodstuffs," Ptolemy said. "And I don't doubt that I can handle the expenses. But I don't like these merchants trying to bargain with me in my own harbor." The satrap of Egypt grimaced, then continued. "In the meantime, get me a slate."

Gorgias looked at Ptolemy as the others left the audience chamber. "It can be done, Satrap. I have been aboard the ship and seen both the strengths and weaknesses of it."

"And what are they?"

"The great strength is simply the size of the thing. That, you can see from here. It would be a climb and we would take losses making it. The ship is like a mountain fortress."

"And the weaknesses?"

"The people on board that ship are sheep for the shearing. Many of them are old, and all of them are fat. If there are two hundred soldiers among the five thousand people on that ship, I'll eat the excess. That is the largest single weakness, but almost as great is the lack of weapons. They wear on their belts a device that is apparently something like a slingshot that throws a small oblong pellet. I doubt they would stand up against bows, even if they had a lot of them. And they don't. They have twenty, perhaps twice that. I didn't want to seem too curious, but they are, at the core, unarmed oldsters off on a jaunt."

"What would be the best way to take the ship?"

"Subversion of the crew, I would think." Gorgias considered. The crew were basically servants, though not slaves. Certainly not war captives. They were paid for their work and under normal circumstances could leave their service. But these weren't normal circumstances, and Gorgias was convinced that the laws that held them in check had been left behind in that place or time they came from. Gorgias wasn't convinced it was truly the future, though he was starting to think it might be. He brought himself back to the question. "Failing that, or perhaps in coordination with it, an attack by galleys, ropes and ladders thrown up to the ports to get our troops in. Once we are in, there won't be much to it. But we will lose men getting in, possibly a lot of men."

Ptolemy nodded, and then said, "Make your preparations, but quietly. And take no overt action until I tell you to." There was a half-smile on the satrap's face. "Such a ship is rulership of the Mediterranean Sea and all the lands surrounding it. If Alexander had had such a ship, he would have indeed ruled the world. And if Perdiccas owned it, I would be dead now. At the very least, we cannot allow it to fall to Antigonus or Seleucus. Attalus would be almost as bad. Hades, even old Antipater would be dangerous with such a weapon. If for no other reason than that Cassander might inherit it when the old man dies. Even Cassander would be brave from aboard such a ship."

"What about Eumenes?"

"No. And not because he's a Greek. He's a good general and Alexander trusted him with reason. No, we are safe from..." Ptolemy stopped. "No. You're right, Gorgias. Eumenes would be the greatest danger of all. Not because of his ambition, but because of his honor. He would try to impose Alexander's empire on us all, out of loyalty to the Argead royal house. He would put demented Philip and baby Alexander on my throne." Ptolemy shook his head. "No, we can't allow that ship to run free."

Queen of the Sea, *Alexandria Harbor*
September 21

"This is so cool," fifteen-year-old Latisha Jones told her brother as they filed into the theater. The entertainment staff had decided to put on Egyptian Karaoke Night in the Queen Elizabeth Theatre. So far, all The Event that brought them here had done was extend their vacation. At least that's what Latisha was telling herself just as hard as she could. It wasn't that she was unaware of the danger they were all in, and the fact that they might never get home again. But she didn't want to face it, not yet. Latisha was in denial, and had every intention of staying there till they got home.

Jason Jones tried to play along. Two years younger than his big sister, he was finding denial harder to achieve. Dad was a high school principal and this was the annual divorced-father-family-vacation. Since The Event, Dad had been spending almost all his time on the shipnet. He was trying to figure out what had happened and what they could do about it. Mom was back at home and Jason was wondering if he would ever see her again.

They filed into the theater, found their seats, and the lights came up to a black-haired guy in a campy Egyptian headdress and a skimpy costume.

"Under the circumstances we have decided that what is needed is a clear and exact description of Egypt at this time," said the guy. Then he went into a lip-synching of Steve Martin's "King Tut."

After King Tut came a woman singing "Cleopatra, Queen of Denial" and then a group of women doing "Walk Like an Egyptian."

Overall, Jason didn't think it was particularly funny, but Latisha seemed to be having a blast.

"How are the passengers reacting, Jane?" Lars Floden asked the hotel manager.

"Restive, Lars. The ship has a lot of entertainment venues, but they are not enough for everyone. It's planned that much of the entertainment on these cruises will be shore excursions."

"We can't risk that sort of thing yet. I'm not even comfortable with the crew's shore leave under Atum's watchful eye. A bunch of Americans with, for the most part, very little in the way of experience with other cultures? That would be begging for incidents."

"I'm not arguing, Captain. But we are going to have to come up with some sort of solution. The *Queen* is a big ship, but it's not big enough for this many people to live on permanently. So the restiveness is only going to get worse. Right now, the main thing preventing riots is that everyone is terrified and intent on sticking together. Once they calm down a little, they are going to start demanding things."

"They started that within minutes of the—"

"No, they didn't. Sure, there were the 'take us home,' 'you have to undo this' types, but mostly people have stayed pretty calm. That's going to change as it sinks in that they aren't about to be beheaded by a bunch of barbarian Greeks, and they'll start to wonder what they are going to do for the rest of their lives. This isn't a stable situation, and I don't see any way of making it into one."

Lars nodded. He knew Jane was right. He just didn't have a good answer. He had *an* answer: dump the passengers. That, at least, would work. But he couldn't do that. He wouldn't. He had a responsibility for everyone on board. In a way, he had even more of a responsibility to the passengers than to the crew. This needed a political solution and Lars wasn't a politician.

However, Lars did have a politician on hand. As much as he didn't care for Al Wiley and distrusted his judgment, he was going to have to call on his skills.

At that moment, Al Wiley was having his own problems. "What can I do for you, Reverend Hewell?"

"We have to go to Judea. The Second Temple still stands and Jesus is coming. We must clear the way for him. Cleanse the temple and protect Judea from the Romans."

"Reverend, that's more than three hundred years from now. We are facing more urgent concerns."

"You don't understand, Congressman. Being a Mormon and all. It's why God sent us here. We are to prepare Judea for the coming Christ."

Al kept his politician's smile, but it wasn't easy. He tossed Amanda a look. Amanda shrugged at him behind Mr. Hewell's back and Al knew what she meant. You had to take support where it was offered in politics. "I will take your points to the captain and speak for them. But right now, it's not up to you, or me, or any of the passengers. It's up to the captain. We are aboard a ship at sea, and the law is clear about that. Until some form of civil government is established, we won't have a lot of say in what goes on."

"That's not right, Congressman. We're Americans. I can't abide dictatorships."

"That's a harsh way of putting it, Mr. Hewell, though I take your meaning. Still, any sort of change in government would need to be done civilly, through the electoral process."

Once Hewell was gone, Amanda ushered in the next complainant. This one wanted the ship to go back out to sea and avoid contaminating the local culture with modernity. Al found he had more sympathy for Mr. Hewell. But he was polite, promised to bring the matter up with the captain, and repeated the spiel about it not being their choice until some form of civilian government was established.

"Boss," Amanda said, "we're pushing pretty close to mutiny."

"I know, Amanda. But if it turns out to be a choice between mutiny and a permanent dictatorship, I'll risk the mutiny." Al threw up his hands in frustration. "Do you think I like this? I'd rather be back in Washington dealing with the Democrats, for the Lord's sake."

"I think Captain Floden has done a pretty good job, sir," Amanda said.

"Captain Floden hasn't yet made a decision or formed a plan," Al said. "He's just reacting. Marie Easley says the best place to go for food is Alexandria, so we go to Alexandria. Now we are resupplying. Fine, good enough, exactly what a pseudo-military bureaucrat ought to be doing. But Floden isn't the man to set policy."

"There really hasn't been a lot of cause for Captain Floden to make long-term policy decisions. It's only been a few days and we've had enough on our plate just dealing with the emergencies."

"I know you're right," Al admitted. "And it may be that we got off on the wrong foot, but I just don't trust his judgment."

Eleanor Kinney was worrying over the same issue, but from a different angle. "We need something to sell, Professor."

Marie Easley looked up from her computer screen. "Excuse me? I thought we had established a list of goods and services."

"We did, and aside from the issues of space, it's working for now. But this isn't a cargo ship. It's a cruise ship. It's designed to carry people, and people are light cargo."

"Light cargo? A human is mostly water. We aren't that light."

"We are when you figure one human in an eight-by-twelve-by-fourteen-foot space, not to mention all the public spaces. We're lighter than a cargo of feathers and a whole lot lighter than a cargo of grain. That's why cruise ships are so much taller than cargo ships."

Marie nodded. "Yes. I should have realized. Also the electricity, the LED lights that have a very long life span, the plumbing and computers. Putting this ship to work as a cargo hauler would be a waste..."

Professor Easley trailed off and Eleanor was tempted to ask her what she was thinking. But she waited.

"A university," Marie said. "Most especially a technical school that will have required courses in political philosophy. If they want to study electronics, fine. But they must also study the Declaration of Independence and the Bill of Rights. The thirteenth amendment and the reason for it."

By now Eleanor had seen the slaves in Alexandria and the welts on backs and arms, the scars on faces and feet. Yes. The thirteenth amendment abolishing slavery was something these people needed to learn about.

It's something they need shoved down their throats. Eleanor was shocked at how violent that thought was. There was a rage building in her that she hadn't realized was there. A little Eleanor Kinney standing up next to Tony Curtis and shouting "I am Spartacus!" along with all the other slaves.

All of a sudden, she was worried. Because as strongly as she felt about it, she knew that they couldn't fight the Civil War with five thousand people, most of them old farts on vacation. Al Wiley said he understood that, but she didn't trust his judgment, not on this.

Triparadisus
September 21

"I don't trust his judgment," Roxane said looking to the north, seeing in her mind's eye the armies that were still days away. Antipater was closest but Antigonus was marching his army to Triparadisus too. She turned to her guard commander, Kleitos. "With Eurydice playing her games, Antigonus will push too hard out of anger and outrage. Ptolemy might have us killed for political reasons, but Antipater is likely to do it just because he's offended or impatient."

"Antipater isn't any worse than Perdiccas," Kleitos said. "He was going to marry Cleopatra and reach for the crown and you know it."

"Maybe. But Cleopatra is thirty-six and if she isn't past her child-bearing years, she will be soon enough. Besides, Perdiccas was made regent by Alexander and the partition at Babylon. That's why Eumenes was loyal to him. The rest of the generals are vultures."

"I know you like the Greek, but the Macedonians won't follow him. I know. I'm a Macedonian."

"And yet you are loyal to me, and my guard as much as my jailor, Kleitos."

"I'm a man under orders, Roxane, and little Alexander is his father's son. I owe him my loyalty, at least what loyalty I have left after all these years a soldier."

Roxane laughed at that. Kleitos was a cynical man, and she knew that if the soldier was ordered to, he would kill her and even little Alexander. But, still, a sort of affection had grown up between them. He was a nice man in his cynical way, even if he was a killer. Every man she had known in her life had been a killer, at least potentially. And most of them had been in fact. That was the world she lived in and the only one she knew. But she knew that world well. She knew how to play the game and how to hide. That was why she was worried now. Ptolemy had abandoned any thoughts of taking Alexander's place. Roxane was confident of that, even though he had stolen Alexander's body. Otherwise he wouldn't have passed on the regency. With him gone, the greatest power among the generals was Antigonus One-eye or perhaps Seleucus. Before Eurydice's machinations, Roxane would have thought that Peithon might have been the strongest, but the little minx had managed to force him and Arrhidaeus to resign as commanders of the army, leaving Seleucus as much in charge as anyone was.

Antipater was old and not that strong, but he might emerge as a candidate who was acceptable to the rest, since Peithon was so recently embarrassed by Eurydice. He was the likely choice, more for his weakness than for his strength. That was why Eurydice had been able to stop Ptolemy's chosen surrogates.

Antipater was better than his son, Cassander, but he hated Eumenes because he was a Greek and didn't like Roxane because she wasn't a Macedonian. What Roxane was afraid of was that Antigonus might have her killed in a fit of rage before he realized it was a bad move politically. That was what had happened to Perdiccas when he had his brother murder Eurydice's mother.

But it didn't matter. She knew Kleitos. She even liked Kleitos. But Kleitos would kill her before he let her escape. Besides, where would she run to? That had always been the true stopping point of her thoughts in the past. No place to go, even if she did get away. But now there was a possibility. That great ship. But she knew almost nothing about it, only that it existed. Even its existence had freed her thoughts, though. What if the great ship did mean safety? What if it was peopled by an army of allies? What if it was Alexander coming back from the grave? Ptolemy had taken Alexander's body to Egypt, after all.

CHAPTER 6

The tension in the bright and airy room could be cut with a knife. Captain Floden was keeping his poker face on, but Staff Captain Dahl was visibly bristling. Marie Easley, Amanda noted with carefully hidden amusement, was unbothered and perhaps even unaware of the tension. She was busy with a slate, checking pronunciations and tweaking the Greek translation program. She had an ear bud in one ear and was apparently paying no attention at all to the looks she was getting from the crew and, for that matter, Congressman Wiley.

"If you don't find us too distracting," Captain Floden said, "we'd like to discuss the warning you decided to issue to the locals about upcoming political events."

Marie looked up. "Why?"

"Because it might have interfered with our negotiations with the locals on any number of matters. We're expecting a visit from Ptolemy later today, and we have no idea how he reacted to your news," Staff Captain Dahl said, and Congressman Wiley—for once—nodded in agreement.

"What are you nodding about, Congressman?" Dahl said hotly. "You've been half a step from open mutiny for the last three days."

"Anders, calmly, please," Jane Carruthers said, then looked at Wiley. "Not that I don't agree with him, Congressman."

"Then you are mistaken, Ms. Carruthers. The passengers are

71

concerned, and rightly so. We have no plan. We simply react. If Professor Easley is to be censured for not following the plan, then there ought to *be* a plan. Not that I think she should have blurted out the predictions like a seeress at Delphi. Certainly not without consultation. But how can we expect her to follow the playbook if there is no playbook?"

Marie was now looking back at the slate.

Captain Floden held up a hand. "Believe it or not, Congressman, I tend to agree with your complaints, though I don't agree that they justify incitement to mutiny." He turned to Marie. "Is that why you went ahead and told them, Marie? Because there was no plan?"

"Not at all, Captain. I said what I said after careful, if quick, consideration, based on *my* judgment. I am an American citizen, even if America is lost in a distant future that will probably not happen at all. No one on Earth, either in the time we left or in this one, has the right to tell me I may not speak my mind. Some may, at some point, have the power to do so, but they still won't have the right."

She turned to Congressman Wiley. "'Congress shall make no law respecting an establishment of religion, or prohibiting the free exercise thereof; or abridging the freedom of speech, or of the press; or the right of the people peaceably to assemble, and to petition the government for a redress of grievances.' My right to speak my mind is not yours to restrict, nor is my right to paint myself blue and worship sacred groves, should I choose to do so. Not yours, or all of Congress, or the captain and all his crew. And, Congressman, you have sworn an oath to defend that right of mine and all the others."

Amanda wanted to cheer. She looked around the room to see consternation on all the faces there. Then Captain Floden spoke up. "No one is trying to restrict your rights, Marie. We are simply asking for a bit of restraint in—"

"Captain Floden, I am not impressed by sentences that contradict themselves. If you are trying to impose restraint, you're trying to restrict. You can't do the one without doing the other." Marie took a deep breath. "Congressman Wiley is right that we need a plan, but the first thing we need to decide is are we to be free people or helots."

"Or whats?" Amanda asked.

"The helots were the—no, *still are*—the slaves of the Spartans, though the status has probably changed by now, from outright slavery to something closer to serfdom. My point is that I am a free citizen, not a helot. I did not yell fire in a crowded theater, so I acted completely within my rights. I, at least, intend to remain a free citizen, and I expect my rights to be respected."

"We take your point," Jane Carruthers said soothingly.

"Yes, we do," agreed Captain Floden. At least, he seemed to be agreeing, until he continued. "But we are in a ship at sea, under what must be considered emergency conditions."

"First of all, Captain, I don't concede that we are in a state of emergency. The word is quite specific. It refers to an immediate threat, not to a generally dangerous situation. But even if we were, absent me shouting fire in that crowded theater or somehow interfering with the crew delivering instructions to other passengers, you would still have no right to restrict my speech."

Congressman Wiley held up a hand, like a student asking for attention. When Marie looked at him, he said, "I'm convinced, Professor. You had a perfect right to speak, whether it was wise or not. But having established that, what were you trying to accomplish?"

"Two things, Congressman Wiley," Marie said. "First, I was proving my claims, and all our claims at the same time. An event that happened in our history hadn't yet happened in this one, and I could tell them about it. If it happens as I said it would, or even if it just starts to happen as I said it would, if for instance Peithon and Arrhidaeus are forced to resign, we have proved that we know at least the outline of their future. Second, if my warning does affect the situation, if, for instance, having gotten word of Antipater's trick, Eurydice manages to foil it, we will know that we can change history.

"But there was another reason. Antipater was a disaster as regent, and the generals, the successors to Alexander, were something of a disaster for the world. Almost any change would be a change for the better. There is a young woman with a mentally challenged husband, and another with a two-year-old—or perhaps three by now—who, in the flow of time, would all die by murder. I was unwilling to sit by and let that happen without trying to change it."

Amanda looked around the room. There were considering expressions on several of the faces.

Captain Floden gave a sharp nod. "I am Norwegian, but we also have those rights and I would be no happier to see them disappear than you would. We will be a free people, be assured of that. That still leaves two major questions. First, what are our plans? Second, how will we determine them? Congressman, I would hear your thoughts on the matter."

"Elections will have to be held. An emergency committee could be established on an interim basis, but elections will have to be held as soon as we can manage. After that, it will be up to the elected body to determine policy."

"I am leery of a majority trying to vote itself a free lunch," Floden said. "I will not allow the expropriation of the *Queen of the Sea* by the passengers."

And they got down to business. The meeting went on for hours and not much was actually settled. What was established were a set of basic principles under which they would build their government.

First, it was agreed that control of the *Queen of the Sea* would remain with the captain and crew of the *Queen* and control of the *Reliance* would remain with the captain and crew of the *Reliance.* However, it was also agreed, at least in principle, that all the transportees had a legitimate interest in both ships and their cargos. That, at the very least, the passengers could not be put off the ship without their consent.

Second, it was established that a civil government based on the principles of representative democracy would be put in place. That the rights of individuals would be protected. Things like free speech and protection from unreasonable search and seizure, would be enshrined in the basic law of the new nation, as would the principle of equality before the law. The issue concerning the right to keep and bear arms was shelved for the moment, since Europeans and Americans had different traditions and attitudes on the question.

Through it all, there was a snake sitting under the table, rattling its rattles and preparing to strike. The snake had two heads; the first was simply that the *Queen of the Sea* wasn't big enough for her population. The second was more subtle. The population was too small to be viable.

Biologically, the population was too small, and would be even if all of them were in their early twenties. The fact that well over half the women on board were past childbearing age made it even worse. Even among the men, a lot of the little swimmers were, nowadays, little waders.

But even worse was the question of cultural viability. They didn't have a culture to be viable. The passengers were from all over the USA and Canada, with a sprinkling from other parts of the first world. The crew was divided into officers—mostly from western Europe—and crew—a majority of whom were from Asia and the Pacific Isles, with a sizeable representation from Africa, Latin America and the Caribbean. It wasn't a naturally cohesive group and it wasn't made up of volunteers. Tensions between ship's complement and passengers were increasing, and so were tensions between staff and crew, officers and lower deck crew.

About the only thing keeping it from blowing up was the threat of being murdered or enslaved by the pre-Christian primitives.

Triparadisus
September 23

Cleisthenes read the message, which was a set of letters. The Greek alphabet was used as both letters and as numbers. Three Greek letters could provide any number between one and nine hundred. Cleisthenes had a code book and what he got was a choice of seven hundred fifty-three phrases, and some number groups that indicated that the next numbers really were numbers. The code was nothing new, and variations on it were used from Carthage to Babylon. So, having received the message, he went to his tent and decoded it. Passage 354 read *Peithon rode at the head of the army*, and the next group instructed him to use only the first word.

It went on like that till Cleisthenes had the whole message. *Peithon forced resign. Antipater captured. Cyclops rescues. Through ruse. Seleucus bribe. Ship from future. Tell queen.*

Cleisthenes leaned back against his pillow on the bench at his work table and thought. Peithon and Arrhidaeus had been forced to resign, and had sent messages to Antipater telling him to hurry. And Seleucus was being very attentive to Eurydice. So was the message that he should bribe Seleucus? Or that One-eye would bribe Seleucus?

Cleisthenes didn't trust Seleucus to stay bribed. Seleucus had tried to short him on the payment for the wheat twice now. He would have a talk with Attalus. There was no way he could get in to see Eurydice, or even Roxane.

Attalus was encamped next to the main camp, with a large contingent of guards to protect the silver coins he had gotten hold of, and merchants were a common sight in his camp. Cleisthenes made no real impression till he reached the tent of Attalus. "I need to see Attalus. I have important news of the giant ship."

The guard nodded and went into the tent, and Cleisthenes was ushered in.

"Has it left the harbor at Alexandria?" Attalus asked quickly. The giant ship had been the talk of the army camp since the news arrived. And such news was of special concern for Attalus, because he had been Perdiccas' naval commander and had kept control of the fleet. A fleet that was in serious jeopardy if a ship the size that was reported decided to threaten it. Such a ship could run over his fleet and leave it kindling, probably without taking any damage at all.

"No, General. It still sits quietly in Alexandria harbor, buying grain and other foodstuffs. And selling the finest quality steel on Earth and other goods of like quality. What I have just learned, or rather had confirmed, is where it comes from."

"You're saying it really is from the future?"

"Yes. I just got a message from Egypt that Peithon and Arrhidaeus would be forced to resign."

"They already...Oh, I understand. They couldn't have known that when they sent the message. So they are from the future, or they have some magi that can see at a great distance."

"That's not all the message said. They report that Antipater will be captured by the army and that Antigonus will come to his rescue with the assistance of Seleucus."

They talked for a while. Attalus paid Cleisthenes a handsome bribe for the information, and to keep it to himself. "Also," Attalus finished, "report any new information directly to me."

Once Cleisthenes was gone, Attalus went for a walk. He needed to think. He moved around the camp with his bodyguard, and saw Seleucus talking with Eurydice.

Attalus had generally good relations with Eurydice, but she was wild. As he watched, it seemed like she was listening to Seleucus a bit too carefully. That decided him. He would tell Roxane, not Eurydice. He turned on his heel and headed across the camp.

Triparadisus was a set of three "paradises," one large hunting park, an orchard of olive and fig trees, and a smaller walled garden with flowers, fruits and vegetables. The hunting lodge was located on the side of the river that held the trees and the vegetables, with the actual hunting park across the river. Across the river was also the direction from which Antipater was expected to arrive. So, while there were scouts on the other side of the river, most of the army was on this side. Both queens and both kings were located in the hunting lodge, though Eurydice wandered the camp at will.

Attalus climbed the three stone steps to the wooden porch of the hunting lodge and faced the guards. "I'm here to speak to Queen Roxane."

"I'll check but I doubt the queen will want to be ..."

The guard trailed off, and Attalus handed him a large silver coin. "Please tell her it's important."

Shortly thereafter, Attalus was let into the presence. The little emperor was wielding—sucking on—a toy sword. It was made of wood, but painted in bright colors.

Roxane was sitting on a couch, leaning against one arm, eating a fig. "What can I do for you, Attalus?"

"I have word of the ship, the *Queen of the Sea*."

Roxane sat up. "What news?"

Attalus looked around at the guards and serving maids, then back at Roxane. But she just shook her head. "I couldn't dismiss them if I wanted to, Attalus, and I have no reason to trust you. How long will I live if Eurydice becomes the head of this army?"

"Longer than you might think. Eurydice may be impetuous, but she isn't stupid."

"Then why are you here?"

"Because I don't trust Seleucus, and he's too close to Eurydice right now."

Roxane gestured to a chair. "Have a seat then. What news from the ship? Is it really from the future as they say?"

"Yes, and it carries some interesting information about what will happen." Attalus took the offered seat and stopped talking. He was aware of the guards and not at all comfortable with their presence.

"Kleitos," Roxane said. "Just you."

A man in bronze breastplate, with a steel sword at his side, made a gesture. The servants and most of the guards moved out of easy earshot. Attalus looked at the man. He was one of Alexander's veterans, going a bit gray now, and like most of them scarred from years of fighting. He was stocky, but well-muscled, with curly brown hair. There was a curl to his lips that Attalus didn't much care for, like he expected to be lied to and wasn't going to believe you no matter what you said. But there was nothing for it. Roxane needed to be told. "They report that Peithon and Arrhidaeus will be forced to resign."

There was a snort of laughter, then Kleitos said. "Excellent. Prove your validity as a seer by reporting what has already happened."

"From five hundred miles away," Attalus said. "They couldn't have known when they sent word."

"*They* couldn't have," Kleitos said, and Attalus started to stand in anger. Kleitos' hand dropped to his sword.

"Stop it!" Roxane hissed.

Attalus got himself under control. He took a breath, then another. "I am not a liar, Kleitos."

"And I'm not a babe, to be taken with fables and stories of magic ships from the future."

"Neither am I, but there are too many reports from too many sources."

"No. They all come through the signal fires and all it would take would be some prankster with more silver than sense bribing some signal man." Kleitos sneered.

Suddenly Attalus relaxed, leaning back in his chair. "No. You're wrong. You know that there are codes used to send the messages. The army has one, the merchants others, the civil government different codes. This latest report came through a commercial agent. A grain merchant. That means that it was encoded by his partner in Alexandria, before it was sent on signal fires. The prankster wouldn't know those codes."

"Unless it's Ptolemy, playing some deep game on us all."

Now it was Attalus' turn to laugh. "Believe or don't, Captain, it makes no difference to me." Attalus turned back to Roxane. "Your Majesty, I believe that the ship is real, and I believe that the messages I have received about it are true. Your husband's name lived on more than two thousand years into the future, and even details of the events following his death are recorded." Attalus went on to repeat the news he had gotten from Cleisthenes, then said, "I believe its true. All of it, not just the parts confirmed."

"It's too ridiculous," Kleitos insisted, then held up a hand. "It's not you I doubt, Attalus. It's...the world, I guess. But I think we need more before we act, if we can act at all. If we can change what is already written in the stars, we ought to be very sure before we do so."

"Are you joining us, my captor?" Roxane asked, running a finger over the scroll work on the arm of the couch.

"For now, Majesty. At least until I get a better offer."

"Then what do you recommend?" Attalus asked. And he couldn't help but smile a little. Kleitos was, in his way, the quintessential soldier of Alexander the Great's army, at least in these days after Alexander betrayed them all by dying. They didn't believe in anything but their pay and their comrades—and sometimes not their comrades.

"You said Antipater would be captured. Wait until that happens. Wait until he arrives and gets captured. That's not something I would guess at happening. If it happens on schedule, then we might act."

"Act in what way?" Roxane asked. "Certainly, we can plan what to do if things fall out as the ship people say."

"That's a very good question," Kleitos said. "Would you rather be in Antipater's hands or Eurydice's?"

"I know you don't trust Eurydice, but will you trust me?" Attalus asked. "If I guarantee your safety, will you side with Eurydice against Antipater and Antigonus?"

"I'll have to think about it," Roxane said.

Triparadisus
September 24

"More news," Cleisthenes told Attalus, standing in the afternoon sun and looking out at the orchards. "Word of the resignations reached Alexandria. Ptolemy released the signal mirrors to Atum based on that word. It proved that the ship folk really were from the future. So he let Atum send me word to protect the queens and the kings."

"Ptolemy did that?" Attalus asked. "He wasn't so loyal when he arranged the murder of my brother-in-law and my wife!"

Cleisthenes was silent and Attalus took a few deep breaths of the fruit-scented air to get himself under control. He knew what the merchant wasn't saying. Ptolemy was being invaded when he had done those things.

But it left Attalus wondering what Ptolemy was up to. He was loyal to Alexander until he died, then Ptolemy was loyal to Ptolemy and no one else. He had been so close to trying for the crown after Alexander died that Attalus had been surprised when he didn't. When he had stolen Alexander's body on its way home to Macedonia, Attalus had been sure that Ptolemy was making his move. That was why Perdiccas had invaded Egypt.

Then, when Ptolemy beat Perdiccas on the Nile and had him and Atalante killed, he had again passed on the regency. But, again, it was because there was enough anger in the army about him and the Macedonian troops he had killed in the fighting to make it chancy. Ptolemy wasn't a coward, but he was a careful man. Perhaps too careful. Attalus was convinced that it was that caution, not any concern for Alexander's family, that had persuaded Ptolemy to allow the message.

Suddenly Attalus thought he understood. Ptolemy wanted the fight. He wanted the rest of the empire under the control of a teenaged girl, a deranged king, a weak widow, and an infant king. What better way to make it fail?

Attalus started to smile. Ptolemy had finally made a mistake. He had misread the women. Roxane was cautious, possibly too cautious, but not weak-willed. And Eurydice, young though she was, could move armies with her words.

Attalus hated Ptolemy almost as much as he hated Peithon, Arrhidaeus, and Seleucus. He would love to see the bastard humbled by a couple of women.

"Go on," he said to Cleisthenes. "Tell me everything."

Triparadisus
September 25

The sun was just setting as Antipater reached the north side of the river. He leaned back in his saddle and rubbed his back. At the urgent request of those incompetents, Peithon and Arrhidaeus, he had ridden ahead of the bulk of his army with only an *ile* of cavalry accompanying him. Two hundred fifteen horsemen, including him, Plistarch, and Cassander, his oldest surviving son. His eldest son Iollas had died at the Nile, serving that incompetent bastard, Perdiccas.

Antipater waved Cassander forward. "Camp the *ile* up near those trees, and have them prepare for the rest of the army." He held up a hand, lest Cassander interrupt. "I know they're tired. I don't give a damn."

"Yes, Father," Cassander said, starting to turn his horse.

"And send me Plistarch," Antipater said, then added loud enough for Cassander to hear: "At least he's killed his boar." Cassander tensed but rode back to the troops without commenting. Antipater snorted a laugh. Then he looked across the little wooden bridge. The river that ran through Triparadisus wasn't much of one. Maybe ten feet across and four deep. But it would slow his horsemen, and when the rest of his army got here, it would slow them even more.

Not that that would matter. He reach up and scratched his beard. Not for Antipater the fad of imitating Alexander's clean shaven face. The boy had only done it because his beard had started out a scraggly thing and he'd been embarrassed. Then it had become part of the legend, and by the time he could have grown a proper beard, Alexander couldn't back down. Now half his generals were imitating the shaved state. *No, these traitorous dogs will come to heel as soon as they are shown a firm hand.* That was why he wanted Plistarch with him, even though the boy wasn't half as clever as Cassander. He had killed his boar and the soldiers would respect that.

Plistarch rode up. "You wanted me, Father?"

Antipater nodded, then shifted in the saddle. His butt hurt. "Get Matelus, Leonidas and Theron. We're going to go have a talk with the army."

"Yes, Father," Plistarch agreed excitedly.

Eurydice watched the old man ride up with his third son. Plistarch wasn't as creepy as Cassander. He was just a bully. Eurydice had known the whole family since she was a girl. She was standing on the front porch when the small group of horsemen escorting Antipater were let through by the army. She was almost surprised that Attalus hadn't tried to block them, even though she had told him not to. The army was no longer a cohesive whole. It was fractured into separate groups under their own commanders and sub-commanders.

Antipater climbed down off his horse and she could almost hear his bones creaking. Then he stomped up the stairs.

"Well, you've made a mess of things, little girl, with your tantrums and complaining. But I'm here now, so you can behave yourself." He didn't say it quietly. It wasn't quite a shout, but he was an old soldier with an old soldier's ability to send his voice out to an army in the midst of a battle. There was no battle now, and at least a hundred men heard him.

"You haven't bowed, Cousin. Perhaps your old bones make it difficult. Or have you forgotten courtesy in your dotage?" Eurydice said just as loudly.

"Not too old to turn a spoiled brat of a girl over my knee!" This time Antipater did shout, and stepped forward as though to carry out his threat. One of her guards started forward, and she could have strangled the man. If old Antipater laid hands on her, it would be a fatal blunder. But the guard's response reminded him of where they were, and he stopped.

He turned around, ignoring Eurydice, and shouted to the army. "Is *this* what you've been brought to? Ignoring your lawful superiors and listening to the prattlings of a girl?"

"Where's our money?" came back from somewhere in the crowd of soldiers.

"Money! What about your honor? You're supposed to be the army of Macedonia. Have you forgotten your place?"

"Have you forgotten our pay chests?" shouted another voice from the army. "Alexander promised us a talent of silver each. Where is your honor? You berate us, but give us no pay! You betray Alexander's promise!"

Eurydice kept her smile hidden. She knew that the soldier was right. Alexander had promised them a talent of silver each, back in Babylon. She hadn't been there, but Roxane had. The generals might equivocate about it—and they all had, from Perdiccas on—but Roxane had been there, not three feet from Alexander, when he had promised the troops that bonus. And the troops weren't going to forget it. Alexander might have gotten away with putting them off, but this old man wasn't Alexander.

"The money's in Babylon. It will take time to bring it."

"Why didn't you bring it with you?" came from the crowd. It was a reasonable enough question. There had been good opportunity for Antipater or Antigonus to send for the money the men were owed. Eurydice knew why they hadn't, too. It was standard practice to delay large payments as long as possible. It was part of keeping the treasury full. Even more important, people you owed money had a better reason to stay with you than people who had already been paid. That was a point she had made to the army on their trip back from Egypt, and Antipater was playing this wrong.

It went on like that. In minutes, Antipater had gone from berating to pleading poverty, and the troops weren't buying it. He tried another round of berating, harping on the foolishness of listening to a girl about matters that should be between men, and got back *where's our money?* again.

By then, Antipater was truly angry. "Get out of my way, you stupid puppy, before I have you whipped back to your kennel!" he shouted at a man on the steps.

The man he said that to was twenty-eight and had been promoted to sub-commander by Alexander himself after a bit of gallantry in Persia. "Try it, you old bastard, and I'll gut you like a pig!"

Antipater carried a riding crop, and now he raised it to strike the man.

That was it.

Swords came out of their sheaths, and Eurydice watched as the blood drained from Antipater's face. The old man had never believed, in his worst nightmare, that soldiers of Alexander might stand up to a Macedonian general.

He should have known better, Eurydice thought. After all, they had acquiesced to the murder of Perdiccas.

Antipater and his son, as well as the others with him, were taken into custody. Arrested by the army, for crimes against the army and not having the pay they were promised.

Not all the army agreed. Seleucus' faction opposed the arrest, and it almost came to blows until the men Attalus had paid came down on the side of the captors.

Roxane watched the whole thing from inside the hunting lodge. She nodded. "All right, Kleitos. Go fetch my co-queen. Attalus was right."

Kleitos grunted sourly, but headed out onto the porch. In a few moments, he was back with Eurydice and her guards. Another guard was sent to bring Attalus, who had carefully stayed out of the direct fight. Attalus was popular with part of the army, but very unpopular with other parts of it.

It took a few minutes for Attalus to get there, and Eurydice and Roxane waited in silence.

"Seleucus is busy making sure that Antipater doesn't suffer an unfortunate accident," Attalus said as he entered.

"That's wise," Eurydice said. "Murdering Antipater would enrage his army. Look at what happened when Eumenes killed Craterus. And that was in battle, not while he was a prisoner."

"Perhaps," Roxane said, "but remember Eumenes is the son of a wagoner. I think Seleucus may have another reason."

Eurydice looked at Roxane curiously, and with what Roxane recognized as suspicion mixed with more than a little resentment.

"It's Attalus' story," Roxane said. "I'll let him tell it."

Eurydice turned her suspicious eyes on Attalus and he began to speak. He explained about the messages from the ship from the future, and waiting for the arrest of Antipater as confirmation of those predictions. "What happens next is that Antigonus gets here, comes across the river with just a small contingent, and keeps the army distracted by a long-winded speech while Antipater escapes. Seleucus is bribed with the satrapy of Babylon to make sure it works out that way. Then they get the army to go over to them and you, Roxane, Philip, and little Alexander go back into custody. I get away, but get defeated at Rhodes. Eventually, all four of you are murdered as the factions fight over you."

"I don't believe it," Eurydice said. "How do I know you aren't making it all up?"

"I didn't believe it, either," Roxane said. "Not that I trusted Seleucus, but it just seemed too weird to credit. However, we tested it. And it's true."

"Send someone to watch Seleucus," said Kleitos. "Find out what he's saying to Antipater, and what Antipater is saying to him."

For a moment Eurydice looked at Kleitos as though the furniture had talked, but then she got a considering look. She called over one of her guards and whispered in his ear. He left.

Triparadisus
September 27

Eurydice listened to the report of the maid, and as she listened a fury grew in her heart. She had trusted Seleucus. He was an older man and had seemed to understand what she was going through with Philip, and what she was trying to do with the army and the regency. But he had been agreeing with Antipater, calling her a spoiled child and a flighty little girl, too stupid to be anything but a mattress, and not pretty enough for a good mattress.

Now, she believed. Now, she believed every word Attalus said about the ship. "He shall not cross!"

"What?" the maid asked. "Who shall not cross?"

"Never mind, Damaris. You have done well." Eurydice gave the girl a silver coin. The who was Antigonus One-eye, even now marching his army up to the river. She now understood that if Antigonus crossed that little creek, she would lose her bid for power. She couldn't count on Seleucus.

"Damaris, have my armor brought. And call my personal guards." As the girl turned to go, Eurydice added one more command. "Quietly, Damaris. No fuss, no fanfare."

Two hours later, dressed in his armor, Antigonus One-eye rode toward the little bridge with a dozen picked men following him. And there across the bridge, came a girl on a large chestnut charger. It had to be Eurydice. What did the girl think she was doing?

He reached the bridge and was met on the other side by twenty horsemen, with Eurydice in the lead, wearing full armor.

"Clear the path, girl. I'll speak to the army."

"Not unless you have their pay with you, you won't!" shouted the girl. "We're tired of false promises!"

Ignoring her, Antigonus walked his horse onto the bridge. She did the same. The bridge was only ten feet wide. There was barely room for two horses to pass one another, if both were cooperating. And Eurydice wasn't cooperating. She angled her horse so that he would have to go through her to go on. Antigonus was six foot two and heavy, all of it muscle. He had one eye, and in armor he made an impressive figure.

Eurydice was sixteen years old and barely over five feet tall. She too wore armor, but the difference in size made her stand all the more impressive to the watchers. Also, her horse was just as big as his, and it wasn't going to be pushed aside, not with her on its back. He would have to knock her down to move the horse and he could see the troops behind her. They would have given way before him, but with the tiny girl sitting her horse before them unmoved, they wouldn't.

He knew all that, and it just added to his frustration. Antigonus was not a man to be balked. He felt the anger building, but he didn't try to control it. He reveled in it.

"Get out of my way, you spoiled little whore!" he bellowed.

She just sat there. Then she grinned at him like she had tricked him. Like she was winning.

He lifted his mace and swung. She brought up her shield cat fast, but it made no difference. Antigonus was every bit as strong as he looked. His mace hit the shield and knocked her off her horse. There was a loud splash as Eurydice hit the water below the bridge.

"Traitor!" shouted a voice. "He attacked my wife!" It was Philip, the idiot who mumbled numbers at state dinners, bellowing like he was Alexander. He even sounded like Alexander, at least a little bit. And he was running at Antigonus, having somehow escaped his caretakers.

Then it was a melee at the bridge. Antigonus had just enough rationality left to order Philip captured before he was in the fight.

With Eurydice in the water, no one knowing how badly injured, and his troops holding onto Philip, the army was in no mood to hear anything Antigonus might want to say.

They wanted his blood.

First were the horsemen who had been with Eurydice. They charged the bridge and when they couldn't get across because Antigonus was in the way, they went into the creek and chopped at his horse's legs. One of them reached down, grabbed Eurydice and pulled her back to their side of the creek. And suddenly Antigonus was going into the water, as his horse reared with a spear in its gut.

"What's happening?" Seleucus shouted. He had seen Antigonus approaching the river and moved to the porch to be there when

Antigonus got there. The porch was where they would stand to address the army. Then Eurydice had ridden by, heading for the bridge in full armor and he realized the plan had gone awry. Now it sounded like a battle had broken out next to the bridge. "Fuck." He turned and ran to where the troops were holding Antipater.

Everything had gone all wrong, but in the confusion he could get Antipater back across the river to his army. And then the old man would owe him. He'd pay too. Seleucus would see to that.

He reached the holding area, and the guards were as distracted as he could hope. He grabbed a second horse and told Antipater, "Come on! Now, if you want to live!"

Antipater looked at his son who was looking scared, but still said, "Go, Father!"

Antipater climbed up on the horse. By now the guards were noticing. He and Seleucus rode them down, the ones in the way, and headed for the creek.

"Shoot!" shouted Attalus. He had a dozen bowmen waiting for just this. He had almost lost them when whatever it was had happened at the bridge, but he had managed to keep them here.

Now, as the two riders came galloping at them, the bowmen fired. They hit the men, but the men were in armor and the wounds were shallow. One shot hit the horse Antipater rode, however. It went down and rolled over the old man.

Antipater lay on the ground after the horse rolled off him, and tried to breathe. Blood bubbled out of his mouth as he exhaled. He couldn't feel his legs, but his chest hurt and his head hurt.

Then the darkness came and nothing hurt anymore.

Seleucus started to turn his horse, saw the mess that was Antipater, and rode for his life. He saw Attalus and the bowmen. He started to turn toward them, then he saw Attalus' face and fled.

That man wanted him dead. He might have killed Antipater for politics, but he wanted Seleucus dead with a passion that Seleucus had rarely seen in years of bloody war.

He turned his horse and sprinted for the river. He took two arrows before he got there and his horse died crossing the river, but he made it.

☆   ☆   ☆

Antigonus came up with a bellow and looked around. He was still angry, but he had spent years as a general of Alexander. He could think through rage.

It was over.

He wasn't going to get across the river, and neither were the others. By now, the Silver Shields who had remained with Perdiccas would be forming on the far side of the river and nothing was going to cross the river in the face of those men. Bellowing his rage, he turned his back and made his muddy way out of the river on his side.

CHAPTER 7

King Philip III of Macedonia was restrained. Wrapped in a blanket and tied up. He had been biting. He was also crying for Eurydice and thereby raising dissension in the ranks. Cassander seriously considered having the idiot strangled. Partly in revenge for the death of his father, but also because the screaming tantrum of the king wasn't good for their legitimacy. Word was all over the camp that Antipater was dead and the army was in an ugly mood, half of it wanting to attack the Silver Shields across the river, and half of it wanting to go home to Macedonia.

He turned back to the tent where Antigonus One-eye was drying off and Seleucus was having his wounds tended. Who would command his father's army was anyone's guess, but it wouldn't be Cassander. No, never. Cassander, who did all the work and was from a good family. Never Cassander, because Cassander had never gone out in the woods by himself and killed a stupid boar. *I don't even like pork. Why should I kill a boar?*

In the tent, Antigonus was dry, proving that a good fire could dry out even a bale of wool, given enough time. Seleucus was not in such good shape. One of the arrows had gone into the muscle and lodged in the bone of his shoulder. They had pulled it out, but it was a barbed arrow and did more damage coming out than going in.

"What shall we do with Philip? He won't shut up about Eurydice."

"We give him what he wants," Antigonus said. "If we have to, we give him back to them. I am not such a fool that I would kill the one true-blooded king of Macedonia. Even if he is an idiot and a bastard. And having him screaming against us is almost as bad. So we give Eurydice what we have to, to get her here to shut him up."

"Be careful, Antigonus," Seleucus said. "You haven't had to deal with her like I have. Eurydice is smart and a powerful speaker. You give her enough rope and she's liable to hang us all."

"Maybe so. But what we give, we can take away again, once we get both kings in our hands."

"And what makes you think that the Silver Shields will let us have both kings? Or, for that matter, that they will let Eurydice leave?" Cassander asked.

"Eurydice doesn't matter that much. Not without Philip." Antigonus frowned. "You probably have a point about the rest of it. But we can always claim that Philip is the legitimate king."

"That's fine as far as it goes," Seleucus said. "But if Roxane and Alexander are in Attalus' hands, we can't afford to let Philip have an accident. With that threat off the table, Eurydice is going to be even harder to handle."

"Just because Philip can't have an accident," Cassander said, "doesn't mean Eurydice can't."

"That won't work," Seleucus said angrily. "I've had to deal with her. She's a wolf bitch, guarding Philip like he's her pup. It was only the threat to him that held her in check."

"If we have to, that accident can be more than a threat."

"No, it can't," Antigonus said. "Not unless you want our 'legitimate king' crying for our heads on pikes."

"So who goes to talk to Attalus?" Cassander asked.

"It can't be me," Seleucus said. "That bastard wants me dead and, at this point, I want him dead just as much."

"And I don't think Eurydice is going to willingly come over to me." Antigonus laughed. "Not after I dropped the bitch in the river."

"Well, that means me, then. But I want my father's satrapy. I want Macedonia," Cassander said.

"What!" roared Seleucus, then winced as his sudden motion pained his wounds. "What makes you think you can hold Macedonia?"

"I have an army," Cassander said. "My father's army. Your army is across the river, selling itself to Attalus."

"Actually, Cassander, *I* have your father's army now that he's gone. It will follow me. You have never commanded an army in the field, and they won't follow you without your father to order them to. They would follow your idiot of a little brother first."

"If he's still alive."

"Well, why don't you go to the bridge and ask them?" said Seleucus.

Eurydice had spent the night crying. The last thing she wanted was for Philip to be hurt. She had always liked him more than his glamorous half-brother Alexander. He was kind and gentle most of the time, if you treated him right. She knew when her mother arranged the marriage that Philip would be her responsibility. She didn't want him hurt and now he was in the hands of Antigonus and they didn't even have Antipater to trade for him.

There was a knock on her door, and a guard called, "Cassander is on the bridge, asking to talk to Attalus."

Eurydice's head came up, and she was all business. "I'll be out in a minute." Quickly she dried her eyes and went out in the main room. Roxane was already dressed and a nurse was watching little Alexander.

"Shall we go see what he wants?" Roxane asked, and Eurydice nodded.

Outside, they walked to the bridge, and there was Attalus. He had Plistarch with him. All of Antipater's guard had been untouched, because Seleucus had only stolen one horse. Only he and Antipater rode into the ambush. Plistarch was looking red-eyed at the death of their father, but Cassander was dry-eyed, almost pleased-looking.

"I'm relieved that you survived the treachery, Brother," Cassander said, oily smooth. "But how is it you weren't with Father?"

"There was only the one horse," Plistarch said. Then, choking on the words, "I urged him to take it, but I didn't know..."

"Of course, you didn't," Cassander said, just a little too quickly. "How could you expect such treachery?" Now Cassander was looking at Attalus.

"Treachery?" Attalus snorted. "What treachery? He tried to escape. Rode down his guards and got killed for his trouble."

"Escape? My father was the ranking general of the army. The natural successor to the regency. Who had the authority to arrest him?"

"I did!" said Eurydice. "In the name of my husband. Roxane did, in the name of her son. And so did the army. He was no more than the satrap of Macedonia, not the regent. It is you and your armies who are in rebellion, not us."

"And who made you regent?" Cassander grated.

"Perdiccas was the only legitimate regent. With him dead, I am my husband's regent. And Roxane is Alexander's. At least until the army declares another. You have ignored my husband's wishes in waging war against his chosen regent, and winning a battle isn't winning a war."

Roxane sniffed. "Murdering Perdiccas didn't mean that Peithon and Arrhidaeus or your Seleucus should inherit his rank, any more than poisoning Alexander would make you Alexander."

Cassander turned white. The charge that he had poisoned Alexander the Great had never been advanced publicly, but it was still widespread in the army. "Are you accusing me—"

"I made no accusations," Roxane said. "There is no proof that I have seen, but there are rumors, disturbing rumors."

Cassander turned away from Roxane to look at Attalus. "I came for my brother."

"And what of my husband?" Eurydice shouted. She hadn't meant to shout like that. She was both more angry and more frightened than she had realized.

"He cries for you, and will not be quieted," Cassander said. "Will you leave him alone without the comfort of his wife? What sort of regent is that?"

"Bring him home!"

"Why, certainly, we will. Home to Macedonia."

And there was the threat, all but open, all without saying anything that she could point to as a threat. Eurydice clamped her mouth shut on her rage.

Roxane moved next to Eurydice and leaned in. Putting her mouth next to Eurydice's ear, she said, "Perhaps it would be best if you went with them. That way each army has one king and neither army can afford to let their king die."

And there she was again. The wife of Alexander the Great, the woman who might not be as brave as Alexander but was certainly as smart. The subtle bedroom adviser who had encouraged the marriages to Persian wives, whatever the rumors said about what happened later.

"I will go to my husband." Eurydice considered. Perhaps if Plistarch was held as hostage for her safety.... Then she looked at Cassander. No safety there. "Let Plistarch go home to his family as well, Attalus. I ask this in the name of my husband, the king."

"And I affirm the request in the name of my son, the king," Roxane added quickly.

Attalus looked at Eurydice, then at Roxane, and after a moment smiled. In a voice that could be heard across battlefields, he proclaimed, "The king's regents being in accord on this matter, I yield to their will."

Eurydice smiled, but that smile hid fear. Now the kings would be separated and there were those stories about Roxane. Stories that she had connived with Perdiccas to murder Alexander's other wives. How hard would it be for her to send an assassin?

"Come, Sister," Roxane said, for the first time using that familiar name. "Let's go pack. You will not go to your husband and king empty-handed, with no good clothing."

Philip was held tight by the blanket and the ropes. He couldn't move, and in strange way that made him less tense. But he was scared. Very, very scared. As scared as he had been when his father had wanted to marry him to that Persian girl. Alexander had stopped that and taken care of Philip. After Alexander died, Eurydice came and took care of him. He had to marry her too, but that wasn't so bad. She knew him and knew he didn't like being touched. He'd even been trying to let her touch him since they were married, but it always made him feel tense. Like he needed to get out of his skin. Now he was scared that they would hurt her. She understood and he needed someone who understood, because most people didn't. And without that understanding, they would kill him.

Philip had always known that he was different. Aristotle had seen what he could do, as well as what he couldn't. Aristotle had shown Alexander, and after that Alexander looked after him and kept him close.

He had to save Eurydice, but he didn't know how. He could calculate the volume of a cube. He could figure out the weight of the world, if he had the tools. He could look at Ares, wandering the heavens and know where it would appear in a week or a year. But he couldn't find the numbers to tell him how to save Eurydice.

His thoughts ran in circles, and he couldn't control where they went.

"That was clever of you, Eurydice," Roxane said as they mounted the steps. "They can't—"

"I heard you the first time," Eurydice said, fear clearly making her angry. "But you could always send assassins to kill me."

"But I won't. Because once you're dead, I lose half my value." It was true too. Not quite as true as Roxane tried to make it sound, but still true. If Eurydice and Philip were to die, Roxane would still have value as a symbol of royal authority. But as long as Eurydice was alive somewhere, losing her would lose Attalus all claim of legitimacy. "Attalus might want you dead, Eurydice. So might Olympias or Cleopatra. But I don't. You, alive and hale, are the best hope for my safety and comfort.

"We need a way to prove to one another that a message we receive is from the other. Something that Attalus or Antigonus can't counterfeit. Because, you must realize, Antigonus and Cassander will want me dead."

Eurydice was looking at her in surprise. "Why should we want to contact each other? Fine, I am safer while you're alive and you're safer while I'm alive. But—"

"To send warnings, of course. I am your best spy in Attalus' army and you're my best spy in Antigonus' army."

"Fine. All we need now is a spy in Eumenes'."

"Cleopatra," they both said together. They started packing. Roxane pulled out a set of gold bracelets that Alexander had given her in Babylon and slipped them to Eurydice. "In case of emergencies."

It wasn't a talent of gold. Barely two pounds in a dozen bracelets, with uncut gems on them. But it was something, something that Eurydice could use to bribe a guard if she needed to.

Suddenly Eurydice's head came up. "I have it." She went to a chest and pulled out several sheets of papyrus, at least twenty. Each sheet was blank on one side and had numbers and formula on the other. "They are Philip's. Put anything you would write me on the back, and I will know it's from you. When I write you, I will use Philip's scribblings on the other side to prove it's from me."

☆   ☆   ☆

When Roxane and Eurydice came back outside, they found a *syntagma*, two hundred fifty-six men of the Silver Shields arrayed before the lodge. The force was divided in half. Roxane looked over at Kleitos and lifted an eyebrow.

"They have appointed themselves your bodyguards," Kleitos explained, and Roxane looked out at them. They were grizzled men, these soldiers who had fought for Philip II before Alexander, and for Alexander all the way from Macedonia to India and back. Hard men, who had grown old on campaign.

"Mine?"

"Well, half yours and little Alexander's, half Eurydice and Philip's."

"Who's paying them?" Eurydice asked.

"I'll be paying the men guarding Roxane," Attalus said. "Cassander will be paying the ones guarding Eurydice."

Eurydice and Roxane looked at each other and each gave a very small nod. It wasn't that Attalus or Cassander were trustworthy, but Cassander would want Eurydice safe as long as Roxane lived and Attalus would keep Roxane safe as long as Eurydice lived. Everyone understood. The rules would change as soon as one of them died.

For two more days the two armies sat on opposite banks of the little river. For two days, soldiers defected from each to the other. Arrhidaeus and Peithon both crossed to Antigonus' side of the river on the twenty-seventh and almost a thousand men had followed them since. On the other hand, almost eight hundred of the men who had followed Antipater to this river crossed over to Attalus' side.

At this point, Attalus had seven thousand men in his army. Antigonus had five thousand in his, and Cassander had four thousand who were officially under the command of his little brother Plistarch, and at least half under the command of Arrhidaeus and Peithon. Seleucus had a couple of thousand of the men in Antigonus' army who would follow him. Together they had a larger force than Attalus, but their command and control was weaker without the old general Antipater to hold them together.

The armies separated. Attalus heading southwest to the coast and the island of Tyre, Antigonus and the rest heading north to face Eumenes.

CHAPTER 8

Mount Ida
September 29

Eumenes sat at a camp stool doing the books. He was making a record of the horses he had taken from the royal herds. He had kept the Argead royal family's books honestly since he was thirteen years old and wasn't about to stop now. It was all coming apart and all he could do was keep the books as the pieces fell. He had defeated Neoptolemus twice and killed the traitorous bastard the second time. Unfortunately, he had had to kill Craterus in that second battle and Craterus was a good and well-respected Macedonian general. The Macedonians hadn't liked that—even his own troops, who had been right there with him. Word was that the troops who had betrayed Perdiccas to Ptolemy had declared him traitor for having the gall to win against Macedonians.

He was making another entry when a knock came. "Enter!"

"A message, General," said Dardaos, one of his Thracians.

"From who?"

"We're getting it from Apelles. He got it from Alexandria."

"What? Ptolemy hates Apelles' guts."

"Ptolemy is in Memphis. The message is from Dinocrates. Well, Crates, but ..."

Eumenes held up a hand. "Give me the message."

Dardaos handed over the scrolls and Eumenes started to read.

Out of fond memories of our time together in Philip's court,
I decided to forward this to you, risking Ptolemy's wrath. It

is unlikely that anything will make him more angry at me than he already is. That man has no sense of humor.

Eumenes remembered the sketch that Apelles had made of Ptolemy trying unsuccessfully to sexually mount a bull. The look of bored disgust on the bull's face had been particularly well done. Still, on balance, he thought that Ptolemy might be justified in his upset. He went back to reading.

> *Crates writes to tell me of a ship that came to Alexandria harbor on the eighteenth of September. The next day he had occasion to board it, and he dictated a detailed report to his scribes. I would think that he had taken to drink, but I know Crates and he is a careful and meticulous man. I believe what he wrote to be true and accurate, though I can't explain it.*
>
> *He sent off several copies and as we have been friends for years, I got one. I am staying here in Colophon with Nausiphanes, a friend and a great wit, if his humor can be a bit cruel, which is why I happened to be so close by. I send you the letter I got from Crates and ask that when you have finished reading it, you send it back. I would go to Alexandria to see for myself, but that would be almost as unwise for me as it would for you.*

Eumenes nodded to himself. There had been rumblings in his own army when Craterus died, and even now his hold on the Macedonian soldiers was not firm. Some of the Silver Shields had come to his defense and had kept the core of the infantry from abandoning him. But the Macedonians, especially the Macedonian nobility, still resented him. That was why he had recruited additional cavalry and why he was taking horses from the royal herds to mount them. "What do you think, Dardaos?"

"I don't know, sir. My gut tells me this changes everything, but I have no idea how."

"All right. Here's what we're going to do. You make two copies of all of this, then send one copy to Cleopatra. I'll write a note to go with it, asking for another meeting."

Eumenes went back to his work, but his mind—all on its own—tried to imagine a ship as tall as a lighthouse.

Queen of the Sea, *Alexandria Harbor*
October 3

Allison Gouch, the sommelier on the *Queen of the Sea*, went over the wine list with considerable dismay. The *Queen* had been in Alexandria for fifteen days now, and the holds were full of food. Not of the quality or the variety that the passengers or even the crew was used to, but edible food nevertheless. Ground grains, frozen meats, local fruits and vegetables. But the wines of half-built Alexandria were not up to twenty-first-century standards. On the other hand, Egyptian beer was a sweet, rich brew, only mildly alcoholic but rich in flavor and nutrients.

Meanwhile, the passengers and more than a few of the crew were getting restless. Two weeks stuck on a ship with little to do but study Greek and look at primitive Alexandria while the food got worse and the crew got less attentive hadn't made the passengers happy. But it had made them thirstier. Before they got to Alexandria the cost of spirits on ship had more than doubled, and now a shot of good whisky cost a small fortune. Ship wines were still for sale, but the price had gone through the roof. It had to. There would be no new rieslings for the foreseeable future. Allison knew that the lack of good wine was among the least of their troubles.

The first of the drugs were running out. The birth control pills were gone, either into the purses of private individuals or used up. Anticoagulants like warfarin were getting low. The insulin was gone, but retired scientists on board and doctors using the ship's mirror of Wikipedia and Encyclopedia Britannica were trying to use jerrybuilt centrifuges to purify insulin from cattle and pig pancreas. They thought they would be able to do it. Whether it would be in time to keep the diabetics on board alive was another question. Two of the Type One diabetics had already died, which was another reason the passengers were restive.

There had been a dozen fights that security had had to break up. In the worst instance, one man had wrested a gun from one of the security guards and had to be shot when he tried to hijack the *Queen* and force it to take him back to Miami.

So far at least, the troubles had all been isolated incidents, but there were almost constant rumblings about holding elections, and signs showing *Wiley for President* were appearing on the ship. Allison was getting scared.

She was also disgusted. There was no question now. Hadn't been since the first. The builders of Alexandria were slaves, *dmōs* in Greek, which Marie Easley said meant "slaves captured in war," but other kinds as well. There was even a word for "human-footed livestock." Like people were cows or goats! Allison wasn't the only one upset. Her husband Pat, who ran the excursions, or had before The Event, was normally an easygoing guy. But what he'd seen while he was trying to arrange a safe excursion for the passengers in Alexandria left him furious.

The problem wasn't the abstract injustice of slavery, either. Even more, it was being forced to witness the actual fact of it in front of their noses. The level of casual, almost unthinking, brutality visited on the slaves was simply astonishing to people brought up in the late twentieth and early twenty-first centuries. Astonishing—and outrageous. In the world they'd come from, even police officers or prison guards caught inflicting that level of violence on convicted felons would be charged with criminal behavior.

Dag Jakobsen and Romi Clarke were ready to kill the Greeks and start the revolution. Romi was just looking for an excuse to use the new steam cannons on the promenade deck.

"You're worrying over nothing, Professor," Daniel Lang said. "I've been looking at the tactics these guys employ. They're toast if they try anything. I don't doubt that individually they are some tough SOBs, but they use pikes. Not even pikes and muskets, or pikes and arrows, just frigging pikes. A hundred guys with crossbows and they are toast."

"Even if you're right—which I doubt—you don't have a hundred guys with crossbows," replied Marie Easley. "You don't have a hundred crossbows. You have twenty-seven. Granted, they are excellent crossbows, low carbon steel bows and machined parts. But still each one had to be individually made and the people and machines that made them had to fit them in between other work."

"We have the steam cannons."

"All four of them. One on the port bow, one on the starboard, and two at the stern. And even at that, Captain Kugan is screaming bloody murder about the *Reliance* being shorted. And not without reason. He has none of the guns and none of the crossbows."

Daniel gritted his teeth. Marie Easley could be irritating. She was one of those people who read all the time and had an excellent command of the facts. What Daniel wasn't convinced of was that she understood the implications of those facts as well as she thought she did. Sure, the Macedonians and their allies had kicked the crap out of all the other late-Bronze, early-Iron-Age countries in their neck of the woods. But even Alexander had started incorporating mounted bowmen, and his Macedonian phalanx had never faced even Henry's bowmen from Agincourt, much less a machine gun. War-fighting technology had moved on. Ptolemy had to realize that without them wasting ammunition or giving away their tricks.

Daniel had people working on a design for a reloader and others looking for ways of making modern gunpowder, but those projects were going to take a while. They would need a lot of charcoal, sulfur and saltpeter even to make black powder. They would probably need some sort of land-based industrial complex to make what they were going to need. In the meantime, every round of twentieth-century ammunition they had was likely to be needed to keep control over the increasingly restive passengers and staff.

Most of the crew were okay. They had jobs and they knew it. But the staff who took care of passengers lacked a lot of the skills that were needed to run the ship. Truth be told, once the passengers were off loaded, they weren't going to need four thousand beds made every day. A lot of the staff weren't needed by the *Queen* unless it was acting as a floating luxury resort. That was the real danger Daniel had to deal with, not some phantom army of hoplites.

Royal Palace, Alexandria
October 3

Ptolemy looked out at the ship and worried. He had been on board her several times now and everything about the thing screamed *disaster waiting to happen*. There was disaffection among the passengers and no weapons to speak of. Even if they made weapons, none of them knew how to use a sword or a pike. He doubted most of them could survive a tavern brawl, much less a real battle. There didn't seem to be a real soldier on the ship, not any. Even their so-called "security forces" would faint like women if they faced a Macedonian phalanx.

But in the hands of a competent general with good troops, that ship could take and hold the coast of Egypt. And holding the coast, it would control all of Egypt. He turned back to Gorgias. "If you fail, I will deny you. Hang you myself, if need be."

"Yes, Satrap. And if I succeed?"

"Carthage to the pillars of Hercules as your own satrapy." He gave his general a hard look. "Don't get greedy once you have the ship. I will have people watching you."

Gorgias nodded.

Ptolemy asked, "How long?"

"Another week. We have the galleys ready, and the towers are half built."

"They should have let me provide them with guards," Ptolemy said and Gorgias was silent. Ptolemy knew that any troops he put on the ship would be his hands and control of the ship would be his, not Captain Floden's. Still, it would have made things easier for everyone.

He looked over at his general. "Very well. I don't want to see you until it's over."

Gorgias smiled as he left the royal apartments. In fact, he knew just who Ptolemy had watching him, and his watchers were going to have some very bad accidents once the *Queen* was his.

Tyre
October 3

Roxane looked out the window at the Mediterranean Sea as Attalus discussed the options. Among the news that they had gotten from the future ship was the information that Attalus would lose to the Rhodians when he tried to gain control of Caria. Though, with the generals in disarray, the Rhodians might not be so quick to fight.

"We still need the link to Eumenes," said Attalus' sea commander, a Carthaginian named Metello. "And we should be able to take the Rhodians. It must have been bad luck in that other time. Assuming the tale of an alternate past where Antipater became regent is true and not just a clever ruse." There was, in fact, almost no information about the fight between Attalus' navy and the Rhodians, except for the fact that it was over Caria.

"Well, what makes you think we will have better luck this time?" Roxane asked the Carthaginian, ignoring the comment about it being a ruse.

"Attalus had better luck at Triparadisus," Metello said. "The army is divided and the orders for his execution have been rescinded, at least for this army. The same for Eumenes and the rest. We're still collecting more forces. We will have a bigger army."

"Eumenes is not nearly so important now that the ship from the future is here," Roxane said. "We need contact with them."

"We need both," Attalus said. "Metello, you go to the coast of Caria and be polite to— No. I will go to Caria. You will go to Alexandria. Stay out to sea, but send a boat into the harbor to make contact with the ship people. Polite contact."

That made sense to Roxane, as she thought about it. Metello was a Carthaginian, and the Rhodians were supporting the other side in the conflict in Sicily. Metello wasn't fond of the Rhodians, and the Greeks weren't overly fond of Carthaginians in general. Metello was probably not the right man to negotiate with a Rhodian admiral. Still, Roxane was more interested in the *Queen of the Sea*. The knowledge of the future had already proven vital. More knowledge might well prove the difference between death and survival for her and her son. "I will go with Metello to visit the *Queen of the Sea*."

"No! The risk is too great. I won't put you in Ptolemy's grasp again."

"Why not? He wasn't interested in keeping me last time he had me in his hands."

"The only reason he let you go was that he wasn't ready to try for the throne. I suspect that now he is. With the failure of Triparadisus leaving no clear successor to Alexander and no clear regent, Ptolemy will make his bid soon. I want you behind walls with an ocean between you and his army. It took Alexander himself over a year to take this island. You're safe here."

"But . . ."

"No, I said. You have had your say and I listened, but I will not risk the heir or his mother in this."

Roxane sat silent. She had lost the argument and she knew it. There had never been much chance that she would win it. She and Eurydice were still counters in the game of empire more than players, whatever Eurydice thought.

It took a couple more days, but soon enough Roxane stood on a balcony and watched two fleets leave. Then she turned, picked up her son, and went inside to wait.

Queen of the Sea
October 10

"How's it coming, Mom?" Josette Easley asked as she entered the corner that had been set aside for Marie Easley's use in one of the ship's internet cafes.

"Tediously. I hadn't realized how much misinformation was in the electronic record. Britannica is as bad as Wikipedia. It's not the outline that they get wrong, but the most recent studies are often missing and—" Marie stopped herself. That they could affect history had already been demonstrated. The butterfly effect—the unintentional effect of their mere presence, or the things they said and ideas they promulgated intentionally or not—was less fully confirmed, but seemed highly probable from the results her warnings had produced in Triparadisus. The exact nature of those results couldn't be predicted in detail, but Marie believed strongly that more knowledge would, as a rule, produce better results than less knowledge. Based on that belief, she had been preparing a book on what was known about this period of history.

"Well, Dr. Miles has a section she wants you to include," Josette said. "A basic outline of germ theory and how to clean wounds. Dag Jakobsen wants something on canning food and handling sewage."

Marie considered. Adding the information was reasonable and made sense, but there were issues. Especially with Dag's part. Canning and canned goods were a marketable product for the ship. She wouldn't prevent Dag from making his own book, in fact she would help him later. But translating canning and sewage processing information was going to take time that she just didn't have. The translation programs were adequate for conversational purposes, where confusion or mistranslation could be questioned and corrected. But a book took greater precision and understanding. That meant that Marie and a few Greek speakers were going to have to translate every word. And even the Greek speakers, like Panos Katsaros, spoke modern Greek, not Ptolemaic Macedonian Greek. On the other hand, leaving out Dr. Miles' section on germ theory would be criminal. "We will include the doctor's section if she can keep it short."

"The steel team has made its first successful pour," Dag reported to Eleanor Kinney. They were in her office and it was just her, Bernt Carlson and Dag, mostly because the chief engineer and all the other engineers were too busy with their work to get away for this meeting. Bernt Carlson was the ship safety officer and between them, he and Dag as environmental officer, were effectively OSHA for the ship, while Eleanor Kinney was the banker.

They were buying food and raw materials. Iron, copper, zinc, lead and other metals in ore form. Also wood, charcoal, hides and hooves, medicinal plants and other stuff. The *Queen of the Sea* had an impressive industrial capacity, but in the nature of things, cruise liners don't haul around a lot of raw materials.

Jackie Ward, the chief electrical engineer, with the help of a couple of retired engineers who were on the cruise and a team of engineering ratings, had come up with an induction furnace and blowers to turn iron ore and charcoal into steel. Well, they had come up with the designs, and as of about two hours ago had a small pilot plant running on the pool deck.

They also had a small plant that was—quietly and with no fanfare—starting to use the lead they were buying to make bullets for the steam cannons. But that production process was being done in a compartment, not out in the open where anyone could see it.

"We need more room," Bernt said. "Putting a steel plant on the pool deck isn't a good idea."

It wasn't a new complaint. Bernt had been making it almost since they arrived in Alexandria. The infrastructure for an industrial base was located on the *Queen of the Sea*, but it wasn't readily transferable. They had the power lines and the electrical capacity to power a small city, but they couldn't pull it out of the ship without effectively destroying the ship. That meant the factories and shops of their small city had to be located on the *Queen*. And there wasn't enough room. It was an ongoing health and safety hazard for the workers and the passengers. It was also not something they could do anything about, and Eleanor Kinney was even more tired of hearing about it than Dag was.

"Rodriguez says they have another load of padded leather chairs," Dag said quickly before it turned into yet another argument between Bernt and Eleanor.

The ship's carpenter was turning out modern furniture for sale to the locals and daily maintenance was being pushed back. Several of the passengers were hired as extra hands for the carpentry shop, but there were only so many saws and planes and sanders.

Eleanor Kinney nodded at Dag, and made a note. "Good. Atum has a list of buyers for it, including His Nibs, who wants a La-Z-Boy for the palace. Between that, the laundry, and other projects that the crew and passengers have started, we'll be buying our food without eating more of our irreplaceable twenty-first century gear."

"If we don't kill people with the risks we're—"

"Alert! Riot on the Promenade Deck!" came over the speakers.

Dag was up in a heartbeat. He ran for the elevators.

"Alert! Riot on the Promenade Deck!" came over the speakers.

Daniel Lang ran for the elevators, cursing Al Wiley under his breath. The congressman had promised to keep a lid on things. He'd been campaigning for an American colony since they got to Alexandria. At this point, Daniel would be just as happy to put the passengers off the *Queen*, but you didn't just drop a colony. It needed support. People needed housing and weapons, seeds and plows, fishing boats and more weapons. And, so far, there was damn little of any of that.

By the time Daniel Lang got there, closely followed by Dag, Lorraine Hebert and Chris Louie had almost restored order, and Congressman Wiley was trying to help them calm things down.

"It wasn't the congressman's fault," Lorraine said in her Cajun-accented English. "He was trying to keep things cool. It was the counter-demonstration by the Jerusalemites."

The Jerusalemites were a coalition faction made up of the "Clear the way for Christ" people and the group of Jews who wanted to discover the true Judaism of the Second Temple before it was lost. That group was headed by Rabbi Benyamin Abrahamson, who had seemed a perfectly reasonable sort till he had met Atum's guard commander and the two had gotten into an argument about what was and was not in the Torah and what was meant by it. For instance *toṭafot*, according to the guard commander, simply meant armor, though it was often inscribed with holy script for added safety. Now Abrahamson had to see for himself.

The Jerusalemites wanted a colony, but they wanted to put it in Israel, at Ashdod. And they didn't seem the least concerned that there were already people living there and that the local Jews were a bunch of mercenaries. No. They wanted to use the *Queen* as a permanent fort to keep the locals in line while they did their religious thing.

"We're trying, people," Al Wiley was saying, "but two colonies would mean almost twice as much work. And each colony, being smaller, would be at greater risk. There is no oil to feed the *Queen*'s engines in Israel and the oil in the rest of the Middle East is, for the most part, both deeper and farther from shore."

"The *Queen* has flex fuel engines!" shouted one of the Jerusalemites. "She'll burn alcohol."

"Yes, she would. If we had the distilled alcohol she needed. But all the beer in Egypt wouldn't be enough. Even if we could distill it, which we can't."

That wasn't entirely true. There was a whole lot of beer in Egypt. But it was damn sure true that they couldn't distill enough to keep the *Queen*'s tanks full. Alcohol wasn't as energy dense as oil and it took more of it—almost twice as much—to get the same amount of power out of the engines. Among other things, that would decrease the *Queen*'s range. Not that that mattered to the Jerusalemites. They didn't want the *Queen* to move, except to Ashdod.

Once the incipient riot had been quelled for the moment, Daniel moved over to Wiley. "Congressman, we have to put a stop to this sort of thing."

"The only thing that will put a stop to it is setting up a colony and giving these people room to breathe, Mr. Lang."

Marie Easley didn't even look up when the alert came through. She was in a private room off the forward internet cafe, working with Cathy Joe Chohan on adjustments to the translation app that the ship had a license on. It was voice to voice, but the Greek it started out speaking was twenty-first-century Greek, not third-century-BCE Greek. Pronunciations, however, were the least of the problems. This time's Greek didn't have words for a lot of the concepts that twenty-first-century English had. In this case, the water pump. Even Archimedes and his screw was a hundred years in the future. What they used in the here-and-now were buckets. Often buckets mounted on wheels and other quite ingenious rigs. But still they were moving water one bucketful at a time. Crates had been entranced by the notion of a water pump. Now they were working on flow rate, and one of Eleanor Kinney's people was trying to get them to buy a low-temperature steam engine to power the pumps. Or a windmill. Or anything at all except slaves on bicycles.

The locals weren't willing to spring for the steam engine, though. Slaves were cheaper. At least, in the short run. The slaves who were carrying the buckets and treading on the treadwheel that lifted the buckets were already paid for and they were going to have to be fed anyway. The steam engine would be a new expense and the fuel to power it another.

Eleanor Kinney's assistant purser's suggestion that they manumit the slaves didn't go over well. It was hard enough just getting them to buy the pumps and the pipes to get the water up to a water tank.

Royal Lounge, Queen of the Sea
October 10

"When can we go to America?" Al Wiley asked the captain. "This ship is a powder keg and it's getting worse. Most of these people are working people. They have spent their lives working. A vacation is one thing. Sitting in a stateroom that is about the size of a prison cell with nothing to do is something else."

"We could leave today if you want us to drop the passengers with nothing but the luggage they brought on the cruise." Captain Floden waved a hand in apology. "I'm sorry, Congressman, but the issues and the time frame are the same as they were yesterday and the day before." He turned to the staff captain. "Anders, where are we on the necessary equipment for the colony?"

Anders Dahl tapped an icon on his slate computer, calling up a spreadsheet. "Two hundred pounds of black powder and fifteen flintlock rifles that we've made since we got here. It's a lot harder to make a rifle barrel than you might think. We're doing better on the crossbows. We have forty of them and they are good, Captain. Their rate of fire sucks, but it's still better than the flintlocks. They have spring steel bows and . . . Well, never mind. It's still only forty for a colony of three thousand."

Dag took a drink of the local beer. He knew the reasoning behind the colony size. Some of the passengers were simply too old for life in a colony. Some had skills that were vital to the ship, but not to a new colony that would have very limited electronics, at least at first. So it wouldn't be all the passengers who were debarking. About half of the staffside crew was going to go with the colony. The rest were staying on board.

Dag looked out the big picture windows. There were a lot of people on the pool deck but they mostly weren't swimming or lying out to get a tan. They were working at the induction furnace or processing furs and fabrics from Alexandria.

The vacation was over, but there wasn't enough room to do all the jobs that needed doing. Meanwhile, the locals were watching everything and word was spreading faster than he would have believed possible before The Event. He wondered if they had heard of crossbows in Tyre yet. If not, they would soon.

Tyre
October 11

Roxane looked out at the Mediterranean Sea as her personal attendant combed her long black hair. Roxane had been looking out to sea a lot since they got to Tyre. She had hoped that Attalus would be better than his brother-in-law Perdiccas, but the pressures of the situation seemed to be making him less stable rather than more. Besides, Attalus was on his way to the coast of Caria, and Metello was on his way to Alexandria harbor, leaving her in the care of under officers, who saw her as a playing piece or a bit of loot. Even the Silver Shields who had taken over guarding her were more concerned with their pay than her safety.

One of the Silver Shields came in then. "Nedelko is here."

Roxane turned away from the window in time to see the commander of the Greek forces in Tyre enter the room. "Well, Commander, what did you think of the drawings?" A couple of days before, a ship from Alexandria had arrived, carrying some sketches. There was a bow mounted on a crosspiece, a gear with pedals and a chain that could fit over the gear to, as the notes said, "do useful work," and a new sort of table called a desk that a chair could slide under to make it easier for scribes to work. Roxane barely got a look at them before Nedelko snatched them away to give to Tyrian craftsmen.

Nedelko stopped at her tone. Which was good. He needed to know that she wasn't pleased. But he didn't apologize, which wasn't good. Instead he looked at her, then said, "I will bring them back, Your Majesty, once the craftsmen have had a chance to study them and make examples of what they show. My guess is that the new scribe's table will be the most useful. I don't see the advantage of tying a bow onto a stick. And keeping the bow bent can't be good for it. The geared wheel is interesting, but slaves work fine and I'm not convinced that letting them lift a bucket with their feet instead of their hands will be any great advantage. The one-wheeled cart might be useful in certain very limited conditions—hard-packed flat ground or paved streets, if the cobbles are even enough. But I don't see what Crates is so excited about. I'm more concerned about Eurydice's latest pronouncement. She's claiming that Philip was the true heir to Alexander's throne. And because Alexander IV wasn't born when the crown passed, he couldn't be the heir."

"You must realize those proclamations are made under the eye of Antigonus One-eye." Roxane grimaced. "Just as my proc-lamations are made under Attalus' eye. You know he's claiming Alexander is the only true heir, even if he hasn't insisted that I sign a proclamation to that effect. At least not yet."

She might have to, even if Attalus didn't force her, just to counter Eurydice's proclamation. It seemed like a good idea at the time. Sending Eurydice off with the other army provided additional security for them both. And it had worked fairly well, at least as far as Roxane was concerned. But there were unin-tended consequences. Aside from claiming that Philip III was the only true heir, the latest word received had Eurydice endorsing Antigonus One-eye as regent. Something that Roxane knew had to have been done under duress.

She changed the subject. "Where is Metello now?"

"Sailing. It will be another few days before he gets to Alex-andria."

CHAPTER 9

Bridge, **Queen of the Sea**
October 15

It was midnight when Apprentice Deck Officer Doug Warren came on watch. Adrian Scott filled him in. Not much out of the ordinary had happened. "They finished up the day's loading of supplies about sunset, and traffic in the harbor has been fairly light except for a small fleet of triremes that's headed to Carthage. Dinocrates says it's some sort of 'show the flag' mission." Adrian waved a hand at the radar screen. "We're tracking them to try and calibrate the radar for the locals' ships."

Doug nodded. Ships were small and the ocean was big. Even back in the twenty-first century when the small craft carried radar reflectors to make it easy to see them, they got missed a lot.

Two hours later, Doug yawned and sipped his coffee as he noted the change in direction of the radar blips that represented the fleet of triremes. The radar reflection from the wooden ships was very weak, so the computer was augmenting the signal and filtering. They didn't appear dim on the display, but the databox made it clear just how weak the return signal was.

Doug took another sip of the coffee. Sort of coffee. Doug, the captain said, liked a little coffee in his cream. Doug was a stocky lad to begin with, and the rich, sweet brew was probably not helping. But the bridge crew still got coffee, even if it was a restricted resource now.

It was a little after two AM. He had the triremes on radar

111

as they made the turn. They were...he checked his radar read-ings...they were 3.4 miles out to the west northwest.

It was the dark of the night, and there was a light mist. To the locals, it must be pitch black. It was a good thing the *Queen* had plenty of sea room. Doug wasn't frightened, or even worried. He was just mildly curious, but kept the radar focused on the triremes. By about four in the morning, it was starting to get a little weird. They were less than a mile from the *Queen*, so they ought to be able to see her lights. It looked like the triremes were shifting course to intercept. He reported it to Julio on the *Reliance*. It was standard practice to share observations.

Reliance
4:32 AM

Dag rubbed his eyes. The ship was moving. That was wrong. The *Queen* shouldn't be moving. Then he remembered he wasn't on the *Queen*. He was on the *Reliance*. He had been in charge of a work party that was helping set up the toilets for the tents they set up on the deck of the *Reliance*. Because they would be back at it early in the morning, they had stayed the night. It was then that Dag's sleep-fogged brain finally snapped to the fact that the *Reliance* shouldn't be moving either.

Dag got up and headed for the pilot house. It took him two minutes to get there and by then the *Reliance* was a hundred feet from the *Queen* and turning away.

"I don't take orders from you, you little asshole!" Kugan was in a shouting match with Doug Warren on the *Queen*.

"What's going on, Captain?" Dag asked.

Kugan whirled on Dag. "Those ships you told me not to worry about? They are headed right for us. A dozen galleys, with some sort of rigging on them. My guess is scaling ladders. And they sailed out, and came around to come at us from seaward, so they could get the *Reliance* even if they didn't get the *Queen*."

"Let me talk to Doug, please, Captain," Dag said. He had told Joe Kugan that the ships were on their way to Carthage, just as he had been told they were when the *Queen*'s bridge watch saw them leave.

"Go for it. Maybe you can pound some sense into the stupid dick."

"What have you got, Doug?" Dag asked.

"Eleven galleys, triremes. They sailed out of harbor for about three miles, then turned around, and headed back. I don't think it's anything important. Maybe they forgot something. And they will come pretty close, but they aren't headed right for us. I think they're using the *Queen* as a lighthouse. There was no reason for Captain Kugan to panic."

Dag's common sense and his education were screaming at each other too. His education said this was impossible and Ptolemy would know that there was no way any ship from Alexandria could attack the *Queen*. It would be suicide. His common sense and experience with these people was screaming just as loudly that this was an attack. It couldn't be anything else, and the locals were all total nutjob tough SOBs who would kill you over a penny in the street.

It was a short fight. Dag had been dealing with the locals since they got to Alexandria. "On my authority, Doug, wake Captain Floden and Daniel Lang." He turned to Captain Kugan. "The cannon will be armed, Captain. The safest place for the *Reliance* is tucked in close to the *Queen*."

"Bullshit, Dag," Kugan said. "The safest place for my ship is out of the line of fire. Besides, it's too late anyway." He pointed at a screen. It was showing a feed from the radar on the *Queen*. Two of the galleys had shifted course and were following the *Reliance*.

"Captain Kugan, I've seen those suckers move. They can get up to fifteen knots in a sprint."

"Which is why we're running at full power. I'm just hoping we can keep ahead of them long enough to wear out the rowers."

"You'd be safer back with the *Queen*."

Kugan looked at him, and Dag could see the fear on the man's face. But all Kugan did was shake his head.

Daniel Lang and Captain Floden reached the bridge at almost the same time. The captain got a quick report and waved at the comm rating. "All hail channel." Then he picked up the mike. "All hands, prepare for boarding from seaside. Man the steam cannons. All watches to stations."

"When do we act, Captain? We don't have proof they are attacking till they do something, and by then it's going to be hard for the steam cannons to depress enough to hit them."

"I'm not waiting. Weigh anchor just in case, but if those ships get within five hundred meters, we will open fire on them."

"Captain, you have to at least warn them," Doug Warren blurted, then blushed at Staff Captain Dahl's look.

Daniel couldn't help but sympathize with the kid. Doug Warren had never been shot at in anger, and he had a deep belief in fairness and the rule of law. Daniel agreed that the rules were what kept people civilized. That was why he was a cop. "He's right, Captain."

Captain Floden looked at them. "You have a good point, Doug, but my first concern must be the passengers and crew on this ship. We'll use the loud hailer to warn them off. But if they don't heed the warning, we *will* destroy those ships."

Daniel looked at the comm rating. "Get Marie Easley up here to deliver that warning."

General Gorgias watched the ship as they approached. It was still showing lights, but fewer than it had the first night it arrived. They were conserving the LED lights, not the electricity that powered them. Besides, at this time of night, they would mostly be asleep, and they were not soldiers, to wake ready to fight at the sergeant's call. They were sheep who would spend hours bleating at each other before they worked themselves up to acting. Kugan was quicker to respond than Gorgias hoped, so that meant that both ships knew they were coming. Their best hope now was speed. He had to get his forces aboard both ships fast.

Then, on the night, there came a voice to frighten a god. At least in its volume. Gorgias knew that voice. It was the voice of the scholar, Marie Easley. "Go back! Any galley that approaches within three stadia of the *Queen of the Sea* without prior authorization will be sunk!" Marie was using Greek units of measurement since the metric system meant nothing to the people she was hailing. Three stadia was about five hundred and fifty meters.

Gorgias turned to the timekeeper. "Increase the rate. We want to get in fast." Then he turned to the artillerists. "Load the catapult with jars of Greek fire. If they have some sort of weapon, we will need to silence them. It won't damage that steel monster. Just clear the decks for our boarders."

☆   ☆   ☆

"They aren't turning, Captain," Daniel said.

"I can see that. Call the gunners and have them put a shot across their bows."

The shot went out and made a splash about a hundred feet in front of the lead galley. By now, lights were coming on all over the ship. Passengers looked out their windows, and then headed for the Promenade Deck to see what was going on.

There was apparently not a consensus among the passengers about whether the *Queen* should shoot.

There was motion on several of the galleys, and a shout hard to hear in the distance. Four of the rigs on the galleys went into action, flinging burning jars of something. None came near the guns, but one reached the Promenade Deck and two hit windows below the Promenade Deck. The windows both cracked, but neither broke. However, the passengers watching from the Hoi Polloi Lounge got a much closer view of the fight than they were expecting.

The results of the one jar that reached the Promenade Deck were much more serious. Twelve people hit, with everything from minor burns to two who were burned to death, and one who went over the side on fire.

As soon as that report came, Captain Floden lost all interest in waiting. "Sink those bastards, Lang. Sink every last one of them."

"About damn time," Romi Clarke muttered when they got the orders. He'd been wanting to shoot this thing since they built it. He took careful aim, using the camera's rangefinder and the little program that adjusted the sights automatically based on range and input windage. Then he pointed the camera at the sucker banging the drum and fired.

As it turned out, either the programming was off or he had guessed wrong about the wind. The wide-angle camera recorded the round hitting the water forty feet to the right of his target. The shot didn't even hit an oar.

Romi adjusted and fired a burst of five. The "potato gun" used steam to propel a heavy object down a four foot long barrel and fired a forty millimeter round that weighed about half a kilogram. They had a muzzle velocity of three hundred meters per second. It took the bullets a second and three quarters to reach the target and the first burst didn't seem to do much. It had hit the trireme but the ship hadn't slowed. So Romi tried again, raking his fire from one end of the ship to the other.

When a one-pound lead bullet hits a thin piece of wood, it doesn't slow much. And if the wood is thin enough, all it does is poke a hole. That was what had happened to the first five-round burst. They had poked five neat holes in the bottom of the galley. The displaced water from their exiting the boat had actually done more damage.

The longer burst hit the rowers on the port side of the galley. The same one-pound round that went through the boat's planking like it was paper, went through the chests of men like they were so many watermelons. Then it went on through the man behind, and the man behind him. The steam cannons weren't silent, but they weren't all that loud either. Besides, the *pop pop pop* of the cannons was over well before the men started to die.

Captain Heron saw the slaughterhouse that the port side of his ship had become and turned away from the battle. He didn't have a lot of choice. He had lost a third of his rowers on the port side, and the rest were trying to get away from the bloodbath.

Gorgias didn't see what had happened to the lead galley. He did hear the screaming but he ignored it. Screams, cries of rage and fury—those were inevitable in a battle. Gorgias was an experienced Macedonian soldier. He had been in battle many times and was not a man to run from a fight. He gave orders to speed up the beat. The remaining triremes raced for the big ship as though their life depended on it.

"Get us moving, Elise," Captain Floden said. "I don't want to be a sitting target if any of those triremes get through."

The huge ship started to move. They had been anchored with plenty of sea room, as much for the comfort of the locals as because they needed it. Now they moved landward to keep sea room from the attackers. And they continued firing the steam cannon.

Two more ships pulled away from the fight after being raked by the stern port steam cannon. But the sonar was showing shallowing. And another, if smaller, volley of Greek fire was flung at them.

"Enough," Captain Floden said. "Reverse engines, Elise. Run over those idiots."

The engines on the *Queen of the Sea* ran generators which, in turn, powered huge electric motors located in turnable nacelles. This allowed the *Queen* to travel forward, backward, or at need, sideways. But even so, it didn't happen immediately. The *Queen* was a massive ship. Even though they had barely started moving, it took them a minute to slow and reverse. But Elise Beaulieu, First Officer Navigation, was a skilled ship handler and no more pleased to be the recipient of Greek fire than her captain.

It took Gorgias a bit too long to realize what was happening. When the *Queen* started slowing, he thought he had won. He was unable to give up that belief in time to dodge. His flagship was run over by a 150,000 ton cruise ship traveling backwards at four knots.

Gorgias leapt over the side just as the *Queen*'s stern contacted the flagship's port quarter. He was a good swimmer and thought he had a chance. He hit the water hard and had both the wind and the sense knocked out of him for a few moments. He managed not to inhale the water. His fingers worked desperately at the leather straps holding his armor on, and piece by sodden piece, he got it off. By that time he was deep in the water. Deep enough that the water pressed on his chest, making his lungs feel even emptier than they really were.

He swam desperately for the surface, but he was disoriented and confused by oxygen deprivation. He had to breathe, but he couldn't.

It didn't really matter. Though he would never know it, Elise Beaulieu had shifted the nacelles and an Olympic swimmer in top form couldn't have competed with the riptides produced by those massive props. Gorgias never saw the propeller blade larger than he was turning at full speed.

It squashed him like a grape.

The reason for Elise Beaulieu's adjustment of thrust was because the trireme behind Gorgias' was rowing with great desperation to try to get out of the way of the *Queen of the Sea*. But like Alice in Wonderland, running as fast as they could barely kept them in place, for the currents of the massive motors caught them and pulled them toward the big ship even as the motors of the big ship pushed it at them. The *Queen* backed over them to the noise of cracking timbers and screaming men. The heavy wooden ribs of the triremes broke like so many toothpicks, and men in those ships were masticated between the *Queen* and the unforgiving sea.

There were no survivors. Not off the flag ship trireme, or the two others that hadn't been able to get out of the way in time. The rest ran for shore. Of the nine triremes that had actually taken part in the attack, four made it to shore. None made it without massive casualties.

The two that had peeled off to go after the *Reliance* had better luck. After an hour of rowing, they gave up the chase. The worst thing that happened to them was the crew of the *Reliance* leaning over the back rail, yelling taunts at them.

Sound carries over water, even for miles. Metello of Carthage, admiral of Attalus' fleet, heard the battle. He heard the strange noises—to him—of the *Reliance* at full power forcing her way through the waves. He gave orders for the fleet, six triremes, to spread out and to douse all lights. And to row quietly. When he saw the lights from the *Reliance,* he ordered his trireme to get to that ship, but as it happened, he wasn't the closest.

Closest was that idiot, Ithobaal. And Metello knew what that meant. The motherless jackal would try to claim the whole ship. Metello leaned over to the *aulates,* whose job it was to play the rhythm for the oarsmen and whispered to increase the pace. He would rather have Ithobaal get there first than have that monster of a ship warned.

The first Dag knew of the new trouble was when he heard a crashing sound on the port bow of *Barge 14*. He looked back and saw the black outline of a mast and rigging. The *Reliance* was attached, slotted into *Barge 14*. That was important because it meant that the people who were scrambling onto *Barge 14* were going to have no difficulty reaching the *Reliance*.

He wasn't the only one who noticed the crash, not that it was going to do any of them any good. They had no guns, none at all. And even as he watched, dozens of men, armed with swords and shields—even spears—vaulted onto *Barge 14*.

"Where the hell did they come from?" Kugan wailed.

"I don't know, Captain," Dag said even as he grabbed the radio mike. "Mayday! Mayday! We have armed men on the *Reliance* and are under attack." He looked at the readings and continued. "By the inertial compass, we are twelve knots east northeast of Alexandria and I see no way to hold the boat." Dag was struck by a thought. "Captain, can you disconnect the tug from the barge?"

"If I had a few minutes," Kugan said, but even as he said it the pirates were running along *Barge 14* to the *Reliance*. Dag guessed the pilot house was the obvious target for anyone trying to take the *Reliance*. Dag had his phone in his breast pocket. Now he turned it off, and slid it down into the crotch of his underwear. In all the old movies, that was the safest place. Though this was ancient Greece, close enough, so that might not help.

Then the Greeks were among them, except these guys weren't speaking Greek. It was a different language. And when they didn't respond, Julio was knocked to the floor with the flat of one of those short, curved machetelike swords they carried.

"We surrender," Dag said in Greek. At least that was what he tried to say. It seemed to work too. Their captors immediately started giving orders in Greek. It was a weirdly accented Greek, unlike what they spoke in Alexandria, and Dag could barely make it out. The rest of the crew were totally lost.

A swarthy bastard with a curly, oiled, black beard started in. He wanted the *Reliance* to stop. Once the *Reliance* was stopped, he started asking questions. "Is this the *Queen of the Sea*?"

"No."

"Then it is the fuel ship?" The word he used was the Greek word for lamp oil, but that was close enough and what they had been using with Atum and the Greeks in Alexandria.

"Strong boat?" That took a little explaining, but apparently the guy with the curly black beard, who Dag learned was named Ithobaal, had gotten some sort of briefing on what the *Reliance* was. And someone, probably Dag himself, had been a bit too free with information about the power and functionality of eleven thousand horsepower engines.

"Good. You will pull my other ship, while we go back to Tyre," said Ithobaal.

Then another voice arrived, and with it another man with a curly black beard. Fancied up whiskers seemed all the rage with these people. This one was called Metello and seem to be in charge of the fleet of pirates that had captured them. Metello said something in the Semitic-sounding language, which Dag was guessing was Phoenician, then in Greek. "I claim this ship as a prize of war since you strangers have sided with the traitor, Ptolemy."

Ithobaal started screaming in Phoenician, and some of the pirates started pulling their big knives. Then other guys were pulling *their* big knives. The knives were a type that Dag saw a lot in Alexandria. They were called *kopis*. They bent forward and were heavier near the end, sort of a compromise between a machete and a cleaver. They were made for chopping. Arms. Legs. Chests.

The new curly black beard, who had claimed the *Reliance* as a war prize, turned out to be the admiral of this little fleet. He worked for Attalus, Roxane and Alexander IV. At least Dag was pretty sure that was what he was saying. Between Dag's poor understanding of Greek and Metello's accent, he couldn't be sure. But he knew that Roxane and Alexander IV were in the custody of Attalus. That much had come back to them by way of the signal fires. Marie Easley was calling it a major change in the course of history.

By now there were other ships tied onto the *Reliance*. Six, including the first one.

Metello was talking again. "You will tow the galleys." He pointed.

Baaliahon looked at the metal and, being a fairly bright guy, figured out that it was a door. After some experimentation, he figured out how to open it. He turned the handle one way, then the other, and then when he thought it was loose, he pulled up the hatch. There was a ladder going down, and Baaliahon started climbing. He took a breath, then another. Then he went unconscious and fell the rest of the way down the ladder into a tank of fuel oil.

Baaliahon had no way of knowing just how dangerous inert gases like nitrogen are. When you hold your breath, you're keeping your lungs full of air, and slowly the oxygen is taken up and CO_2 takes its place. But when you go into an inert atmosphere, you exhale all the oxygen in a couple of breaths and there is no buildup of CO_2 to warn you that something is wrong. So you lose consciousness quickly, with no warning. Baaliahon was with Baal before his mates knew he was missing.

☆   ☆   ☆

In the pilot house of the *Reliance* a light went red, indicating that the port three hold had been opened. Then, when it stayed open, an alarm sounded. Not a very loud alarm, but an alarm, and a sound that none of the locals had ever heard. It was a *beep beep beep* in a pure tone and it caught the attention of everyone in the pilot house.

"What is that?" asked Metello.

Joe Kugan looked at the console and grinned grimly. Joe didn't have Dag's daily practice at understanding Greek and spoke not one word, but he knew his instruments. He saw the light and said in English, "Looks like one of these assholes opened the P3 tank. Think they used an oxy mask?"

Dag looked back and forth between them, Metello curious and Joe smiling, and wasn't sure what to do. He knew what Joe meant about the oxy masks. Also, some of the safety systems had been let slide in the days since The Event. They were reworking the fuel barge to multi-purpose and Joe Kugan had been protected in some ways. He hadn't dealt with the locals the way Dag had and he hadn't seen the level of casual violence that was an everyday event on the docks in Alexandria.

"Joe, if they didn't, then one of these guys is dead and the rest of them are probably going to take it out on us. So grinning is a pretty bad idea, don't you think?" Then Dag looked at Metello and explained what the alarm meant.

Joe didn't get the grin wiped off his face quite quickly enough. Julio wasn't even trying.

Ithobaal was frowning, but Metello seemed almost as amused as Julio. Metello ordered everyone to stay out of the holds, but it took some time. Several more people had either followed the first guy down the hatch or opened another. Two more lights came on and a total of seven of the pirates died in the holds of *Barge 14*.

Metello didn't seem all that concerned with the deaths. He went on with business, asking what job each person on the *Reliance* had. "What is this one's task on the ship?" He pointed to a crewman and was told his job, then another, and another. He got to Julio and asked in the same tone of voice as the ones before. He identified all the crewmembers of the *Reliance* and Dag's work crew. When he had everyone's job, he turned back to Julio.

"It is *unknown word* to see your enemies die from their *gibberish maybe stupidity maybe ignorance.*

"You thought it was *unknown word* that Ithobaal's crewman didn't know of your *unknown word* air. Well, so did I. But I am an admiral, not a deckhand. For you to show *unknown word* was as *stupid, maybe ignorant,* as breathing *unknown word* air." He gestured to two of his men. "Kill him." And never lost his smile.

They fought—the rest of *Reliance*'s crew, Dag and his work crew. But the truth was they weren't nearly as good at hand-to-hand fighting as the locals. They weren't SEALs or Green Berets. They were working people who spent their time working, not training to kill. They were quickly restrained, then beaten for fighting.

Dag looked at the admiral through bruised eyes. "Even admirals can face consequences. It's worth remembering."

Metello looked back at Dag and shrugged. "Maybe, but life is risk."

CHAPTER 10

Queen of the Sea, *Alexandria Harbor*
October 15

"Do we go after them?" Anders Dahl asked. Not that there was any doubt.

"Captain, there is a ship heading out from the docks at Alexandria. It looks to be Ptolemy's galley."

"I am tempted to say to hell with it and leave now," Captain Floden said. "We have people on the *Reliance*, even if Joe Kugan has been being a horse's ass about weapons and fuel."

"Well, he was apparently right about the weapons, Captain," Daniel Lang said.

"Was he? If he had just stayed with us..."

"He would have been in our way when we ran over the triremes," Elise said. "Sorry, Captain, but he would have been. It would have made maneuvering more difficult and dangerous for all of us."

"Fine. He was right and I was wrong. All the more reason to go after him now."

"I'd like to agree, Captain," said a new voice as Congressman Wiley stepped onto the bridge. "But we are still going to need Alexandria for some time, and showing that level of disrespect for Ptolemy isn't going to make that easy."

"That bastard was behind this attack, Congressman. We had the ships on radar from the time they left the harbor to the time the last of them limped home."

"I don't doubt you, Captain. But we still have to deal with him." Wiley waved a hand. "We don't have to let him off easy. We can charge him through the nose. But we are going to have to let him save face publicly."

"Fine. We'll need Marie." Lars looked around. "Where is she?"

"In the wardroom, having breakfast, Captain. After she delivered the warning, she didn't want to be in the way," Daniel Lang explained.

"Doug, would you go fetch her, please."

It took Ptolemy's galley fifteen minutes to reach the *Queen*, and almost the first words out of his mouth were protests that he had never authorized the attack, and that Gorgias had acted completely on his own and against Ptolemy's orders. He didn't try to convince them that it was anyone but Gorgias who had done it, which Marie thought was wise of him. For this meeting, Marie simply watched and translated. Wiley played peacemaker, with Floden in the background, muttering darkly about burning Alexandria to the ground in retaliation. It was a good bargaining ploy, and it worked in terms of getting the royal treasury to pay for the damage and loss of life, while letting Ptolemy save face and act as magnanimous innocent.

But it took time.

It was after nightfall by the time all was settled. By then they had received a phone call from Dag informing them that he was pretty sure they were going to Tyre. In a way, that made it less urgent to go after the ATB, articulated tug barge. They knew where they would be, and could go fetch them once the more immediate business was taken care of.

Internally, the attack cut the legs out from under the Jerusalemites. Yes, the *Queen* would defeat anything on the sea, but once they got on land, they could be taken prisoner and held for ransom. Not a good plan. Wiley's plan of going to Trinidad or perhaps Spindletop, Texas, and setting up the United States of America early gained a lot of credence and the consensus was that Trinidad was the best place. It was an island, so there would be some protection. And it had oil that was easy to get to.

They got a second call, but it was breaking up. Dag was out of range of the cell tower, even over water with no competing signals, well before the *Reliance* got to Tyre.

On learning that the *Reliance* had been captured and was on its way to Tyre, Ptolemy again offered a contingent of Greek soldiers to help them. Captain Floden started talking about the Trojan horse, and Marie didn't have to translate that, as Ptolemy's next words made clear. "I understand the captain's concern, but I am not Agamemnon."

More time as Wiley smoothed things over.

Then the issue of burying their dead came up. There was a dive shop on the ship. Two of the entertainments available on the *Queen* were scuba diving and snorkeling, so there was extensive scuba and snorkeling gear. They had been able to recover the body of Eileen Sanders, the woman who had gone over the side in flames during the attack. They had three bodies to bury and they couldn't afford the bad feeling that would be generated by ignoring the desires of the grieving loved ones.

Reliance, *approaching Tyre*
Dawn, October 16

Dag, bloody and subdued, watched a bloody and subdued Captain Joe Kugan show Admiral Metello the sonar depth gauge. Dag knew Joe Kugan well enough to know that Joe was protecting the *Reliance* from going aground more than he was protecting himself from another beating. The *Reliance* and *Barge 14* together made up a seagoing ship that was more seaworthy than anything from this time. They were designed to transport fuel across the high seas. In essence, *Reliance* and *Barge 14* constituted a small tanker, except at need the massive fuel bunkerage in *Barge 14* could be separated from the *Reliance* so that one of the two could receive maintenance or repair while the other part of the system was still in operation. That had happened several times before The Event. About half the time the *Reliance* had been attached to *Barge 15*. For a moment Dag was distracted by the question of whether the *Reliance* and *Barge 14* would ever be separated again. It almost certainly would, he decided as he looked back toward the stern. It was a waste of fuel to lug around *Barge 14* when you were towing triremes.

From the pilot house, Dag could see the steel cables that went from the stern of the *Reliance* to the bow of a trireme. After that was another cable from the stern of that trireme to the bow of the next, and so on until all six of the triremes under Metello's command trailed the *Reliance* like ducklings. After Julio's death, the crew had cooperated. In exchange, they had been mostly left alone.

Most of the crews of the flotilla were camped on the *Reliance*, with only steersman and a few sailors on the triremes. The campers were being careful to avoid dark places, the holds especially, and mostly not touching anything. Partly that was because of the guys who had died from the fire suppression system, but it was reinforced by how strange this giant ship made of steel was to them.

Dag had managed to make one covert phone call shortly after dark on the fifteenth, and confirmed that they were headed for Tyre. Everyone in the work party had phones. They were standard issue for the *Queen*'s crew. Pretty decent phones—not the most recent, but about two generations back. After making his point, Metello was surprisingly gentle with them. He had taken all the cell phones, but they hadn't searched anyone and missed Dag's.

Keith Seiver had a cell charger in his pocket, but there had been no opportunity to use it. The charger was, in Dag's opinion, a silly gadget. At least, it had been before The Event. It was a battery to recharge your cell phone through the USB port. But this battery was shaped like a cell phone and had one side covered in solar cells. The idea was that you could just leave it in the sun and it would charge the battery, which could then charge the cell phone or tablet computer. The problem was the solar panel was small. It would take the solar panel a couple of days in the sun to fully charge the battery pack, then you could use the battery pack to charge the cell phone in a couple of hours. Given enough time, the solar panels would charge a cell phone, a slate, even a laptop, but that meant putting it out in the sunlight. As soon as they did that, it would be seized. At the moment Dag's cell phone and Keith's battery pack were both fully charged because they had managed to plug them into the ATB's power grid last night. But who knew how long it would be before they had another chance to do that.

Dag looked out at the island they were approaching. Tyre was an island with an artificial causeway to shore. The causeway was about ten meters wide and nearly a kilometer long. Dag knew the history. Alexander the Great had built the causeway under the eyes and arrows of the defenders, then sacked the city. It hadn't yet fully recovered, though a lot of Phoenicians still lived there, and the defenses had been mostly rebuilt. Now it was Attalus' home base on the east end of the Mediterranean and currently the residence of Roxane and Alexander IV.

Dag and his work crew were pulled off the *Reliance* when they got to Tyre and put on a galley that took them into shore. A very beautiful, dark-haired young woman, surrounded by a bunch of grizzled old vets, was there to meet them.

"Why are these people tied up and what happened to them?"

Dag didn't find the girl's accent hard to follow. It was a bit different than the Macedonian accent, but was a lot closer to it than Metello's. The girl had black hair done up with a sort of gold chain hat, dark eyes, pale olive skin . . . and she was built. This must be the famous Roxane. She looked a bit like Elizabeth Taylor.

The commander of the galley started to answer back, but apparently thought better of it and just said, "Admiral's orders," in a sulky tone.

"Release them."

"Admiral said to . . ."

"I don't care what Metello said, and I doubt Attalus will either," Roxane said.

"You are not Alexander," the commander said. "You're not even Macedonian." That struck Dag as strange, because from his accent and appearance, the commander was probably Phoenician from right here in Tyre. Not that Dag was an expert.

Roxane looked like she was about to back down, then an older guy moved up beside her. "I am! Release them."

Hours later Dag felt better. He was washed, bandaged and even to an extent, briefed, by Kleitos, the guy who had backed Roxane. There was another man in the room, the commander of the Silver Shields, named Evgenij. Older and harder looking than Kleitos, he didn't talk much. Kleitos was something between her bodyguard and jailor. Not one of the official bodyguards who had been appointed in Babylon, four for Philip and three for baby Alexander, but none of them were present. They were all out trying to raise armies to bite off their own chunk of Alexander the Great's empire. Kleitos was a man for hire who would keep her safe or kill her, depending on the orders from the paymaster. That paymaster had been Perdiccas before his untimely demise, then Peithon for a couple of weeks, then Attalus. The Silver Shields were almost worse. They had appointed themselves and were halfway between guards and extortionists. As long as the money kept coming, they would keep Roxane and little Alexander safe. If the money stopped, they would sell her to the highest bidder.

And they were all quite disgustingly straightforward about it.

Kleitos had backed Roxane because he didn't like Phoenicians, and the Silver Shields had backed him because they were mean old bastards who didn't take crap from anyone.

"Roxane is pretty enough, I'll grant, and smart too," Kleitos explained. "But she has all the guts of a rabbit. You, on the other hand, look like you have at least a little bit of guts." Kleitos waved vaguely in the direction of the *Reliance*. "So tell me all about the ship out there."

Dag looked at the old reprobate and did. "First, you need to know that Metello made a bad mistake by taking the *Reliance*. The *Queen of the Sea* is almost twice as fast and a lot bigger."

"The sea is a big place. It's going to be hard to find a single ship. Even a ship the size of that one."

"Not that hard. They know we were headed for Tyre."

"How would they know that?" asked Evgenij in a voice like gravel. He had a scar along his neck and apparently didn't like to talk.

"I told them," Dag said. "Building big ships isn't all our people can do."

Evgenij looked frightened, then angry.

Kleitos, though, looked intrigued. "From what we heard and from what I saw, you people are just very skilled crafters so if you told them, you had to have some way to signal. Some device? That's right, isn't it?" He was watching Dag like an eagle watching a mouse hole, and Dag wished he'd kept his mouth shut.

Kleitos was still watching him, not saying anything, and Evgenij was starting to fidget like he was getting ready to do something Dag would regret.

"Yes, that's right." Dag said. He was being careful now that it was too late. And he realized that Kleitos would make a really good poker player if someone taught him the rules.

"Is the device still on the ship?"

Dag started to lie, hesitated, then told the truth. "No." He pulled the phone out of his pants and Evgenij laughed and said something that was probably obscene.

Kleitos laughed too, then said, "Show me how it works."

Dag turned it on and Kleitos lost his smile. Something approaching wonder was on the face of Evgenij. Gears and springs these men understood. Even ships made of steel made a kind of sense to them. But a flat piece of black glass that glowed to life with images and strange symbols? The Greek of the third century BCE didn't have distinct words for science and magic. Learning and trickery were all one to them. Invoking the favor of the gods, just another skill, like knowing how much to slant an aqueduct, or how to arrange a phalanx of infantry to best advantage in a battle. And if invoking the gods didn't always work, neither did arranging the phalanx. This was magic. This was learning, but of power and subtlety well beyond anything they had ever seen, even the *Reliance* sitting out in the harbor.

"There are devices like this on the *Reliance*, and other devices. And though this small one is out of range now, the emergency beacons on the *Reliance* will lead the *Queen of the Sea* straight to her." Dag had tried to say that in Greek, but Greek didn't have all the words. At least, Dag's Greek didn't. He had the phone out, so he used the translation app. It was out of range of the ship, but it had been updated with the most recent lexicon only day before yesterday.

Kleitos exchanged a look with Evgenij that Dag couldn't read. He suspected it was something to do with the *Reliance*, and Dag wondered if they would warn Metello about the beacon.

As it happened, they didn't. Neither Kleitos nor Evgenij was fond of Metello, who was arrogant in a way that Macedonians found objectionable in anyone but another Macedonian.

"It will run out of power soon if I use it too much," Dag explained, then turned the phone off.

"Well, you're wealthy enough," Kleitos commented. "You should be able to pay your ransom, so you won't end up a slave. Will your people pay the ransom of your common soldiers?"

Dag froze for just a second. Somehow, unconsciously, he had been thinking that he was still in the twenty-first century. No. He hadn't been thinking at all. He had just assumed that there was civilization here. Then he spoke, parsing every word carefully. "I think you should assume that the *Queen of the Sea* will do whatever is necessary to get us all back."

Queen of the Sea, *Alexandria Harbor*
October 19

Eileen Sanders, Jose Clavell, and Owen Kalusza were buried in Christian ceremonies in the Gabbari necropolis two hundred thirty years before the birth of Christ. That, at least, is what archaeologists would call it upon rediscovery in 1997. The locals just called it the necropolis. Josette Easley attended the funerals both as a representative for her mother, and because she had met Eileen. Their staterooms were just across the hall from each other, and they had drinks together at the first night party. Eileen was killed by Greek fire. Her husband wanted her buried, not "dumped in the ocean." Ptolemy was most accommodating.

More delays while they had people in the hands of pirates. Meanwhile, the signal fires confirmed Dag Jakobsen's report. The *Reliance* arrived at Tyre at dawn on the sixteenth. Now Josette, back on board in the Nobles Lounge, was having a drink in memory of a woman she barely knew.

"Why are we wasting time going after them?" the drunk Mr. Stuart whined. "We should just go ahead and go to America. Let these European barbarians kill each other. And let that stuck-up bastard Kugan take care of his damn fuel barge himself. He was busy telling everyone the barge was his. Let him and his crew protect it. We don't need them. There's oil in Trinidad, plenty, and the engines will use it without refining. We should go to America and never come back to this hellhole."

"We have people on the *Reliance*, Mr. Stuart," said Romi Clarke. This was said more in the way of a threat than the simple providing of information.

"We have people right here too," Stuart said. "Paying passengers." One of the changes over the weeks in 321 BCE had been the dropping of the rules about belowdecks personnel staying below decks. Crew and staff were, by the captain's orders, allowed into all the public areas of the ship. They could buy booze at the bars, swim in the pools, and so on. Not all the passengers appreciated that, but Captain Floden had been firm. Apparently, Mr. Stuart was one of those displeased by the crew's admittance into passenger territory.

Josette Easley wasn't the history scholar her mother was. She was an electrical engineer who had gone on the cruise to celebrate her recent divorce from her mechanical engineer husband. Since she was on the ship, she studied it and was working part-time with the electrical systems managers. So she knew the specs pretty well. "Mr. Stuart, the *Queen of the Sea* has a full tank range of just over eight thousand miles. But we don't have full tanks. Even sitting in one place, just running the lights and other electronic devices, plus air conditioning and water purification systems . . . all that takes power. From here, Trinidad is over five thousand miles. We might have enough to make it to Trinidad, but we would be close to out of fuel when we got there. We need the *Reliance*. We need her fuel and we are going to need her in the colony, to take that oil from shore to the *Queen*. And to do all sorts of things that a very powerful tug boat can do, like helping to dredge canals and harbors.

"But even if none of that were true, it takes a truly contemptible coward to advocate leaving our people in the hands of barbarians when we have a height advantage of over a hundred feet, not to mention steam cannons."

Suddenly there were people standing and applauding. Romi looked at the skinny little white girl. He'd seen her around, but hadn't really noticed her. Now he decided he liked her. He walked over, took her hand, bowed with a flourish, and kissed it. "Well said, pretty lady. On the money."

Meanwhile, something similar was going on all over the ship. Joe Kugan and, to be honest, most of his crew had been less than subtle in harping on their newfound wealth, and the need the *Queen* had for their fuel. And how rich that made them. Finally, Captain Floden got on the ship's intercom and made an announcement saying basically what Josette had said. Then the *Queen of the Sea* headed for Tyre.

Royal Compound, Alexandria
October 19

Ptolemy watched the *Queen of the Sea* sail out of the harbor and worried. He hadn't imagined the steam guns, and he should have. He had seen ballistas and catapults. He had underestimated the ship people. But he hadn't been wrong. They *were* soft. The loud lamenting over casualties so light as to be meaningless proved that. He simply hadn't realized how powerful their tools made them.

Ptolemy turned from the harbor and re-entered the palace. "Call Dinocrates," he told a guard. "And Crates and every scholar in Alexandria. We need a library."

Hades, Ptolemy thought, *I'll even send for that idiot, Apelles.* He was a very good artist and a fair scholar. And Ptolemy was going to need all the scholars he could get. There was no way that he was going to be able to reproduce the *Queen of the Sea.* But he might produce the steam cannon on another ship. Cannon like that, on the Nile with a powered ship, would control the Nile.

Royal Compound, Tyre
October 20

The sun was setting and Dag decided to check his phone. He was rationing his checks, especially since the *Reliance* had sailed off. He didn't know where the ship was headed. He hadn't had a meeting with Roxane. Kleitos had kept him busy, then let him check in with his work crew. They were being treated well. He pulled out the cell and turned it on. He had bars. Well, he had one piddly little bar. But it told him the *Queen* was on her way. He needed to find out where the *Reliance* was going.

Dag put his phone away and went looking for Kleitos. Dag wasn't entirely sure why Kleitos and Evgenij had let him keep his phone. He would like to think it was because they were afraid to touch the magic, and there was probably something like that in their attitude, but it felt more like a plumber insisting they get an electrician in to work on the wiring. They knew that there was potential danger in it and wanted it left in the hands of the expert.

"I would like to speak with Her Majesty." Dag smiled. "In fact, there is someone else who would like to speak to Roxane, even more than me. A scholar who studies your time, as some of your scholars study Troy."

"A storyteller, then." Kleitos laughed.

"She knows a lot," Dag explained.

"She? A woman scholar?" Kleitos laughed again, though there seemed a bitter edge to it. Dag didn't know why. In any case, Kleitos finally shrugged. "Why not? She's been pestering me all day, wanting to interview our ship people."

"Isn't she in charge?"

"Rabbit," Kleitos said. "I told you that. Rabbits aren't in charge of anything when the foxes are around, and that girl's been surrounded by foxes her whole life."

Dag struggled through the greeting and the woman seemed to be almost enjoying his difficulty.

"Thank you for your greeting," she said. "I know it must be difficult for you. I had a great deal of trouble with Macedonian and I already spoke some Greek. Please sit and tell me of the ships from the future."

About then, a little boy with a painted wooden sword came running in, shouting about the hydra, and chopping off the imaginary hydra's imaginary heads.

Well, he was yelling "Hydra" and chopping the air. Dag went to one knee to put his head on eye level with the tyke, and said, "Greetings, O great warrior." At least, that's what he thought he said. Whatever it was that actually came out, it was enough to stop the kid in his tracks and the little replica of a *kopis* stopped chopping hydras and went into the kid's mouth like a pacifier. Dag, without thinking, reached out and took the sword away from the kid.

Little Alexander resisted, but it came out of his mouth if it stayed in his hand, and the co-king of the Alexandrian empire started screaming. "Quiet," Dag said, and for just a moment there was quiet. Following up quickly, Dag looked around for something, anything, to distract the kid from the painted sword. Nothing in his pocket. It wouldn't help to keep the kid from lead poisoning, then have him choke on a button or keys.

There, in his back pocket, a plastic comb. He gave it to the kid.

Then he looked up at Roxane. She had come out of her chair when Dag grabbed the sword, and was now kneeling next to Dag, ready to snatch her son out of danger. Dag tried to explain, but he didn't have the words for paint, lead, or poison. All that came out was "Sword bad."

"Not for a son of Alexander the Great, they are not."

Dag pointed at the teeth marks in the sword blade and said, "Sick." He pulled out his cell phone and turned it on. Then he called up the translation app that Marie Easley had been working with programmers to tweak. He spoke in English. "Poison in the paint." The app translated.

Roxane grabbed the blade away from her son, and threw it across the room. "How do you know?"

Dag was ready and pushed the translate button and got the words in English. But Roxane was still talking and the app only worked one way at a time. It had to record the words in ancient Greek, then translate them, or record the words in English and translate them the other way. It couldn't just work in conversation. Dag recorded a message in English. "You have to say the words to the phone, then wait for it to translate them, then say another phrase. Just say the words when the front of the phone is facing you."

Then he had the phone translate. Roxane looked at him and nodded slowly with emphasis. Then she waited.

Dag pushed the record button and turned the phone to face her. Then she spoke two phrases with a short pause between them and nodded again.

Dag had it translate and "How did you know?" A pause, then, "Who tried to poison Alexander?"

"No one tried to poison him. It's the lead in the paint that is a slow-acting poison. It takes a lot of it over a long time, but it's unsafe, especially for children."

The guards were all watching this. "So, not a plot," said Kleitos. Dag had enough Greek to make a good guess, and shook his head no.

Roxane pointed at the phone imperiously, then at herself. Once Dag had pushed record and had the phone pointing at her, she asked, "How does that work?"

Dag tried to explain using the translation app and pointing at symbols on the phone's screen. In the process, he noticed that the little battery was less than half full. So he explained that.

"So it will be useless when the charge is gone?" Kleitos asked.

Dag thought he understood, but had Kleitos repeat the question to the phone.

"Yes, sort of. There is a charger, but it's not mine." More questions and answers. Finally Keith was brought from holding.

"What's up, Mr. Jakobsen?"

"What would you want for your charger, Keith?"

Keith looked around the room. It was a luxurious room with golden candelabras and expensive wall hangings. The chairs were thronelike. Dag could see Keith getting greedier by the moment.

"Don't go overboard, Keith. They can always just take the thing. And kill us both in the bargain."

"How about a couple of talents of silver?"

"Are you trying to get yourself killed?"

"I'll let them talk me down, Mr. Jakobsen," Keith said with a grin. "Let's see what they say."

Kleitos was playing with the hilt of his sword, so Dag guessed that he had at least understood the term "talent." A talent of silver was enough to pay the two hundred man crew of a trireme for a month. A trireme crew weren't just casual labor. It required skill to handle those oars, and the men were also the boarders in battle.

Dag made the offer. Roxane started cursing in Greek and some other language, and all the guards were fingering their swords now.

Finally, she calmed down and pointed out that the charger wasn't of any use without the cell phone. Apparently she had understood Dag's explanation fairly well. Then the real haggling began, using Dag's phone with the translating app. Roxane called Keith the worst kind of thief, and Keith protested his desperate straits. It went back and forth, and a couple of minutes in, Dag got the feeling that Roxane was enjoying herself.

Kleitos was clearly amused and a bit impressed by Keith's audacity, and was kibitzing. It was Kleitos who pointed out that if they bought the charger and not the phone, they had nothing. Suddenly Dag was in the bargaining too.

They finally settled on one silver talent for both charger and cell phone. Dag was to receive two-thirds of it, while Keith Seiver got the remaining third. Since both were necessary, Keith wanted an even split. That didn't fly with Roxane. She was very clear on the issue of officers versus common sailors. Dag was an officer/noble, he would get more. Dag would be required to help Roxane handle her new cell phone. Keith was sent off to fetch his solar power charger.

Dag checked his bars. He had three now. The *Queen* was on its way, but was still probably a hundred miles out.

He borrowed Roxane's new phone and used the app to ask, "Where has the fuel ship gone?"

"Rhodes. That idiot Metello has decided that he will take the island and all of the Rhodian ships."

Quickly, Dag pushed the button and called the *Queen*. He had enough bars. The call went through and he was talking to Adrian Scott. "Adrian. First, the *Reliance* is headed for Rhodes. Now I need you to get Marie Easley up to the bridge so that she can talk to Queen Roxane. Then I need you to come get us."

"You're on your way to Rhodes?"

"No, not us. When we got here, they dumped me and my work party off and took the *Reliance*, with her crew, off to conquer Rhodes. They have her packed to the deck heads with soldiers."

"That could be a problem, Dag," Adrian said. "The passengers are pretty mad about the attack and the *Reliance* running off like that."

"Hey, Adrian. *I* didn't run off. That was Kugan's doing."

"I know that, and you know that, but the passengers don't want to believe it. I'll tell you, Dag, I'm starting to think we ought to dump the whole bunch of them off in Ashdod and let them stew in their own pot. Hold on, I have Professor Easley on the line. Patching her through now."

Dag handed the phone to Roxane, and was then left out of the conversation while Marie Easley talked to Roxane about what was known, and Roxane explained what she knew about the players involved. It was a few minutes later that Roxane looked up and said something in Greek. She listened to the phone again, then handed it to Dag.

"Dag, this is Captain Floden. We need to get the *Reliance* back before it gets us involved in the political mess that Alexander's successors are involved in."

Dag felt the color drain from his face. He understood. He wished he didn't, but he did. Right now the *Queen of the Sea* was walking a political tightrope. She was virtually impregnable, but she needed food and supplies that she couldn't force anyone to sell them. So she couldn't afford to be banned from any port, especially not Alexandria. That was why the captain had decided to go after the *Reliance* before rescuing them.

But it might be worse than that. It might be that they would have to leave Dag and his crew right here in Tyre rather than alienate Attalus. Dag could be here for months.

Dag Jakobsen was a nice guy, but he was neither an idiot nor a coward. He realized that they were liable to need some form of weapon and that his captors were unlikely to sell them swords. Not that Dag could use a sword if he had one. But Dag had known how to make black powder since he was a small boy. His family made their own fireworks. Besides, he was a fan of Nobel and had studied the arms manufacturer's life in school. "Keith, I want you to do me a favor."

"What's in it for me?" Keith asked resentfully. He wasn't pleased that Dag got the lion's share of the money for the phone and charger combination.

"Get over it, Keith. We don't have time for that crap."

Keith came to a parody of attention, snapped an open-handed British-style salute and said, "Sir, yes, sir. Anything the officer requires, sir."

"Sit down, Keith. We need to make some black powder."

Keith looked around sharply and Dag shook his head in disgust. He wished he had Romi Clarke with him. "Keith, how many people on this island know what the term black powder means?"

"Seven. You, me, and the other members of the work crew."

"Right. So just don't make a big deal of it. You want to make a poultice. For your aching backside, or your legs, or your forehead. I don't give a crap. The poultice will contain..." Dag proceeded to give Keith the ingredients for black powder, along with some other stuff that was essentially useless, but would mask the purchase of the ingredients a little bit. "Any of the local apothecaries ought to have all of it, so we are going to have to be fairly careful. One thing about black powder is it needs to be ground moist, and then dried, then ground again. For that second grinding, you want a brass mortar and pestle to avoid sparks. We're also going to need clay or iron pots, little ones. Hand grenade size. And nails or other bits of metal for shrapnel."

"What are you planning, sir?" Keith asked, serious now.

"I don't know, but we're prisoners. I believe the captain is going to come for us, but what do you think these people are going to do when he does?"

"They won't turn us over. They'll try to ransom us."

"Right. How much are you worth?" Dag asked. "How much will Wiley and his people think you're worth? I can hear him now, being noble. 'We will not negotiate with terrorists or kidnappers.'"

"Yeah. Me too. Funny thing is, I sort of agree with him in principle."

"As do I. However, it feels a bit different when you're the one being sacrificed for his principles."

"Don't it just?" Keith agreed.

"The day we arrived, Kleitos asked me if the *Queen* would ransom us or not. If not, we will be sold as slaves. I figure they can get a really good price for us on the auction block, considering we're such unique items. I'd rather avoid that, Keith. So I think that we might want to be in a position to get out on our own. Or at least close enough to out that the captain will be able to come get us."

"You think there'll be enough time to make black powder grenades before the *Queen* gets back from Rhodes?"

"Again, I don't know. I do believe it's better to try than not."

Keith saluted again, but this time it was casual and real. "I'll get right on it, Mr. Jakobsen." He coughed experimentally. "I think I'm developing a chest cold."

CHAPTER 11

Queen of the Sea
October 20

Captain Lars Floden felt like a coward and a traitor as he turned the *Queen* to go after the *Reliance*. But he had a responsibility to the passengers and crew of the *Queen*. They needed that fuel. They couldn't afford the chance that some accident in the battle at Rhodes would leave the *Reliance* aflame and all her fuel up in smoke.

So he did what he had to, hating himself all the while. The *Reliance* had left on the route to Rhodes almost twenty-four hours ago, which put the *Queen* well behind. It was going to be close, even with the *Queen*'s higher speed.

Reliance
October 21

Rhodes was in sight and the *Reliance* had clearly been seen. In the dawn's early light, the Rhodians were putting to sea. Three triremes were heading out to meet them and Joe Kugan wondered where the rest were. Metello was sure there would be a bunch here.

"Run them down, Captain," Metello said. "Steer straight for them. My men will deal with any of the crew that manage to board."

Joe did as he was told. The *Reliance*, with *Barge 14* attached, wasn't exactly spry. She had powerful engines and controlled thrust, but a barge full of fuel wasn't easy to shift. She was close to as fast as the triremes, but she couldn't maneuver like they could.

So what followed was a slow-motion game of tag. The *Reliance* would head for a trireme, and the trireme would turn and race away, then try to come at the *Reliance* from the side or rear. One unfortunate trireme managed to close on the *Reliance* and found out what the backwash from eleven thousand horses did to the local currents. It survived but lost about half its oars, and was out of the fight for a while.

"*Reliance*, this is the *Queen of the Sea*. What are you doing?"

It blared over the speakers in the pilot house, and Metello went a little white. He had no idea what was said, but he had to know what it meant. Joe checked the radar and there it was, big as a mountain rising out of the southwestern sea. Still half an hour out, but coming on.

Joe still didn't have much Greek and he wasn't of a mind to try just now. He turned to Metello and said in English, "You're toast, sucker!" Then he grinned like an idiot through his busted lip and missing teeth.

"Go there!" Metello pointed at the harbor, where until just a few years ago the Colossus of Rhodes had stood.

Joe started to comply. He was cowed by this bastard, as much as he hated to admit it. But an ATB the size of the *Reliance* doesn't do anything fast. There was time for Joe to consider the consequences. He realized that if the *Reliance* grounded *Barge 14*, there would be no escape. In desperation, he hit the emergency stop, and the engines came to a stuttering halt.

Metello looked at Joe, and Joe looked back. Metello reached for his sword, and Joe lunged. He was desperate, but Metello was just that much faster, with reflexes honed by years of combat. Joe never laid a hand on him as Metello sidestepped and brought his *kopis* down on the back of Joe's neck.

With the ship stopped, the Rhodians saw their chance and pulled alongside to board. But they didn't have it all their own way. There were two thousand troops camped on *Barge 14*, and by now they were at least fairly familiar with the hardware that dotted the hull, making defensive works.

By the time the *Queen of the Sea* actually got there, the Rhodians had been pushed back to their ships, with considerable losses on both sides.

Queen of the Sea
October 21

"Are there any of our people in view?" Captain Floden asked Staff Captain Dahl.

"Not that I can see, Captain."

"Fine, then. Clear that deck, but keep the muzzle velocity low. We don't want any of our shells poking holes in the *Reliance*." One of the nice things about a steam cannon is that, to an extent, it has a modifiable muzzle velocity, and therefore adjustable penetrating power. The power a one-pound lead bullet needed to pulp a human chest, even an armored human chest, is considerably less than the muzzle velocity necessary for that same shell to punch through a one-eighth-inch steel plate.

The crew of the *Queen* had made lots of bullets for the steam guns.

Two thousand armed and armored soldiers crowded onto the *Reliance*. They couldn't have spread out if they wanted to and they didn't know enough to want to. They clumped together to provide mutual protection and support and the one-pound rounds of the steam cannon went through two or three men to finally lodge in a fourth.

It didn't take long for the deadly rain of lead bullets to have their effect. People started screaming that they surrendered. These were tough men who would readily face other men in battle with sword and shield, but invisible death that ripped a man in two and sounded like Zeus on a rampage...? That they weren't willing to face.

They surrendered, but could that surrender be trusted? Could Lars send people across to the *Reliance* without knowing that?

"We're ready, Captain," came Daniel Lang's voice over the speakers.

"All right. Pull us alongside." Then, into the mike, "Dan, don't take any chances. If any of them give you any trouble at all, just shoot them."

"Right, Captain. Police brutality coming right up."

The *Queen* came up alongside the *Reliance* and a massive porthole opened to reveal men in glowing white uniforms with little metal things in their hands. The little metal things looked harmless, and the only ship people these men had contact with till now were the unarmed crew of the *Reliance* and the equally unarmed work crew. They didn't know. Still, the rain of death from above kept most of them in check.

Most of them.

Daniel Lang would never know whether the Macedonian soldier who charged him was desperate or just saw an opportunity. Ultimately, it didn't matter. Dan had done twenty years as an MP and another ten as a cruise ship cop, and never even drawn his gun in anger.

Didn't mean he didn't know how.

The gun came up, he hollered half in Greek and half in English. He'd been practicing. The man didn't halt.

Dan fired. *Blam, blam, blam!* Three in the chest. They punched right through the guy's bronze armor. That halted him and more. He went down on his back. It was close enough to what had been raining on them, louder even. Now they knew.

The order to drop their weapons was given again. Those who hadn't already done so dropped their weapons.

Goran looked at the men. *Wait! Is that a woman?* Yes, it was. Dark-skinned, long black hair tied back, wearing the same whiter-than-white clothing as the rest. And holding death in her right hand, just like the men. But she had tits. Nice ones too, best he could tell. And no man had a waist and hips like that.

His observations nearly got him killed. Not because the woman was offended, but just because he was so busy staring that he almost missed the order to get on his knees. Fortunately, they were repeating the orders twice before they killed people over them.

Goran got to live. He went to his knees on the decking wet with blood and waited. He put his hands behind his head and interlaced his fingers just as the voice from nowhere told him to, and as he did he realized that it was an effective method of restraint. Not because you couldn't unlace your fingers, but because it took time and was pretty obvious. These people must be great slavers, they were so practiced at restraining captives.

He looked over at the woman. By now he had seen other women among their captors, but he thought of her as *the* woman. She had a set of bindings and was going along behind the kneeling men, taking one hand and binding it behind their back to the other hand, while a man with death in his right hand held death pointed at the captive.

Goran let his hands be bound. She wasn't gentle about it, but neither was she vicious. She was just efficient.

There was a shout in their tongue, and then what sounded like orders. About half the white suits went off to do something. Goran considered. Probably they had found the crew. Goran had come on at Tyre, so he hadn't had much to do with the crew of the little boat that pushed the big boat.

"Captain, we have a ship. A galley, but only two rows of oars. It's heading for us and there is some guy in the front waving some branches at us. I don't know if he's suing for peace or trying to drive off evil spirits."

"I'm not entirely sure, either, Captain," Marie Easley put in. "I would guess suing for peace. I think those are olive branches."

"Talk to them, Professor Easley," Captain Floden said. "Tell them to stand off while we deal with the *Reliance*. Tell them we'll send a boat to talk to them after we're done."

Marie waited for the comm officer to cue her, then spoke. The ship stopped, but the guy with the branches started yelling. It was too far and the accent was weird enough that she wasn't sure what the guy was yelling about, but it seemed urgent. Or at least, he seemed to think it was urgent.

"I think I'd better go have a talk with them, Captain Floden," Marie said. "The Rhodians were the England of the eastern Med at this time. As in 'Rhodes rules the waves.' They probably have more in common with our modern form of government than the Athenians do."

"Fine, Marie. After Mr. Lang has secured the prisoners on the *Reliance*, I will have him provide you with an escort and one of the converted life boats to go chat with the Roadies."

It took time. There were a lot of troops on the decks of the *Reliance*, nearly two thousand before the shooting started and nearly fifteen hundred after it was all over. After twenty-five percent casualties, there was no organized resistance, but Daniel Lang was taking no chances on people going there. And rightly so. There were two more shooting incidents when individual mercenaries from Tyre went berserk.

It was just on three hours later and approaching noon, when

Marie Easley, Daniel Lang, and Officer Arti Young boarded the converted lifeboat for the trip to the Rhodian ship. It was fancy and sleek, if smaller than the warships, a ship of diplomacy.

"We will need to go aboard," Marie told Daniel. This was less from her reading than from discussions with Atum, Ptolemy, Dinocrates and other merchants and military officers after they arrived in Egypt. Refusing to board was both an admission that you were afraid and an insult to the integrity of the other ship or people. That was why Atum had been willing to board the *Queen* in the first place. On the other hand, taking guards was just prudence.

Once they boarded, they were met by *Nauarch* Demaratos, who informed them that the ship—he pointed at the *Reliance*—had been involved in an act of piracy in the very harbor of Rhodes and was therefore the property of Rhodes. And, while Rhodes and its people were thankful for the aid, that didn't entitle them to seize the property of Rhodes.

"We have a prior claim. The ship was taken by an act of piracy a few days ago and we have been following it to get it back. Many of the crew are still alive and were taken prisoner by the pirates and the captain of the ship was killed only a short time before we arrived."

"So you claim. But there is no evidence, and even were it true, it doesn't change the fact that the ship was part of an invasion attempt, and someone has to pay for the deaths of our people killed in that attack."

Marie was not just a scholar anymore. She had been, of necessity, involved in the negotiations in Alexandria everyday, ever since their arrival...and she had learned. This was a starting position of negotiation, but the negotiations were going to take some time.

Anders Dahl looked out the bridge windows, down at the *Reliance* and its still blood-soaked deck. "With Joe Kugan dead, the *Reliance* is going to need a new captain."

"You want it, Anders?"

"No, I do not, Captain. With all due respect to the *Reliance* and even considering the new circumstances, captain of an articulated tug barge is a demotion from staff captain on the

Queen. I was thinking Elise." Elise Beaulieu was the first officer navigation, which was the senior navigation watch stander. While not next in rank after the staff captain, it was the next in line of ship's command. And with the loss of navigational satellites, her training in navigation was even more vital. Both ships had radar and sonar, so with care were unlikely to run up on the rocks. They had radio communications and shared observations and could sometimes get directional fixes. But both ships would be using clocks, sextants and star sightings to determine their locations, along with inertial and magnetic compasses.

"I will pass, *mon capitaine*." Though French, Elise spoke with very little accent unless she was upset. "I will stay here on this large ship, with good food, clean sheets, and laws against rape."

Everyone turned to look at Adrian Scott, the second officer navigation. "Hey, wait a minute, Captain," Adrian offered. "This is ancient Greece. I have more to worry about in the rape department than Elise does."

"Don't worry about it, Adrian," Elise said. "You're no Johnny Depp."

"I do all right, Elise."

"I know, Adrian. I just don't understand why," Elise said. Then she turned back to the captain. "Still, Captain, if someone is going to be sent off to be raped by barbarians, I vote for Adrian."

"Gee, thanks," Adrian said to general laughter.

The laughter might have had a slightly hysterical edge to it. The deck of the *Reliance* was still covered in blood and gore, and the captain they were getting ready to replace had been murdered earlier in the day.

"Well, Adrian, do you want it, or do we send out poor Doug?"

Adrian looked over at Elise. "You sure? You deserve it, you know, and I don't want to step on your toes."

"I'm sure, Adrian," Elise said.

"I'll take it, Captain," Adrian said. "We must protect Douglas here from the rapacious Greeks at all costs."

Captain Floden nodded. "Thank you, Adrian. I hate putting you off the ship, but someone has to captain the *Reliance*. It's bad enough that Dag and his people are sitting on Tyre while we negotiate with yet another group of rapacious Greeks."

Tyre
October 20

Young Alexander had not liked losing his chew toy. He screamed himself hoarse and managed to develop a cough.

Roxane heard about Keith buying materials for a poultice, and after consulting with Keith about it, Dag agreed with the queen that a black-mud poultice would be good for Alexander. Just make sure it was kept moist.

For the next three days, Dag and Roxane used the translation app on Dag's phone to discuss politics and their situation, with Kleitos looking on. Dag was six foot two, with blond hair and blue eyes. He had a square jaw and was clean-shaven when he could manage it, and with the money he had made from the sale of the phone, he could manage it. To put it another way, he was a handsome young man and Roxane was an acknowledged beauty. Maybe not up to Helen of Troy, but only maybe. They played with the baby and talked.

"Should we put a stop to it?" Evgenij asked Kleitos.

"What difference does it make?" Kleitos shrugged. "You know she's going to be married to whoever wins."

"That or dead. Sure. But a little blond bastard might confuse things."

"We won't let it get that far. It's not like they have time alone."

"Might not be a bad thing at that," Evgenij said. "Did you see the size of that ship? And it was just the fuel tender for the other. Those ships change things."

"No. Men are men. Always will be. Things stay the same."

Queen of the Sea, *Rhodes Harbor*
October 25

Captain Floden smiled at the new captain of the *Reliance*. "You'll do fine, Adrian."

"Not a problem, Captain. *Reliance* and *Barge 14* together are as seaworthy as the *Queen*," Adrian Scott, the new captain of the *Reliance* said, and it was almost true. The ATB was smaller than the *Queen*, but it locked up tighter. Fully battened down, *Barge 14* was as watertight as a submarine and constituted a massive flotation device that would keep the tug part of the system protected from the worst of any storm. It wasn't the ocean that worried Captain Floden. It was pirates.

"How about the crossbows? You have enough?"

"One for every man in the crew and another twenty in the arms locker," Adrian said. This time his smile was a bit twisted. Adrian was getting the worst of the malcontents from the *Queen*. Only about three hundred of them, but the really bad ones. They would be in tents set up on the hull of *Barge 14*. Those people would not be armed, except during designated practice times. And the reason for that was neither Lars Floden nor Adrian Scott trusted them with weapons. They weren't prisoners, not exactly, but the choice to travel on the ATB rather than the *Queen* hadn't been entirely voluntary.

"Stay well away from land as much as you can and don't put into shore till we reconnect," Lars said, knowing even as he said it that Adrian knew it all perfectly well. "We'll probably be stuck here until you're past Gibraltar, then we have to go get Dag and his work crew. I don't know how long that's going to take."

Tyre
October 27

The phone rang and Roxane almost dropped it. She was playing chess against the computer and losing, not surprisingly. Dag had showed her the game only days ago. She barely knew how the pieces moved. It rang again and the little green symbol had a circle around it that was expanding. Roxane had been playing with the phone whenever it had enough charge since she had bought it, either using it as translator or playing games. She knew about tapping or swiping. She tried tapping first, then swiping. Swiping worked and a voice came over the phone. Not the voice she knew from the translation app, but a different one, speaking Dag's English. Roxane had maybe ten words of English. She tried one. "Hello?"

"Hello," then gibberish ending with "Dag Jakobsen" came over the phone.

"Roxane," Roxane said. "Phone mine."

Roxane turned to one of the Silver Shields who was always with her. "Find Dag and bring him."

The Silver Shield nodded, but didn't leave. Instead he gestured at another guard, who ran off in search of Dag.

Dag was showing Alexander how to make a paper airplane, or rather a papyrus airplane. He had just tossed the airplane when the guard came in and it flew right past the startled man.

"Roxane wants you," the guard said.

That phrase was familiar to Dag and he picked up Alexander—decked out in a black powder poultice—and headed for the queen's sitting room. Dag now had a pouch at his waist with a grenade in it and a Zippo lighter loaded with lamp oil in his pocket.

When he got to the sitting room, Roxane held out the phone. "It talked English," she said in Greek.

Dag walked across the sitting room and exchanged the toddler king for the phone and saw bars. He called up the phone function and found a recent call from the ship. He called back and got Captain Floden asking for a situation report. The conversation ended with, "We'll be there in about three hours, Dag. Be ready."

By that time, everyone was watching and apparently getting a bit impatient.

"The *Queen of the Sea* is coming to get us," Dag said, looking around the room. There were half a dozen Silver Shields in the room, including Evgenij, who had apparently arrived just ahead of Dag.

"What about the fuel ship, the *Reliance*, you called it?" Kleitos asked, coming into the room.

"What about the *Reliance*?" Dag asked the phone.

"The *Reliance* is now in our hands," Doug Warren explained. "Captain Scott has been given command and the remaining crew have agreed to the sale of the *Reliance* to the government of the ship people for a fee in ship's dollars. It's a pretty damn large fee, but not unreasonable, Ms. Kinney says. Dag, those steam guns are murder, absolute murder. You know how they talk about stuff being awash with blood? Well, the *Reliance* really was."

Dag wished Doug were speaking Greek. It might persuade the locals to be reasonable. He looked over at Kleitos. Or...maybe not. If one thing more than any other had impressed him about the Macedonian mercenary, it was that he didn't scare easily. That was actually something Dag liked about the man.

"They took it back from your pirates," he told Kleitos.

"Not my pirates," Kleitos said. "What happened to Metello?"

"What happened to Metello?" Dag asked the phone.

"That was kind of a mess, Dag," Doug said. "The Rhodians wanted all this stuff in recompense for the *Reliance* being involved in attacking them. First they wanted the *Reliance*, then they wanted all sorts of promises about the *Reliance* and the *Queen*, then they wanted all the Macedonian troops as slaves, and on and on. Anyway, when Wiley heard about the slave part, he started screaming that he would not see free men made slaves. 'It was hard enough to stand idly by while the horrible inequity was practiced.' As though the captain would have done it anyway. And then . . . well, never mind. The captain finally had enough. He had Metello tried for piracy on the high seas and hung right in front of the Rhodies. And the passengers."

"What did Wiley say to that?"

"Funny thing. He backed the captain right down the line. He's still making speeches about it."

Dag turned back to Kleitos. "My captain had him hung."

"Your device said more than that."

"Apparently, he did it right in front of the Rhodians. I'm not clear on the details, but they were making claims against the *Reliance* or something, and the captain decided to make a point."

Dag was watching Kleitos as he spoke, and Kleitos was looking more grim at each word.

"The rest of the soldiers?" Kleitos asked.

Dag remembered Doug's comment about awash with blood and started to feel a bit grim himself. But he passed on the question. "What about the rest of the pirates? I know they loaded up a bunch when they got here. You can't have killed them all."

"No. Mostly they decided that the soldiers were just following orders and not responsible. But there were a couple, the ones directly involved in killing Julio, that they hung. Most of the soldiers are on the *Queen*, disarmed and locked in, eight to a stateroom. The captain wants to put them off here, but not as slaves."

Dag considered quickly. "What about the rest?"

"Dead," Doug said. "Either in the fight or soon after. Like I said, those steam cannon are murder."

Dag turned back to Kleitos and the rest. "A lot of your fellows were killed in the fighting. The rest will be returned after my companions and I have been freed. And, of course, the young king and the queen can come with us." Dag wasn't sure, then or ever, why he had said it. Something in Roxane's expression, or maybe just something he wanted to be there. But the idea of sailing off on the *Queen of the Sea*, leaving her and little Alexander to the not-so-tender mercies of these hard men was more than he could face.

Right up to Dag's mentioning Roxane and Alexander, Kleitos had been half nodding. But as soon as the suggestion about Roxane left Dag's lips, his face changed.

"I have my orders," Kleitos said. "Attalus doesn't want Alexander to leave the island till he gets back."

"I'm not leaving my son," Roxane said instantly. Then she added to Kleitos, "But you have no authority to prevent me from leaving."

Dag was looking around the room. The Silver Shields seemed of two minds about what to do. Then he saw Evgenij's expression and somehow he knew. Evgenij was in on it with Kleitos. At any moment, he would give the order. Dag was sure. So sure that he turned away, put the phone in his pocket, and pulled the grenade out of its pouch. With his other hand, Dag reached into his pants pocket and pulled out the Zippo lighter.

"I have the money I was paid and Attalus' orders. That's all the authority I need," Kleitos said. Then, apparently seeing Dag's movement, "What are you doing?"

With a flick of his thumb, Dag opened the lighter and struck the flint. He turned back to Kleitos and lit the fuse. "Making a point." Dag watched the fuse as it burned, then tossed the grenade. "Catch."

As soon as the grenade was out of his hand, he turned, spread his arms wide, and pulled Roxane and Alexander to the floor behind the couch.

There was a pause and Dag though he hadn't let the fuse burn down enough, that it was all going to end in disaster... then *boom*.

A boom and screaming. Dag stood up and looked around. Kleitos had been holding the grenade when it went off. He was dead and his right arm, the one that held the grenade, was gone to the elbow and shredded beyond that. Not that it mattered. The shrapnel, small bits of iron that were in the casing with the powder, had filled him with more holes than Dag could count. But the shock wave had probably killed him. There wasn't that much bleeding.

Not from Kleitos, anyway. One of the Silver Shields had apparently stepped over to see what the grenade was. He was still bleeding and screaming. The rest of them were staring at the mess in a sort of shocked horror.

Then Evgenij looked over at a Dag. "Stop!" Dag shouted. "That was what we could make in a few days while under guard. What do you think will come off the ship if you do us harm?"

Evgenij stopped and stared. By now the outer edge of the room was crowded with Silver Shields.

A voice from behind the Silver Shields came in "You want us to blow our way in, Mr. Jakobsen?"

"Hold what you got, Keith," Dag shouted. Then to Evgenij, "Choose now, Commander; whose side are you on?"

Evgenij looked at Dag, then the mess on the floor. Then, oddly enough, he looked at Roxane and he wasn't looking at her like his prisoner or his charge. He was looking to her for orders. Dag could see it in the old man's expression. This was so far beyond his experience that a horse might as well have sung Pavarotti right there in the sitting room. Roxane might not be brave, but everyone knew that she was almost as smart as she was beautiful. Smart was clearly what was needed right now.

Roxane saw it too, and Dag wasn't altogether pleased by the little smile that lit her face. It wasn't a very nice smile. It was calculating. "The Silver Shields," Roxane said, "are the royal bodyguards. They will remain loyal to me and my son." A short pause. "Won't you, Evgenij?"

"Yes, Your Highness."

"Very well," Dag said. "Now for the important question, Roxane. Are you and little Alexander staying here or coming with us?"

For just a moment, the queen mother of King Alexander IV, co-ruler of the Macedonian Empire, stood like a deer in headlights. Then that little smile came back. It was still small, and still calculating, but there was a little less frost in it. The hint of warmth that might be there, hidden under the habit of fear and caution. "We will go with the ship people. That is the wisest course."

"Evgenij, have your people let mine through." Dag gave the order now, confident that it would be obeyed. "I'm going to let the ship know what's going on."

CHAPTER 12

Queen of the Sea
October 27

"We don't have room for a hundred Greek soldiers and their families," Jane Carruthers complained.

"Oh, come now. We have a thousand men locked up right now," Marie Easley said. "Besides, the Silver Shields are famous for their ability and loyalty. They were Alexander's elite infantry."

"And that's supposed to make the passengers feel better?" They had spent eight days in the harbor at Rhodes, part of it in negotiation, part in modification of staterooms into jail cells to transport the prisoners back to Tyre. And altogether too much time negotiating down an incipient mutiny of the passengers over the question of whether they should go to Tyre at all.

"At this point, Jane, I don't much care how the passengers feel," Lars Floden said. "I want them off my ship just as much as they want to get off. And even more since they wanted me to abandon my people."

Increasingly, a large contingent of the passengers wanted to get on with the trip to America so they could get on with their lives. What is a vacation for a week becomes a prison after more than a month in which you can't leave the ship. It wasn't that they were happy about the prospect of starting over, but not being able to was getting to them.

"Well, just getting them to Trinidad isn't going to be enough, Cap—"

Lars waved off the explanation. He knew it perfectly well. The *Queen* would be staying in the new world for at least two months to help with the construction of the new colony and setting up the oil wells. In fact, there was considerable doubt that they would be able to get it done in two months. It might be next summer before the *Queen* headed back to Europe. The *Reliance* was already on its way, with three hundred of the most anxious to get started camped out on its decks. It would take the *Reliance* longer, nineteen or twenty days to get to Trinidad. The *Reliance* left on the twenty-fifth, so unless the *Queen* was unduly delayed here it would probably get to Trinidad ahead of her. But many of the most obstreperous of the passengers chose to take the longer trip because they didn't want to stay on the *Queen* with "Captain Bligh" in command.

Captain Floden turned back to the comm and waved at the comm tech to put it on speaker. "Dag, hold in place there. We're going to give them some of the prisoners as a show of good faith."

"Why, Captain?" asked Anders Dahl.

"Because I want someone on the other side who knows what the steam cannon can do. I am sick and tired of killing these people to convince them we're not too soft to defend ourselves. Let them know what the steam cannon can do, and maybe they will see reason."

Captain Floden was an easygoing man. It was a job requirement. A cruise ship captain is more entertainer and host than autocrat. But for right now he had taken on the aspect of a Caesar or—given the time—an Alexander. What he said was going to happen, was going to happen.

Jakov climbed into the small boat he would have called a ship before he saw the *Queen of the Sea*. He was relieved to be getting back to Tyre alive, much less as a free man. He had been wounded by Zeus' hammer, what the Greek prisoners called the steam guns. It had broken a rib which had then punctured a lung. But they healed him. The boat people had healing magic almost as powerful as their killing magic. Most of the people on this boat had been wounded by Zeus' hammer. And Jakov was sure that was why they were being sent back, message and messenger all in one. He settled on the bench with a grunt, and a man he didn't know and who sported a bandaged arm sat down next to him.

☆   ☆   ☆

They docked at Tyre and the men were herded off the boat by the white-suited guards who carried death in their right hands. Then the boat left and the next one docked. Jakov looked around and headed for the gates in the walls. He was called over by a *lochagos*, file leader, roughly a sergeant. "Come with me. The general wants to see you."

Jakov was a soldier, but just a common soldier, not a *lochagos*. "Why me?"

"Why not you? Can you think of any reason we shouldn't take that boat out there?"

"Are you insane?" Jakov shouted.

The *lochagos* stopped and looked at Jakov. "Ares blood, man. What did they do to you?"

Jakov looked at the *lochagos* and tried to explain. "They just shot me and I was four ranks back. The bullet, a lead bullet this long—" He held up his thumb and forefinger three and a half inches apart. "—and this big around—" He held his finger and thumb an inch apart "—pointed like a quarrel, but made of lead dipped in copper! It went through three men, the ones in front of me! Broke my rib. They had a machine, manned by two men!" Jakov held up two fingers for emphasis. "And it fired so fast that..."

Jakov had run out of words. "Here is what you do. You fart in Nike's face, and after that you charge that boat. But don't expect me to be anywhere near you when you do it."

The *lochagos* looked at him and must have seen something in his face, because he grabbed Jakov by his arm on his good side and pulled him along. "The general will need to hear this."

So Jakov got to explain to the *strategos* in charge of the defense of Tyre what the battle on the *Reliance* had looked like from the point of view of a Greek foot soldier.

Strategos Nedelko didn't believe him. Officers are good at disbelieving privates who tell them things they don't want to hear. But he was a good officer, an experienced one, and so before attacking anyway he asked other soldiers and even other officers. Some of them had survived. Every story was as horrible as the last, but those stories took time. By the time he heard a dozen he was starting to think in terms of mass cowardice, but the boats were back at the *Queen* and two hundred of the soldiers Metello had taken with him to Rhodes were ashore, talking to the troops on the island.

He could give the order and the galleys would put to sea and attack the *Queen*. But his men would be nervous and upset. If there was any truth at all to what the returning troops said, his army would come apart all the quicker for the prior knowledge. He had mostly discounted the sheer size of the *Queen* but, no, he couldn't. He might still be able to use the prisoners as a tool...but the prisoners were holed up with the Silver Shields. And he knew about the magic talking device. He would waste his strength against them and probably only end up with dead prisoners anyway.

Royal Compound, Tyre
Evening, October 27

The *strategos* of Tyre, roughly the equivalent of a colonel, came up to the royal encampment and requested a parley. Dag looked over at Evgenij. "What do you think?"

"Let him in. Nedelko is a good man, honest."

Dag nodded agreement, and the officer was let in. They met in Roxane's sitting room. Kleitos' body had been removed, but the blood stains were clear on the wood floor and spots of blood dotted the rugs and hangings. Alexander was being quiet, sucking on Dag's comb. Roxane was being quiet too.

The *strategos* saluted Evgenij and then turned to Dag. "What is *nonsense words, more nonsense words*."

Roxane held up the phone and pushed a button. "What is the device that throws sling bullets and quarrels from the great ship?"

Apparently the app was having some trouble with the Greek words, but Dag managed to work it out. He motioned for Roxane to hold up the phone. "It's a steam cannon."

The translation had everyone looking at him like he was insane. He motioned for the phone again, and Roxane passed it over. He pushed a few icons and had the thing translate back. "The cooked ballista" was what he got.

He tapped the record symbol and said, "It's hard to explain. Doesn't translate well. What do you want to know about it?"

What followed was a tale of horror and clearly one that *strategos* Nedelko didn't quite believe. But Dag knew about World War I, and the machine guns in the trenches, and those poor bastards on the *Reliance* had been stuck in no man's land with no trenches to retreat to, and no way of getting to the enemy's trenches. It had to have been utter slaughter.

"I know you don't believe me, but think of men caught in the open with no armor and no place to hide while arrow after arrow rains down on them. No place to escape and no room to scatter. No place to hide."

"They would surrender."

"Ever since we got here, you people have assumed we are weak. You assumed it when you attacked the *Reliance*, when Ptolemy attacked the *Queen*. As you held me and my people here. We don't like to kill, but it's not because we aren't good at it. It's because if we let ourselves, we could kill the whole world, down to the insects." Which wasn't true in the here and now, but wasn't that far from the mutually-assured-destruction doctrine that kept the nuclear powers from blowing up the world back in the last half of the twentieth century. Dag didn't remember much of that, but his parents talked about it.

Royal Lounge, Queen of the Sea, *off Tyre*
October 28

Nedelko looked across the table at Marie Easley. "I will need some explanation for Attalus and Eumenes."

Marie slid a folder over the smooth surface of the table. It was a manila binder with a picture of the ship and a picture of a monarch butterfly on the cover. It had one hundred seven pages of Greek lettering in a twelve-point type face. "That is an outline of what we know of the history of this time. There were a lot of scholarly works about Alexander's era, but not much hard information. Very few of the original sources survived. What we got was quotes, often taken out of context and always incomplete. I have learned almost as much in the month we have been here as I learned in the thirty years of study back in our time. In spite of that, the details about what would have happened if we had not arrived are sketchy at best."

Nedelko listened to the scholar as he flipped through the pages. He stopped at a drawing, little blocks on a map. He read the inscriptions. "The battle of Paraitakene." The Macedonian date six years after the joint kings had been proclaimed, with no month given. Three and a half, maybe four, years in the future. Eumenes managed a draw with Antigonus One-eye. Nedelko hadn't imagined that the Greek would be alive in a year, much less fighting Antigonus to a draw, maybe winning if the casualties were to be believed. And four years from now. But Marie Easley was still talking. "We have given a copy of that to Satrap Ptolemy of Egypt and another to Nauarch Demaratos of Rhodes."

"I request several copies, one for me, one each for Attalus, Eumenes, Cassander, Cleopatra, Olympias, others."

"Cassander? Didn't he go with Antigonus?"

"This is going to change who goes with who. This is going to change everything."

"It already has. The first time someone saw this ship, it changed everything. The first page after the table of contents is a short description of what we call 'the butterfly effect.' When you have some time, you should read that section carefully. Just what I told Crates in Alexandria changed history drastically. In my history Antipater was named guardian of the kings and *strategos* for the whole empire. Antigonus got possession of the kings and Cassander as an aide and a watcher, then was sent off to capture and execute Eumenes."

"Well, old One-eye is still going after Eumenes. And he still has Philip and Eurydice."

"But he hasn't been empowered to arrest Eumenes by the regent, and Roxane has endorsed Attalus as regent."

"Is that still the case?"

"We'll know that when Roxane is on the *Queen of the Sea*."

"And that's my problem. If Roxane, from the safety of the *Queen of the Sea*, endorses old One-eye, Peithon, Seleucus, or anyone else, all the rest are going to blame me for letting it happen."

"And they are all going to claim that we coerced the endorsement out of her," Marie agreed. "That's why she isn't going to endorse Captain Floden, Dag or Congressman Wiley. And we aren't going to endorse anyone to her. We're going to give her that history book we compiled—the one with the butterfly on the cover—and let her read it. Then she can make up her own mind."

Nedelko swallowed.

Royal Compound, Tyre
October 28

Roxane read the small writing with some difficulty. Her father hadn't seen any point in teaching a girl to read. Alexander had, though. He had her tutored and she could read now, but it didn't come as naturally as if she had started as a child. This, however, was easier to manage than most writing. The letters were all exactly the same and there were spaces clearly separating the words. There were even little dots to mark the ends of specific thoughts, and double-sized letters to start thoughts and to delineate the beginnings of names. By about halfway through, she was reading it more easily than anything she had read before. In spite of that, she read well into the night.

As Roxane read, most of her goods were packed up under Dag's guidance and the eagle eyes of the Silver Shields. Rooms had been assigned and part of her guard contingent was already there. The rooms for her guards had cost thirty silver talents and her rooms had cost another two talents, but she was paid in advance for the next six months. She had a royal suite, the men shared staterooms, and Evgenij was positively loquacious over the quarters.

Meanwhile, over half the survivors from Rhodes were shipped back to shore. The exchange was being done a little at a time, even as negotiations were ongoing.

Dag came in carrying a cloak. It was a heavy cloak with a hood and it clinked.

"What is this?"

"This is an armored cloak. It has steel plates sewn into the lining and the hood. It also looks just like two others that we are going to have other women wearing for the transfer to the ship."

"No!"

"What? Why not? It's a good idea. It will keep you safe from assassins with bows."

"I have to be seen," Roxane insisted. "If I am not seen getting on the boat myself, they will assume you killed me and buried me in the garden."

"What are you talking about?"

"When Alexander was sick, the men almost rioted until he showed himself. For all I know, going out like that when he was so sick killed him. But he had to because the rumors said he was dead and the generals were hiding it. I have to be seen and so does my son."

Dag muttered and pulled out the new cell phone he got when he got back to the *Queen*, and started talking to it.

☆   ☆   ☆

"No, not for nothing. I know the formula, and if you don't pay me two talents of silver that knowledge is going to sail away with me." Keith Seiver grinned, showing even white teeth in a brown face. Curly black hair topped his head and he had the bare beginnings of a beard, even though he had himself shaved just that morning.

Dareios wanted to punch out the teeth of the arrogant bastard, but he smiled, keeping his mouth closed. Dareios had always been comfortable with his teeth until he met these people. His teeth ground together in frustration. The shipman had him, and he knew it. He couldn't use force. The grinning Silver Shield behind the shipman made that very clear. He paid the money.

Keith handed two pounds worth of silver in electrum coins to Hermogenes. The old bastard had to be sixty and had a son in the Silver Shields as well. He also had a wife, a daughter, three grandchildren, and four slaves who would be going along on the trip. He was a right bastard in a lot of ways, and had never risen higher than private, but he knew how the world worked and was always out for the main chance. Keith was looking forward to the bastard's expression when he learned there was no slavery on the *Queen of the Sea*.

"Is good," the guy said in English, then some words in Greek. Something about them working well together. Keith nodded agreement, and they headed for the boats.

Tyre Docks
October 29

Roxane, in shining steel plate armor with a lion's head helmet over her black hair, waved at the crowd as she walked out on the docks. It was a copy of Alexander's famous lion's head headgear, made by the jewelry shop on the ship. It was a rush job and not great in quality, but they had buffed the steel to a high shine. The lion's head had glass eyes that looked almost real. The rest of her armor was steel plate, breast and back plate, greaves and bracers, all shined.

It was a pageant, and not bad for a rush job. Anyway, the people seemed to approve. There was a lot of cheering.

Dag stepped ahead and handed her into the converted life boat, then took little Alexander—also in armor and not happy about it—in his arms.

Then the rest of the party boarded and they headed for the *Queen.*

In the Royal Lounge, Captain Floden, Congressman Wiley, and Marie Easley were waiting, and so were Nedelko and Evgenij.

Marie Easley spoke before anyone could get formal. "Have you decided who you are going to endorse as regent?"

"As regent? No one. I will act as regent for Alexander. But for *strategos* of the kingdom, I endorse Eumenes. He has always been loyal to my husband's house. He will countenance no harm to come to Alexander or his uncle.

"I place command of all of my husband's armies in his hands, to distribute as he sees fit until our return."

Dag had learned a bit of Greek, and had no trouble recognizing Nedelko's muttered "Oh, shit." Evgenij didn't look pleased either.

But Roxane was still talking and now seemed to be speaking to the two Macedonians. "I know that many will not like being placed under the orders of a Greek, but that is part of the reason I chose him. He can never be more than council to the kings. Never be tempted to seize the crown for himself."

Marie Easley nodded firmly, and gave Roxane an approving half-smile, as if a student in one of her classes had come up with a good answer to a question in the lecture hall. "Very well, Your Highness, we will have the documents drawn up for your signature."

Queen of the Sea
Two hours later

"What?" Evgenij asked. "You're stealing our slaves?"

"No," Dag said quite calmly. "We're emancipating them." The word he used was *cheirafétisi*, which translated as "manumission," though, as a rule, you could only manumit your own slaves. The English "emancipation" didn't imply prior ownership the way manumission did.

"They aren't your slaves. You can't manumit them," Evgenij used the word *cheirafétisi* too.

"Slavery is illegal on the *Queen of the Sea* and it's going to be illegal in the colony we'll be setting up in America too. Consider yourselves lucky you're not being arrested for being a slaver." Dag looked the angry old bastard dead in the eyes. "You grabbed me and my people. You held us hostage, and I'd be ready to see you thrown over the side for that."

"We treated you well."

"In expectation of ransom, yes, you did. But if the *Queen of the Sea* hadn't come to our rescue, you would have sold us."

"Yes, of course. That's what happens when you lose." By the end of that statement, Evgenij was sounding querulous, but with the next sentence, he was back to belligerent. "We didn't lose. We came aboard the ship by agreement. You have no right to seize our property."

"You should have looked into the laws then, because we have made no secret of the fact that slavery is illegal on the *Queen*." They hadn't either. They just hadn't specifically said that yes, those laws did apply to the Silver Shields.

Dag saw Evgenij's hand moving in the direction of his sword. "Be careful, Commander." Dag slapped the holster and the old man flinched.

"This isn't over," Evgenij blustered.

"It had better be," Dag said.

Roxane's Suite, Queen of the Sea

"You betrayed us," Roxane said coldly.

Dag didn't want this fight, not the way he had wanted the fight with Evgenij. "I guess in a way we did," he agreed. "But it was necessary for your safety and your son's. Would you have come knowing that your slaves would be freed? And even if you would have, would the Silver Shields have let you?"

"But my servants have been with me for years."

"Then hire them. Pay them a wage and keep in mind they can leave if they want to," Dag said hotly. Then, with an effort, he got himself under control. "Think, Roxane. If we were willing to set aside our laws at your desire, what protection would those laws be when you needed them? You can't have slaves, but neither can you be made a slave. Not a slave or a playing piece of Alexander's successors."

"If you will take my property without my consent, what else will you take?" Roxane said. "Leave me!"

Dag left.

CHAPTER 13

Queen of the Sea, *Straits of Gibraltar*
November 2

"Ptolemy is a cold man," Roxane agreed. "Eumenes is almost as cold, though. And I am not at all sure that he would have come down on my side, even if I were still in Attalus' custody."

"I'm surprised by that statement," Marie Easley said. "Eumenes was recorded as unfailingly loyal, though some scholars gave that loyalty baser motives. Besides, you endorsed him." She glanced past Roxane at the grizzled Silver Shield who stood by the door of the dining room in Roxane's suite. He was standing straight in what looked to Marie like something between attention and parade rest. His feet were apart, but one hand rested on the hilt of his sword, and the other was tucked into his belt. What struck Marie was his expression. He didn't look happy. Then Roxane's next words brought her back to the politics of the *diadochi*.

"Eumenes was Philip's man. He was a wagoner's son King Philip took a liking to. He was always loyal to Philip II, and he studied with Alexander and Philip III under Aristotle. He knew about Philip III and he knew that the king loved him and so did Alexander. But Philip II was willing to put aside his love for his children for the dynasty. Eumenes will do the same. Philip and Eurydice are both Argead and Philip's mother is Macedonian. That puts Philip's son, if he were to have one, closer to the Argead royal house than my son, at least the way most Macedonians see it and probably Eumenes as well. Olympias, on the other hand,

163

hates Philip III because he is the result of Philip II's infidelity to her. And even if she doesn't think I'm good enough for Alexander, I am the mother of her grandson so she will come down on my side. I'm not sure how Cleopatra will decide. She doesn't hate Philip III, but she was devoted to her brother Alexander. In any case, I have no desire to be left in Eumenes' custody. I feel a lot safer endorsing him from a distance."

"Historically, Olympias had Philip murdered and forced Eurydice to commit suicide."

"That's because Olympias doesn't care about the Argeads as much as she cares about her own blood lines. That's Alexander and Cleopatra, no one else."

"What about Heracles?" Marie Easley asked.

"Who?"

"Barsine's son, Heracles?"

"What about him?" Roxane asked, confusion on her face.

"It was reported," Marie said cautiously, "that Heracles is Alexander's illegitimate son."

"Alexander and Barsine?" Roxane's eyes were wide in shock, then she started laughing. "Alexander would have rather stuck it in a thorn bush. I actually sort of like Barsine, but the woman does have a tongue like a *kopis*. Heracles is a nice child and practical, but like most Rhodians, he's all about ships."

"Tell me about Antigonus," Marie said.

"He doesn't think anyone who isn't a Macedonian is quite a person. That applied to me, and even to my son Aristotle. At a guess, right now he's going after Eumenes. In fact, that was already decided. He'll probably be in Cappadocia in another month or so."

"What about Eurydice and Philip?"

"She'll be endorsing him. She doesn't really have any choice. And, knowing Eurydice and Antigonus, he probably has her locked up by now. Antigonus keeps to his wife, but Stratonice is the twisty one of that pair. Antigonus doesn't trust women, except Stratonice."

"Why does that mean he'll lock up Eurydice?"

"She will want a say in the government. In truth, what she really wants is to be a ruling queen. Antigonus will never agree to that. So she will make speeches and he will lock her up."

Marie nodded. They had already discussed Philip. He seemed to have something of an autism spectrum disorder, and was perhaps some sort of savant into the bargain.

Queen of the Sea, *North Atlantic*
November 3

Tyrimmas watched the girl and fumed. He had taken her in a battle four years ago and she had been his. But the ship people had stolen her, and now she was swimming in the artificial pool, flaunting herself in front of him. They were thieves, that's what they were. She was Tyrimmas' wench to do with as he pleased, not a citizen. Who ever heard of a woman citizen? But at fifty-eight and as a veteran of the Silver Shields under Philip II and Alexander, he knew discipline. He forced his eyes away from the bitch and looked around the pool deck, looking for doors and access ways. This was a prize like no prize ever seen, and whoever controlled the bridge would control the ship.

Daniel Lang looked at the roster and worried. They'd gotten a lot of the malcontents off when the *Reliance* left, but quite of few of the younger passengers—the sort to be recruited into the ship's security contingent—were among the three hundred who left. Meanwhile, Daniel had ten security guards, most of whom had never fired a shot in anger. They examined IDs and ran people through the metal detectors. They weren't the frigging Marine Corps.

He wanted to recruit from the passengers. There were two hundred eighty-two veterans among the passengers, but two hundred fourteen of them were over sixty-five. Of the remaining sixty-eight, only three were active, and none of them were in combat arms military occupational specialties. Two were cooks and one a truck driver. There were half a dozen vets under sixty-five with combat experience, and about twice that number who had combat arms training, but had never been in combat.

For the battles using the steam cannon they had used regular crew, and his people had done a good job of rounding up the prisoners and keeping them locked up while the *Queen* made her way to Tyre. There they had picked up not just Queen Roxane and the baby king, but a contingent of Alexander the Great's elite infantry.

That was what Daniel needed. The Silver Shields. They had experience in combat, decades of it, and it was the combat of this time. He took one last look at the spreadsheet on his computer and called the bridge. "I need to talk to the captain."

☆   ☆   ☆

"We should have stayed on Tyre," Evgenij told Roxane as she paced around the room. Even a luxury suite just wasn't large enough for a good pace. It was bigger than anything there would have been on any ship she had ever seen before now, but you couldn't go very far before you had to turn back around.

Roxane wanted to agree with Evgenij. She was furious with Dag for not warning her about the crazy laws the ship people had, and even more the ridiculous notion that she—Roxane, Alexander's widow—would be required to abide by them. At the same time, Roxane understood the political situation back in the empire better than Evgenij did. She believed Marie Easley's book about what would have happened to her and to the Silver Shields. The changes that the ship people had made were as likely to make things worse for her and the Shields as they were to make them better. "Perhaps we should have. But we are here now and we need to deal with this situation. All they have taken is the slaves. The ship restaurants serve food, the laundries..."

"That's not the point. Those slaves were a good part of our wealth. An ongoing source of funds. We put them to work or rented them out. Now that's gone."

"I know. I lost my slaves too, at least the ones that were with us." The truth was that Roxane owned hundreds of slaves back on her father's lands. Also in Babylon and other places around the empire. Alexander had been generous with her whole family, and he had a great deal of booty, including slaves. She just hadn't had that many with her in Tyre. And now that she knew, those slaves weren't coming anywhere near the *Queen of the Sea.*

The Silver Shields, on the other hand, carried all their booty—including the slaves—with them. And the slaves were at least half the wealth of most of them.

"Give me some time, Evgenij. Let me try to figure something out."

Evgenij opened his mouth, then closed it and nodded. There was something in that nod that made Roxane nervous, but she wasn't sure what it meant.

"What about this offer of employment?"

"Yes, take it as long as there are enough left over for my personal guard contingent." Roxane and Alexander IV had five guards with them at all times, like a Secret Service detail, though Roxane had never heard of the Secret Service until Dag mentioned it. But that only took a small number of the force at any given time. "Learn what you can of the way they make war."

Daniel Lang didn't speak Greek, so he wasn't following the comments made by the Silver Shields as he showed them around the ship. Tyrimmas, who was a leader of sixty—something between a sergeant and a lieutenant—seemed all business, though. Looking for access points and potential blocking points. Every once in awhile he would raise his hand and gesture for Daniel to use the translation app and ask pertinent questions.

Good questions. Sometimes questions Daniel hadn't thought of. He answered them as well as he could, and gained a respect for the man's abilities while he did.

Amateurs, Tyrimmas thought, as he followed the white-suited but unarmored man around the ship. The place was a maze, but Lang had conveniently provided him with a map.

It would be hard to take this ship. Harder than he had thought before the tour, but not because of the crew. Just because of the size of the ship, and the number of narrow passageways. Passageways that would let one or two men with shield and spear hold back an army for hours or days. Tyrimmas smiled to himself. Once they took the ship, they would be able to hold it, as few as the Shields were.

"Captain, this is insane!" protested Marie Easley, doing her best to keep her temper under control. "You might as well recruit tigers or lions—hungry ones, fresh from the jungle or savannah— to your security force. I keep telling you, these people are *not civilized*. Not in the sense of the term that you and I mean by it, at any rate. And to make things still worse, the Silver Shields think they have a grievance against you—us—because we stripped them of their slaves. From our standpoint, that was simply social justice. From theirs, it was outright theft. And they are people for whom theft isn't even a 'crime,' it's just another element that's added or subtracted to their ledgers of acquisition and revenge."

Lars Floden wiped his face with a hand. In that moment, he looked inexpressively weary and Marie had a moment of sympathy for him. Great sympathy, in fact. The man had been under tremendous pressure since The Event and, all things considered, had handled it extraordinarily well. But the moment was still brief. This was a disaster in the making.

"I am sorry, Marie, but I don't see where I have much choice. Daniel Lang is insistent and it's not just him—our entire security force is feeling completely overwhelmed. There aren't enough of them, it's as simple as that. And they were never trained for this kind of an emergency."

Marie pursued the matter for a few more minutes, but the captain wouldn't see reason. As much as she respected Floden— was coming to like him personally, too, more and more as time passed—he could be as stubborn as the proverbial Swede, even if he was Norwegian.

So, eventually, she left off the argument. And went in search of a sane Frenchwoman.

"How well do you shoot? I know you were in the French navy."

Elise Beaulieu cocked her head and studied Marie for a moment. "I shoot extremely well, as it happens. Especially with a sidearm, where I was at competition level when I was a young woman. Why?"

"Because the captain—meaning no disrespect—has lost his . . . ah, what's the way to put it?"

Beaulieu smiled a little. "You think he and Daniel are being incautious, allowing Silver Shields to join the security force?"

"Not exactly the term I would choose. 'Incautious' is sticking your head into the gaping jaws of a crocodile. Letting Silver Shields into the security force is utter recklessness."

Beaulieu's tips tightened. "I have doubts myself. But the fact remains that Lars Floden is the captain, and I am not. And the fact also remains that I am not at all inclined toward mutiny."

Marie waved her hand in a downward, patting motion. "No, no, of course not. I am not suggesting that you be in any way insubordinate. Just make sure you have your sidearm with you at all times."

The Frenchwoman shook her head. "I can't walk around carrying a holstered sidearm." She looked away, her expression thoughtful. "What I will do, however, is make sure that I have it available whenever I'm on the bridge."

"And keep one in your stateroom as well."

Elise smiled more widely. "Marie, pistols—good ones, which

mine certainly is—are *expensive*. I am not one of your American—what are they called?—'gun nuts,' I believe. I only own one pistol."

Marie looked grim. "I'll get you another one."

"Captain, I *insist*. I know Lang has some spares available."

Floden's smile was very crooked. That was not like him at all.

"Fine, Marie. I will order him to provide a pistol to Officer Beaulieu. But on one condition. No, two."

"What?"

"Call me 'Lars,' please. And join me for dinner tonight. I could use..." He made a gesture with his hand that could mean most anything. "Company."

Marie stared at him. "But... I'm considerably older than you are. Lars."

The captain's smile got more crooked still. "Your passport is on file with us. You are exactly five years, one month and three days older than I am, Marie. Not so much, really. Not even in the world we came from—much less this madhouse."

Queen of the Sea, *North Atlantic*
November 4

One of each guard contingent was a ship person and one was a Silver Shield. The ship person was armed with a pistol and the Silver Shield was armed with a short spear, six feet long instead of ten, and a shield. This let the ship's personnel instruct the Silver Shields in ship procedures. The first day they were checking in every few minutes, not because Daniel didn't trust the Silver Shields, but just because they weren't trained.

The day went smoothly, with only a few incidents where passengers approached the pair of guards and the Silver Shield responded more belligerently than Daniel would have preferred. But he reminded himself these were infantrymen, not professional security from the twenty-first century. They hadn't been trained in "firm but polite."

Daniel shut down his phone and went to talk to the captain.

"I think we should start training them on the crossbows, sir," Daniel said as soon as he got to the wardroom.

"Is there any hurry, Daniel?" Captain Floden asked. "I have

heard some rumblings. They aren't fully reconciled to the loss of their slaves. I think it might be better to give them a few weeks to become more acclimated to the new situation."

"In that case we shouldn't have them guarding passageways," Daniel said. "I passed two of them on the way to the wardroom."

"I know. But your people have been overworked since The Event." On a normal cruise there wouldn't be any sort of a watch on the hatches or passageways on the ship because there wouldn't be any need for such a watch. But between the dissidents among the passengers and the external threats, Daniel and the captain had agreed that they needed more than just the cameras and smart cards.

Queen of the Sea, *North Atlantic*
November 5

The group of eight Silver Shields walked to the door from passenger country to crew country, and the ship person guard stood up, along with the other Silver Shield at that post.

"Everything under control here?" Tyrimmas asked in Greek, and was answered with a nod and grin.

The ship person, a girl who looked absurdly young, pulled out her phone, probably to access the translation app. But as she did, her fellow guard reached out and grabbed her arm. As she turned, he showed her his other hand, the one with the knife in it. He put the knife against her throat and backed her to the wall. Then he reached down, unbuckled her gun belt, and tossed the gun, belt and all, to Tyrimmas, who put it on.

The ship people were about to learn that there were consequences to robbing Silver Shields.

The guard opened the door to crew quarters with the smart card and the small party slipped through. Then he grabbed the girl by her ponytail, took her into crew quarters, locked her in a broom closet, and went back to stand watch on the door.

A light blinked on a short time later in the security room and Rui Jorge, the second deputy security officer, noted it in his log but didn't call the guard post. That same door had opened and closed fifteen times since he came on shift. Each time it was a crewman going back to crew quarters after having a meal in passenger country.

Just a minute later, the light came on again. And again two more times. The *Queen of the Sea* had clocks and the Silver Shields had learned to use them. The concept of a coordinated attack was anything but new to them. They were all veterans with plenty of combat experience. Four of the *stichos*, eight-man squads, were involved in the attempt. Not all the Silver Shields were as incensed about the freeing—as they saw it, stealing—of their slaves.

Koinos watched as Tyrimmas led his two squads to the forward elevators. He was nervous about this and had argued for waiting, but Tyrimmas outranked him and was a mean bastard besides. Koinos wasn't going to go up against Tyrimmas, not when it would mean betraying the men in his squad as well. Koinos waved and his two squads headed aft toward the elevators that would take them to the engine room. "Don't kill anyone you don't have to," he said again. "The Gaul was right when he said even the floor moppers might know things we need to find out. Besides, a ship person slave will bring a high price."

"We know, Koinos," Archelaus said. "You've said it before."

Koinos wasn't ambivalent about the plan because of any warm fuzzy feelings for the former slaves or the ship people who had taken them. He was just afraid that thirty-two men weren't enough to take and keep control of the ship. Tyrimmas had assured them that once they got control, the rest of the Shields and even Roxane would come over to their side. Koinos didn't doubt that. He just wasn't sure that even all of them together and their families were enough to keep the ship. It bothered him how quickly their slaves had abandoned them when the ship people emancipated them. He expected more loyalty. Less than half the slaves chose to stay with them, and even the ones who had had mostly insisted on getting paid.

They reached the elevators and called up two of them.

Jon Sonnenleiter, assistant engineer, said, "Knut, the waveforms are still too rough on the induction furnace," as the elevator reached deck seven and the doors started to open.

Knut Hedlund, engineering mate, answered, "With all due respect to your exalted rank, Jon, the iron ore is melting and we have too much that is broken or at least in real need—" He stopped as he saw the Greek attire of the men standing at the elevator door. "What are you people doing in crew country?"

The captain had allowed belowdecks crew into passenger country, but not the other way around unless they had special permission. And none of the locals had permission. None of these Macedonian hoplites knew enough to be of any use.

Knut wasn't armed, but he was belligerent. He grabbed his phone and that was all it took.

Argaeus of Macedonia grabbed Knut's arm and chopped his hand off with the *kopis* he was so fond of.

That started Jon Sonnenleiter yelling. The one thing that the squads absolutely could not afford.

Koinos cut Jon's throat, in the process spraying the bunch of them with blood. "Damn you, Argaeus. I said we wanted prisoners, not corpses." *I hope Tyrimmas is doing better on his end*, Koinos thought.

The first anyone on the bridge knew of the coup attempt was when the doors opened and sixteen men in the arms and armor of Silver Shields came in. The bridge of the *Queen of the Sea* was a large, airy, room with lots of big windows. It had comfortable seats and computer consoles that allowed the bridge crew to access any function of the ship from the rudders to the nacelles that pushed the *Queen* through the sea. They hadn't been designed to offer cover and concealment.

In moments, the bridge was taken and everyone was in custody. Captain Floden had a black eye and a split lip, but was otherwise unharmed. Tyrimmas looked around and smiled happily.

That was when it all went to hell.

When Elise Beaulieu saw the Silver Shields piling onto the bridge she understood immediately that Marie Easley's worst fears had come to life—and also knew immediately what she would do herself.

She had, as Americans would put it, an ace in the hole—or two, rather.

The first was the obvious one. Positioned in the center drawer of her work station, ready to hand as soon as she opened the drawer, was a MAB PA-15—a fifteen-round 9 mm automatic pistol designed by the *Manufacture d'armes de Bayonne*. France's armed forces chose not to officially adopt the pistol, but most of the services purchased some for competition. They selected a model especially designed for that purpose, known as the *Pistolet Automatique de Précision (PAP) Modèle F1*. Which was the model Elise owned herself.

Her second ace in the hole was more subtle, but ultimately more important. Because she was female, the Silver Shields would immediately dismiss her as a factor in the military equation. They wouldn't even "dismiss" her, really, because that term implied that they would briefly consider her as a possible threat whereas in actual fact it would never even occur to them that she might be.

So, none of them noticed—none of them was even looking in her direction after an initial glance—that she was quietly opening the drawer and taking the pistol in her hand.

She considered, for a moment, firing from her seated position. But she was a competition shooter by training and decided the extra time it would take her to rise from the chair was worth the advantage she'd have from taking a stance she knew and was sure of.

Only three of the Silver Shields looked at her when she rose to her feet and none of them kept their eyes on her for more than a split second. Their attention was focused entirely on the male members of the ship's complement, especially Captain Floden.

On her feet. In the Isosceles stance. She fired.

Tyrimmas was standing less than twenty feet away. Elise was a bit excited, so she brought the gun up too far. Instead of hitting him where she'd intended, just above the armor, the bullet caught him in the upper throat and clipped the underside of his jaw before exiting his neck. An artery was severed, producing a gout of blood that covered Doug Warren.

"Merde!" she hissed.

Never, not then, not years later, would Elise admit that she hadn't been aiming at his neck. She claimed that she was afraid the armor, if hit at an angle, might deflect the bullet—which was true enough, but she hadn't been aiming more than a few millimeters above the line of his armor.

But all that would come later. Right then, right there, she was furious with herself and leaned on her training. Which was years in the past—but had been taken very seriously by her young self. And she'd trained for the 25-meter quick-firing competitions as well. The men she was firing at were nothing but targets now.

She shifted aim to the left. *Fired.* The bullet struck right where she'd aimed—at the base of the throat just above linothorax that served Macedonian soldiers as chest armor. Blood sprayed from the man's back and gushed out of his mouth. She'd severed the aorta.

But her aim had already shifted by then. In competition, at her prime, she'd been able to fire four aimed shots a second. She was a little slower now, but not much.

Fired. Further to the right. *Fired.* Back to the left where a Silver Shield was finally starting to react. *Fired.* As he slumped forward, a companion behind him was exposed. *Fired.*

Beaulieu had trained as a competition shooter, shooting bull's-eye style, not as a police officer or a special forces soldier. So she was firing only one shot for each target.

It didn't matter. Except for that first high shot, every bullet had struck where she'd aimed. All but one of the men she'd hit since had had his aorta ruptured, and the one exception had had his spine severed—as had three of the others.

She brought the pistol back around to the right. *Fired. Fired.* Two more down.

"Elise—stop!" shouted Floden. But a Silver Shield was moving. Away, but he was moving. *Fired.*

"Stop, I tell you! That's an order!"

That half-shriek broke through her total concentration. She managed—barely—not to squeeze the trigger again. Vaguely aware of the shock and terror on the face of the Silver Shield who'd come so very, very close to dying that moment.

She lowered the pistol—slightly—and glanced around.

As had... *That many?* She was quite surprised. As had always been true in competition, her mind—her training even more—had kept her concentration completely focused. Nine of the Silver Shields had already died or were mortally wounded. Seven of them from bullets striking right in the upper chest where she'd aimed. There was...

Blood everywhere. Especially on the surviving Silver Shields, of whom there were...

She counted quickly, using the pistol barrel as a pointer. Without realizing it, completely stifling whatever thoughts of further resistance might have crossed any of their minds. Beaulieu was simply taking a count, but to everyone who watched—especially the battle-hardened Silver Shields—it was blindingly obvious they were all dead men if she chose to start firing again.

There were only seven survivors. Some of the Silver Shields

she'd shot were still alive but they wouldn't be for more than a minute—and there was no way to keep them from bleeding to death. Not with those wounds. Probably none of them had still been conscious before they fell to the deck, except perhaps the one she'd shot as he turned away.

Then Captain Floden pushed a button. A siren started and the motors stopped. Not the engines. The electric motors that powered the screws. It was the emergency stop control.

Captain Floden spoke in English. "The ship is stopped and will not move again until certain codes are input. So whatever mischief others of you may be attempting will be of no purpose."

Elise blinked. That was sheer nonsense. She had no idea why the captain said it. She kept her pistol level, though. No one was moving.

"And now," Floden said, "put down your weapons." He considered the surviving Silver Shields for a moment, with a very cold gaze. "And take off all your armor. No, strip completely naked."

He pointed to a far corner of the bridge. "Go sit over there. And do it quickly, or I will order my officer to kill the rest of you." There was nothing in his tone of voice, any longer, of the gracious and cordial captain of a luxury cruise liner. But Elise had no difficulty imagining that tone of voice in command of a Viking longship.

The Silver Shields obeyed instantly. Occasionally they would glance at Elise, but only for an instant before looking away. She realized that she must have slid her way into their own myths and legends. *Diana, whose bow never missed.* No, Diana was the Roman goddess of the hunt. Elise couldn't remember the name of her Greek equivalent.

There were two doors onto the bridge of the *Queen of the Sea*, one to port and one to starboard. There was a banging on one of the doors, and Captain Floden shouted, "Hold what you have, Mr. Lang."

Elise wondered if it really was Mr. Lang. If so, he had gotten here really fast.

Then, slowly, Captain Floden reached into his shirt pocket and pulled out his phone. He repeated what he had said about the motors and added that the most the Silver Shields could do was to strand themselves in the middle of the ocean until they all died of starvation and thirst.

☆　　　☆　　　☆

The ship changed. There was something different.

It took Koinos a moment to figure out what it was. By the time he had, there was an alarm sounding. He didn't know what that meant either, but the ship stopping hadn't been part of the plan. They were almost to the engine room, and with two dead bodies and his squad covered in blood it was way too late to abandon the plan. "Move!" shouted Koinos.

They ran.

They burst into the engine room just as an announcement came over the loudspeakers. It was in English, which wasn't good news.

Almost Koinos ordered a slaughter. He wasn't a stupid man and he was well aware that losers were not treated well. He had seen infantrymen trampled by elephants at the orders of Perdiccas. There wasn't much for him to lose. What stopped him was the emancipation. He, like Tyrimmas, Evgenij, and the rest of the Silver Shields had taken it to be weakness. Softness. Wishy-washy indecision. Now he prayed to Ares and Athena, to Nike and Zeus, that the ship people would prove just as soft as he had thought.

"Stop! Put up your swords!" Koinos shouted.

Argaeus turned on him, sword out. "Are you crazy?"

"You think you can defeat them now that they are ready?"

"We take hostages! They are weak! They will back down."

Koinos considered. It might work. There were perhaps a dozen ship people visible here. Eight men and . . . no, just three women.

Edith Wild looked up at the captain's announcement.

"A group of the Silver Shields has attempted to take the bridge. All crew go to alert status."

Then she looked over at the blood-soaked bastards who had just come pouring into the main engine room and thought, *Now you tell us.*

Edith was wearing sound-damping earphones because even with the insulation, the big turbines were noisy. She was distracted because the captain's—she assumed it was the captain's—killing of the motor had put a major spike in the ship's electrical grid. She had been busy trying to compensate for that when the captain's announcement came over the comm channel in her earphones. She looked at the Greeks again, then went back to balancing the power system by pouring passive current into the gyros.

The *Queen* balanced power just like any power plant. It used a massive gyroscope to store excess power as mechanical energy.

The Greeks were talking, then they started waving their swords, collecting people.

"Jackie!" Edith shouted. "Tell these assholes that we have to watch the engines unless they want to get burned to death!"

That wasn't true, but Jackie Ward, chief electrician, didn't hesitate. She pulled out her phone and called up the translation app. While the engines weren't going to blow up, pulling the sort of stunt the captain pulled could do real damage to the electrical control systems if they weren't managed. And everyone by now knew that the ship's engines and electrical center were completely irreplaceable.

One of the Greeks pointed a bloody sword at Jackie. "Show me phone."

Jackie seemed to understand. She held up the phone and the Greek spoke, then gestured again. She ran the app and got, "Call captain and tell him we have the engine room. We will make deal to kill you all."

He must mean that if they can't make a deal, they will kill us all, Edith thought. The translation app was not perfect. It put in words like to and as, but sometimes misinterpreted colloquial Macedonian Greek. And, according to Atum and Dag, often did the same the other way.

Jackie called the captain and reported. "There are sixteen Greeks down here and they have everyone under guard. They say they want to negotiate or they will kill us all. Captain, they have swords but no distance weapons. One of the swords and about half the Greeks are spattered with blood. I think they have already killed someone."

The Greek with the bloody sword waved it threateningly at Jackie, and she stopped talking.

Five minutes later, everyone on the ship knew at least a part of what was going on because Captain Floden made an announcement.

"There was an attempt to take the ship by members of the Silver Shields who boarded ship in Tyre. The attempt failed and the Silver Shields who survived are in custody, and will be tried on a charge of piracy on the high seas." A short pause, then

Captain Floden corrected himself. "Attempted piracy, which carries the same penalties. Some of the perpetrators are holed up in the engine room and have taken hostages."

"Gee, I never would have guessed," Edith muttered.

David Sayre, a motorman, snorted and one of the Greeks hit him with the butt of his sword. That was an almost-good thing. The Greeks had proven in the last five minutes that they were willing to hit women, but they weren't as fast to do it as they were to hit men.

They would generally threaten the woman first. The guys they just slugged.

Lars Floden looked around the bridge of his ship. Two crewmen were mopping up the blood and he had just received word from Daniel Lang of the deaths of Jon Sonnenleiter and Knut Hedlund.

He called Dag Jakobsen. "Dag, these Greek bastards have killed some of our people. You find Marie Easley and get her and that Greek bitch up here. And bring the commander of her guards too." The normally cool-headed and phlegmatic Norwegian's face was pale with fury.

"I'll bring them, Captain, but I don't—"

"I don't want to hear it, Dag. Get them here."

Dag ran. It took him two minutes to get to Roxane's suite, and by the time he got there, there were a dozen Silver Shields with swords out. Also, the short version of their spears. Dag pulled up short. He was looking at a porcupine of spear points. He slowly and carefully took out his phone, then spoke into it. "Do you stupid bastards want to die?" Then he pushed the translate button.

Evgenij pushed his way through the massed Shields, and spoke in Greek.

By now Dag had a little Greek. Not much, but a little. He understood what Evgenij was saying, or at least he thought he did.

"Some of your men tried to take the ship. If you don't come with me, and right now, the captain is going to—"

He had no idea what Floden was likely to do, but saw no reason to downplay the possible consequences. "—execute you and everyone with you."

"I know nothing *nonsense nonsense.*"

Dag set the phone to record and held it out. "I know nothing of any attempt to take the ship. Tyrimmas and one of his platoons are missing, but they are off duty."

Dag knew the Greek word the app was translating as platoon. It meant a group of four of the eight man squads, or files, that made up part of a Macedonian phalanx. Platoon was close enough.

Dag called the bridge and got Doug Warren. Doug was not exactly covered in blood, but his wiping of his face had been less than complete. "Doug, the ones who attacked, was one of them Tyrimmas?"

"Hell, Dag, I don't know any of them. Wait one."

A moment later, Dag's phone beeped in Doug's ringtone. He switched calls and saw a picture as Doug said, "This is the one who was wearing the gun."

The picture was of a man with the bottom left quarter of his face blown away, but Dag recognized him. He held out the phone to Evgenij. Once he was sure the man had seen the picture, he called up the translation app and said very carefully, "Didn't what happened to Kleitos teach you people anything?" He spoke the next phrase to the app. "You and Roxane will accompany me to speak to the captain, or people with guns and hand grenades will come here and kill you. They will keep killing you until you comply or you're all dead."

"And Alexander?" Roxane shouted from behind the Shields.

"Alexander is safe. We don't kill children any more than we allow slavery."

Then Roxane forced her way through the Silver Shields. When she got to Evgenij, she turned to face him, said, "Come with me," and came.

Evgenij gave some orders in Greek and joined Dag and Roxane.

Dag started to lead them away, then stopped. He pointed at the *kopis* on Evgenij's belt and said into his phone, "Leave that and any other weapons unless you want them seized. The captain is not happy."

Roxane followed Dag onto the bridge and saw the blood on the uniforms. Then she saw the face of Captain Floden and began to be afraid. She'd thought she was safe for the first time in years when she came aboard the *Queen of the Sea*. She knew what the ship people could do, at least in a small way, because she had seen Dag toss the hand grenade to Kleitos. With the ship people between her and the danger of her husband's generals, she was safe. Her son was safe.

But now, looking at Captain Floden, that all disappeared.

"What has happened?"

"Your bodyguards tried to pirate my ship," Floden said. His tone was icy cold and seemingly emotionless, which just made him scarier. "But you must know that. They are your men, after all."

Roxane's eyes, of their own accord, leapt from face to face around the bridge. None of those faces showed any support. Not until she got to Dag's face, and even he was not happy with her.

"Captain, I had no knowledge of what they were planning," she protested. "If I had, I would have stopped it, by informing you, if nothing else. I promise you, Captain. I swear on my son's life. Before all the gods, I swear." She said it and hoped they believed, for it was true. She hadn't known they were planning this.

She had known that her Silver Shields were not happy about the ship people's trick. Not happy that the ship people had taken their property. Evgenij hadn't been happy. She turned to face the commander of her guards. "Did you know?"

"No, my queen, I didn't know," Evgenij said, but there was something in his voice.

A new voice spoke from the door to the bridge. Marie Easley said, "Did you suspect, Commander?"

Evgenij turned quickly and his hand moved in the direction of his empty scabbard, then stopped.

"No!" he said firmly. "I knew they were unhappy. None of us are happy to have lost so much of our wealth when you took our slaves from us. But I did not know that they had anything like this in mind."

"Captain," said Staff Captain Dahl, followed by "*nonsense nonsense nonsense.*"

Roxane looked to Dag. Dag pulled out his phone and said the same words into it.

"All this can wait," said the phone. "For right now, we have a bunch of Silver Shields holding our people hostage."

"Evgenij," Roxane said, "order them to surrender. Send his voice to wherever they are," she added to the bridge in general.

Dag started to use the app, but Marie Easley translated Roxane's words before he could. She said more than that, but Roxane didn't know what. She had left her phone in her suite, and Dag had put his away.

Captain Floden looked at Evgenij, then he spoke to Marie Easley, and she said, "Captain Floden will let you speak to the people in the engine room, but I will be listening to everything you say."

Evgenij's gaze went from the captain to Marie, then Dag. He nodded.

"This is Evgenij," came over the speakers in the engine room. "Put down your arms and surrender."

"Fuck," Koinos said.

"What?" Orestes asked querulously. "Evgenij's on our side. It must mean we're winning." Orestes was a good man to have at your back, but not the sharpest sword in the armory.

"Evgenij wasn't in on the plan, you fucking ox," Koinos said. "That means they have him. The ship people have Evgenij." He pulled out a phone he had taken from one of the prisoners and called up the app. "How do I talk back to wherever that voice is coming from?"

By now the doors to the engine room were blocked by the ship's soldiers in their white clothing. And Koinos was pretty sure that they weren't going to be able to get past them.

One of the prisoners pointed to one of the metal desks with buttons on them, and Koinos motioned him to do whatever he had to do.

"What's going on, Evgenij?" Koinos asked into the device. "Where's Tyrimmas?"

"Tyrimmas is dead, you stupid shit," Evgenij said, and he didn't sound happy. "What were you idiots thinking?"

"It wasn't my idea!" Koinos said. "Tyrimmas ordered it."

"Well, you'll probably get killed over this."

"I won't die alone, you bastard. You tell them that!" Koinos shouted into the thing.

"I probably shouldn't have told him that," Evgenij muttered as the shout came over the bridge speakers.

"No, you definitely should not have," Marie told him.

"Give me the microphone," said Roxane. When she got it, she said, "I order you to surrender yourselves to the ship people. You have endangered Alexander's son and heir. Throw yourselves on their mercy. You don't want to face my wrath."

"It's all your fault! You let them take our slaves!" Koinos shouted back. Apparently Koinos didn't understand that you didn't have to shout to use the ship people's telephones.

Roxane could hear Koinos saying, "We could make a break for it."

Another voice, "But where?"

"It's a big ship and they don't know who we are."

"They know who I am, you fucking coward."

"Well, fuck you. I'm going to make a break for it."

At that point, Marie Easley said, "Someone is about to make a run for it. Warn..."

Doug Warren was already talking, and then there were shots.

"Fuck, fuck, fuck," Koinos said.

"Who is dead?" Roxane said coldly. "And it had better be one of yours, not one of the ship people."

"It's Argaeus," Koinos said. "The cowardly bastard."

"Surrender. I am running out of patience," Roxane said.

It took a while longer, but they did surrender, leaving twenty-nine Greek prisoners, four Greek dead, and two dead crew. As well as a frightened and angry security guard who'd been locked in a broom closet.

And a major political and legal mess for everyone.

CHAPTER 14

Queen of the Sea, *North Atlantic*
November 6

"You can't try them, Captain," Allen Wiley said. They were in the captain's office, a large room behind the bridge. "The maritime law of the twenty-first century doesn't allow for it. They have to be tried by civilian authority."

"Congressman Wiley," Captain Floden said, quietly for all the steel in that voice, "I will not have you interfering with—" There was a short pause as Captain Floden realized where this was going. "—ship's administration. Besides, we tried that bastard Metello in the harbor at Rhodes."

"I'm not trying to interfere with ship's administration, Captain, and I think you have realized that," Allen said. "Maritime law in the twenty-first century was all about capturing criminals and transporting them safely back to shore, where the relevant civilian court could try them. Even military ships didn't do shipboard court-martials. In Rhodes, we were dealing with the local maritime law, and you could have crucified Metello rather than just hanging him. Now we are on the high seas and twenty-first century law applies. Either that, or we use Roxane and let her apply contemporary legal practices."

Captain Floden's expression was a study in discontent as he said, "I'm still not convinced that she was unaware of the situation. And I'd lay you good odds that that bastard Evgenij knew something was up, even if he didn't know the details."

183

"I don't disagree. But unless we are going to throw them all over the side—including the women and children—and raise the Jolly Roger, we have to deal with them. And if we are going to *be* anything more than just the newest barbarian with the biggest stick for the moment, we have to respect laws. We have to stand for something, Captain, not just be one more trade ship."

Captain Floden rubbed his eyes. "What do you want, Congressman?"

"I'm reminded of a line from *Jesus Christ Superstar*. And as much as I dislike playing the role of a Pharisee, if we want them executed we'll need to go to Roxane for the legal justification to do it."

Floden's expression was a bit haggard. "I am Norwegian, Congressman. We abolished capital punishment in my country over a century ago. We didn't even execute that terrorist swine Breivik when he killed over seventy people back in 2011. Whatever my personal feelings might be at the murder of my crewmen, I support that stance—and I am not about to agree to participate in what amounts to mass murder."

Wiley's expression was a little on the haggard side as well. He raised his hands. "Then, what do you propose to do? We have no laws to go by—and won't until we've established the colony at Trinidad and written some maritime law. After that the *Queen* can be registered out of that nation and you will have legal authority to act within certain broad bounds."

"I'll want some input into the writing of those laws, Congressman," Floden said, then quirked a smile. "Either that, or the *Queen* might change her registry."

"I'd expect nothing less, Captain," Allen said with a smile of his own. "In fact, why don't you write them, or have someone on your staff write them, and I'll see about getting them passed."

Floden nodded. "I will do so. But in the meantime..."

Dag had remained present when the discussion began, mostly because no one had ordered him to leave. Perhaps Floden and Wiley shared his own self-assessment, which was that he understood the people they were dealing with at least as well as anyone else aboard the *Queen of the Sea* and probably better.

Now, he spoke. "We don't have to do any of that, Captain. Congressman. What we are faced with is not a thorny issue involving law and justice, it is simply a practical problem."

Floden looked at him. "Explain."

Dag shrugged. "It is true that they murdered Jon Sonnenleiter and Knut Hedlund. On the other hand, thirteen of them were killed also. Let that cold arithmetic be enough to satisfy anyone's desire for vengeance. For the rest of them, we have neither the authority nor—more importantly—the need to do anything except get them off the ship. We don't have to try them, we don't have to punish them. All we have to do is maroon them."

Wiley frowned. "On a desert island, you mean?"

Floden shook his head. "Almost thirty men? That would be tantamount to a death sentence. We don't need to do anything so..." His thin smile even had a bit of real humor in it. "So traditional, let us say. We can simply disembark them on one of the islands of the Lesser Antilles."

"That might get pretty rough on the natives," Wiley said, dubiously. "Whatever else you want to say about them, those Silver Shields are some tough bastards."

The icy cold expression came back to Floden's face. "I didn't say we would let them take their weapons ashore with them. Let the Silver Shields find out how tough they are facing armed natives with their bare hands. They might very well wind up becoming slaves themselves—which would serve them right, as far as I'm concerned."

He looked at Dag. "Make the arrangement, please. If any of them give you any trouble." He paused and took a slow, deep breath. "Shoot them and throw their bodies overboard."

"Captain Floden will not allow Evgenij to remain in charge of the Silver Shields who are staying aboard the ship," Marie Easley told Roxane and Evgenij together.

Evgenij bristled, but Marie stared him down and continued. "His argument is that if Evgenij did know about it, he can't trust him. And if he didn't know, he should have, as their company commander. And, frankly, it's a very good argument."

"Well, Evgenij?" Roxane asked.

"It's not that simple. You fight with men at your side for decades and you can't betray them. I didn't know, Your Majesty, I swear I didn't. But, yes, I suspected they were planning something. Maybe I should have told you. but I've known those men longer than you've been alive."

"Which is Captain Floden's point," Roxane said. "What do you —What about Dag? He could be the commander."

"I think Captain Floden would accept that," Marie said consideringly. "Though there are legal questions." She looked to Evgenij. "What about the Silver Shields? Would they accept him?"

"Those are my men—" Evgenij stopped at Roxane's raised hand.

"No. Those *were* your men . . . until you lost control of them," Roxane said. "If they are going to continue to serve me, they will have to serve me in truth. Can they do that, or must I dismiss them all when we reach Trinidad in two days?"

Evgenij was staring at her and then he nodded. No. It was more as though he bowed his head in submission. "We will obey Your Majesty."

Roxane turned back to Marie. "What sort of legal issues?"

The legal issues were simply that Dag was an officer on the ship and therefore under the orders of the captain, and making him the commander of the Silver Shields would put him under Roxane's command. "A man cannot serve two masters. Not and give full measure to both."

"No, it's not an issue," Roxane said. "Your captain's objection to Evgenij maintaining command of the Silver Shields is that he doesn't want an independent force aboard his ship. That is the truth behind the legal conflict. Very well. While the Silver Shields are aboard the *Queen of the Sea*, I will officially place them under the authority of an officer that the captain and I agree on. That officer will be Dag and I will not gainsay him in their command save to leave the ship."

"I'll take it to the captain," Marie said. "Now tell me a bit more about Eumenes."

Outside Sardis
November 8

Eumenes sat his horse well. He'd had plenty of practice. He had his wife, Artonis, and his brother-in-law, Pharnabazus, with him as he rode up to Sardis for the second time in three days. Cleopatra had been less than welcoming two days ago. Not rude, but not happy to see him. And definitely not ready to endorse him as regent for the kings. The news he brought of the ship convinced her not to order him and his army away, but only barely. She told him that if Antigonus were to arrive before further word, Eumenes would have to leave.

The guards let them in and they rode up to the royal compound. He dismounted and helped Artonis down from the horse. Artonis was pregnant and Eumenes was concerned.

As he was helping his wife down, Cleopatra came down the steps to greet them. Cleopatra was thirty-six and her dark brown hair was starting to be sprinkled with gray. She had a long nose and wide dark eyes, and there were lines around her eyes and mouth. Some laugh lines, but more worry lines. "There must be news?"

"Yes. I understood you, Your Highness. There is news. I am endorsed by Roxane as *strategos* for the armies of her late husband, your brother."

"You? Regent? How did you manage that?"

"Not regent." Eumenes took the sheet that was worth a thousand talents of gold from the saddle bag and passed it over. It had already been read to the army, and Attalus was not happy with it. "Roxane will be acting as her son's regent and endorses Eurydice as the regent for your brother Philip. I am simply her choice as general of her husband's army. It's the ship. It showed up at Tyre and collected her. So this is apparently her free choice, not coerced at all."

That brought a derisive laugh. Cleopatra was well aware of the level of coercion that could be brought to bear on a ruling monarch, much less on a king or a queen who didn't control their army.

"No," Eumenes said. "It appears to be true. I, at least, put no pressure on Roxane. I couldn't have."

"Not if the ship people really..." Cleopatra's voice trailed off as she looked at the sheet. It wasn't just paper. First, it was in color. The writing was black, but there was a picture of Roxane and Alexander IV in the top left corner. The quality of the picture was such that no painter in the world could paint it. In the top right corner was a picture of the ship, rendered with the same precision. Below that was the notation in Greek "Certified by the *Queen of the Sea* Notary Department." Then Roxane's full name and titles, followed by the body of the text. Cleopatra turned, still reading, and walked back up the steps, followed by Eumenes and his companions. He understood her distraction, as he had found the text rather distracting when he first read it.

> *In order to provide for the welfare of all the lands inherited and taken by right of conquest by my late husband Alexander the Great, I take upon myself the role of regent and instructor for my son Alexander IV. In acknowledgment of the declaration of the army at Babylon at the time of my husband's death, I do hereby acknowledge the co-rulership of the empire of Alexander the Great by his son, Alexander IV, and his brother, Philip III. I endorse Eurydice as regent for Philip III.*
>
> *For the safety of myself and my son, I have moved to the* Queen of the Sea. *For the welfare of the realm, I name* Eumenes strategos *of the empire and reconfirm him in the satrapies that he was granted at the Council of Babylon. I likewise endorse the satrapies granted to Ptolemy and...*

There followed a list of satrap appointments that pointedly did not include Menander, Antigonus or Peithon. The satrapies that had been granted to them were granted to others instead. What had been Antigonus' to Eumenes, what had been Menander's to Eumenes, and what had been Peithon's to Atropates.

Attalus was named commander of the Companions, the post that Seleucus held after the partition at Babylon. Seleucus got nothing. At least, he got nothing from Roxane. Word was that under the influence of Antigonus One-eye, Eurydice had appointed him satrap of Babylon.

Finally, she appointed three bodyguards, Dag Jakobsen, Evgenij, and Amyntas, the brother of Peucestas, who Eumenes knew to be a good kid, if a bit conceited like most Macedonian nobility. He didn't know the other two, though he recognized Evgenij's name.

"Who," Cleopatra asked, "is Dag Jakobsen? And what kind of name is that?"

"I'm guessing it's a ship people name," Eumenes explained. "There is also a letter and a book."

For the next hour or so, Eumenes and his companions dined at Cleopatra's table while she read and questioned them about what she read. They didn't have many answers, mostly just what was in the papers.

"I assume," Cleopatra finally said, "that you have shown this to the troops."

"The proclamation certainly," Eumenes said. "The butterfly book and the letter, I wanted to show you. But I will have copies made, to be given out to the troops. The galley only brought a few copies, and a member of the garrison from Tyre who went to Rhodes with Metello. There is a vague mention that there is another form of weapon made by Dag Jakobsen. Nedelko sent a man to report to Attalus, and I haven't had a chance to talk to the messenger yet. I intend to have a talk with Attalus about that, but he was made commander of the Companions by the same proclamation, so there is very little I can do to the man."

"That was clever of Roxane," Cleopatra said. "Also more courageous than I would have expected of Alexander's pretty little flower."

Eumenes kept his expression bland. Cleopatra was not beautiful, and had a tendency to resent women who were. It could affect her judgment.

Cleopatra looked at him for a moment, then shrugged in annoyance. "Very well. I will need to consider this. I didn't think that Antigonus would have me killed. Polyperchon has little to recommend him as satrap of Macedonia, save for his blood lines."

"You would have been a better choice," Eumenes agreed.

"If it weren't for the fact that I am a woman, you mean," Cleopatra said with disgust strong in her voice. She had lived with the Macedonian attitude toward women rulers all her life and that attitude was shared by most of the Greek states, including Thrace, where Eumenes was from.

Eumenes himself had considerable sympathy for Cleopatra's situation. He, like her, was banned from ultimate authority. In his case because he was a Thracian and the son of a wagoner, not a Macedonian noble. On the other hand, Eumenes had never wanted the top job. He was by temperament as well as objective circumstances a man who was most comfortable as a lieutenant for someone else.

"As I said, let me think about this. I will give you my answer in a few days."

Eumenes agreed. It was what he expected. In her own way, Cleopatra was almost as cautious as Roxane.

Camp of Antigonus, Eastern Cappadocia
November 10

Paskal of Macedonia rode with a leather messenger pouch slung over his shoulder. When he reached the camp of Antigonus, he was met by an infantry contingent. "I have a message for Queen Eurydice."

"The general sees all her messages first."

Paskal sat back on his horse, his bronze breastplate proclaiming his rank. "Is she then a prisoner in the hands of a usurper?"

"She's a woman and that's enough."

Paskal looked at the group of Macedonian infantrymen and asked quietly, "Can any of you read?"

"I can," said a grizzled old veteran.

"Fine. Then I'll let you see it and you decide." He handed over the proclamation from Roxane.

The veteran looked at the sheet and showed it around to his fellows. Most of these men had seen Roxane, and the picture was an amazing likeness. Then he started to read aloud. He read slowly and haltingly, literate but not highly literate, and struggled with the words, sounding them out. The breaks between words made it easier, and the man did a decent job.

With every word, the crowd grew larger. Eventually, one of the Silver Shields who had appointed themselves as Eurydice and Philip's bodyguards joined the crowd. He listened for a moment, then turned and moved away quickly. Soon there were Silver Shields coming back to listen. And they were carrying their shields. While they weren't carrying their long spears, they were armed.

By the time the proclamation was read, there was the next best thing to a riot between the Silver Shields who were insisting that the messenger be sent directly to Eurydice, and the Companions Cavalry, who were insisting that the message belonged to Antigonus and Seleucus. One of the infantrymen—not a Silver Shield, just an ordinary Macedonian infantryman—shouted "What are you arguing about? You work for Attalus now! Queen Roxane said so!"

"Roxane is a woman!" one of the cavalrymen said. "She has no authority!"

"She's the mother of King Alexander!" a different infantry man shouted. "You bastards were the ones who insisted that Alexander be co-king with Philip. Live with it!"

After Alexander the Great's death in Babylon, a dispute had arisen over the succession between Perdiccas and another distinguished officer by the name of Meleager. The cavalry had supported Perdiccas; most of the infantry, Meleager. Perdiccas had gained the upper hand and executed Meleager and three hundred of his men—the men by having them trampled by elephants, a hideous death which had never previously been used by any Macedonian commander. Resentment over what had happened at Babylon had not faded away, and the split between the cavalry and the infantry was as wide as ever.

Someone else was passed the proclamation. This was a cavalry-man, and he was both wealthier and better educated. He read it quickly and easily, then shouted, "It's true! Roxane has assigned Attalus as commander of the Companions."

"I'm commander of the Companions!" Seleucus roared from the edge of the crowd.

"Not according to this!" the cavalryman shouted back, hold-ing up the proclamation.

Paskal faded back and dismounted. He handed his reins to one of the Silver Shields and asked, "Can you take me to Eurydice? I have messages for her."

The Shield nodded, motioned to another Shield, and Paskal was whisked away to see Eurydice while the fight over Roxane's proclamation was approaching full-fledged riot status.

Eurydice was watching from her tent. The army was encamped in the countryside and Antigonus had claimed the village build-ings for his officers, not granting her one. It was one of the many little slights that Antigonus heaped on her daily to make sure that she, as well as the army, knew her place.

She recognized Paskal from his armor. The bronze breastplate was in the form of a man's chest, complete with nipples. The man had paid almost two pounds of silver for the thing.

"What news?" she asked, and Paskal grinned. He was a bit on the stout side and wore a bushy black beard.

"Your co-queen sends news!"

"Come in then."

She gestured him into the tent. Philip sat on a camp stool, drawing shapes and writing numbers. Philip looked up, then went back to his numbers without acknowledging Paskal.

"What does Roxane have to say?"

Paskal pulled a sheet of papyrus from his pouch and handed it over. Eurydice read the note. Mostly all it said was "Read the butterfly book." There were a few more comments, and Roxane said she thought Eurydice and Philip would be safer on the *Queen of the Sea*, but Eurydice wasn't convinced. By the time she had finished her reading, order had been somewhat restored in the camp and Antigonus was demanding her presence.

She stood before him in the headman's house in the little village, while he sat on a chair that resembled a throne altogether too closely.

"You will proclaim this to be a false proclamation."

"I would look like an idiot," Eurydice shot back. "It's a true proclamation, and she wrote it freely."

"How could you possibly know that?"

"Because of this," Eurydice said, holding up a piece of papyrus. The moment she did it, she knew she had been a fool. The use of the papyrus with Philip's formula on it as proof of truth was supposed to be a secret shared only by her and Roxane. And she had blurted it out to Antigonus the first time she got a letter. She covered as well as she could. "This is Roxane's own hand." But she wasn't at all sure that Antigonus believed her, even though it was common practice to use the back side of any papyrus.

"I don't care if she wrote it. And even if she did, there is no proof that she did so willingly." Antigonus was scowling at her. At the same time, the room was full of people, Seleucus and Cassander, as well as the commander of her small contingent of Silver Shields. Not that Trajan was likely to back her against Antigonus. He would protect her physically, probably. If the odds weren't too bad. And his very presence would make any attempt on her life or Philip's obvious. That was protection in itself, because if Antigonus had her killed, he would have no credibility left.

"A letter I write with your sword sticking in my back isn't going to mean much." Eurydice looked around the small, crowded room pointedly. Then she backed down a little. "I can decline to endorse Roxane's edicts, especially when it comes to your satrapy, but I can't claim she didn't make them. Not and be believed."

"Then deny them. All of them—" Antigonus started, then stopped. The man wasn't a fool, after all. "No. I will go over Roxane's proclamation, and have a proclamation made up for you to sign." Then he dismissed her.

The next day, Eurydice received and read Antigonus' proclamation. It outlawed Eumenes and condemned him to death, in fact.

It named Antigonus as regent for the empire, as well as *strategos*. It made Seleucus satrap of Babylon, and generally undid everything Roxane had done that wasn't just a continuation of what had been decided at Babylon, with Antigonus in Perdiccas' place.

Eurydice gritted her teeth and signed it. She even wrote to Roxane in her own hand that the proclamation was her will. She wrote it on the back of a merchant's account sheet, but she wrote it.

Royal Compound, Alexandria, Egypt
November 10

Ptolemy looked at the royal proclamation from Roxane, then he looked at Dinocrates. "So, how do they do it?"

"It's called printing, Satrap. And they use something on the ship called a 'laser printer.' But there were other ways of doing it. The one we can do most readily is probably the mimeograph process, though the movable-type process would be better for when we want to make a great many copies of something. I must tell you that none of the techniques we know will make the coating that is on Roxane's proclamation. You note that it's not on the butterfly book or the letter. I'm not totally sure, but I think they coated the paper in what they call 'plastic.'"

"Put people to work on both the memio...whatever it's called, and the movable type.

"We also have a report of that young officer of theirs—Dag something—using some device at Tyre to kill Kleitos. Kleitos would not have been an easy man to kill, and from the reports, Dag tossed Kleitos a pot of lightning. How could he do that?"

Dinocrates shook his head. "I don't have any idea, Satrap. And no one I..." Suddenly Dinocrates stopped and just stared at nothing. He remembered the engines and the use of fire. He remembered that the ones he saw were called turbines and spun in a circle as the fire pressed against the blades. But there had been another kind that pushed a cylinder back and forth with little flames and high pressure. "Maybe I do at least have an idea of what they did. Not how they did it, Satrap. That could take years of study, but the basic form of what they did."

Ptolemy had been sitting in a chair and Dinocrates standing before him. But now the satrap of Egypt leaned back and examined Dinocrates. Then he made a gesture and a slave brought in a chair for Dinocrates to sit on. "Very well, Dinocrates. Tell me the form of this thing that Dag Ja...that the boy did."

"When you heat air, it expands. When you heat water, it expands even more. That is how their steam guns work. What if you had a clay pot full of water and you were able to heat it all to steam at once? There would be no place for the steam to go unless the pot broke. Then it might strike you, much as lightning might. It might even seem to be lightning."

They talked on, and Ptolemy studied the state of science and the dozens of new things that had been created just from seeing the ship. Alexander would have loved this, he thought, and Aristotle even more. For himself, Ptolemy wasn't at all sure he was pleased. But the time of the philosophers was upon the world, and Ptolemy was not one to deny reality just because he didn't like it. What concerned him more was Wiley, and the comments he made about slavery. All the ship people seemed to be fanatical in their opposition to slavery. You might as well oppose the tide, but the ship people didn't appear to be willing to face that fact.

The science was scary in its way, but Ptolemy was convinced that when all was said and done, the true danger of the ship people was their political notions.

CHAPTER 15

Queen of the Sea, *off Trinidad*
November 10

"We see Trinidad, *Reliance*," Doug Warren said over the radio. They'd passed the *Reliance* en route, but the maritime radios had greater range than the phone, so the *Reliance* was still in contact.

"That's good. What part of Trinidad?"

"The Dragon's Mouths. We're at eleven degrees, one minute forty-five seconds north by sixty-one degrees, forty minutes, thirty-eight seconds west, and we can see promontories on both the Trinidad and the Venezuelan sides of the straits."

"Better. We're on track about a day out from you. We should make the Boca Grande strait tomorrow around noon and La Brea around three."

"How are your passengers?"

"Not happy, but calm enough. They are ready to conquer America, all by themselves. How are yours?"

"Dag is now in command of the Silver Shields. And Queen Roxane paid the Shields for their former slaves, then officially manumitted the bunch of them. Made a ceremony of it and the slaves seemed to appreciate it."

"You think you can trust the Shields now?"

"I don't know, but Dag thinks we can and he was with them in Tyre."

Doug and Adrian continued their chat, while in another part of the ship Marie Easley and Roxane discussed the politics of what was left of Alexander's empire. It was an ongoing discussion. Marie had spent thirty years studying this time and the two hundred years that followed it, and Roxane had spent most of her life stuck in the middle of it. They had a lot to talk about. The Greek city states, art and artistry, the future prospects of little Alexander. What Olympias was like in person, what Cleopatra and Eurydice were like. The generals and their wives, many of whom only made it into history as names, if they made it at all. Marie was combining Roxane's knowledge and hers to try to build a database about the players in the politics of Europe. Roxane wasn't her only source. She had talked to most of Roxane's Silver Shields, and most of their wives and former slaves as well.

To Marie the trip to Trinidad was mostly an unavoidable delay. That wasn't true for Congressman Al Wiley.

"So, Amanda, what do we know about the people here?" Al Wiley asked. It was a set-up question. There were eighty people in the small theater room. Mostly passengers, but a few from the staff side of the ship's crew and even a couple of the ship side. Also, Evgenij was there representing the Silver Shields, and so was Bilistiche, representing the freed slaves. Bilistiche was one of Roxane's maids who had decided that she wanted to stay in the colony.

"Not nearly as much as I would like, Congressman. Mostly, we think—and it's think, not know—that they aren't one people at all. There are probably half a dozen different tribes, some that are related to each other and speak the same language, others who have entirely different languages. But all that is speculation, and even at that we are going on very sketchy data. There simply isn't a lot of information on the ship about this part of the world at this time. We don't know what language or languages they speak, and we certainly don't know those languages. The software on our translation apps can't do much with an unknown language."

"That's going to change, Amanda, isn't it? Once we get to talk to them and can get a sample of their languages?"

"Yes and no, Congressman. We can program in sounds and if we learn their word for water or wood, we can add it to the app's lexicon. With experience, we can work out grammar. But for the foreseeable future, it's going to be pidgin and gestures."

Lacula's Trading Post, Trinidad
November 10

Lacula looked out at the gigantic ship and casually slapped a mosquito that bit his left shoulder. He was barely aware of the mosquito, in part because this was the end of the wet season and the mosquitoes would be thick for another month or so. But mostly it was because of the big ship. The big white ship flooded his mind with a combination of avarice and dread.

In a different timeline, archaeologists would call his grandchildren Saladoid. Lacula had never heard of the word, and his name for the location that name was based on was not Saladero. It was Tupky. He wasn't from there, but he had been there several times.

He had just arrived a few weeks ago because he preferred to be here in the dry season. Fewer mosquitoes. What he was, was a trader. He traded pots to the natives for fish and turtles, birds and deer. He also harvested the tar from the pits and sold it back home. The natives he dealt with here on the island would be called Ortoiroid by those same archaeologists, though in fact they were from five different tribes, spoke three distinct languages, and were generally fighting with each other over something or other.

The reason Lacula was afraid wasn't so much because he thought the people from the giant ship would kill him. Oh, he was afraid of that, deeply and profoundly. But the thought that drove the blood from his gonads and shriveled him up to the size of a worm was the pure and certain knowledge that anyone with a ship like that would have pots to put his to shame. A ship that size could carry more such pots than he could carry on his family boat for the rest of his life. The market for pots was destroyed. Even if they were selling something else, the dumb natives would be offering up their goods for whatever those ship people were selling. They wouldn't have any left for his pots.

The avarice that brought the blood back to his manhood was the knowledge that that monster ship must be carrying goods that he could sell up the Orinoco River in his homeland. That meant he could buy here and sell at home. And who knew what the ship people might need? There was a whole new possible business, one that might make him rich.

That was what kept him standing there as the natives ran

back into the woods, leaving their flint arrowheads and bone fish-
hooks, their baskets of crabs and other goods, lying on the sand.

The little ship that the giant ship sent out was bigger than
his largest canoe. A lot bigger. It was sort of like the catamaran
canoes that Lacula was familiar with, but it was all one hull,
just shaped like two, and it made its way to shore with no sail
or rowers.

Lacula stood on the beach about a hundred yards in front of
his palm leaf shack and waited for the future to arrive.

Dag grinned at the nervous Amanda Miller. The congressman's aide had insisted on coming. Or, to be more accurate, the
congressman had insisted on Amanda coming. Something that
hadn't pleased Roxane at all. Roxane was used to being the pret-
tiest girl in the area, and in Dag's opinion she still was. But the
competition was a lot closer. Most of the women on the *Queen
of the Sea* had straight white teeth, clear eyes, and unblemished
skin. Amanda, even with the darker roots showing in her hair,
was very attractive, well built, and had a wardrobe to envy.

Amanda grinned back, though it was a little forced. Dag
knew that Congressman Wiley had wanted to go himself, but
he couldn't, for the same reason that Captain Floden couldn't.
For right now, his place was on the ship, not trying to buy the
land for a colony.

And buy it they would. That much had been agreed. They
would found a new nation here, and that new nation would no
doubt have to fight wars. But it wouldn't be founded on theft, not
of land, not of anything. Dag found himself in agreement with
the congressman on that, though Roxane and the Silver Shields
thought Wiley was being an idiot.

The boat beached when they were still fifty feet from the shore
and the front opened up. Dag climbed out, then jumped down
into the surf and waded to shore. He was followed by half a
dozen Silver Shields, each carrying a crossbow and a short sword.

The presence of the Silver Shields in spite of Tyrimmas'
treachery was political, and Dag's decision. It was proof of trust.
And, perhaps oddly, Dag did trust them. He was certain that
the Silver Shields left on the ship after the mutineers had been
disembarked on Guadaloupe no longer entertained any notions

of rebellion. Partly, that was because—once again—the seemingly soft ship people had proven to be much more dangerous than anyone had thought they'd be. Partly, it was because Roxane's reimbursement of the losses they'd suffered from having their slaves freed had removed their chief source of complaint. And, partly—not such a small part, either—he thought they had come to have real confidence in Dag himself.

He was more worried about an accidental discharge than about one of the Shields intentionally shooting him in the back. Dag needed the Silver Shields to know that he trusted them and didn't hold a grudge. He wasn't going to be able to do what Antigonus did in that other history, and cut them up into penny packets and use them up on dangerous missions. They were too necessary to the survival of the colony for that. They might not be all that familiar with crossbows. Almost no one was. But the Shields were very, very, very familiar with war. Far more familiar, he was sure, than the natives of any island in the Caribbean. The Silver Shields were the veterans of decades of war in Eurasia against the toughest opponents in the world—who were usually other Macedonians like themselves.

Dag looked over his shoulder as a Shield reached up and helped Amanda down. Then he faced front at the tall, brown man with the sides of his head shaved and a slicked down black lock on the top of his head. He was also painted in patterns of white and red, diamonds and cross hatches. That was easy to see because, aside from a loincloth, he wasn't wearing anything. And considering the temperature, he probably had a point.

As Dag reached the shore, the man held up a hand palm out, like a cop telling you to stop, and said something. Dag was already recording, using his new phone. He stopped, held out his own hand and said, "Hello." Then he pointed at his chest and said, "Dag Jakobsen." Then he pointed at Sideburns.

Sideburns pointed at himself and said, "Lacula." And they were off and running. They named everyone in the party, then they named body parts. Hands, fingers, head, feet, legs. Lacula lifted up his loincloth and named those bits as well.

He laughed when Amanda blushed, then he pointed at her chest, and said in passable English, "What called?"

Gamely, Amanda said, "Breasts," and Lacula pointed at Amanda's crotch.

Blushing more, Amanda said, "Genitals."

Dag probably should have kept his mouth shut at that point, but he didn't. "I think he means the specific for females, Amanda. Genitals refers to both men's and women's bits."

Yep. From Amanda's look, Dag certainly should have kept his mouth shut.

"Mound of Venus and vagina. And you can ask someone else to display which is which. Maybe the little queen you're so hot for."

Yes, I certainly should have kept my mouth shut, Dag thought as his face turned red.

Lacula wasn't following all of this, but he was clearly aware that something was going on and probably was making some shrewd guesses about what it might be.

It was about then that a new figure came out of the trees near the shore. The trees were mostly palms, but there was also heavy underbrush. Out of that underbrush came a man also wearing nothing but a loincloth. He wasn't painted like Lacula and didn't have the sides of his head shaved. He didn't have a beard, but Dag figured that was natural for him. He was also a leaner sort. Lacula was a stocky man, with a bit of a paunch. This guy looked like he could use some more calories in his diet. *No*, Dag thought, *he's just thin.*

He was also carrying a spear about six feet tall with a bone blade. The blade had a hook in it and Dag was sure its primary purpose was for spearing fish. "Stand down, guys," Dag said in his limited Greek. "That's for fish."

The bows went back down, but not all the way. Now they had four languages going, English, Greek, Lacula's and this new fellow, whose name turned out to be Bueli.

Bueli was local, they figured out after a few minutes. Lacula was, they now discovered, a trader from across the ocean. Dag guessed the mainland of South America, probably what would become Venezuela in that other history.

The attentive, almost relaxed attitude of the two natives no longer surprised Dag. Whatever notions he might have once had that "primitive people" would be so awestruck by the *Queen of the Sea* that they would be reduced to gibbering or complete silence had long since vanished under the impact of experience. Human beings in the year 321 BCE were certainly ignorant in many ways, but they were not stupid—and they certainly weren't bashful.

Dag invited them to come aboard the *Queen*, but they declined politely. As the sun set, Dag and the party got back in the boat and headed back to the *Queen*.

The *Queen* was anchored almost half a mile offshore, and if the sonar on the boat was any guide, the *Reliance* and *Barge 14* weren't going to get in much closer until a channel was cut. And that was a problem. Refilling *Barge 14* a bucket or a barrel at a time wasn't going to be an easy job, even after they got a working oil well.

While they had been on shore, the phones—Dag's and Amanda's—had been sending the new words back to the ship, and the programmers were busy encoding the sounds of the words spoken and starting the lexicons of the new languages. Once they got back, they were questioned about what other meaning the words might have. It was still by guess and by golly, and would be for a while, but they were trying.

Lacula's Trading Post, Trinidad
November 30

The locals and the *Queen*'s colonists managed to get enough of a common language so that, with the help of maps and showing people around and marking bounds, they bought a chunk of Trinidad that was almost twenty-five square miles of the Kaluga hunting ground. The Kaluga tribe claimed the southern tip of Trinidad around where Siparia would be back in the world the *Queen* came from, all the way to the southwest tip of the island. It wasn't that the *Queen*'s colonists were asking the tribe to move out, not quite. But they had explained—or tried to—that they would be planting crops, raising livestock, and that hunting and gathering in their fields and among their herds would be frowned upon.

The colonists also learned enough to know that the land on Trinidad was in constant dispute and almost every square foot of the island was claimed by at least two tribes, and often by three or all of them. They had made their deal with the Kaluga, but the Kapoi were not likely to respect it.

Based on that agreement, the colonists started building beach-front homes on the island, and started the process of finding the oil well. They knew that the first successful well was dug at Aripero and they knew the coordinates of Aripero. But they didn't know exactly where. So far they had drilled two hundred-yard-deep dry holes and were getting ready to try a third.

Reliance, *Gulf of Paria*
November 30

Adrian watched as the fishing net poured out of the rack rigged
on the *Reliance,* and the floats made a circle around the school
of tuna. It was a big school and they were some big tuna. This
project was a joint venture between the *Reliance* and the Kapoi.
The Kapoi would receive half the catch and would respect the
borders of the ship people. It wasn't exactly extortion. The Kapoi
provided most of the fishing crew, and they had a fleet of canoes
coming out to gather up the catch and take it in to shore and
back to the *Queen* where it would be processed into tuna steaks
and flash frozen. Some of the Kapoi's share would be frozen too,
but much of it would be taken into shore and smoked or dried.

The circle was complete and the winch went to work tightening
the net. The tuna could, if they realized it, swim down below the
net and escape, but tuna were not really bright. Most fish weren't.
Instead, they crowded together and the net tightened until there
was a boiling mass of silver next to the Reliance.

The Kapoi fishermen were dancing around like loons. Then
the killing started. They used long, weighted poles with heavy
hooks on the ends and pulled the fish out of the water. It generally took two or three men to pull a fish from the water, and it
wasn't unusual for one of the tuna to be eight feet long.

The canoes of the Kapoi were surrounding the net and pulling in tuna too. One or two tuna, then the boat would have to
head to shore. The canoes didn't have room for more. But as soon
as they got to shore, they unloaded and came back, leaving the
women to do the butchering and cutting.

Meanwhile, the *Reliance* was covered in fish and made its
own trip to the *Queen* to unload, and the lifeboats were also
being pressed into service. They kept at it through the night and
through most of December first. By the time it was over, they
had more fish than they had smoking racks. The Kapoi were
forced to trade some of their share of the catch to the Kaluga,
who piled in with a will once the deal was made. They didn't
have winter in the tropics, but having a nice reserve of smoked
or dried tuna was going to make life a lot easier for both tribes.

The farmers who were preparing the land for the first crop
grabbed up the fish offal and fish bones, those that the natives

would give up, and ground it up for fertilizer. And the *Queen* ended up with almost ten tons of frozen tuna steaks.

Fort Plymouth, Trinidad
December 5

Even December is way too hot to be pulling a plow by hand, Bob Jones thought, as he placed his right foot down on the grass covering the sandy soil and leaned forward. Latisha mirrored his movements and the plow moved forward, the blades cutting the soil and the roots of the grass. The ship bought cattle and pigs in Alexandria, then they butchered said cattle and pigs and froze the meat. In all of that, no one had thought to buy a mule or an ox and keep it alive to pull the plows.

Someone should have. Someone most certainly should have. Perhaps a high school principal turned agronomist. Bob straightened and placed his left foot forward. Especially since that agronomist had a great-grandfather who had been born a slave and died a sharecropper in Georgia. A man who had listened to stories from his grandparents about how they had pulled the plow by hand after they lost their mule. Bob wasn't the only one who failed to think about the need for working animals. No one was expecting to do any large scale farming at this time. There were, as it happened, a grand total of two farmers on the *Queen of the Sea* when The Event happened. And they had grown cotton, not wheat.

This wasn't a real farm. It was an experimental ten-acre plot designed to study seed to yield ratios, local insect predation of imported wheat plants, and a host of other things to start the process of breeding better wheat plants, and setting up an agricultural industry.

"I quit," Latisha complained though she still pulled. "I am not a slave."

Fort Plymouth, Trinidad
December 5

"You need slaves," Roxane told Amanda Miller. They were sitting in the royal embassy, a compromise between Wiley and Roxane that had been worked out by Dag and Marie Easley. Roxane, partly at the urging of her Silver Shields, had wanted a Macedonian, or perhaps an Alexandrian, colony here in Trinidad. Wiley had invoked the Monroe Doctrine. Then someone pointed out that an embassy had its own laws and slavery was legal back in Europe. Wiley had gotten on his high horse—Roxane loved that expression—and proclaimed that the newly founded nation on Trinidad would not grant embassy status unless Roxane agreed to forgo slavery. Which she couldn't do as a matter of law, even in theory, because Eurydice was her co-regent. But she had reluctantly agreed to the ban for the royal embassy. The natives, especially the Kaluga, were taking to the notion of money fairly well and the paper currency issued by the ship was accepted by them readily enough. That had helped with the labor shortage, but the tendency was for them to work just long enough to get the money to buy what they wanted, be it a knife, a bottle, or a blanket, then go back to their hunting and gathering.

"We need engines," Amanda said, and Roxane threw up her hands. Yes, the magical engines that moved the *Queen of the Sea* and the *Reliance* through the water were amazing things, but they had a very limited number of them. One hundred and three, to be precise. The engines on the *Queen*, the engines on the *Reliance*, the engines in each of the lifeboats—both the big fiberglass ones and the little inflatable ones—three internal combustion-powered air compressors for scuba diving. And one motorcycle engine that a member of the crew had smuggled on board to fix, then hadn't had time to work on. The rest of the magic motive power on the ship was done with electric motors—everything from blenders at the bars to winches was electric. Dag had explained it to her. The electricity was there and keeping the mechanical generation of power concentrated made sense both in terms of efficiency and control.

"We need Zeus to come down from Olympus, turn himself into a bull, and pull the plows," Roxane complained. "That's going to happen before you get your steam engines to work."

"Then he'd better get down here, because Paul Howard is getting pretty darn close."

"No doubt. But you're missing the point. Right now, today . . . and tomorrow and next year, if we are honest about it . . . we don't have the engines to power tractors, bulldozers, cars, airplanes or—most important of all—factories."

"The *Queen* . . ."

"The *Queen* is leaving! Granted not this month and probably not next month, but certainly soon. And when it goes, so does ninety percent of your industry. And your high-minded ideals will not plow a field or power a grinding wheel when the crops come in. Greeks, Egyptians, and certainly Persians, know about work, but not these Indians." Roxane used the ship people term for the hunter gatherers of the island with a certain degree of relish.

"Locals" and "natives" had become the general term for people from this time, just as "ship people" had come to mean all the people from that future world who had arrived on the ships *Queen of the Sea* and *Reliance*. A term to distinguish the natives of Trinidad from the Macedonians had become necessary. The ship people, much to Marie Easley's annoyance, had fallen back on the mistake of Christopher Columbus—whoever that was—and called them Indians. It was shorter than calling them Trinidadians, after all.

Not that Roxane had any intentions of staying in Trinidad, but she was going to be leaving some of the wives and kids and thirty of her Silver Shields here. Thirty of the oldest and most worn, as a retirement post. She had even bought a few hundred acres to support them. She was concerned with the colony for the same reason that Dag and Captain Floden were—because it was going to supply the ship with both fuel and cargos to sell in Europe.

And with the amount of time they had already spent here, and the still more time they were going to have to spend here to make sure the colony stayed viable while they were back in Europe, she was starting to wonder what she would find when she finally got back.

CHAPTER 16

Tyre
December 7

Boom!

Nedelko looked up from the crossbow drill he was supervising in the courtyard of the palace. The crossbows were something that the survivors from Rhodes had seen and not suffered from. But they were something that once seen, could be reproduced.

For the moment, Nedelko was less interested in that than in the mushroom-shaped cloud he could see in the town.

"Follow me!" Nedelko shouted and ran. By the time he got to the powder mill, it was ash and pot shards, and the two buildings next to it were mostly flattened too. Tyre, the city, was a warren of narrow streets and two-story buildings, but now there was a good-sized hole in the center of it.

Dareios survived, but he was bleeding from both ears and had a broken arm and two broken ribs. He would be dead if he hadn't been behind a large stack of urns when the explosion happened. The buckets of water of the fire brigade were way too little and way too late, at least for the powder mill. They weren't even trying. They were throwing water on the buildings that were knocked down.

Two days later, Dareios, still deaf, stood in the throne room, insisting they rebuild the powder mill. And all the merchants in Tyre were right there, insisting that the powder mill not be rebuilt anywhere near them.

The world of Alexander's empire had just learned the first lesson of gunpowder production: put it out in the country, away from fragile things like buildings. And people.

Also, until now the knowledge that they knew how to make gunpowder had been something of a secret. But now it was known all over Tyre...and that meant Ptolemy and Antigonus—not to mention Eumenes—would know.

Sardis
December 15

"What do you hear from Tyre?" Eumenes looked over at Attalus with a lifted eyebrow. Eumenes was situated in a secondary building of the palace compound. He was sitting on a couch with a lap desk on his lap and a pot of ink, doing the books.

"The same thing you do. There was an explosion at the powder mill," Attalus admitted. "And no, I didn't get the formula. Dareios is keeping it a family secret, even now that his son died in the explosion. Perhaps especially now."

"It would have been polite to let me know that there was a powder mill in Tyre," Eumenes said, then waved that issue away for the moment. "You know that Ptolemy knows about the black powder that explodes by now, and he will have heard it's powerful enough to knock down buildings."

"I don't think that he will be able to do much with the knowledge," Attalus said.

Eumenes wasn't reassured. He had been informed by his friend, Apelles, that Ptolemy was actively recruiting scholars. Apelles hadn't gone to Alexandria and, with some difficulty, he had convinced his friend, Nausiphanes, not to go. However, a youngster he liked, Epicurus, took a ship to Alexandria to see what the new library was going to be like.

There was a knock at the door and a moment later an officer came in. "We have more defectors from Antigonus' army. Fifty of the Companion Cavalry."

"Go ahead, Attalus," Eumenes said. "No doubt they will be more comfortable with you than with me." The Companions were made up almost exclusively of Macedonian nobility. They would be willing enough to take Attalus' orders, but not Eumenes'. That was why Eumenes was developing his own cavalry force and drilling them constantly.

"Before I go, what does the latest message from Antigonus say?"

"I believe he's claiming my mother was a nanny goat and my father was a rabbit."

"Interesting cross, that." Attalus laughed.

"*Baaaaaaaaa!*" Eumenes said.

Artonis came in as Attalus left, and Eumenes smiled. The Persian girl Alexander had married him to had proven to be a blessing. She was a pretty enough girl, but more than that, she had a ready wit and a warm nature.

"Are you letting your ancestral tongue loose again?" She smiled.

"At least I'm not hopping."

Artonis put her feet together and hopped. She was in her eighth month and everything jiggled. Suddenly she stopped, and went to a chair. "I shouldn't have done that," she said.

"Are you well? Should I call the healers?"

"No, I'm fine," she insisted, though to Eumenes' eye she didn't look fine. She looked pale and there was a sudden ripple across her belly.

"You're not fine. I'm calling the healers." Eumenes set the lap desk aside and stood.

"Everything is fine, Eumenes. They were false contractions. It's not unusual this late in the pregnancy," the healer said.

Cleopatra nodded in agreement. "I had them with my son. And Artonis seems healthy."

A week earlier, Cleopatra had endorsed Roxane's appointment of Eumenes as *strategos* for the empire. She watched the political winds and decided that Eumenes was the right horse. Being Cleopatra, she offered an olive branch to Eurydice and even to Antigonus, to some extent, offering to host Eurydice and Philip and guarantee their safety while any disagreements between Eurydice's and Roxane's proclamations were ironed out.

Eurydice—or at least a letter signed by Eurydice—questioned her veracity, based on the report that Cleopatra's mother, Olympias, had Philip murdered in that other history. Olympias called that report a blatant lie, but Eumenes wasn't so sure. Neither, he knew, was Cleopatra.

"Don't worry about Artonis, Eumenes. Worry about Antigonus. Not everyone is happy about your promotion to *strategos*, and some of the generals—Menander, for instance—are going over to him just because they're angered by that."

"I know. I was half expecting him to attack by now, though Menander always was a snake. I expect the butterfly book is right. He would be fighting against me even if he had gotten to keep Lydia."

It was all settling out. The generals were choosing up sides. Ptolemy was ostensibly neutral, but neutral in favor of Antigonus. The old-line Macedonians, those most offended by Eumenes' promotion, were going over to Antigonus. And then another contingent that didn't like Eumenes, but didn't trust Antigonus, was staying out of it. And, finally, there was a surprisingly large group that was taking Roxane's proclamation at face value and supporting Eumenes out of loyalty to Alexander.

"It's coming soon," Eumenes said as he looked out at the hills surrounding Sardis. "The battle for the heart of Alexander's empire is coming and we have to be ready. That's why I want the Shields' baggage train safely inside your walls, Cleopatra. And I'll be leaving Pharnabazus here with a force of the new crossbowmen to guard the walls. Most of the Shields know what happened in the other history, and they are all at great pains to assure me that it won't happen that way again. But we'll all be happier knowing their wives and wealth are safe here."

Army camp of Antigonus the One-eyed, Cappadocia December 20

Cassander shifted in his saddle to try to ease the not-quite blisters. He could ride—everyone in his station had to be able to ride—but he wasn't truly comfortable on a horse the way his younger brother was. Now he sat on his horse, next to Plistarch, watching the infantry march by. Most of the Silver Shields were with Eumenes, and of those who were left, most had gone with Attalus after Triparadisus. At this point, the only Silver Shields in the army were the one hundred and twenty-four men who acted as guards for Eurydice and Philip. The infantry he watched weren't the Silver Shields. They were veterans, but not elite. They carried the long *sarissa* pike, and they marched in good order. But they lacked the élan that the Shields had.

The army was approaching Celaenae on the Persian road to Sardis, and Cassander wasn't thrilled with the plan. Mostly he wasn't thrilled because he and his brother were being left out here with most of the infantry and only a small contingent of cavalry, as bait to draw Eumenes away from Sardis. Antigonus had read the butterfly book, the book of the future, and had determined the weakness of the Silver Shields and, for that matter, of Eumenes' army. That weakness was the baggage train, the wives and children and the decades worth of loot that the army had gleaned over the course of the wars.

Eumenes had figured out the same thing, so their spies had reported. That was why the baggage train was being left secure in Sardis. Antigonus had already left with most of the cavalry, to swing around wide and hit Sardis once Eumenes came out to fight.

"Well, now we see," Cleopatra said with a bitter laugh, "that Plutarch, as you might expect from someone born so near Delphi, gets the outline of the thing, but is misleading."

Eumenes tried to keep his laugh less bitter, but it wasn't easy. It was true that he would much prefer to fight here near Sardis. The mostly flat ground was better for cavalry and his cavalry was better than Antigonus'. He also had more of it and it was mostly not Macedonian, so more trustworthy. Roxane's proclamation had gone a long way to stiffening the Silver Shields and other mostly Macedonian infantry in his command, but it just wasn't as effective as the cavalry. Not as flexible. Alexander had always used the infantry as the anvil, to hold the enemy in place while the cavalry pounded on them from unexpected angles. According to Plutarch, in the butterfly book, Cleopatra had ordered him away because she was afraid of Antipater, and that might have been true in the other history. But Eumenes expected that, even then, it had been as much a tactical necessity as it was going to be here.

Celaenae was in the hills. It was not good cavalry country, but the small city controlled the main road to the east and was wealthy in its own right. If Antigonus took it, he could use it as a base and block Eumenes from most of the eastern empire. Besides, Eumenes had obligations to the people of Celaenae. One of the disadvantages of being the legitimate *strategos* of the empire was he had to act like it. All of which meant that he was going to have to take his cavalry and infantry up into the hills.

"The wives of your soldiers will be safe here, *Strategos* Eumenes, and so will their loot."

Eumenes slapped his leather gloves against his thigh and nodded sharply. Then he marched down the steps of the royal apartments, took the reins from his aide, mounted his horse, and rode out to join his army.

The hills outside Celaenae
December 25

Celaenae was holding out. That was a surprise. Antigonus should have taken the place by now. Even with the smaller army that he had out of Triparadisus, he should have been able to take Celaenae. Its walls were barely twelve feet tall and it was not well defended. Old men and boys. Though Eumenes had reason to respect old men in war.

It was almost as though they were—

Eumenes stopped and looked at the army again. It was too small. Not just because it was almost entirely infantry. Eumenes doubted there were five hundred horsemen over there and half of those were officers.

He'd been fooled. That wasn't Antigonus' army. It was just his infantry.

Almost, Eumenes was tempted to turn around and go back to Sardis. He knew now that Antigonus was already there, besieging Cleopatra. But no. He had to fight here and now, for two reasons. First, he had to relieve Celaenae. To come to the gates and turn away would stink of betrayal all the way to Zeus' throne.

Second, Alexander's third rule of war: Attack them separately when you can. Eumenes didn't know it, but that rule would travel down the ages as the adage "defeat in detail" or, in the pithy phrase of Nathan Bedford Forrest, "Hit 'em where they ain't."

Eumenes had Antigonus' anvil before him, with no hammer to protect it. He could pound it into plowshares at his leisure, and what real use is a hammer if you don't have an anvil?

He called over Attalus, Alcetas, Polemon, and Docimus, then gave his orders. They took them, Alcetas insisting that he wouldn't have been fooled by the ruse. Attalus looked at his brother-in-law with a half-smile on his face, and simply nodded at Eumenes' orders. Polemon looked to Attalus and when Attalus nodded, he did the same. Docimus looked at Attalus too, which was just a bit worrying. Eumenes would either have to get Attalus more firmly on his side, or do something about the emerging clique.

Attalus was in charge of the Macedonian cavalry and Eumenes took personal command of the non-Macedonian cavalry he had been recruiting and training since Babylon.

Polemon was in nominal command of the infantry. They would take his orders as long as they believed that they came from Eumenes because of Roxane's proclamation—Hera bless the girl for it.

The infantry moved out first, and there was much shouting and cheering from the walls of Celaenae. At the center of the infantry line were the Shields, their silver-embossed shields shining in the sun. Eumenes watched as the enemy infantry shifted from the attack on the walls to face the new threat.

As Eumenes watched, he began to feel better. The knot in his guts began to unknot. For, with every step, the march was firmer.

It was the Shields, those tough old bastards who had marched with Alexander to India and back, and were the only ones who had ever faced the great man down. They knew they were unstoppable and as they moved forward, the phalanx on their left and right came to know it too. Eumenes could see it happening and he could see its effect on the infantry in front of them. Gods.

The enemy's *sarissa* came down without orders and way too soon. It was hard to keep a *sarissa* in combat position. To hold it out for any significant amount of time was an exercise in torture. A *sarissa* was heavy, and the weight of the iron blade was as much as twenty-three feet in front of you. Eumenes had never heard of Archimedes since the great scientist wouldn't be born for another thirty-odd years. But any Silver Shield could explain the lever principle from the point of view of the fulcrum. They knew that you waited until the last possible moment before lowering that long pole into position.

The Silver Shields marched up to about a hundred feet from the enemy infantry, then Polemon shouted a command, "Halt!" then another, "Rest!" The Silver Shields stopped before the enemy infantry, their *sarissa* pointing at the sky, and rested. There was a ripple of laughter from the Silver Shields. It started with one or two individuals, then swelled and was taken up by the rest of Eumenes' infantry. It never got to the point of rolling on the ground, as they had to hold up their *sarissa*, after all. But they just stood there, laughing while the enemy infantry held their *sarissa* out in front of them, unable to reach the Shields while their arms turned to fire, then to water.

There was a shout. Eumenes recognized the voice. It was Cassander's little brother, Plistarch. "Forward!"

Eumenes was expecting Polemon to order the Shields to lower their *sarissa* in preparation for the enemy advance. But Polemon didn't. Instead, he rode out in front of the Shields and—utterly ignoring the approaching infantry—ordered the Shields to dress ranks.

It was a studied insult, and Polemon didn't carry it off as well as Alexander would have. Not nearly as well. But it was good enough. The Shields dressed ranks and Polemon ordered the *sarissa* down, and barely got his horse out of the way in time. "Advance!" The *sarissa* came down like a breaking wave, and in a number of cases they banged the enemy infantry's *sarissa* right out of their hands.

A *sarissa* can be manipulated, even as long as it is. It takes muscles like iron and years of experience, but you can almost fence with the things if you're good enough and fresh from a good laugh.

Eumenes' infantry was good enough.

They knocked aside the enemy's *sarissa* as they marched forward, and the enemy started to crumble. That was when Cassander should have used his cavalry, once Eumenes' infantry was fully occupied. But he couldn't. He didn't have any cavalry to speak of.

But Eumenes did. Eumenes had almost ten thousand cavalry in three contingents. The Macedonians on the right; his own men in the center; and Attalus' Companion Cavalry, the part that had defected to their side after the proclamation, on the left.

The Macedonians stayed with the infantry to hold off any attempt at a cavalry response. And the rest of Eumenes' cavalry swung around the army and along the walls of Celaenae to take the baggage train.

Cassander got away. His brother stayed with the army, but Cassander ran, and was probably still running on a new horse. And Eumenes was stuck here.

Stuck here because he couldn't quite trust his officers not to commit an atrocity by massacring the enemy infantry if he left them on their own.

Eumenes wanted that infantry. He wasn't sure of everything in the butterfly book, but he was starting to suspect that the role of infantry was going to change, but not be eliminated. The anvil would still be needed, even if the needs of the smith required its shape to change. He had captured the infantry under Craterus, and that was a big part of his present infantry force. That force, with the Silver Shields strengthening it, had just won a massive victory—and proven itself to itself in the process. If Eumenes could integrate these new men into his force, he would have an anvil bigger than any since Alexander. Combined with the cavalry, he would be difficult for anyone but Ptolemy to take on.

Assuming, of course, his army didn't sell him to Antigonus to buy back their wives and goods from the sack of Sardis. For three vital days he was stuck reforming his army and convincing Polemon to take care of the prisoners, not just murder them and take their stuff. Then and only then could he take his cavalry and head back to Sardis.

Sardis
December 29

Seleucus rode up to Antigonus. "The Companions are ready."

Antigonus turned so that his remaining eye could see the man. Seleucus liked to approach from his blind side. It was one more sign of the subtle disrespect Seleucus showed almost everyone. He pointed to any flaw he could, always in a way that you couldn't take offense at without sounding like a vain fool. It was part of the man's arrogance and it was getting tiresome, but aside from Eurydice's endorsement, Antigonus had no more rank than Seleucus, not the way Macedonians counted such things. He held a satrapy, but to get Seleucus' support he'd had to grant him Babylon as his satrapy, and get Eurydice to endorse it.

"Those of them who are left," Antigonus said sourly. A number of the Companions left after Roxane's proclamation to go to Eumenes. Not all of them, thankfully. Even with Roxane's endorsement, some weren't willing to put themselves under the orders of a Greek peasant. Many of them had simply gone home.

Seleucus' smile got a little tighter and Antigonus cursed himself for letting his temper get the best of him. He needed the smarmy bastard. "Very well. You'll take the right flank, as we discussed."

Antigonus' cavalry charged for the gates and along the wall. Cavalry using their horses to get in fast, then trying to scale the walls from horseback. But they ran into a rain of arrows.

The arrows came over the wall in sheets. Seleucus rode at the head of the Companions, and it seemed like every arrow was coming right at him. It just seemed that way, and he knew that. He had been in battle before. He rode on as the arrows scythed through his troops. He got to the wall, reached up and grabbed the top of it. A sword came down half an inch from his hand, striking sparks on the stone. He jerked himself up with all the energy of his terror and bowled over the boy holding the sword. It was a boy, Seleucus realized in a moment of clarity. The walls of Sardis were being defended by women and boys, with only a sprinkling of mature warriors. Then a crossbow bolt took him in the chest and he went back over the wall.

As he fell, he never saw that the arms holding the crossbow were the arms of a middle-aged woman.

The first attack was pushed back with heavy losses, but there were enough men who had looked over the wall for Antigonus to realize that the town's defenders were mostly women, old men, and boys, with only a few warriors.

"We should attack again," Peithon insisted. "They are women—"

"There are a lot of them," said Hypatos.

"So—"

"You don't understand. It wasn't that there were only a few warriors. There weren't a lot, it's true. But everyone in the town was put to work defending the walls. And even if they are women, they can still shoot a bow. Most of our losses were before we got to the walls. They were firing at an angle from behind the walls, and we couldn't touch them. When we got to the walls, we were facing seasoned fighters supported by old men and boys, not just old men and boys." Hypatos turned to Antigonus. "General, if we take that city, we're going to end up putting everyone in it to the sword. After the losses we'll take, there will be no holding the men. Where are your hostages then?"

That stopped the conversation and Antigonus was glad of it. He needed time to think. Cleopatra—and he was sure it was Cleopatra—had done this. Eumenes wouldn't have thought of it. Hades! Antigonus knew he wouldn't have thought of it himself. A sacked and destroyed town would simply produce an enraged army. He had to find another way.

Sardis
December 30

"Boil the bandages," Cleopatra said to her clerk.

There was a small section in the back of the butterfly book, called Germ Theory. It said that disease was caused by small organisms too tiny to see, and that they could be killed by boiling water. The whole section was less than a page long, but Cleopatra decided that it was probably accurate. It, after all, agreed with much of what the best physicians said. So the bandages would be boiled and the wounds would be cleaned with wine. She had found surprisingly little resistance among the wives of the Silver Shields. It fit with their own wisdom. Mostly, there had simply been concern over the cost of the wood to boil the water, which was what her clerk had been complaining about. There were a lot of wounded, and a lot of bandages needed. More than they had been prepared for.

She looked at her town. There was a pall of smoke in the morning air. It covered the city like a cloud. The walls stood unbreached, but there was constant noise, people screaming in pain, too far away and too many to separate the individual cries.

The clerk left while she was watching the city. Artonis came in. "It's not bad."

"Not bad?"

"Battles in the field are worse. Only tents and no fireplaces, save for rock rings. How are we set for food?"

"A month, perhaps two, with all the local villagers who have crowded into town."

"That's plenty, then."

The young Persian woman sounded so confident that she drew Cleopatra's attention from the cries. "You're so sure?" Cleopatra had managed a kingdom, but never ridden to war.

"That's cavalry out there. All cavalry. And if the reports are true, it has to be most of Antigonus' cavalry."

"And that means?"

"It means that Eumenes will face nothing but an infantry force. The phalanx are a powerful tool, but take away the cavalry that guards their flank and rear, and they are helpless. I don't know what caused Antigonus to forget that, but I promise you, my husband has not."

"Desperation!" Cleopatra said, suddenly feeling a great deal more confident. She might not know war firsthand, but she knew politics and she understood the dispatches. Without official sanction—well, without uncoerced sanction—Antigonus might as well be a bandit. That was why she decided not to show anyone her mother's letter.

Olympias, in Macedonia, had a copy of Roxane's proclamation and declared that since Roxane was not Macedonian, the regency of Alexander must go to her instead. Then she declared that Philip III was not heir to anything and opened up the bidding for the position of general to anyone who would bring her Eurydice's head.

There was no way of keeping it secret for long, but Cleopatra didn't want to do anything to weaken that legitimacy of Roxane's proclamation. Not now, not when it gave their side such an unexpected advantage.

Sardis
January 5, 320 BCE

Eumenes looked out at the army of Antigonus One-eye and smiled. Antigonus hadn't taken Sardis, and now he never would.

The infantry was still a day behind and that limited Eumenes' options. But just the presence of Eumenes and his cavalry meant that Antigonus couldn't focus his entire force on taking the city.

And Antigonus' army wasn't the army that had followed Alexander to India. They were holding together, more or less, but they were a rough and ragged group. Mostly cavalry and mostly Companions, but there was an air of desperation about their actions.

Eumenes looked back at his own cavalry. They were calm.

Attalus was smiling, almost grinning. "Can you see Antigonus?" he asked.

Eumenes looked. Yes, there in the plumed helmet with the right eye covered. Eumenes nodded and pointed.

"What about Seleucus?" There was an edge in Attalus' voice now. This wasn't all about Roxane's proclamation. It was partly about the butterfly book and a lot of it was Attalus wanting the men who had caused the death of his wife. Roxane, and even the book, had simply convinced the stubborn Macedonian that Eumenes was his best chance of doing that.

"I don't see him, but I think that's Peithon next to Antigonus." He pointed. It was impossible to be sure at this distance, but it looked like Peithon's clothing.

"Let's go get them, then."

"Not yet," Eumenes said. "I'm not at all sure this is a battle we want. If they simply retreat, we might gain as much as if we beat them—"

"Peithon is over there. And Seleucus."

Eumenes held up a hand. "Attalus, I know you're angry and you have every right to be. But we have a war to fight and a dynasty to restore. We have obligations beyond our own needs. And it's those obligations that keep this army from becoming nothing more than a crowd of bandits."

It was a hard thing to put into words. Philip II had done it, and Alexander even more. Taken hard men who were little more than hill bandits and turned them into an army and a nation. Almost a nation, anyway. It had all started to come apart as soon as Alexander died. That was why Eumenes had supported Perdiccas. Not out of love for the man, but to hold together the world Alexander was trying to make. Perdiccas had failed, and so would any of the generals. They didn't understand, not really. They just saw it as taking what they wanted. Now there was Roxane and Eurydice, with an almost alliance. Perhaps the empire could form around them. But all Attalus cared about, for now at least, was revenge on the murderers of his wife.

Eumenes sometimes wondered if anyone saw what he saw. It was a bitter thought, though not a new one.

And it distracted him, so Eumenes failed to notice for a few minutes that Antigonus had come to the same conclusion he had. He gained little from battle here, but Antigonus lost a great deal by quitting the field before him. Antigonus had to do something that would at least let him claim victory. And so did his followers. They were forming for a charge. The pride of Macedonia's cavalry against Eumenes' mostly disciplined forces.

Eumenes turned in his saddle and grabbed Attalus by the arm. "You keep your head, Attalus. If you go haring off after Peithon and leave Antigonus an opening to claim victory, I will kill you myself. Now, get to your command."

A few minutes later, the armies clashed. It was a cavalry fight on both sides, a cavalry melee, with no infantry to act as a center. It was a cool day, as was normally the case in January this close to the Aegean Sea. But, unusually for this time of year, it hadn't rained in weeks. The ground was very dry and it took only minutes before the clashing cavalry forces turned the dust into a choking fog, with men and horses panting as they flailed around in confusion. Eumenes managed to keep his mercenaries together and in formation, but the Companions went off into a melee with the other Companions, and the rest of the cavalry on both sides lost cohesion.

It was still possible most of the time to see Mount Tmolus rising above the dust clouds, so everyone knew more or less where Sardis lay. But everything else was uncertain. Even the location of Hermos River was uncertain except for the cavalrymen who stumbled onto its banks—some of whom immediately followed the discovery by spilling themselves and their mounts into the water.

Eumenes rode through the dust with his mercenaries and came across clumps of horsemen fighting each other. It was hard to tell who was who. The cohesive, disciplined, and trained unit cut through anything in their path, but almost from the beginning Eumenes had to guess who was on his side and who was the enemy.

Attalus led his part of the Companion's Cavalry. Some of them, about a quarter of the force, had come over to their side after Roxane's declaration. They fought well, even in this mad dust storm, because whatever else they were, the Companions were among the most ferocious fighters in the world.

Then they ran into themselves. The Companions who had stayed with Antigonus and been given into Seleucus' command by Eurydice, came out of the dust-filled air, and it was brother against brother, Macedonian noble against Macedonian noble.

Attalus blocked a spear with his buckler, and another from the other side glanced off his armor. It was that sort of a fight. He jabbed his lance at someone—he thought it was Heron, but he wasn't sure. It might have been Heron's cousin. Whoever it was was screaming curses and bleeding from his left arm. The arm came up anyway, and blocked Attalus' spearpoint, then the melee pushed them apart.

Peithon was in front of him and Attalus forgot everything. He had held himself in check since his wife died, but now—already in battle—his bitter rage took him. He charged with no thought at all but to rip out Peithon's throat. His spear went wide, but his horse ran right into Peithon's and they both went down. They managed to get loose from the horses, and Attalus pulled his *kopis* and charged in. Peithon blocked with his left arm. It was cut deep, and blood gushed. Attalus smiled, then Peithon, using the back half of his broken spear, jabbed at Attalus' gut. It burned and Attalus screamed. He let go of his sword and with both hands reached for Peithon's throat. With fingers strengthened by years of wielding sword and spear, he grabbed and twisted. He felt cartilage breaking. He held on until the world went dark.

Arrhidaeus, in command of a battalion of cavalry, realized that the battle was lost and decided that at the very least he wanted to show the Silver Shields the cost of following a wagoner's son. He turned his battalion toward the walls of Sardis and charged.

Artonis stood on the walls and saw her husband in the distance. She walked along the walls offering encouragement and support to the men and boys guarding them. Those men and boys kept demanding that she should get back to safety, but Artonis had read the butterfly book and she had drawn her own conclusions from it. If the sons and grandsons of Silver Shields must face the army of Antigonus, she must face that army with them.

"There!" She pointed. "It's starting."

Artonis watched the armies clash and saw when a battalion of cavalry turned to the walls of Sardis. She rushed to meet them, waddling to the section of the wall where they would arrive. And with her came the people of Sardis.

There was a crowd on the wall where Arrhidaeus' force arrived, and the attack was beaten off almost before it was well started. But as the cavalry turned away, they fired a volley of arrows at the defenders.

One arrow, by mischance, struck Artonis in the side. It missed the baby but hit the uterus, and the water of the uterus spilled out into her.

Quickly she was carried back to the palace, but she was bleeding internally. And along with the uterus, part of her intestine had been perforated.

Antigonus pulled out and away. Not far. Just enough to get a feel for the battle. He was good at this. He had years of experience reading battles from subtle clues of sound and sight, even smell. He knew that this one was turning against him. It had started well, and if it weren't for Eumenes' mercenaries, he would be winning. But they were disciplined, and staying together in a solid formation. He got to a flautist and ordered a retreat.

It was a slow disengagement, and he lost more men than Eumenes had, but he got them out.

And Eumenes let them go.

After the battle was over, the people of Sardis came outside the walls. They collected up the wounded. At Eumenes' order, they collected up the enemy wounded as well as their own. They found Attalus, his hands still around Peithon's neck. Peithon was dead. He had died within minutes of having his wind pipe crushed by Attalus.

Attalus was still alive, but was unconscious. One of Cleopatra's doctors thought he could save him with surgery, and Cleopatra agreed. It was worth a try, anyway. The Companion Cavalry was losing commanders at a phenomenal rate.

Artonis' situation was much worse. Her wounds were not as immediately life threatening, but the healers agreed that it was likely that her intestines had been punctured. They knew that her uterus had been cut and that the birth waters had been released into her body. Artonis was awake and insisted that they take the baby. "I'm dead anyway, but my child will live."

The operation was a success, but while they were in there they found a perforation in her intestine. The doctors knew what that meant. When the operation was done and she came to, they explained what they had found and what it meant.

By that time the battle was over, and Eumenes was inside the walls of Sardis.

☆   ☆   ☆

"We have a son, my husband. You will need to find a wet nurse."

"What were you doing on the walls?" Eumenes asked furiously.

Artonis quirked a smile at him and said, "Don't be angry, my husband. Alexander wrought better than he knew in our marriage. We have made a fine, noble son, Persian and Greek. And we made a love too. A love to sing ballads about. Don't let it end with angry words. It will end soon enough without them."

"Why?" Eumenes pleaded.

"Because they had to see. They had to see that your wife, your child were at risk just as theirs were," Artonis said with a cold pragmatism that surprised him.

She died soon after. And the thing that Eumenes found hardest to accept was that she was right. Her death in this way had welded the Silver Shields and the whole army to him in a way that his calm deliberation could never have accomplished.

CHAPTER 17

Royal Compound, Alexandria
January 20

The news from Sardis was disheartening in a way, Ptolemy thought. Eumenes had held and now had Sardis. And with it, most of western Anatolia. Antigonus still had Eurydice and Philip, but he was losing troops and he would need to find new allies. Meanwhile, the butterfly book of the ship people had as much as proclaimed that Alexander's empire was dead.

"It could hold together," Eudemus of Rhodes said. "It didn't in that other history, but there were reasons. I have examined the book left by the Easley woman and I must admit it is well organized and clear. The empire was held together by Alexander. Without him at its center, there was continuing warfare till eventually it was split into separate nations. In that other history, it was Antigonus who acted first, some fourteen years from now. By the ship people's measuring, in the three hundred and sixth year before their calendar starts. What they label 306 BCE. But all the other generals who survived quickly followed suit. The important point, though, is that by then both kings Philip III and Alexander IV were gone. And even—" He laughed. "—Alexander's bastard, Heracles, was dead. With a live heir to Alexander, it might well remain an empire." There was a measuring pause. "But it can never be your empire."

Ptolemy looked at his old ally. Eudemus was fifty, three years older than Ptolemy, but he carried his age well. "So you think I should declare Egypt independent?" Eudemus was an excellent

225

recorder and organizer, which was why Ptolemy had offered him the post of curator of the new library.

"That is not for me to say. But if you are to be king, it is Egypt of which you must be king. And Egypt can be the key to it all."

"Tell me."

"Crates managed to get hold of a ship people map of the world." Eudemus pulled the map from a tube and spread it on the table. "This is a tracing with the ship people's political boundaries left out and our own added."

There were many fascinating aspects to that map, but the feature that Ptolemy found most striking was that Alexander's empire, seen against the whole world, was so small. Not tiny, no. But...small. And they had thought at the time that they were conquering almost everything!

Eudemus was still talking. "The world is larger, much larger, than anyone thought and mostly covered by water. However, see here—" He pointed. "This is what the ship people call the horn of Africa. To get around that would take months, perhaps a year or more. But the spice trade is vital and there are more goods to buy and sell in India." He pointed again. "The shortest route from the Mediterranean Sea to the spices of India is by way of the Red Sea. And by compiling the reports of those who talked to the ship people, especially to a Greek sailor, Panos of Katsaros, we have learned that they had a way of setting their sails so they could sail almost directly into the wind. Also, they had steam engines that can move a ship with no wind at all. With those things, transport by sea becomes much more profitable. But there are choke points where the land blocks the best sea route. For Egypt, it all turns on this fulcrum." He pointed to the land between the Gulf of Suez and the Mediterranean Sea. "There was, in the ship people's world, a canal here."

Ptolemy looked at Eudemus. It was nearly a hundred miles from the gulf to the Mediterranean, most of it desert.

Quickly, Eudemus continued. "I'm not suggesting we try to duplicate their canal, but they had things called trains, planes and automobiles. Trains seemed to be a way of moving large loads over land. Planes...well, planes are just ridiculous. Automobiles are like trains, but don't need a track."

"What's a track?"

"We don't know yet. The prostitute who entertained Panos of Katsaros failed to ask him because he was ready to go again. Apparently, the whole thing came up in a discussion of plays and a comparison of Greek comedies with ship people plays that they call movies." Eudemus shrugged. "We will have a great many questions for the ship people when they return."

"If they return," Ptolemy said. Though he thought they probably would, unless the gods decided to move their great ship to yet another world and time.

"Even if they don't, just knowing that such things are possible is having an effect on the scholars at the library. One of our people put a lid on a pot with just a small controlled gap to direct the steam. He put a wooden copy of a propeller in front of the steam pipe and it moved. Not much, granted, but it moved."

"Eudemus, what does this have to do with anything?"

"I'm sorry, Satrap. My point was, even without the ship people, the knowledge they brought us will change things. We will build steam engines. It might take a while, but we will. And we will figure out what tracks are. Or, in looking for them, we will find something else. And knowing that, we know that in some way that stretch of ground right there is the key to trade between the Mediterranean and India. So we must find a way to cross that ground."

Studying the map, Ptolemy saw something else. The Red Sea, then around the Arabian Peninsula, put him on the other side of Alexander's Empire. Also, the mouth of the Red Sea was narrow. A fort there and a small, well-armed fleet, and he would own the whole of the Red Sea. That, by itself, would be almost a doubling of his territory.

But for now at least, he would not declare Egypt independent. He wouldn't declare himself traitor to Alexander's memory, or to Alexander's family. Not with Roxane and Alexander IV on the *Queen of the Sea*.

Royal Suite, **Queen of the Sea,** *off Trinidad*
January 20

Roxane lounged in the hot tub, glorying in the moving water. This was luxury. She drank a glass of wine. It was expensive now. There was very little of the ship's wine stock left, and the wine from Egypt wasn't nearly as good. At least, not as consistently good. Setting her wine down, she picked up a crab leg and used the tool to crack it open. She dipped the meat in butter sauce and ate it. Then the phone rang, proving that not everything the ship people brought was good.

She climbed from the tub and wrapped a terry cloth robe around herself, then went to the phone. "Yes?"

"The representative of the Tupky is here." The words were in English, spoken by her concierge. Almost all of the *Queen of the Sea*'s hotel staff had gone to the new colony on the shore, but the *Queen* would be hosting quite a few guests on a permanent basis. The crew and workers in the new ship factories were also in need of the same services. So a core of the staff had stayed, and many of the natives had been hired to replace the ship people who had changed jobs. The *Queen* would now hold only two thousand passengers and five hundred crew. Even at that, for now the *Queen* was less than half full. The rest of the room was being put to use as factory floor space, where they were making everything from steel to bread.

Some industries, like papermaking, were going on to shore. They had a producing oil well. All of which was important, but what had brought Roxane out of her bath was the fact that she was the regent for the king of Alexander's empire, and could make binding trade agreements with the locals for importing things like wheat, rye, and woad. At least in theory.

Roxane got dressed and went to meet the pot makers of Tupky.

"Welcome," she said in Greek and her phone app translated it to Tupky. The app for Tupky wasn't as good or as complete as the Greek version. It often got words or syntax wrong, but it was being improved daily and was perfectly adequate for greetings. The Tupky were sort of like the Egyptians, in that they had made their royalty into divinities. Their kings, like Pharaoh, were considered the gods made manifest, or at least related to the gods. That was another of those confusing bits in the translations.

The representative said something and bowed deeply. The translator said, "Wife of the god of the eastern sea, we welcome you to the lands of the Tupky and wish only peaceful relations. But we do not give to you the land. Be satisfied with the island of Trinidad." Yes, the translation program needed tweaking, or Lacula had been fudging again.

"You will need to speak to President Wiley about that," Roxane said. There had been an election not long after they got to Trinidad and Congressman Wiley got about two-thirds of the vote. The other third was split between several people. Captain Floden, who had insisted all along that he wasn't running, still pulled a solid ten percent of the vote. Rabbi Benyamin Abrahamson got eight percent. Marie Easley had six percent she didn't want. A Baptist minister who wanted to pave the way for Jesus got four percent. And Roxane, who also hadn't been running, got most of the rest, aside from people voting for personal friends and family. Meanwhile, Lacula seemed to be setting up for a run in four years, by which time the locals would be citizens. At least, some of them would. The congressmen and women, all thirty of them, were working out the rules for acquiring citizenship in the new nation.

More talking back and forth, then the spokesman who had the same shaved sides that Lacula did, and what looked to be dried blood under his fingernails, spoke again. "But he is not even a priest, just a *drisket*." The word didn't translate, but the tone was contemptuous.

Roxane realized something. Macedonians weren't deeply enamored of the Athenian democracy, or even the Rhodian's representative system, but they did listen to the people. That was why they had gotten so angry when Alexander started requiring the Persian-style bowing. These people were more like the Egyptians. "God" and "the boss" were the same, and the people did pretty much what they were told or bad things happened to them.

All right, she thought, *I can deal that way too.* "Be very careful here, gentlemen. If your godking disrespects our president, the queen of the eastern sea will be very angry. All sorts of bad things could happen then. Hurricanes, avalanches, floods."

After that, they got down to business. Gold and silver were available from upriver. So were things like corn, latex from rubber trees, cocoa beans, and other goods. Roxane was finding that she had more of a job now than she'd had when Alexander was alive. She was also finding that she liked it. She had always understood politics. She'd grown up with it in her father's court, and life in Alexander's court was what Marie Easley would call a graduate course. But, while Alexander had been willing to listen to her and consider her advice, this was the first time she was in a position to make real policy decisions. And it was fun.

Fort Plymouth, Trinidad
January 21

President Allen Wiley looked out the window. There was no glass, but there was a fine-mesh screen. It was made of black-dyed thread and it was tight enough to block flying insects. Malaria might or might not be a consideration, but why take chances? And who knew what kind of other insect-borne diseases there might be in this era? The good news for the natives was that the ship people hadn't brought smallpox or the other plagues that the Conquistadores had. Wiley hated the name "ship people." It reminded him too much of the Vietnamese boat people from when he was a kid. But like it or not, it seemed to be sticking.

The door opened and Amanda came in. "Mr. President, Queen Roxane is here."

"How is the queen mum?" Al asked.

"The queen mum is fine, Mr. President, but you're not going to be," Roxane said as she entered behind Amanda. The Bactrian woman's English was becoming very good, to the point of being fluent and often idiomatic. But her accent was still quite pronounced.

"Surely you're not taking offense..."

"What? Oh, I have learned to ignore your plebeian silliness, Mr. President," Roxane said. "No, what is likely to cause *you* problems is what I suspect was under the fingernails of the delegation from Tupky yesterday."

"I've never been one to condemn a man for having a little dirt under his nails, Your Highness?"

"What about blood?" Roxane asked. "And I'm guessing human blood."

Allen Wiley was a pretty hard-bitten politician, and had done some pretty iffy things in order to garner support in his political career before The Event. Even after The Event, his hands had not been entirely clean, in that he had been pushing for this office since less than a week after it happened. And he had skirted awfully near mutiny on the high seas to get it. But now he was feeling the blood drain from his face. He had known that the pyramid cultures from the Aztecs on back had often engaged in human sacrifice to appease their false gods. He had learned since The Event that the Carthaginians did, on certain religious occasions, practice child sacrifice.

In at least one version of the Jewish Torah that was still in use at this time, Abraham had not been stopped from sacrificing his child to God. He knew and understood that these were barbaric times. But to sit down across the table from someone who had removed a human heart in a religious ceremony . . .

He couldn't do that. Nor could he send in the 82nd Airborne Division to put an end to the vile practice, because he didn't have the eighty deuce. He had a bunch of Greek hoplites equipped with crossbows and a total of ten modern pistols. There was a gunsmith—actually a retired pipefitter off an oil rig—who was using the induction-melted crucible steel to make single-shot pistols, but he'd only made one of them, and they were still working on the primers.

What it all came down to was that as much as he would like to, he didn't have the power to stop human sacrifice, either here in the new world or in the old. No more could he end slavery, save on this island, and only part of that.

"Very well, Your Highness. I have myself under control. I will not order out the army and march them upriver."

"For now at least, Mr. President, it's going to be worse than that," Roxane said.

"What do you mean?"

"We are going to have to deal with them," Amanda chimed in. "They are our only source of latex. With latex and the chemistry we can do on the ship, we have rubber. There are literally hundreds of goods like that. Queen Roxane gave me a list."

"So the *Queen of the Sea* will return to Europe with tons of goods." Allen nodded sadly. For this he was going to need a long spoon indeed.

"Not for months yet. The oil well, singular so far, is producing. But it's going to take quite a while for it to produce enough to fill *Barge 14*."

"Speaking of that, how is the harbor work going?" At the moment there wasn't a nearby harbor that was deep enough for the *Queen* or even the *Reliance* to dock. Both of them were anchored out at least a quarter mile from shore. The *Reliance* was acting as the muscle for the construction of a harbor deep enough to let at least the fuel barge dock, because without that it was going to be like filling a swimming pool with buckets. Doable, but a whole lot of work.

"It may be ready before the *Reliance* is filled by barrel load, but I wouldn't count on it," Amanda said. "And that will probably be after the *Queen* is on her way back to Europe."

"What do you think is happening there?" Wiley asked Roxane.

"I wish I knew, Mr. President. I wish I knew."

Approaching Mugla
February 5

Eurydice looked out at the village. She didn't know its name. It wasn't much of a place, mostly a fishing village, but also a stop on the coastal trade route between Idrias and Idyma. They could find a ship here to send a message to Rhodes. And Antigonus needed allies, a state of affairs that didn't bode well for her and her husband Philip.

Olympias had always hated Philip. Eurydice's guards were just as nervous as she was. And feeling like they had backed the wrong queen into the bargain.

She looked over at Trajan. The old man was watching her and not happily. She wondered if she could trust him. The gold Roxane had given her was still hidden away, and Antigonus and Cassander were paying her guards, just as Attalus had been paying Evgenij and Roxane's guards.

Cassander was looking even more ragged than the rest of them. Perhaps a hundred men escaped from the infantry forces, all of them mounted, so all of them officers. At that, most of the officers, including Cassander's brother, died or were captured. The baggage train was captured, so much of Cassander's wealth was gone. At least the cash on hand. He was still heir to his father's estates back in Macedonia, assuming Olympias didn't seize them.

Antigonus was in better shape. They'd been traveling through land that was his satrapy before Roxane's proclamation, and he had authority to collect taxes, or at least he had a solid claim that he did. He'd been collecting those taxes with fire and sword all the way from Sardis.

Eumenes was going to have a mess to clean up and Antigonus was well supplied with silver.

She looked over at Trajan again. "Can I trust you, Trajan?"

Trajan looked back at her. Trajan didn't shave. Instead he trimmed his beard short. It was gray now, shading to white, as was his hair. The lines on his face were deeply etched. It was a hard face, like worn away iron. "No."

Then he smiled, and it was like fifty years had fallen away. "Not unless you have a good plan." Now the hard old man was a youth, a sneak thief ready to try, but only if he thought he could get away with it.

"What would be a good plan, Trajan?"

"Not stealing a ship," Trajan said. "Not unless you know some place it can take us."

And that was the rub. Where was a safe place for her and Philip? Eumenes was loyal to the dynasty, but Roxane made him *strategos* for the entire empire, and he only needed one of the kings. She would like to think that she could trust him, but could she?

Olympias wanted her dead. That was a given. In the world of the butterfly book, she'd had Philip killed and forced Eurydice to commit suicide.

Then there was Cleopatra, Alexander the Great's only full sibling. Eurydice and she had never been close but Cleopatra didn't hate Philip the way Olympias did. Cleopatra had doted on her dashing little brother, Alexander, and Alexander had liked Philip.

Also, Cleopatra had never thought Roxane was good enough for Alexander, which might incline her to Eurydice's side. On the other hand, little Alexander was her nephew and Roxane was little Alexander's mother. Cleopatra was possible, but risky. Especially since Eurydice hadn't been in touch with her at all since the *Queen of the Sea* arrived in the world.

Ptolemy? Maybe. He was satrap of Egypt, and he didn't have the endorsement of either her or Roxane, not as anything more than satrap. The question was, did he want anything more? Ptolemy was good at the friendly public face, but underneath he was a cold man. So Eurydice's mother had told her. Careful and cautious, as quick to retreat as to advance. And the butterfly book seemed to support that contention. He occupied and retreated from Syria four times. His caution might make Alexandria a safe harbor. Or maybe not.

But the truth was Eurydice didn't want a safe harbor. She wanted her own army. She wanted to contend with Antigonus on the field of battle. She wondered how she could get Ptolemy to give her an army. What about Attalus? She had worked with him before and with Seleucus and Peithon dead, he might be more reasonable. But no. He was probably going to die from the belly wound. At least, that's what she heard.

Sardis
February 10

Euphemios of Athens felt Attalus' forehead and called for damp cloths. He had read the butterfly book, combined that with his knowledge, and done everything right. Yet still the wound had become infected. Attalus burned with fever. They must have left something out. Euphemios resented that. He resented it mightily, even though he knew that the resentment was unfair.

The *Queen of the Sea* had only been in Alexandria for a month, Rhodes for a week, and Tyre for a few days. The book was apparently completed while they were still in Alexandria, which was an amazing thing in itself. He knew that the appendix on medicine was just that, an appendix. Only a few pages added to the back of the book at the insistence of their chief doctor, but he had seen half a hundred men die of infected wounds since the battle. And if that number was less than half of what he would have expected without the boiled bandages, the sulfur and wine washes, and the stitching up, it was still too many.

His eyes fell on the slave, Hermes, grinding sulfur into a paste using a splash of wine. The book said that wine and beer contained something called alcohol that killed the germs as well as boiling, but it didn't explain how to extract the alcohol. Sighing, he got up and went to the door. "Paint the wound with the paste again, Hermes. I will be talking to Cleopatra." Then he left.

Hermes watched him go with a troubled heart. Hermes had been sold into slavery for nonpayment of debts when he was little more than a child and had spent his life as one of Euphemios' slaves and attendants. He made the medicines, emptied the chamber pots, and did all manner of other jobs. He hadn't had access to the book. There was only the one copy here in Sardis and it was reserved for Cleopatra and important courtiers like Euphemios. But there was, according to rumor, a section in it on the rights of people that condemned the practice of slavery. He looked around the room with its polished floors and beautiful hand-crafted wall hangings, then at the not-quite-rags he wore and wondered.

He was afraid of the notion of being on his own. Who would feed him? How could he make his way in the world? At the same time, he resented the restrictions placed on him. He always had, but slavery had just been the way the world was, his lot in life. Now he was beginning to wonder if there might not be another way.

He wasn't the only one.

Eumenes took the goblet of wine from the slave and sipped as he listened to the doctor's report. It was still touch and go for Attalus, even after six weeks, and it would be months more until he recovered. If he recovered.

"It's time and past time to replace Attalus as commander of the Companion Cavalry," said Alcetas.

"But Attalus has access to Perdiccas' funds at Tyre," Cleopatra said.

"So do I. Or I should, at least," Eumenes pointed out. He was talking about the appointment as *strategos*.

"Attalus is Perdiccas' brother-in-law," Cleopatra said.

"And I am Perdiccas' brother!" Alcetas said. "I should be strat— I should be the commander of the Companion Cavalry."

"Not after your part in the death of Cynane," Cleopatra told him.

Cynane had been Alexander the Great's half-sister. Fearing her influence, Perdiccas had sent his brother Alcetas to put her to death. He'd done so, but the army had been so furious they had almost mutinied. Perdiccas was now dead himself, murdered by his own officers after the disaster he led his army to on the Nile. And no one had forgotten Alcetas' role in the death of an Argead princess, least of all the Macedonian troops who were still largely devoted to the dynasty.

"That wasn't my fault! The stupid woman—"

Cleopatra held up a hand, and Alcetas fell silent. Red-faced, but silent. "It doesn't matter if she forced you to it. You almost had a rebellion in the ranks and it's the reason that Attalus was given access to Perdiccas' funds instead of you in the first place. Also, the woman you killed was Eurydice's mother and Roxane has proclaimed Eurydice as regent for Philip, effectively the co-ruler of my brother's empire. If we give credence to the part of Roxane's proclamation that makes Eumenes here *strategos* and grants him the satraps, then we have to acknowledge the part that makes Eurydice Philip's regent."

Cleopatra turned to Eumenes. "Who do you think for commander?"

"I'd appoint Pharnabazus," Eumenes said, and Alcetas started to interrupt again as Eumenes continued. "But the Macedonians won't accept him because he's Persian. Besides, he has naval experience, and it would almost be a waste to leave him as a cavalry commander. No, I think it will have to be Docimus."

Cleopatra looked around the room. Alcetas was not happy, but Eumenes' suggestion of Pharnabazus had worked. Alcetas would accept it. Cleopatra wasn't happy with it, but it was the best choice they could make work.

CHAPTER 18

President's Office, Fort Plymouth
February 10

"We're in the wrong fucking place!" the large, gray-haired man roared as he banged through the door, and Allen Wiley wished that the New U.S. had a Secret Service.

"This is, of course, Sean Little, our chief petroleum geologist."

"Oh, bull, Wiley. I'm just an old roughneck with lousy luck. And you know it." The gray head turned and brown eyes looked out at the collection of natives and ship people. The natives were the tribal sort from here on Trinidad, and the ship people included Bob Jones, Amanda Miller, Nick Pacheco, and Eleanor Kinney.

Wiley saw the penny drop as Sean Little realized that this might not be the best time or the best company for one of his rants.

"I'm guessing that Mr. Little is a bit upset with me and wishes to vent. Is it urgent, Mr. Little? We are discussing the pricing of ship-produced ceramics and..." Allen let his voice trail off.

By now Little's anger had cooled a bit and he was thinking again. "I guess I can wait, but it's important, Al. I'll be in the library at the computer when you get done here."

"Is there anyone I should bring?"

"Amanda, and maybe Bob. And we are going to need the *Reliance* in this, so Adrian Scott."

"What about the *Queen*?" Eleanor Kinney asked.

"Just came from there. Besides, it's not the *Queen*'s business."

Little wasn't a fan of Captain Floden. He felt that the passengers had gotten a raw deal. He turned and marched out of the office.

"What's got his panties in a knot this time?" Eleanor asked.

"I'm sure I'll find out," Allen said, putting all the long-suffering patience he could manage into his tone. The truth was Allen was reasonably fond of Little. He was a hard-working, hard-partying sort who came on the cruise to gamble in the casino. He had been a roughneck for thirty-five years. And by now, near retirement, he knew every aspect of a drilling rig, from the mud loggers to the pipe fitters. "In the meantime, we were discussing the price of ceramic storage vessels?"

"No," said Botoka, a middle-aged stocky woman who was wearing a single kola feather in her straight black hair and not much else. "We talk about cooking pots for cassava."

The translator app wasn't ready for prime time when it came to Akpara. The Akpara were from the hills on the north side of the island, and combined hunting and gathering with limited farming. Mostly cassava, *guinep* trees, and some herbs. The ship people had been a bit disheartened to learn that coconuts hadn't reached the Atlantic yet. A lot of the modern cassava recipes involved coconut milk or meat. Still, the cassava were a staple food source of the region already. They were a product that the colony could buy in exchange for clay pots and steel implements, from machetes to cook pots.

It took another hour before the discussion of prices was done and Allen could find out what had—as Eleanor put it—Little's panties in a knot.

Amanda brought Sean Little in, and Allen spoke before Little could. "I called and the *Reliance* is dropping nets in the north of the bay. Can I inform Captain Scott about it in the morning? Whatever it is?"

Little looked around. Now the room held only him, Amanda, Allen Wiley and Bob Jones. "I shouldn't have popped off like that, Al, but we're in the wrong place, the wrong part of the island."

"I got that part. But what do you mean and how do you know?"

"You know that Aripero number five isn't producing for crap, right?"

"Yes. I approved of the saltwater injection well you proposed."

"Right. And that's the problem. I knew about that trick from a

hundred wells on as many fields. When the oil field isn't producing much anymore, because the pressure has dropped, you drill
another well a bit deeper than the first and pump in saltwater.
Saltwater is heavier than oil, so it pushes the oil up and increases
the pressure, so you can get oil out of an old well. Problem is,
this ain't an old well. It's a brand new well. That bugged me.
They didn't know about that trick in the eighteen sixties when
Walter Darwent drilled his well. Poor sod didn't go broke and
die because he was underfunded, like Wikipedia had it. He went
broke because there wasn't enough pressure to push the oil. You
know where the first commercial oil well on Trinidad was drilled?
Out in the forest, near a village that was called Guayaguayare
in our time. Guayaguayare is on the other side of the frigging
island. Thirty-four miles from here." Sean pointed at a spot on
the map in Allen's office. The spot was in the southeast corner
of the island, and well outside the area the colony bought.

"Are you saying your injection well won't work?"

"No. It'll work. For a while. But there probably isn't all that
much oil down there, at least not recoverable oil. We can make
the sucker produce for a while. But there's a reason injection
wells like this one are sometimes called salting the field. They
make the field produce, but they use it up fast too. I figure two
years if we're lucky, six months if we ain't."

"How deep are the wells in Guaya-whatever?" Amanda asked.

"I don't know. They can't be too deep for us to reach, since
they were drilled in 1902."

"I'm afraid that is not the most urgent issue," Bob Jones said.
"The Koksy don't like us, and they hold that land. They use blow
pipes and poisoned darts to hunt the howler monkeys, and they
occasionally hunt each other too."

Bob was using the term "hold" advisedly. Ownership of land
wasn't an official sort of thing on Trinidad. It was an issue of
who could hold it, and that changed frequently, with tribes and
even families fighting each other over the land. The locals were
surprised at the ship people's willingness to pay for the land they
bought. The anger of the Koksy tribe had to do with a lot of their
young people running off to get jobs with the ship people. There
were six on the experimental farm Bob and his family set up.

"They have a tribal hierarchy set up with the elders running
everything. The youngsters don't have a lot of choice but to

toe the line or live on their own, which is uncomfortable and dangerous. With us over here offering jobs, food, and housing, the young people are running off to work for us any time the elders decide they have to do something they don't like. Like become their uncle's third wife. We have two teenage couples on the farm and a couple of girls looking speculatively at my thirteen-year-old son."

Allen was looking concerned, and Bob grinned. "Don't worry about it, Allen. We have more important issues." Allen, Bob knew, was worried about the issue of polygamy because of his Mormon heritage. Being a Mormon politician in the world they'd come from meant you had to be vociferously opposed to polygamy or you got accused of all sorts of unnatural appetites.

Meanwhile, here on the island and among the tribes in Venezuela proper, all sorts of marriage customs were in practice, from monogamy to every form of group marriage. In the here-and-now, no one with any sense had time to spare for worrying about that sort of crap. And, aside from a very few people who had not accepted the new situation, no one was very worried about it. They were too busy catching and freezing fish, harvesting and freezing wild fruits and vegetables, and the other necessary jobs to make sure there was enough food and shelter to last them until the *Queen* got back with live cattle and mules to pull plows and let them start farming seriously.

Plymouth Bay
February 15

Leonard Wechsler breathed deeply several times, then let go of the side of the outrigger boat and sank down in the water. He was wearing his snorkeling mask and a set of weights to let him sink fast. He was also wearing a harness so that he could be pulled up without dropping the weights. When he reached the bottom, he started to walk along, looking for issues that would make the dredge work more difficult. They were trying to get a canal deep enough for *Barge 14* to navigate up to shore.

The problem was, they were doing it with cobbled-together tools. The sandy bottom here was only ten feet deep, and what Leonard was looking for were rocks that would have to be blown up, like stumps in clearing a field. Once the rocks were out of the way, they would drop the dredge, the *Reliance* would pull it seaward, and dig a trench. It wasn't efficient—or environmentally sound—but it would let them get *Barge 14* close enough to shore to pipe oil into it. Leonard saw a rock protruding up from the sand and went over to check it out. He reached for the rock and shook. It was firm, but there was a place a rope could be attached. Leonard pulled a cord from his belt, tied it around the rock protrusion and pulled his signal cord. Then he swam back up to the boat.

"Gimme the tank and a balloon, John," Leonard said.

"What you got, Lenny?" John Harvell asked.

"Got a rock. Pretty big one, but I think it's just sitting there. Not bedrock. I want to see if we can lift it and use it as part of the canal wall."

John passed over the rope and leather balloon, along with the small air tank. Leonard took several more deep breaths, and went back down. He found the rock, tied the rope around it, and used the tank to inflate the balloon. It was a good-sized balloon, but it didn't shift the rock at all. Leonard left it tied to the rock and headed back to the boat. This was taking a long time.

Queen of the Sea
February 15

Georgios Iconomou checked the settings on the vacuum pump and started the motor. He was an American Greek who had two words of Greek, *ouzo* and *retsina*. And one of them, ouzo, didn't exist yet, except for a couple of bottles on the *Queen*. So rather than being a translator, Georgios was working on making tubes. It was proving surprisingly difficult, in spite of the fact that the *Queen* had vacuum pumps of excellent quality. The problem was that you had to pump out all the air, then let the sucker sit for a week or so, so that the gas molecules that had been stuck in the glass or metal of the tube slowly migrated out. Then you had to pump it out again, and then set off a match to use up the last few atoms of oxygen. And even at this, you had to have all the wires in the right place.

The reason they needed tubes was twofold. One, the ships only had a limited number of radios. Very limited. Two, even those radios, at least the powerful ones, used tubes. Tubes that were eventually going to wear out.

Georgios watched the gauges and waited. Then he sealed the pipe, and turned off the pump. This one would wait a week, then be sucked out again, and they would see if he had gotten it right this time.

All across the *Queen of the Sea* there were people like Georgios Iconomou, using their knowledge and experience, along with the knowledge available in encyclopedias and technical reference works—not nearly enough technical reference works—to try to build the tools to build the tools to start an industrial revolution two thousand years early.

Southeast Trinidad
February 15

Pelio waited and watched as the howler monkey moved from branch to branch, somehow never giving him a shot. Pelio was furious. It wasn't fair. Just because his stupid little sister ran off, *he* was in trouble. The Koksy elders just needed someone to punish, so he was going to have to wait another year to marry, and he wouldn't be getting Leasook as his wife.

His foot came down in the black mud and he cursed. Then he stopped. His stupid little sister talked about the ship people liking the black mud. They burned it. Well, Pelio knew you could burn it, but he didn't like to use it. It stank and made the food over it taste bad. But if the ship people used it, maybe he could trade it for some of their knives. He slipped away, the howler monkey forgotten.

Experimental Farm, Trinidad
February 16

Jason Jones listened to the girl who worked on the farm and her brother—or boyfriend, or something—and tried to figure out what they were talking about. Not that he was particularly happy to see the guy. Whether he was brother or boyfriend, he wasn't good news as far as Jason was concerned.

Then the guy, apparently frustrated with Jason's failure to understand, reached down and rubbed a finger over the side of his ankle, then brought the finger back up and rubbed the greasy black crap on Jason's face.

Wait a second. Greasy black crap. Oil.

"Right!" Jason said. "Dad! We have a guy here who knows where there's an oil seep."

Using the translation app helped a little, but not very much. The Koksy language was unique on the island and apparently hadn't survived in any form into the twenty-first century. Also, the workers on the farm weren't bilingual with any of the other tribes, at least not very. As a result, the app had only a few words programmed in and even less syntax. So it was gesture, point, and guess, but over an hour of point and shout. Bob got the idea that the young man, Pelio, was the brother of Safsa, a girl who worked on the farm, and that Pelio knew where oil seeped out of the ground, and would show them in return for a machete.

At that point, Bob Jones called Fort Plymouth.

"I need to talk with Al, Amanda. We have a kid here who knows where there's an oil seep."

"In Koksy territory?" Amanda asked.

"Probably. The kid is Koksy, anyway."

Southeast Trinidad
February 18

It took a couple of days to get the expedition organized. The team had a canister of black powder, half a dozen microphones rigged for ground pickup, and a computer to record the echoes and hopefully find a salt dome to drill through.

The *Reliance* gave the team a ride most of the way around to the south of the island, and they put into a small bay that, on their maps, was marked Guayaguayare Bay. Then they made their way inland, with Pelio making what were probably snide comments about all the noise they were making. Robert Waters sympathized with the kid a bit. He'd never been much of an outdoorsman, but he had shepherded suits around his shop, and spent most of the time wishing they would go away and not interfere with his work.

It took the team a couple of hours to make the trek inland. The team was Sean Little, a former roughneck, Jeffrey Zeitlin, their seismologist—that is, he had taken a course in seismology while getting his early modern lit degree thirty years earlier. John Bogan, one of Sean's crew, recruited after The Event. He had been a mechanic at a lube and tire shop in Mississippi and was on the cruise with his wife for their thirtieth anniversary. And David Dove, who was carrying a black powder rifle made after The Event. Robert Waters and the rest were carrying crossbows.

They reached the area, and Pelio pointed out the pool of oil.

Sean Little scooped some up, took it over a ways, and tasted it with the tip of his tongue. Then he lit it with a Zippo lighter. "Sweet crude. Guys, you could almost run the lifeboats on this stuff without refining. Jeff, where do you want the charge set?"

"I'd like to get a bit of distance. I want to be sure that the echoes are distinct. It would be best if it was on a rock, so the sound transmission to the bedrock will be clear."

All of which he had said before, any number of times. On the other hand, Robert had to admit that between Jeff Zeitlin and Katy Borman, a programmer on the *Queen*, they had done some pretty good seismology, and spotted the well where they finally hit oil.

It took several hours to get the charge and all the microphones in place. The microphones were hooked up by way of long wires, so they could be placed at a considerable distance. But as with the charge, Jeff wanted them put on rock whenever possible and there wasn't a lot of exposed rock here. They were in what the government was calling a forest, but what Robert thought of as a jungle. There were vines everywhere and all manner of trees. Robert could barely see the sky, and the area was densely wooded, except right next to the oil seeps. Even there, there were dead trees. Apparently they were fairly recent seeps.

The howler monkeys were screaming in the trees and a bird about twice the size of a turkey was making its call in the distance.

Finally, they were ready, and Jeff waved. Sean lit the fuse on the charge and took off running. Everyone except Pelio ducked. Pelio was looking at them in confusion when the charge went off. He ducked then, went flat to the ground and when everyone got up, he started screaming something.

Robert didn't have a clue what Pelio was screaming about, except he was gesturing for them to get gone and right now. He kept pointing to the south and waving for them to move. "Hey, Sean, Pelio seems upset and he knows the area. You think maybe we don't have permission to be here?"

"Maybe not," Sean said, holding up his crossbow, "but what are they going to do about it?"

Robert wasn't so sure. "The kid seems really upset."

"Don't worry, kid," Sean said. "As soon as we've gathered up Jeff's gear, we'll be out of here."

They gathered up the gear and started back for the shore. Pelio was getting more and more agitated as they did, and it was rubbing off on Robert. He scanned the jungle as they went back and he saw Jeff, with the little dart sticking out of his neck. There was another sticking out of Jeff's shirt and Robert couldn't tell if it had broken the skin beneath the shirt. What he did know was that Pelio didn't have a shirt on and he saw someone, a movement in the jungle, who seemed to be pointing at the kid. It was all happening way too fast for Robert to think about but he jumped forward to protect the kid. In the process, he knocked Pelio down and got hit with three of the darts.

Robert Waters felt a cramp in his neck and it spread. All his muscles cramped and it was agony. But it didn't last long. His heart cramped too. It contracted and stayed contracted. He was dead in minutes.

The poison dart frog found on Trinidad was purple with blue spots, but it was about as poisonous as the golden poison frog of the Pacific coast in Central America. They were a different subspecies and in the original timeline would have been killed off in another three hundred years. Along with the Koksy, whose lifestyle didn't endear them to their neighbors. The Koksy were actually a very pleasant people, open and gracious, but they didn't count a male a full adult until he had killed another adult male. There was constant low-level fighting between the various Koksy villages, and they accepted the death of other tribe's male members as proof of virility. The Pleck, a coastal fishing tribe, were often their victims, and the male Pleck stayed out of the wood. There was a prohibition among the Koksy against killing women, so the Pleck women often gathered plants and foods in the Koksy jungles, and even traded with them. Occasionally, one of the women was taken as a wife, but that was less common. The Koksy wanted to keep the trade open for the addition fish and turtles made to their diet.

The Koksy heard the bang of the charge used for the sonar, and came to investigate. They found the party, and the young

Koksy in the hunting party simply couldn't resist the opportunity. Six men in their forest. Pelio was of the Koksy, but not of their village and shouldn't be here either.

They attacked in a group and got four of the men in the first salvo. Then they started arguing over who had killed who. Sean Little was hit by three darts, one in the backpack, one hung in the sleeve of his shirt, and one in the leg of his pants. That one actually nicked the skin, but most of the poison had been rubbed off by the camouflage fatigue pants that were something of a fashion statement for Sean. They were also very comfortable. And in this case, between the fabric wiping much of the poison from the dart and the bagginess of the pants slowing the dart so it nicked but barely penetrated the skin, Sean's leg cramped, but the poison didn't stop his heart or his breathing.

The others, except for the kid, were dead.

Faskly, the leader of the hunting party, hadn't taken part in the slaughter. He had already killed his man. In fact, he had killed several over the years, mostly in retaliatory raids on other Koksy villages. He knew about the big boat and had not wanted this fight.

Pelio was shouting that they would be sorry when the ship people came and killed their whole village. Tokis pulled out a stone knife to silence him, but Faskly shouted, "Stop! We need to know what they were doing on our land."

Pelio shut up then, apparently realizing that once they found out what they needed to know from him, they wouldn't need him anymore.

Faskly was mildly impressed by the fast-thinking youth. He looked around and cursed under his breath. This was supposed to be a training hunt, before they heard the *bang*. The boys were mostly too young to be going on raids. They had spoiled each other's kills and probably none of the kills would be counted by the tribal elders, because how could they tell whose dart killed a stranger, when the stranger was hit by three darts.

Another of the kids started to pull a knife and Faskly shouted at him to stop.

"But he's still alive," Topkady complained. "I—"

"You can be dead," Faskly shouted and lifted his pipe almost to his lips. All the boys were staring at him now. This was a dangerous time for young men, after they stopped being children, but before they had killed their man. It wasn't unheard of for elders to be killed by boys on a rampage. It meant that Faskly had to get control back, but he couldn't push too hard before they got back to the village where the other elders would be able to support him. "You just settle down. We have to get all of them back to the village for the elders to question. And the elders haven't decided that the new people are fair hunting yet."

"They are in our jungle," Topkady insisted.

"So they are. But this is the border lands. It's possible that Pelio's village has an agreement with them."

Sean was in agony. His right leg was curled up, his muscles were contracting like to break his bones, and he couldn't move it at all. For that matter, his butt was contracted and his left leg was twitchy. His heart was stuttering and he wasn't sure whether it was from the poison or the fear. It was hard to breathe, and this kid who couldn't be more than fourteen grabbed him by the hair and jerked his head up like he was going to cut his throat. Then the old guy shouted and he got dropped again. Being very careful, with shaking hands, Sean checked himself for more darts and pulled two that didn't reach him through the clothing. And suddenly he knew just how these people could be defeated. Their little darts were light. Very light. A bit of light cloth held away from the skin would be very effective armor.

It was strange, the stuff you thought about when you were scared out of your mind.

The older guy got two of the kids to carry Sean and another couple to guard Pelio. Sean's first thought was that Pelio had led them into an ambush, but that didn't fit with the way the other natives were acting.

The poison was still there and he was still feeling it, but he was better able to think now. He waited as they were dragged back through the jungle and to a small village.

The village was a set of the roofed, but not sided, huts that were common on the island. All the villagers used them, even the traders like Lacula. Sean was dropped in a hut and left. He managed to pull out his phone and call the ship. He reported the attack and mentioned his thoughts on the defense against blow darts. Both *Reliance* and the *Queen* picked up the signal and the two directional reports gave a good location for the village, 10 12' 18" N by 61 5' 47" W.

As Sean looked around, he started to realize some things. There were something like three women to every man, and while everyone was dressed in islander standard—a loincloth and not much else—these people also wore paint. The men wore it in jagged patterns with sharp points, the women wore theirs in curved lines that often emphasized breast and hip. They weren't, to Sean's modern western eyes, a particularly attractive people.

One of the older women came over and examined Sean, then she went out again and started giving orders. People ran off to obey her instructions, and a half hour or so later, she came back. Using a stone knife, she cut his leg just where the dart had cut him and pushed a paste into the wound. It hurt, but an hour after that the cramping started to ease a little.

President's Office, Fort Plymouth
February 18

"We have to go get them," Allen Wiley said, "and we are going to have to make an example."

"If you had—" Captain Floden started, but Al cut him off.

"Captain, this is a New U.S. decision. And, to be frank, your presence in this meeting is strictly a courtesy." Floden had made his lack of responsibility for the New U.S. quite clear, even while helping set up the colony. Al knew why that was. Floden didn't want the *Queen* held responsible for any action the colony might make. But there was another side to that. If Floden didn't have responsibility, he didn't have authority either.

Floden shut up, and Al hoped he hadn't soured relations between the colony and the ship too much.

"You do indeed have to go get them, and the example should be the eradication of the Koksy," Roxane said. "And before you point out that I am here by courtesy, remember it's probably going to be my Silver Shields who are going to be the ones who go get your Sean Little and the bodies of the rest of your survey party."

Which nicely expressed Al's biggest problem in administering the colony. He was the President of New America, as they'd decided to call their nation. "New United States" had been suggested also, and that had been Al's own preference. But the objection had been raised that there was only one "state" to begin with so how could it be "united with itself"—and then some people started muttering that it was all a plot to let illegal aliens become citizens so they could set up new states of their own . . .

Al had dropped the issue, at that point. Not that he hadn't been tempted to point out to the conspiracy-mongering cretins that *of course* they were going to have to accept immigrants because the breeding stock that had arrived on the ship was way too small, on average much too old—and the majority of the ones who were still young enough to have children weren't U.S. citizens to begin with.

But Wiley was a firm adherent to the Biblical saws, among them Jesus' advice in the Sermon on the Mount that *sufficient unto the day is the evil thereof.* He'd fight the issue of who could and could not become a citizen at some point in the future. So, New America the new country became.

All twenty-five or so square miles of it. But there were other power groups that weren't under his authority. The *Queen of the Sea* was owned by the crew now, and most of the passengers had sold their share in the ship in exchange for its aid in setting up the colony. The *Reliance* was owned jointly by the *Queen of the Sea* and the colony. Roxane was not a citizen of New America, but the recognized ambassador for the Empire of Alexander the Great, and her Silver Shields were an allied force. Not part of Al's army. Al's army was a hundred guys with crossbows and three breech-loading black powder cannons on the walls of Fort Plymouth. They could hold the fort against anything on the island, but to go out in the forest hunting native tribes, they were going to need the Silver Shields. And Roxane was going to want some concessions for that.

It took hours to work out, but the Silver Shields—in mosquito-netting armor—would be the striking force. The ship people had arrived at the end of the wet season, and no one had known what diseases the local mosquitoes might be carrying. One of the first things they did was produce a tight-weave net, or very loose-weave cheesecloth that was dyed black to put on windows and doors to keep the mosquitoes and other insects out while letting the breezes in. Everyone wanted it, and it was a lot easier to produce than either metal screens or glass windows. Now it was one of their local export products, along with the pottery and the steel.

Approaching Kaland Koksy Village, Trinidad
February 20

The Silver Shields were wearing the netting over their armor and the little sticks that held it out away from their skins, but they weren't happy about it. What they were happy about were the crossbows. Each Silver Shield was equipped with a crossbow, and between the modified phalanx formation and the four ranks, they could fire volley after volley of crossbow bolts. It was a new technique, developed between Evgenij, Dag, and Carey Chilcote, a sixty-five-year-old man who had been playing war games and studying the history of warfare for the better part of forty years. He had read of Alexander and his hoplites, but also of Napoleon and his Imperial Guard. The two men worked out a formation that would allow the use of crossbows, but not seem too weird to the hoplites, who were used to fighting in a tight mass.

Carey pointed out that against something like the ship's steam cannon or the fort's cannon, the formation was mass suicide, but "against wild injuns with blowguns, it ought to work all right."

Evgenij smiled at the memory of the conversation as they approached the clearing. Then the air was full of little darts, and Evgenij was a lot more happy about the netting than he had been a moment ago. A two-inch long bamboo needle with a feathery back got hung in the net just short of his cheek.

"Hold your line!" he shouted as an automatic reflex. It was probably unnecessary. All his men were veterans, but it was automatic to shout that. Besides, this was a new formation, even if they had practiced it. And they were in amongst trees, not out in the open as they would have been back in Europe. "Anyone see them?"

"I have some, Captain," shouted one of the men. He pointed with his crossbow. Evgenij followed the gesture and saw a flash of red body paint disappear behind a tree.

Faskly ducked behind the tree and cursed the day those boys were born. The darts had always worked in fighting the enemies they hunted. Those enemies wore almost no clothing. Even when Sean Little survived the darts, Faskly hadn't thought about the connection. Now, though, he realized that it didn't take much to stop a blow dart. He made Pelio explain how the crossbows worked and was impressed by the force, but he hadn't thought about what that might mean. Now, in an instant of terror, it was all perfectly clear.

They were going to die. All of them. Because those idiot boys jumped in too fast.

He put a dart between his lips, put his pipe to his lips, and stepped out looking for a target. But all he saw was the strange nets. Then it was too late. Three quarrels ripped into his body—chest, belly, and thigh. There was no poison on the quarrels, but they didn't need it. They ripped gaping holes in his body. The one in his chest opened a lung. The one in his belly ripped open his lower intestine in two places. The one in his thigh wouldn't have been deadly, just debilitating. But that didn't really matter.

The Silver Shields marched on, and the natives melted before them. Some standing and dying, most running into the jungle.

They caught the villagers packing to leave, and the men folk ran off. Some of the women did too. Others, though, knelt on the ground and were left alone by the Shields. Mostly left alone... by Macedonian standards of "left alone." And even that was fairly restrained. The Macedonians hadn't lost anyone. Not one dead Macedonian, which was good luck as well as good planning. Even the net armor didn't cover everything. All it would have taken was one dart getting through to kill a Silver Shield, and things might have gotten ugly. Or perhaps not. Dag Jakobsen was here. He hadn't given any orders, just been with them, but he was their new commander and they all knew the ship people had delicate sensibilities. And they respected those delicate sensibilities, because they went with hand grenades and handguns.

As it was, between Sean Little calling for calm and the easy acquiescence of the village women, a massacre didn't happen. But all the women and children were collected up and brought back as spoils of war.

Which led to a conflict with the New American government, as said government didn't allow the taking of slaves.

Evgenij and the rest of the Shields were expecting it, knowing the attitudes of the ship people. That attitude had lost them their slaves. And they were expecting to lose these slaves too. But they weren't going to give them up without compensation. Roxane was actively planning for it. The prisoners would not be slaves, but concubines. When that didn't work, she would pay the Shields a bounty. Not buy the prisoners. Pay a bounty for prisoners, and get the government of New America to reimburse her for the bounty. Then let the New U.S. figure out what to do with them.

Dag didn't exactly sympathize with the Silver Shields' viewpoint, but he did understand it. This had been part of their pay in all the years that they had served with King Philip II and Alexander the Great. Now their new commanders were denying it to them, and they were giving it up. Just not without compensation.

Wiley wasn't happy with that, but Roxane—and to an extent, Dag—were finding it easy to live with his displeasure.

There was no official end to the Koksy war, but within days of the fight, word was all over the island. Over the next couple of weeks, they learned that the men of that village had not fared well. They were mostly killed by other Koksy fighters and the consensus among the Koksy was that fighting the ship people was not a good idea.

In fact, a negotiating party from Pelio's village showed up to work out drilling rights in their newly acquired hunting ground. In exchange for several steel knives and certain other goods, ship people and workers of the oil company would be considered off limits. They would be expected to wear a symbol, a cloth badge on their hats. The badge was a black oil rig on a white field.

By the time the *Queen of the Sea* sailed for Europe, Al Wiley was more concerned about the Tupky than the Koksy.

CHAPTER 19

Queen of the Sea
April 14

Sailing was put off one more day because they didn't want to sail on Friday the thirteenth. That wasn't just the Americans. When the locals heard of the superstition, they adopted it for their own. Lars Floden was thankful that there were no black cats on the *Queen*, but the winter in the tropics was used to good effect. The *Queen* had holds full of dried corn and frozen fish, tanks of live crabs, not to mention latex, steel blades, and all manner of other goods. There were twenty-two pounds of gold and over a hundred pounds of silver in coin form in the ship's vaults, and the tanks were full of oil. It was crude oil, but it was enough to get to Europe and back here, if they didn't spend more than a month or two in Europe.

"The *Reliance* is on the comm, Captain," Doug said and Lars picked up the mike.

"Just calling to wish you good luck, Captain," Adrian Scott said. "We'll be along as soon as we can."

"Right, Adrian. You get those tanks full. We'll arrange docking and tankerage in Alexandria or, failing that, Rhodes." The *Reliance* now had only two of its tanks filled with fuel oil. The rest were slowly filling with crude. They were going to need that fuel oil in Europe, because the lifeboats used it, and there weren't a lot of places deep enough for the *Queen* to dock.

"I will."

The *Queen* was underway and Fort Plymouth fired one of its cannons in salute.

Capitol Building, Fort Plymouth
April 14

President Wiley watched the *Queen of the Sea* leave with mixed feelings. The loss of Lars Floden and Roxane didn't bother him at all. It was the loss of the behemoth in the harbor that worried him a bit. The natives were restless. Some of the locals, but mostly it was the pot people, the Tupky and their allies along the river. They were looking at the very wealthy, by local standards, colony with avarice in their eyes. Refrigeration was available in Fort Plymouth, and a cold drink on a hot day was a luxury that had proven to be very impressive. The Tupky were trying to buy refrigeration units... and trying to buy the ship people who could make them work.

"We're going to have trouble, Mr. President," Lacula said.

Allen turned around. "You think?" Lacula no longer wore the sides of his head shaved. His hair was cut and trimmed in the ship people style and he was wearing a pair of khaki pants and a polo shirt. He was even wearing shoes. Well, flipflops. He had brought his wives and family out in February, and had a decent account in the First New America Bank. Nor was he the only one. Many of the local tribesmen had jobs in Fort Plymouth, though most of them worked just long enough to get a payday, then took their money, bought the tools they needed, and disappeared.

By now the population of Fort Plymouth was about four thousand, with three thousand ship people and a constantly shifting population of locals. There were also a hundred or so farms that were owned by ship people and employed locals on a part-time or full-time basis. They weren't producing much yet, and wouldn't until the *Queen* got back with work animals. Like the Jones experimental farm, they were mostly preparing the ground for later planting and studying the needs of local agriculture. The farms accounted for another three hundred ship people and a like number of locals.

What they didn't have was much in the way of electricity. The *Queen of the Sea* was a very integrated system, with just about all its electricity generated in the engine rooms, and the *Reliance* was the same way. *Barge 14* had no electrical generation capacity. Instead, it had a battery pack to power its thrusters, and the batteries were charged by the *Reliance*. The *Queen* actually had two complete engine rooms, well separated in case of emergencies, but Floden wouldn't agree to giving one to the colony on Trinidad. Allen Wiley understood the reasoning behind that decision, but that didn't make it any easier for the colony.

They had spots of electricity and not very many of them, the capitol building, the hospital, a few industries that had to have electricity to function. And almost all of it had been built since The Event. Over the months that the *Queen* was in the Gulf of Paria, they had built some steam power plants—small ones with small generators. Only one of the doctors from the *Queen* stayed in Trinidad and there were only three among the passengers, two of them retired and in poor physical condition.

With the *Queen* gone and the *Reliance* getting ready to go, things were going to be much harder for a while.

Queen of the Sea, *Mid-Atlantic*
April 17

Dag kicked the pipe and coughed as the dust filled the compartment. It was true that the flex fuel engines would burn anything, but that didn't mean that the level of maintenance work was the same for crude oil as it was for refined fuel oil. Crude left more soot and the pipes needed more cleaning.

Romi Clarke looked down the compartment at Dag, grinning like a demon.

"What are you grinning—*cough, cough*—about? You're going to have to come down here and clean out these pipes."

Romi lifted the filter mask into place, hiding his grin, but Dag could still see the laughter in the little man's eyes. Romi seemed to like the third century before the birth of Christ. He was studying Greek and Tupky and doing pretty well at both. Which made sense. He was multilingual before The Event, just like Dag. Most of the crew had at least two languages, their own and English, and more weren't uncommon.

Dag climbed up the ladder and shot Romi the finger. Discipline and rank were still there and still important, but since The Event the crew had gotten closer. They were all ship people. The ones unable to accept that mostly got off in Trinidad. Mostly, but not entirely. Rabbi Horse's Ass and Reverend Jackass and their followers insisted on going back.

And Wiley—the bastard—supported them on the basis of individual liberty and religious freedom. Dag was pretty sure that Wiley was mostly happy to see the troublemakers out of New America. Dag pulled up his breath mask and got to work.

Alexander IV was not, he felt, being given the respect he was due. This wasn't because he was the king of Macedonia. Alexander had no real idea what king meant. It was just part of his name. No, the *lèse-majesté* was because he was two and a half now and Dorothy Miller was only two and a quarter and had just had the temerity to dispute with him on which hole the plastic peg fit in. She insisted that it was the round hole and then laughed at him when he failed to insert the round peg into a square hole, something that clearly had to be tried. So Alexander of Macedonia called her "Poopy head!" and hit her with the peg, at which point the silly girl started crying and Alexander was sent to the dreaded time-out.

The world is an unfair place when you're two and a half, king of Macedonia or not.

Berenike was of two minds about time-out. Berenike was very much a "spare the rod, spoil the child" caregiver. But Alexander was royalty and you didn't spank royalty. Berenike was the woman of a Silver Shield. She was forty and he was sixty, and they had been together twenty-two years, ever since the Shields had taken her home, back when Philip II was king of Macedonia. Being nanny to the next king of the Macedonians was a step up, and the quarters that she and her family now enjoyed were positively palatial. But it all felt wrong somehow. Too much change, too fast. She tried to talk to the daycare workers of the ship's crew and the new hires from Trinidad.

"I know what you mean," said Sally Chin. "Before The Event, I was saving up to go to college to study education. Now I'm an expert in early child care, and I don't know what I'm doing."

"At least you admit it," complained Gupatok, a new hire from Trinidad. "It's the ones who think they know it all that I can't stomach."

Gupatok was wearing a white T-shirt and black bikini bottoms.

Even that was a concession to the rules of the ship. The normal mode of dress of her tribe was a loincloth and even that was discarded casually. She found the whole notion of a nudity taboo to be foolishness.

And that was Berenike's problem. There were all sorts of people on the ship, most of them not even Greek, much less Macedonian. They came in every shade of hair, from the ones with pale hair like Dag, to black-haired people like Sally Chin, and none of them seemed to think it mattered at all. Sally Chin's eyes were different from any eyes Berenike had ever seen, and Gupatok had a facial structure that was almost as strange. And no one seemed to care. Well, some did, but they cared about the most ridiculous things. Like skin color.

Berenike was experiencing culture shock and her life hadn't taught her that change was a good thing. It left her waiting for the disaster that all the strangeness presaged. Her phone rang, and Berenike answered.

"Berenike," Roxane's voice came over the phone, "I'm going to be tied up with the rabbi for a while longer." Roxane, Berenike knew, had been raised in the Zoroastrian faith, which was, in a way, the precursor of the later monotheistic faiths, Judaism, Christianity, and Islam. But Alexander was in no way a respecter of Zoroastrianism. It didn't leave room for him in the pantheon. He had trashed the library in Bactria, or at least his troops had, and he hadn't tried to stop it.

"Yes, Your Majesty. The king is in a time-out."

"What did he do now?"

"He hit Dorothy Miller with a plastic peg and called her a poopy head," Berenike said and Roxane laughed.

"Rabbi," Roxane said as she put away the phone, "I can't guarantee you much of anything in Judea. Not won't, can't. Unless I miss my guess, Ptolemy and Laomedon of Mytilene will be at war in short order. And while Ptolemy may not have declared himself pharaoh yet, I think he will, and sooner in this timeline than in the other one. In the meantime, he is the satrap of Egypt, and Judaea in the satrapy of Syria is territory in dispute. He might invade at any moment."

"But we must have protection, and Captain Floden refuses to see reason."

"All I can suggest is that you appeal to Ptolemy. Or, if he is still in charge, Laomedon."

It went on like that with Rabbi Benyamin Abrahamson and Reverend Laurence Hewell trying to gain her support, and Hewell being insulting of her religion in the process. He knew little of Zoroastrianism and almost as little of the Greek pantheon, so he condemned both as superstitious twaddle while proclaiming the fables about his carpenter's son being the king of heaven as absolute truth. Roxane was raised at court and schooled in diplomacy and keeping her own counsel from an early age. She declined to dispute with him on the subject and let him believe her overawed by his arguments. All the while, she wondered what Ptolemy or Laomedon would do with him should they get control of him.

That was a serious concern. Hewell had what the ship people called a BS degree in Pastoral Ministries. It had not apparently focused on electronics or steam power generation, but it was a college-level education, so the man had to have learned something, even if Roxane hadn't yet seen any evidence of it. No, that wasn't true. The man could move a crowd and he could be very persuasive among his followers. His church had twenty-three members, most of whom were in their forties or fifties, generally with some education and quite a bit of experience at jobs like plumber or electrician. Those followers, and perhaps even Hewell himself, would be a valuable source of ship people knowledge. Whoever got control of them.

Roxane was convinced that if they continued on "their mission," they would all be slaves within a few months, whether their master would be Laomedon, Ptolemy or some Jewish merchant or priest. And that thought didn't bother her. Not at all.

Jerusalem
April 17

Laomedon looked across the floor at Ptolemy's agent and felt rage and caution at war within his heart. He had read the butterfly book. He knew that in that other history, after he refused to sell the satrapy to Ptolemy, the bastard just stole it. Laomedon was caught, and he knew it. And what was worse, he was almost certain that Ptolemy was offering less this time around than he had in that other history.

Forcing himself, he nodded stiffly.

"A wise decision, Satrap," said the envoy, and then went into details of how the money was going to be delivered.

Ptolemy now owned Syria, a Syria that included the two kingdoms of Judea and Israel. And, just as in that other history, he got it without spilling a drop of blood. Laomedon proved cheaper to bribe than the Pharisees of the Second Temple.

Alexandria
April 20

Ptolemy read the report and called for Eudemus. Ptolemy was quite sure that Judea and Israel were important to the ship people, even if he couldn't keep track of their ridiculous beliefs.

When Eudemus arrived, he waved the man to a chair and said, "Tell me about the ship people's religion."

"Actually it's religions, Satrap. There are three major ones, all of them related. Judaism, Christianity, and Islam. We think that Judaism is the most important of them, but that could be the bias of the priest of that religion who was doing most of the questioning about our religions. He was a Jew, and was asking one of Atum's guards about Judaism. According to the guard they are all—even the ship people's Judaism—nothing more than heresies of true Judaism. Aside from those big three, there are Buddhist, Wiccan, Hindu, Baha'i—which may be another heresy of Judaism."

"Why are there so many versions of Judaism running around? Did the Jews rise up and conquer the world the way they are always claiming they will?"

"Rather the opposite, if I have put it together right. What happened was they were totally defeated and scattered to the winds, but kept to their beliefs. Then those beliefs were picked up by others and adopted. There is something appealing about having one great and powerful god that you can blame everything on. Apparently, they think that after you die, he judges you and the ones that believe in him have wine, women, and song for all eternity. The ones that don't believe are thrown into a fiery pit, also for all eternity."

Ptolemy snorted, and Eudemus shrugged. "For whatever reason, it became accepted. Or they became accepted, I should say. Some of the reports claim that one sect—I think it's the

Christians—insist on blowing themselves up to punish the unbelievers. But why the sudden interest?"

"I have just gained Syria, and I understand that Jerusalem is of importance to them."

"Yes, important, but I think the Christians revere Mecca even more."

"Where's Mecca?"

"I have no idea. Maybe near Jerusalem or Bethlehem."

"Bethlehem?"

"The birthplace of Muhammad."

Ptolemy shook his head. "Never mind for now. But we are going to need to understand the ship people's superstitions if we are to deal effectively with them. Try and get a clearer understanding. The reason I asked was that we made a deal with Laomedon, so we own Syria, and that means we control the Jews and their temple. Can we use that to tempt some of the ship people to our service?"

"It might well work," Eudemus said. "And that could be vitally important. You know that they don't have slaves?" Eudemus' voice had taken on a cautious note, as though he knew what he said sounded ridiculous, and Ptolemy nodded.

It was ridiculous, but from everything that Ptolemy had seen it was also true. "They have machines that are magical in their effect. That was how they explained it, and it appears to be true."

"Yes. They can wind thread and do unimaginable things without human labor, or at least with very limited labor. The nation that gains that knowledge will be the richest nation on Earth. And some of that knowledge is in the minds of the most menial of their sailors."

"Find me a way to acquire some ship people. But under no circumstances anger the ship people on the ship in the doing of it. I saw those steam cannons in action. That ship could destroy Alexandria and never come within range of our most powerful ballista."

"We can make a steam cannon," Eudemus said. Then visibly stopped himself. "That is, we are fairly sure that we will be able to soon." More hesitation. "Soon means within a few years, not a few days."

"Fine. Then all we need concern ourselves with is what the *Queen of the Sea* will do between now and a few years from now."

Queen of the Sea, *Straits of Gibraltar*
April 20

Dag sat down in Roxane's suite and a waiter brought a tray of rock crab from Trinidad. There was also fresh baked bread and tubers that were clearly relatives of potatoes, but different. They had a brown flesh and an almost nutty taste, almost sweet, but not quite. It was a variety that the Tupky grew on their river.

"How goes the conversion?" Roxane asked.

"It's ongoing," Dag groused, then tried to clarify. "The forges and machine shops have been moved to decks five and six inboard, but we are keeping the outboard cabins."

They'd started even before heading for Trinidad, and in the months spent in Trinidad they had converted about a quarter of the staterooms on the *Queen* into factories for the production of all sorts of stuff. And the process was ongoing.

The *Queen* was actually a decent industrial base. It had lots of electricity and lots of wiring to get that electricity to wherever it was needed. They could run saws, induction furnaces, centrifuges and electrolytic conversion plants all perfectly well. What they couldn't do was export any of those industries to the rest of the world.

"And you can't install the factories in Bactria?" Roxane asked again.

Dag grimaced. "I'm not dissembling. Yes, we can make a saw or a spinning wheel, even a spinning jenny or a carding machine. But those are eighteenth-century industries. Sometimes sixteenth- or fifteenth-century industries. They aren't the twenty-first-century industries that we can do on the *Queen*. Even on the *Queen*, we can't make integrated circuits or microelectronics in general. And a bunch of the really high-end stuff, like artificial materials and genetic engineering, is beyond us."

"Don't ask Ahura Mazda for still more aid after the aid the world has gotten in the *Queen of the Sea*. A spinning jenny and a carding machine allow a few women to do the work of a hundred."

"Right," Dag said, "don't ask for butter on your popcorn."

"We have plenty of butter. Did you want popcorn?" Roxane sounded confused, and Dag explained. Roxane had done an excellent job of learning English in the months on Trinidad, and Dag hadn't done all that badly with Greek either, in spite of the fact that they had both been learning the languages of the natives of Trinidad at the same time. And it was languages; there were three on the island, plus Tupky. In spite of that—or maybe because of it—English was becoming the *lingua franca* of the island of Trinidad. But in spite of all that, they could both get tripped up by idioms.

"Yes," Roxane agreed with a warm smile after he had explained. "Popcorn is good, even without butter. And even without electricity, spinning wheels and steam-powered lathes and looms will change the world. But after Alexander took Persia and emptied out the thresher houses, there was what your economists call inflation. Prices for everything went up. They are still high, but they have been dropping in the last couple of years. One of the passengers, a Mr. Jack Carroll, is an amateur economist and says that what is happening is that the economy is catching up with the money supply. I had just assumed that the silver was finding its way back into the vaults of the satraps."

"It's probably some of both," Dag agreed. "But what's your point?"

"I'm not sure. But what will be the effect of your saws and lathes and spinning wheels? Also the plows and reapers and the milling machine for the wheat. What will those things do to the cost of cloth and the cost of bread?"

"Not to mention the quality of bread," Dag agreed, holding up a roll. It wasn't a new question. It had been discussed before and no consensus had been reached. Well, one reason was that the ship had its own money, called ship credit, that was recorded in the ship's computers, and Eleanor Kinney determined how much ship credit she would give for so much silver, gold or latex. "I don't know, but I know that the captain hopes it will eventually put an end to slavery."

There was a tightening of Roxane's mouth. The queen of Alexander's empire wasn't an abolitionist. In fact, aside from some Stoics in Athens, the only abolitionists on Earth seemed to have arrived on the ship. Even the Stoics more trivialized slavery than opposed it. Roxane had managed to restore peace after the Silver Shields' attempt to take the ship by, in essence, buying the slaves from the Silver Shields so that she took the loss, then by pleading their case before Captain Floden. She still hadn't quite forgiven Dag for not warning her of the problem before they had brought her retainers and their families and slaves aboard. But she didn't say anything. She knew that this wasn't something that any of the ship people would give on.

Dag knew slavery was wrong. Knew it with a bone-deep certainty that made it difficult for him to see how she could fail to understand the evil in it. Slavery was theft. Theft of the labor and the liberty of the slave. But the truth was that Roxane didn't see much wrong with theft either. It was what armies did when they conquered new territory, after all. And that was what her late husband had been all about. Morality at this point in the history of the world really was something that was only applied sporadically.

Slavery was one of the issues that they avoided talking about. Dag changed the subject to the schedule of stops in the Mediterranean. "We think a week in Alexandria should be enough. We mentioned the possibility of a university at sea to Dinocrates before we left, so there may be some students coming aboard."

"I know the *Queen* is not carrying nearly so many passengers, but do you think that Eleanor will be able to buy enough food for the cruise in just seven days?"

"If she can't, we will just be eating a lot of tuna steaks and potatoes. We're carrying enough food for two months, and we'll be back in Trinidad before we run out."

"Assuming there are no delays at the other stops," Roxane said. "I still don't see why you insist on going to Rome. Carthage makes some sense, but the Romans are barbarians."

"Even worse, Samnium," Dag grinned. "We are planning a day in Salerno, well, what will become Salerno, and another in what will be Naples. Both of which are part of Samnium at this time."

"All Italians are barbarians," Roxane agreed. "I will grant you that in a couple of hundred years Rome might become civilized, but at the moment it's a bunch of farmers without much to trade. I'd rather deal with the Tupky."

"They have iron and are just a bit of knowledge and practice away from steel," Dag disagreed. "They are working on aqueducts and good roads."

"The Tupky have steel now, or will by the time we get back. They live on a river, so have less need of roads and aqueducts. Their knot writing is different from Greek writing, but in some ways it's superior. All the Romans have, they got from the Greeks, who stole it from the Persians."

"Rome gave the world pizza," Dag proclaimed, one finger pointing to the ceiling, then started laughing.

They were both uncertain about how well the goods they were carrying would sell. Latex from South America was potentially very useful for things like rubber tires on wheels, but would the locals see the value?

CHAPTER 20

Alexandria Harbor
April 24

The lookout spotted the *Queen* over an hour before she sailed into Alexandria harbor, and the galleys were waiting, but making it very clear with white flags that they had peaceful intent. The notion that the ship people considered the white flag a sign of parley was promulgated by the library and everyone was making sure to use it.

Atum Edfu was not first to board the *Queen*. That was Dinocrates' privilege, as the representative of Ptolemy, Satrap of Egypt and Syria.

"So he got Syria in this history as well as the other," Roxane said as Dinocrates bowed. "Did he wait until the Jewish holy day?"

Dinocrates stood back up and smiled. "No. Having read the butterfly book, Laomedon agreed that resigning his post in favor of Ptolemy was his wisest course. I understand several talents of gold changed hands, but everyone is being quiet about how many."

Jane Carruthers waved them to the elevators, and they chatted as the next group came aboard.

Ten minutes later, seated in the Royal Lounge with sweet potato fries and a glass of wine, Dinocrates got down to business. "Satrap Ptolemy wishes to hire ship people to work in the Library of Alexandria and to consult on the opening of a route from the Mediterranean to the Red Sea."

Roxane nodded. "I think Ptolemy may be able to find employees for that, but you need to know something. When my Silver Shields came aboard the *Queen* with their wives, concubines, and slaves, the slaves were emancipated by the ship people. I ended up having to compensate my bodyguards for the loss of their chattel, because the ship people flatly refused to. It's possible that once away from the ship, some of them will develop a more reasonable attitude, but I wouldn't count on it. Their opposition to slavery is fanatical. You will do better to use hired employees, people who are at least technically freed of bondage, as their servants and supports."

"Is it really that bad?" Dinocrates asked, more curious than offended. "I knew that they were opposed to it. There is a section in the butterfly book that condemns the practice. But it doesn't offer much in the way of how we are to manage without slaves. Someone has to chop the wood and empty the chamber pots. How is a man to get any work done if he spends all his time on menial chores?"

"They have devices…" Roxane started to explain, then stopped herself. There was a great deal to explain about how the ship people's society worked, and there was no way she could get to it all now. "Never mind all that. What is the situation now? Where are Eurydice and Philip?"

"In a small fishing village on the Aegean coast, called Mugla. They are still in Antigonus' custody and Eumenes seems satisfied to leave them there. He's busy up north trying to bring order to chaos. Meanwhile, the Greek city states are declaring independence in droves."

"It's all coming apart," Roxane said sadly. "Even faster in this history than in the other."

They discussed the political situation and Dinocrates offered to let Roxane move into Alexandria. She politely declined. Then they talked about the role of the *Queen*.

"It's what they call a university," Roxane said. "Or a college, like Socrates or Aristotle set up, but more formal, to teach people science and law—whatever they want to learn. They will charge tuition and a fee for living on board. But remember what I said about slavery. There is no slavery on the *Queen of the Sea*. Any slave brought aboard is free the moment its foot hits the deck."

"I can't imagine that you can learn much if you're spending all your time cleaning your clothing," Dinocrates repeated the complaint he had voiced before. "Besides, who would go to their school with such a restriction?"

"There are employees who work for the ship. Or you can hire people to do the necessary chores. But don't worry about emptying chamber pots. Their toilets..."

"I remember," Dinocrates agreed.

Just then a waiter brought in a cart with a variety of cakes on it. They were served and Roxane thanked the waiter as he left. "It's not that they don't have servants, but the servants are free to leave and seek other work if they choose to."

Atum Edfu got aboard and was reintroduced to Eleanor Kinney, the chief purser. "Eleanor, dear lady, how badly are you going to cheat me this time? I warn you, our smiths are producing good steel now, so I have little interest in your steel knives."

That was a lie. The smiths of Alexandria, armed with the knowledge the ship people had let drop, were making steel. But it wasn't good steel, not nearly as good as the steel of the ship people. And it cost a fortune. Slaves were cheap, but they had to be fed. And pumping a bellows to force air into melted iron to remove the carbon was not work for weaklings.

"That's fine then," Eleanor said. "We'll keep our steel knives for sale at Rhodes. We have plenty of silver, and even quite a bit of gold that we got across the Atlantic." Eleanor was using the translation app. She was finding Macedonian Greek difficult to master. And besides, the delays as the app translated gave her time to think.

"Still," she continued after the app translated, "you might want to have a snack before we get down to business. Here we have Trinidadian tuna salad and corn chips. The bowls are made from processed latex."

She dropped an empty bowl on the floor and it bounced.

"Woman, I must bring my wife to protect me. Your beauty blinds me and I can't bargain fairly," Atum complained mournfully.

Alexandria Harbor
April 26

"How are we doing, Eleanor?" Captain Floden asked.

Eleanor had been smiling from the moment she entered his office. "Unbelievable, sir. It's a feeding frenzy out there. While we were gone, the stuff we sold last time—including the stuff we made, what little there was of it—has been being passed around and gotten more expensive with each trade. Those steel knives especially. They hold an edge like nothing these people have. So they were waiting for us when we got here, with goods ready to sell and silver to buy. Then they saw the stuff we brought from Trinidad, the new foods and the latex. Also the llama wool and dyes. It was all new and the feeding frenzy pushed the prices of the South American goods higher than I ever thought possible."

"So, our silver supply?" Captain Floden waved her to one of the leather arm chairs.

"I think we're ready, sir." Eleanor sat down, then passed her slate computer over to the captain.

"This soon?" Captain Floden asked, glancing at the spreadsheet displayed on the computer screen, then handing it back.

"Yes, sir."

While Marie Easley was studying Alexandrian-era politics with Roxane, and Dag and others were learning how to make steam cannons and steel, Eleanor was studying money. She, in cooperation with President Wiley and Captain Floden, came up with a silver-backed partial-reserve money. The ship was one of the two reserves.

The paper money was a way for the ship to issue more money than they had silver, without adulterating the silver with copper. But to do that, they first needed to make sure that they had plenty of silver. It was only partly about making sure that the ship had enough money to cover its expenses. It was also about making sure that there was a consistent money for them to use in dealing with other people. Something they could set prices in, for things like tuition and room and board on the ships while studying.

The machine shops had made up the plates, but they weren't going to start printing the money till they were sure that there was enough silver.

"We're ready," Eleanor repeated.

"And the university?" Captain Floden asked, leaning back in his chair.

"We're ready there too, Captain. We have a faculty for electronics, for modern English, for steam power, basic metallurgy, medical stuff, and we have the layout of the Advancement of Civilization course." That was the "seeds of liberty" course they developed to try to convince the locals that slavery was a bad thing, that it was evil in its nature. The course also argued that it was no longer a necessary evil, because of the knowledge and technology that the *Queen* brought with her. They all knew that it was going to be a hard sell. Even getting the local slave owners to realize that it was evil was proving a lot harder than any of them expected.

Mugla
April 29

"The ship people are back," Trajan reported. "The news just came over the signal fire network."

"Does Antigonus know?" Eurydice asked.

"He's probably being told right now."

Eurydice had spent the winter and early spring in this little fishing village writing letters and trying to judge the situation. The kings of the far eastern edge of Alexander's empire declared independence, and the satraps of the eastern empire were busy trying to bring them to heel, with mixed success. Babylon was given, by her, under Antigonus' instruction, to Seleucus, then to Cassander's little brother, Philip. Who, in Eurydice's view, couldn't pour wine out of an amphora without guidance. Roxane, in her proclamation, gave Babylon to Peucestas, who wasn't much better. The arrogant bastard wasn't someone Eurydice would want at her back with a dagger, anyway.

By now this stinking little village had just about driven Eurydice insane, and Antigonus was nearly ready to deliver her head to Olympias, dumping the rest of her body, and Philip's, in the bay.

"Can we get loose?" she asked.

"Possibly. But to go where?"

It seemed that Trajan was always asking that question. Every time she asked about escape, he came back with "to where?" Now, though, Eurydice thought she might have an answer. "To the ship. The *Queen of the Sea*."

"Can we trust them?"

"We'll know soon. If Roxane is well, then we can probably trust them. If she is dead or held against her will, then we must look elsewhere for our escape."

Royal Lounge, Queen of the Sea
April 29

"So, Eudemus, who do you plan to send to the university?" Roxane asked once he was seated on the couch. She waved at a waiter, who brought good Egyptian beer and potato chips.

"Would that I could attend myself. Unfortunately, my duties prevent me. There is still the issue of personal servants." Eudemus looked at the chips curiously, and Roxane demonstrated. They were ridged potato chips and there was a cassava-based dip on the tray.

He tried it and Roxane looked at him, trying not to show how much she sympathized with his complaint. The *Queen of the Sea* university was opening for students and would be making a tour of the Mediterranean, picking up more students. Then it would go back to Trinidad and then come back here, on a set schedule. The whole trip would take three months and would constitute one semester, at a fixed rate that included food, lodging, and training in two subjects. All of that was fine and acceptable to Eudemus and the scholars, especially after they saw the rooms and the other facilities. This was still a luxury cruise liner, after all. But almost to a man, the scholars expected to bring at least one slave with them on the trip.

Captain Floden made it clear, though. Once a slave set foot on the *Queen*, he or she was no longer a slave and would be allowed to leave the ship anywhere they chose.

That had forced a question to the front of the minds of the scholars. Would their slaves, their personal servants, remain loyal if they had the option of leaving? That question ate at them.

It ate at the slaves too, the idea that there was another option than slave or master. They wanted the question to go away. Roxane wanted the question to go away. One of her servants stayed in Trinidad. Another stayed with her on the ship and was her employee, who received pay every week out of Roxane's account.

Neither the slaves nor the masters knew how to approach the idea of liberty. But the slaves were starting to adapt to the notion a lot faster than the masters were.

And that was a truly scary thought.

"They are firm, Eudemus. They will not budge on this and only the knowledge of how few they are prevents them from putting every city within the range of their guns to rubble until the practice of slavery is abandoned."

"Monstrous," Eudemus said, and Roxane was tempted to agree. As fond as she had grown of Dag and as much as she respected Marie Easley and Jane Carruthers, she found some of their attitudes deeply offensive.

They got back to business. "I'm sending Crates of Olynthian. Most of the work on the sewage system is done and he wants to study refining techniques. You know he works with mines as well as sewers. Also a young scholar called Epicurus of Samos."

"Samos? I would have thought Athens." Roxane said.

Eudemus looked at her curiously. "In fact, his parents are Athenian and were thrown out of Samos when Athens lost the island. Epicurus was doing his two years military service to Athens when his parents had to move to Colophon. He had just joined them there when Satrap Ptolemy called for scholars to come to Alexandria and form a library."

"It almost has to be him," Roxane muttered. At Eudemus look, which had gone from curious to irritated, she explained. "There is an Epicurus who is the founder of the Epicurean philosophy. The Wikipedia has more on him than it does on me."

"Well, I hope it's not the same one. He's irritating and opinionated. Half the reason I'm sending him is to get him away from me."

"Who else?"

He named three more scholars, none of whom had survived the weaning of history. Then said, "Ptolemy is sending Thaïs and his children on the trip."

"Why?" Roxane asked, though she could make a good guess. Ptolemy was keeping his options open. He hadn't married Thaïs or made any of the children legitimate, but he had apparently decided to provide them with an education and get them out of the way while he negotiated with the other satraps.

Eudemus just shrugged. And Roxane gathered up the notes and documents and went to see Jane Carruthers.

Jane waved her into her office and Roxane gave her the notes.

"There are twenty-three scholars who have raised the tuition money on their own," Jane said. "Also about forty regular passengers who just want to make the trip in comfort."

"Has everyone..." Roxane started.

"Yes, everyone has been told that there is no slavery on the *Queen* and that even former slaves will have to have their passage paid before boarding. Oh, Atum is sending his son, Aristotle Edfu."

"Where? To the university?"

"No. As trader aboard for about twenty tons of cargo. It's partly seeds and partly sample goods that Atum wants to see if there is a market for in Trinidad. He's not the only one. Three other Alexandrian merchant houses are sending merchants aboard to look after their cargos. Aristotle is going to be studying ship people business and banking. I think that Atum wants to be Ptolemy's bank."

"Thaïs would be a better choice."

"Oh." There was a lot less warmth in Jane Carruthers' voice. "What do you know about Ptolemy's hooker friend?"

"Don't underestimate her. Jane, I don't really understand how you people did things back in your world, but a hetaera is the only class of women who can own their own property and sign their own contracts in this world. Or at least in the Greek states, including Macedonia. Granted, Egyptian women have more rights. As for Thaïs, she has been with Ptolemy for twelve years and has three children by him. Alexander liked to have her around because she is one of the smartest people there is." Roxane waited while the ship woman worked it out.

"In a way," Jane said consideringly, "it may not be all that different in our world, but we are a lot less open about it. And most of the people in the world, including me, are still prone to think in Victorian terms. Momma didn't approve of such women, so neither should I. Add in the burning of the palace, and you get my reaction."

"That wasn't Thaïs' fault. They were all very drunk that night. Besides, it was Alexander's idea to burn the place. Thaïs was just telling stories, which was part of her job."

Thaïs manumitted her slave Delphinia as soon as she learned of the ship people's strange notion. Delphinia had been thankful, but concerned about how she would live. "Why, I'll hire you to take care of the children." So when Thaïs and her family boarded the *Queen* with Delphinia in tow, there was no problem. They had a suite, two rooms. And though it was cramped by land standards, it was gloriously roomy by any standards of sea travel Thaïs had ever imagined. She was looking forward to the voyage, though she was more concerned than she liked to admit about what Ptolemy would do in her absence.

She bowed politely to Roxane as she entered the queen's suite. "It's good to see you, Your Highness. How have you been?"

"Well, very well. At least since Dag rescued me from the generals."

"I know. Isn't it horrible? They were all so loyal before Alexander died, but now it's all this mad quest for empire."

Roxane lifted an eyebrow at that, and Thaïs laughed. "Well, they were loyal. They might not have always wanted to be, but they were. At least mostly. Your husband was all that held the empire together. Now it's his name and, of course, you and your son." She watched Roxane carefully to see how she would respond.

"Philip and Eurydice," Roxane said quickly. "Don't put all the burden on us."

"I'm surprised," Thaïs said, and she was. There hadn't been any love lost between Roxane and Eurydice, not that she had ever heard of. "I had thought you had been forced, or at least encouraged, to include Eurydice and Philip in your proclamation."

"I was, sort of. Marie Easley, who studied this time, pointed out the advantages. But even in Triparadisus, I would have been willing enough to share the burden with Eurydice, if I had been able to trust her."

"So why trust her now?"

Roxane laughed. "Because she can't get at me. It's a gesture of trust that helps her, and doesn't endanger me. As long as I stay on this ship or in my embassy in Trinidad, I am safe from them all. But enough about me. Tell me, why has Ptolemy packed you and the children off like this?"

Thaïs would have liked to have heard about the embassy in Trinidad, and she didn't particularly want to talk about the effect independence had on Ptolemy. He had been negotiating with Antipater before Triparadisus on the subject of putting her aside to marry one of Antipater's daughters. And he was still looking for a royal wife. Thaïs was a hetaera and though she could keep the company of kings, she could never be a queen. She had been born a slave, sold to a school and worked her way up. She sympathized with the ship people's dislike of slavery, though she couldn't imagine how society would work without it. She sighed. "Ptolemy enjoys me, but he has become obsessed with the potential to become Alexander. Or, at the very least, pharaoh of Egypt and Syria. So he is looking for a wife who will buy him the support of one of the other generals."

"Do you think he will try for the empire?"

"Not as long as Alexander or Philip is alive. He is too careful for that. And I don't think he will try to do anything to you. He truly loved Alexander, and for Alexander's sake wouldn't murder you or Philip."

"But he wouldn't cry at our funerals," Roxane said with some bitterness.

"No. He would cry, and real tears. But he would be calculating his chances even as he wept." *It was the relief,* Thaïs decided. The relief at not having to watch every word that had made her so free with her speech. That, and she was more angry at Ptolemy than she had realized.

"Well, you will enjoy the ship." Roxane changed the subject, to Thaïs' relief. "It truly is a school, and there is a great deal to learn."

They talked then about the *Queen of the Sea* university, and the courses available on it. Then about the schedule of the trip. "From here, we go to Pelusium, just a short stop to see what is available over the trade route from the Red Sea. Then on to Ashdod."

"So I heard. Ptolemy is anxious to get the ship people situated there. He's sending documents to guarantee their safety and support."

Roxane nodded. "So I heard as well. Reverend Hewell took it as a sign that God favored their endeavor. Along with Hewell's church, there will be Rabbi Benyamin Abrahamson, his family, and a small community of Jews, seven in all."

"Why so few?"

"There aren't as many Jews as there are Christians on the ship. In fact, there are even more Muslims than Jews, though the Muslims are mostly in the crew. There were about a hundred Jews on the ship, and most of them stayed in Fort Plymouth. A lot of them were pretty secular. Others are going to be teachers at the university."

"Secular?"

"Jewish by birth, but not religious."

"And the Muslims and Christians?"

"They believe in one god and that it is the same god. But they argue about what that god wants." Roxane held up a hand and shook her head. "There will be a course in Comparative Religion, if you're interested. Personally, I find it all very confusing and not very important."

"What is important then?"

Roxane stopped and examined her fingernails. "The electricity and the steam. The machines and the treatments for illness. And something more, I think. Hope, as Pandora released from her box, but bigger and more."

Thaïs took a moment to think about that, then changed the subject. There would be time to make her own judgments. "After Ashdod?"

"Cyprus, then Rhodes," Roxane said. "After Rhodes, up the coast of Anatolia with several stops, then to Macedonia and back down to Athens. It's all been published in the schedule."

"I've read it, but it seems awfully fast."

"No, not really. This ship isn't just bigger than anything else on the ocean. It's faster."

"Could you stop at Mugla?" Thaïs asked. "Pick up Eurydice and Philip?"

"I asked, but it probably won't happen. First, because the captain is nervous about the depth of the water in the area, but mostly because if we go to Mugla, Antigonus is likely to do something desperate. Certainly, he will take Eurydice and Philip away from the shore."

"Don't underestimate Antigonus, Roxane. He may have lost a couple of battles, but most of the Macedonian generals despise Eumenes, whatever your book says about him. Because of what your book says about him, and how it disparages them, Antigonus is getting support from a lot of important people."

"Ptolemy?"

"Not officially, but yes. Ptolemy has sent him money. He doesn't want Eumenes trying to impose Philip or your son on him as his new lord."

"There are several issues about radios," Chief Radio Officer Joshua Varner said. That was certainly true, but he wasn't going to be mentioning any of them besides the technical ones. And those he was going to be exaggerating or distorting almost to the point of outright lying. There were a whole host of political factors involved in leaving a radio station in Alexandria or anywhere else in the Med. They must either give the basic technology to the locals or leave someone there to manage the radio system.

Neither Captain Floden nor Congressman Wiley was willing to do either of those things. Not yet, anyway.

The radio itself wasn't that hard. A tube from a microwave could be used, and so could integrated circuits scavenged from any number of places. There were all the phones and slate computers on the ship, each one of which could be hooked into a downstream signal amplifier to produce a radio that with atmospheric bounce and digital signal enhancement could reach a great distance with decent consistency. For that matter, with the sort of vacuum pumps available on the *Queen* and their knowledge of how radio worked, they could build radios from scratch. They would still need some computerization for frequency tweaking to match the changing atmospheric conditions, if they wanted to get signals from the other side of the world. There just wasn't any major technological barrier to putting a radio station in Alexandria or another major port on in the Med.

"Radio waves travel in straight lines and the surface of the earth is not flat," he said to his assembled audience.

The statement was true, in and of itself—and never mind the fact that radio waves could be bounced off the ionosphere. That was a *different* fact. Which was not crying out to be blabbed in public.

"Also the signal strength diminishes at the cube of the distance," he added. He saw no need to mention that that depended on the shape of the antenna.

Dinocrates asked him questions, and so did the other philosophers. Joshua never actually lied. Mostly because the philosophers didn't know enough to ask the right questions.

At best, though, this was a stopgap measure. Joshua wasn't one of those morons who thought that because people of the ancient world were ignorant, they were stupid. Whatever he might or might not know—yet—Dinocrates had been remembered more than two thousand years after he died. What were the odds that he wasn't as smart as a twenty-first century radio specialist?

About as bad as the odds he would hit the progressive slots in the casino seven times in a row, Joshua figured. They'd be lucky if this subterfuge lasted half a year.

CHAPTER 21

Royal Lounge, **Queen of the Sea,** *Pelusium*
May 1

Thaïs looked at the city sitting between the beach and the swamps. They'd left Alexandria as the sun was rising and here it was only just after noon, and they were looking at the fortified city of Pelusium. She sat with Roxane and Marie Easley in the Royal Lounge, drinking some not very good wine and eating some decent cheese, while looking out at the fortified city.

"Will you tell me about Olympias?" Marie asked as they watched the boat head for the Pelusium docks.

"Must we?" Thaïs complained. "Why spoil a lovely day? Kiril is on that boat along with Roxane's Dag. On their way to buy up all the linen in Pelusium in exchange for a few spinning jennies, and a couple of your new looms with the flying shuttles. The sun is hot but the air conditioning is cool, and if the wine is so-so, the cheese is tasty."

"Dag is not..." Roxane started, only to receive rather condescending looks from both older women. She quickly changed the subject. "Kiril will be delivering Satrap Ptolemy's letters of authorization, and Atum's son, Aristotle, will be buying spices from the Red Sea traders."

"Why are you both so reticent when it comes to talking about Olympias?" Marie asked.

"We're not. It's just that stories of ghosts, ghouls, and Olympias should be told on a dark night when you're very, very drunk. Just before you burn down a palace," Thaïs said.

"Did Olympias..." Marie started, and Roxane laughed as Thaïs held up an hand and protested.

"I honestly don't remember. But we were all very drunk, and Alexander had a strange relationship with his mother. He loved her dearly, but by preference he loved her from a distance. And Olympias didn't like anything Persian, so burning the Palace of Persepolis probably would have pleased her." Thaïs looked over at Roxane and smiled a bit sadly. "Your husband ruled the world with whims. He ruled us all with his whims. Ptolemy would have followed him anywhere. He had something about him...maybe he *was* Zeus' bastard. I wouldn't put it past Olympias. All in all, I like your Dag better. He's a serious boy, and he cares about people deeply. Alexander's passions ran hot, but not deep."

"I know. Alexander was always the tiger lashing his tail and baring his teeth. But he was so smart, he could see through people."

"What about Philip II?" Marie asked.

"In a way, he was more like Ptolemy than Alexander. King Philip was a plodder. A careful general, except that Olympias could always get under his skin."

"Is there any truth to the reports that Ptolemy is Philip's son?"

"No, none. The 'reports,' as you call them haven't really started yet. Some of Ptolemy's advisers are suggesting that he float that as justification for declaring himself pharaoh, but so far Ptolemy is unwilling to do it. He loved his father, even if they had all the normal father-son conflicts."

They talked about the other generals and their wives, and Alexander's moving the court before his death in Babylon. They discussed the partition at Babylon and explained to Marie that Ptolemy's role was less than history recorded. "Perdiccas had the ring, and Alexander had given it to him," Roxane said, and Thaïs nodded.

"Ptolemy would have followed Alexander, like I said, but he didn't want to," Thaïs said. "We were all tired of it by then, all except Alexander."

By the time they finished talking, the boat was on its way back. And four more were headed in to load up on Egyptian linen. They left for Ashdod as the sun set and were there by morning.

Ashdod
May 2

"It really ought to be April first," Dag muttered as the religious emigrants offloaded. Kiril was watching them like a farmer watches his chickens. Looking forward to lots of eggs and an eventual stew pot.

An older woman, Christine Boonie, walked down the ramp to look at the small town, nodded sharply, and marched down the dock toward the town. She was pulling a wheeled suitcase behind her, and Dag knew that it now contained books on medical procedures and homeopathic remedies. Christine, a devout Christian, had spent thirty years as a nurse's aide in hospitals and old folks' homes. She was now the closest thing to a twenty-first-century doctor in Ashdod. The rest of the religious emigrants were heading up the docks, now mostly with local Jews leading them. And with a great number of gestures and a lot of confusion.

Kiril reached out a hand to Dag. "I'll be back in a few hours. Don't leave without me." He spoke in Greek and now Dag could follow his comments without the translation app.

"Well, hurry up. The captain wants to be in Tyre tomorrow morning."

"I'll be back by dawn, I promise." Tyre was barely thirty knots away. An hour and a half would see them there.

Dag wandered along the docks with an escort of two Silver Shields. They carried their shields, which had been polished and then lacquered, and they also carried the traditional Greek *kopis* and wore polished armor. Dag carried one of the ship's pistols in his belt, and was under orders not to fire it unless absolutely necessary.

This was a rare day off for Dag. It was turning out that the environmental officer had a lot to do when industry and residence were all on the same ship. The gases and fumes from chemical processing had to be gotten away from the passengers. A new smoke stack had been added near the stern of the ship, which worked fine while the ship was underway, but not so well in dock or at anchor. Though, at anchor, they could mostly put the stern downwind. Plus Dag had his duties as the commander of this contingent of the Silver Shields.

Dag put away thoughts of his jobs and looked around the food sellers' carts to see what was on offer. There was less variety than would have been seen in the twenty-first century, but more than he had been expecting.

Panos Katsaros headed for the nearest brothel, as was his habit. And, as was custom since The Event, he was followed by a group of the crew. After this amount of time, some of them spoke Greek, but none of them spoke it well. Panos had managed to parlay his skill at parlaying into getting the other guys to pay for his entertainment.

What he didn't know was that a Greek soldier had been sent ahead to the brothel to make sure that things went well and to encourage the girls to question Panos and the others about anything they could find out. The girls, and their pimps, would make more from reporting on Panos' discussion than they made from Panos directly, and the ship people were overpaying in the first place.

Tyre
May 3

Nedelko met the boat in person, and was just as happy to see that Evgenij was still beside the big Gaul. "So, how are the ship people?" he asked.

"Crazy to a man. They have outlawed slavery. I think they plan on outlawing sex next."

"No," said the big Gaul. "Sex is natural."

"You've been learning," Nedelko said. Then he pulled a small clay jar from his cloak. "So have—" He stopped speaking and moving. He almost stopped breathing at the reaction. Evgenij had his crossbow pointed at Nedelko. The big Gaul had a little thing pointed just as unerringly. "I was simply pointing out that we had been learning too." Very carefully, Nedelko put the jar away.

"How did you figure out the formula?" Dag asked.

"Trial and error. With one of the errors blowing up several buildings. We have the powder plant out of town now." Nedelko wasn't going to explain about buying the formula. Tyre might want to buy more information from Keith Seiver.

Roxane didn't accompany them. For this first trip, at least, Roxane and little Alexander were staying on the ship. Well, mostly. She did take one of the boats in and sail along the dock, waving at the crowd. She had done the same at Alexandria and

Ashdod. But she was being very careful not to put herself or her son anywhere they might be grabbed by any local potentate. She wondered how Eurydice was doing in Mugla.

Mugla
May 4

"The packet boat from Rhodes was carrying the ship people's schedule," Trajan told Eurydice. "I got it from Niko, Antigonus' clerk. They are making a loop around the sea, then going back to the colony they set up on the other side of the world."

"Roxane?"

"She was seen and so was King Alexander, but they didn't leave the ship. No one is sure whether that's because they didn't trust Ptolemy or because they weren't allowed to."

Another guard came in and Trajan shut up. The Shields in her guard were paid by Antigonus, and some of them reported anything she said to him. This was one of his spies, Jovan. "The general wants to see you," Jovan said.

"The *Queen of the Sea* will be passing near here with the false king," Antigonus said. "For your safety, we are moving you and Philip inland for the next few days."

"I take it that is from the boat that just arrived." The boat Eurydice spoke of was a small thirty-foot lateen-rigged sailboat with only four oars on a side, and those not used save in harbor or in dead calm. The rig had been changed since the *Queen of the Sea* visited Rhodes the first time, and the boat was faster than before.

"Yes. They announced their schedule to the world. They don't appear to be concerned about pirates." Antigonus sounded annoyed.

Eurydice laughed. "I wouldn't be concerned with pirates either, if I owned such a ship."

"Then you're as much a fool as they are," Antigonus said. "Any ship can be taken or destroyed if need be."

He sounded even more irritated as he said that, which Eurydice took to mean that Antigonus hadn't figured out a way to take the *Queen of the Sea*. Eurydice was starting to wonder if these great generals of Alexander's were so great after all. Yes, Alexander had conquered half the world with them, but without Alexander to do their thinking for them, it seemed they couldn't accomplish anything.

Eurydice was not modest. In fact, she was about as arrogant as a seventeen-year-old girl could be. But even she was surprised at the level of success she'd had. She'd ousted Peithon and Arrhidaeus from command of the army, and stopped Antipater from getting control. She had only fallen into Antigonus' hands through bad luck, and what advantage had the man gained from her? Not much.

"When will they be arriving?"

"They aren't coming here. They expect to be at Rhodes in eleven days. From there, they will go to the port of Izmir. From Izmir to Macedonia, then to Athens."

"Did Roxane send any message to me?"

"No," Antigonus said, but Eurydice didn't believe him.

"Can you find out what word Roxane sent me?" Eurydice asked Trajan.

"Maybe. What's in it for me?"

Hesitation warred with Eurydice's need to know and—as was usual with Eurydice—hesitation lost. She slipped a small gold ring from under her gown and passed it over.

"Thought so," Trajan said. "How many of these did Roxane give you at Triparadisus?"

"A few," Eurydice admitted. "There will be more if we flee. I am a member of the Argead dynasty." Assuming Olympias didn't have her killed, she was a member of the royal family. "And Philip is the king of Alexander's empire."

Three days later she got the letter from Roxane. It was written on the back of some of Philip's scribblings, so she knew it was genuine. The letter read:

> *Eurydice,*
>
> *There may be help for Philip. The ship people were rich in their time, and their time was rich in wonders developed over the centuries. They may have a treatment for Philip's condition. I don't know the details and there are no promises. All I know of it is from a movie, a sort of recorded play, that you will have to see to understand. This movie,* Temple Grandin, *is about a woman who had a condition that at least seems like Philip's, if not quite so severe. She found treatments for herself and became a successful scholar in her field.*

Eurydice wondered what that field was, and why Roxane didn't mention it.

> *One of the treatments was a hugging box that Grandin developed. Another I've heard about is weighted clothing, which was described to me by Doctor Laura Miles. It is also a possibility, though she doesn't have much faith in their effectiveness. But there are educational techniques that will make it easier for him to interact and might allow you to have sex with him and produce an heir.*

Eurydice stopped dead. Why would Roxane offer that? If Philip had a child, that child could inherit. Wait...maybe Roxane was hoping for a daughter who could marry her son? But that would be a risk unless Roxane had a means of insuring that only daughters survived. No. Roxane was conniving enough for that, but not brave enough to try it. At least she hadn't been.

> *The ship is safe, and as long as I stay on it or in Trinidad, I am safe, as is my son. You could be safe here too, though I know that safety was never your goal. But there is much for you to learn and experience should you find yourself able to take the risk and trust me a little.*
>
> Roxane, Regent to Alexander IV,
> Co-king of Macedonia and Persia

Queen of the Sea, *Off Tyre*
May 5

Epicurus, one of the university students, was a stocky young man with a large nose that had apparently been broken at least once. *He looks like a thug in a dirty bathrobe and he is interested in food, whatever Marie Easley says*, Patrick Gouch thought as he led the group of Greek philosophers and scholars on a tour of one of the *Queen of the Sea*'s kitchens. The other guys were interested in the induction stoves.

"No," Pat explained "It's true that they are efficient but because of the loss in running the generators, they aren't actually more efficient than direct flame would be. The real reason the *Queen of the Sea* was designed with so much of the cooking done with induction and microwaves is because of safety. Even on a steel ship like this, open flames can be dangerous. Induction heats the pots and pans directly. A towel left too close to an induction heating element just sits there. A towel left too close to a gas burner catches fire and people get hurt."

Epicurus motioned for the use of the translation app and asked, "What are those brown tubers?"

Guillaume Dubois came over to look at the party. He was a short man with a shorter temper. He had spent twenty years working his way up to master chef of one of the restaurants on the *Queen*, only to be dumped in the third century BC and lose three-quarters of his staff to the colony. The staff had been replaced by natives who didn't speak English, Guillaume's native French, or German or Italian, Guillaume's other languages. After giving Pat an irritated look, he said, "They are *tova*, which are a sort of potato grown in this time in Venezuela. They managed to get lost somewhere in the two thousand years between now and then. They have an almost nutty flavor and our dietitian says she thinks they may be higher in protein than modern Irish potatoes."

"If they are so good," asked Aristippus, "why did they die out?"

Guillaume sniffed. "There could be any number of reasons. The Irish potato famine happened because a variety of potato was subject to a disease. That sort of potato is rarely grown anymore. Or it could be that the people who are eating these now switched over to corn for some reason."

Epicurus asked about cultivation and asked to try one. "These are marvelous." He grinned.

"You should try them with sour cream and chive dip," Guillaume said.

"I will," Epicurus said with a big smile.

Queen of the Sea, *Port of Izmir*
May 17

After a week in Tyre, they went to Cyprus, where they spent two days, then to Rhodes, where they spent four days and left with full holds. From Rhodes, they went to Izmir, near Sardis.

In Izmir, they were met by Eumenes.

"Welcome aboard, *Strategos* Eumenes," Queen Roxane said as Eumenes boarded the *Queen of the Sea*. Cleopatra was not with him, which disappointed her a little bit, but didn't really surprise her.

"It's interesting to finally see it," Eumenes said with a smile. "You are lovelier than ever, Your Majesty."

"Thank you. The beauty shops on the *Queen of the Sea* are something no woman should miss."

"And how is His Majesty?"

"Quite well, even if he spends altogether too much time in time-out."

"What's that?"

Roxane explained and Eumenes asked, "Can such a gentle reproach truly do any good?"

"It seems to," Roxane said. "He spends less time in trouble than he used to, and he seems to be learning quite rapidly. He is starting to recognize his letters."

"I look forward to seeing him."

"You will. Don't worry, Eumenes. The ship people are not threatening me or little Alexander. I can leave any time—" Roxane stopped for a moment. *It might be worth it.* She gave Eumenes a very measuring look.

"Your Majesty?"

"I trust you, Eumenes, I do. But to put myself in the hands of one of my husband's generals after the partition at Babylon and what happened at Triparadisus... I'm not sure if I can bring myself to do that."

"It would help, Your Majesty. In fact, it would help a great deal. It would even help were you to come ashore for a few days, examine the army with your son, then come back here. That last might help most of all. It would be proof that I am willing to let you come and go as you see fit. Please consider it."

"I will. But why is Cleopatra not with you?"

Eumenes nodded. "For the same reason you are hesitant to go ashore. She wanted me to make sure that the ship people didn't hold you against your will, and that they wouldn't kidnap her if she boarded."

"In the meantime, come with me. We will sit in the Royal Lounge and converse as though we are civilized people."

"Aren't we civilized?" Eumenes asked.

"I used to think so, but I am beginning to wonder."

☆   ☆   ☆

"I am here to coordinate a little demonstration, just in case some of your troops are getting ideas," the short woman told Eumenes.

He'd been told she was Dr. Marie Easley, an expert on this time. He found her appearance somewhat disorienting, even disturbing. The gray hair drawn back in a bun and the stern demeanor suggested a woman old in both years and authority. But that fit very poorly with Easley's superb even white teeth and rather attractive appearance. She had the complexion and clear hazel eyes of a woman in her thirties or possibly forties, not a woman whom he guessed from her bearing to be well into her sixties; at the very least, in her late fifties.

"We failed to do that in Alexandria," she continued, "and that had unfortunate results. Not for us, you understand. For Ptolemy's army and the ships carrying his soldiers,"

"What sort of demonstration?" he asked.

"Pick a place in sight of the ship. Any place. It doesn't matter to us. Make sure that it is empty of people. Put up some targets, shields, that sort of thing. Then we will demonstrate the guns. After that, perhaps Roxane will visit your army."

Port of Izmir
May 19

Roxane rode in a carriage. It was a wheeled carriage, with latex tires and shock absorbers that had been made up by the ship's machine shop. It was pulled by two white horses. She waved as she passed the lined-up phalanx of Alexander's army. Silver Shields, in armor, stood guard in the carriage, and seated next to her was Dag Jakobsen. Alexander, in his walker, was standing in the opposite seat and waving at the army too. The carriage was a combination of ship people tech from their century and earlier centuries. When she had it made back in Trinidad, she'd doubted she would ever get to use it. It was trimmed and inlayed to look as royal as she could make it, and there were platforms for the guards to stand on. All the pomp and ceremony needed to impress the troops, and comfort as well.

The demonstration had gone very well. Eumenes put his target on a hilltop almost a mile inland, which was rather clever of him. But when he heard about the distance, Dag just laughed. They angled the guns up almost thirty degrees to get the range, and accuracy suffered. But they walked their shots across the field and the targets were ripped to shreds.

Eumenes' army was impressed. "In shock" was probably a more accurate description.

So Roxane decided that she could afford a demonstration of her own. A demonstration of trust. Hence the inspection of the troops, and the waving happy little Alexander.

And that demonstration too was going very well. Her personal Silver Shields standing on the corners of the carriage were important to that, almost as important as Alexander was. These were men who would be recognized. Not by everyone in the army of Eumenes, but by enough so that everyone would believe that the Silver Shields did indeed support Roxane and Alexander, and by extension, Eumenes. They reached the end of the infantry phalanx and were now passing through the cavalry, the young men of noble families from all over Macedonia, and by now the rest of the Greek states and half of Persia.

Roxane kept waving and thanked the gods she wouldn't be expected to speak.

The carriage rolled to a stop in front of the house Cleopatra had taken as her residence while in Izmir. The door opened. Roxane picked Alexander up from his walker and the tall, blond Gaul stepped out of the carriage and handed the queen down.

Cleopatra watched them and wondered. There were rumors about the ship people Gaul who was now one of Alexander's bodyguards. Cleopatra was fairly sure that the interest was there, whether they had acted on it or not. She considered the advantage that might bring. Roxane was already a foreigner. If she married or became pregnant by someone from the ship, especially a blond barbarian, the army might rebel. She glanced over at Eumenes. He was frowning slightly. He saw the problem too.

Eumenes spoke, "Please come in and we'll talk."

Roxane carried King Alexander into the building, and the blond Gaul followed. Eumenes entered behind Dag, and Cleopatra followed Eumenes. The Silver Shields split up, two following them in and two taking up positions by the door.

Everyone except the Silver Shields was seated, and Roxane looked over at Cleopatra. "You should come back to the ship with us."

"Why?" Cleopatra asked. She was seated in an ornately carved wooden chair. Ornately carved, but with no padding. The room was open to the air. The day was a bit chill and the fireplace fought the cold breeze from the windows.

"Because if you are on the ship, you will be able to visit every port in Alexander's empire, and be safe in them all," Dag said. "On land you are, to some extent, under the authority of a general—whichever general happens to have an army close to you. On the ship, you are in a citadel that can keep you safe while letting you move around."

"You will go where I tell you?" Cleopatra asked, disbelief clear in her voice.

"No, but we have a published schedule. Is there some place you want to go that we won't reach?"

"Assuming I'm allowed..."

Dag pointed at Roxane.

Cleopatra shook her head. "It looks good, but those bullets of your steam guns could reach her even here, were you to call them in."

"They could, but I won't. Ask her."

"I can speak for myself, Dag," Roxane said. "Cleopatra, I am here of my own free will. And when I go back to the ship, that too will be my free choice. I like hot tubs and lobster thermidor."

"With Spam," Dag said, and Roxane gave him a dirty look while Cleopatra wondered what the look was about.

Roxane looked back at Cleopatra. "The ship people have some entertainment that I don't find all that entertaining. It's not important. I was simply saying that the *Queen of the Sea* is still a luxury cruise ship, even if it does have a factory complex and a university in it now."

Cleopatra and Eumenes exchanged glances. Eumenes said, "We have discussed the possibility. I would actually prefer that she stay here. Her presence has helped provide me with some sorely needed legitimacy. But I know that Cleopatra is concerned, now more than ever, about her safety." He pointed at the rather dog-eared copy of the butterfly book.

Dag looked at it and smiled. "We have a new edition, you know. It includes little new about what would have happened in our timeline, but rather more about what is different in this one. Marie and Roxane consulted about it off and on while we were in Trinidad."

CHAPTER 22

Izmir
May 22

Eumenes read through the new butterfly book. This one was different. Dag said it was printed using print plates. And they had over ten thousand copies of it printed, and had been selling them at every stop on their trip. They sold three hundred copies to the new Library at Alexandria, most of which were to be resold, but some of which would be kept in the library. This copy was a gift and, as valuable as he thought it was, he considered it a poor exchange for Cleopatra. She had finally decided to go, and was moving her property onto the ship. Some of it, anyway.

Cleopatra had considerable wealth in Sardis, wealth that she had not wanted to risk on the trip to Izmir. Captain Floden had been unwilling to wait, so the *Queen* sailed for Amphipolis. They would be coming back in four days, though. The purser managed to convince the captain to make the trip to pick up the gold, silver, and jewels Cleopatra was having shipped from Sardis.

He turned back to the book. It had a page in Greek, then a page in the ship people tongue, English they called it. It was also longer and had an extensive section of maps and a warning that while the maps were accurate in their time, the ship people knew that there were inaccuracies in this time. But those were in the details.

The scope of the thing, the size of the world . . . that was accurate. And it made Alexander's empire a tiny thing, and his dream for ruling the world a fantasy.

The world was an enormous place—full of wonders. And the ship people offered access to all of them.

Queen of the Sea, *Off Amphipolis*
May 22

"Captain," Rolf Olmstead, the comm watch rating, said, "we have a signal from the *Reliance*. They are on their way to Alexandria and want to confirm arrangements."

"What's their location, Rolf?"

Rolf gave the coordinates and pulled up a map. The *Reliance* was about a hundred miles southwest of Crete, staying well away from land. The *Queen* was working diligently on radios, and was getting close to making some reasonably powerful ground-based radio stations, but a lot of draw on the time of the skilled techs and the equipment meant that the radio project was getting pushed back. So there was no radio of any strength in Alexandria, Tyre or Rhodes. There was no way to warn Alexandria that the *Reliance* was on the way, or that the *Queen* would be going back to Alexandria to refuel before continuing its circuit.

"Here, let me have the mike," Lars Floden said. He took the mike and said, "We made arrangements and Atum is setting up a wooden fuel barge that will be in Alexandria when you get there. At least, it should be. What took you so long?"

"There was less oil than we thought in Aripero number five. They started pumping up salt water a week after you left. They have a producing well near Guayaguayare, but the delay slowed things a lot."

"What else do you have?"

"Latex, Captain. Tons and tons of the stuff. They have a regular industry back up the Amacuro. They produce rubber shoes for half the natives in Venezuela."

Lars Floden had known that, vaguely. The native technique for making shoes was to heat the sap of the rubber trees and dunk their feet in it. The sap would cool to rubber, then you had a flexible pair of shoes till they wore out in about six months. That didn't take very much latex per pair of feet, but there were a lot of feet in northern South America.

"Well, we have the sulfur processing system worked out, so we ought to be able to produce some good hard rubber. What else?"

"Some food, not all that much, and the oil. That's about it, Captain."

"We're here for another few days." Floden wanted to tell Adrian to wait out at sea till they could meet. To do all the transfers in mid-ocean to keep the *Reliance* safe and away from the barbarians that populated the world, but he couldn't. More importantly, he shouldn't. It was Adrian's ship. "We have no reason to question Atum, but no reason to trust Ptolemy. Use your own judgment, Captain."

"We'll be careful, Mama. Besides, we have our own steam cannons now," Anders said. "You'll be refueling at Alexandria after we leave?"

"No. Unless you're in a hurry to get back to Trinidad, we'll meet you at Alexandria."

"Well, there is this little wahini . . . We'll wait for you in Alexandria."

Floden put down the mike. He hoped Cleopatra was having better luck with Olympias.

Amphipolis
May 22

"What happened to your mind?" Olympias said.

Cleopatra of Macedonia noted that her mother had a furry voice. There was a soft roughness, often at odds with what she said. Her mother had been raised in Macedonian politics, as had Cleopatra, and Olympias had used her presumed magical abilities as a threat for most of her career. When Philip III developed his problems as a small boy, Olympias encouraged the belief that she was the cause. Just part of the ongoing war between her parents that had only ended with her father's death.

No. It hadn't even ended there. Olympias was still trying to kill off any of Philip II's children by other women. Cleopatra bit her tongue and said nothing. She didn't want a fight with Olympias. Mother knew drugs and poisons.

"Well?"

Olympias wasn't going to let it go. It was only a faint hope, after all. "It allows safety and transport while I negotiate."

"You can't trust the ship people. They don't respect the gods."

Cleopatra blinked in surprise.

"They are Jews. And the Jews worship a bastard god from Tyre's old pantheon."

Cleopatra looked around the room for a distraction. The floor was white marble pieces in red cement. The walls were hung with tapestries, mostly tapestries of Alexander. Cleopatra loved her little brother, but Mother had taken Alexander worship to an obsession.

Unfortunately, nothing in the room offered any change of subject. "She won't come, Mother, and she won't send Alexander's son, either."

"I will order out—" Olympias started, then stopped.

Cleopatra knew that her mother had started to threaten to order out the army of Macedonia to arrest her daughter-in-law, but she didn't have the authority to do so. And even if she had, what could the army of Macedonia do against the *Queen of the Sea*? Cleopatra looked at her mother and waited.

"She must. I am Alexander's mother."

"No," Cleopatra said. "Roxane is Alexander's mother. You can visit the ship, but be aware they have rules."

"What sort of rules?"

"No slavery, no human sacrifice."

"The gods will have their due," Olympias said.

"The gods have put the ship people here!" Cleopatra shouted, then cursed herself for the shouting. She had intended to keep her temper, but Olympias always seemed to know how to get inside her armor. "Will you visit the ship?"

"I will not. And you are forbidden to return to it."

"If you try to keep me here, Mother, the ship people will knock down the palace."

"Then it's true. The ship people hold you prisoner. I knew it."

"No. But as a paying passenger, I am under the ship's protection."

"How would they know?" There was a clear threat in the furry voice now.

Cleopatra looked over at Evgenij and nodded. She'd borrowed Roxane's Silver Shields for this visit. Not all of them. One eight-man contingent, headed by the former commander of Roxane's personal guards, who was also one of Alexander IV's bodyguards. More importantly in this case, Evgenij was equipped with Roxane's phone.

Evgenij pulled the phone from the pocket he'd had sewn onto his tunic and pushed a button, then another. Suddenly, from the phone, came a voice.

Cleopatra had seen it before and had it explained to her, but still the voice emanating from the little handheld slate sent a chill down her back. Olympias went pale as the blood drained from her face.

Evgenij looked at Cleopatra and lifted an eyebrow.

Cleopatra looked at her mother, and saw the shock congeal into anger. She nodded at Evgenij again.

"Proceed with the demonstration," Evgenij said to the phone in Greek. It had to be Greek. They needed Olympias to understand.

The city on the hill surrounded by the river was about a nautical mile from the shore, about a mile and a quarter from the *Queen of the Sea*, which was barely within the effective range of the steam cannon. But there was an empty spot—well, a field—in sight of the palace, about a quarter-mile down the hillside. The sighting had been done and Evgenij's order sent a fusillade of a hundred rounds at the field.

A round from a steam cannon—or at least these steam cannons—left the muzzle of the gun at just under the speed of sound and it slowed as it went. So it took the rounds about seven seconds to go from the muzzle of the gun to the field. The steam cannons were not silent, not even close. They resembled any other cannon in sound. In fact, the four steam cannons on the *Queen*, when fired on full automatic, sounded a lot like an antiaircraft gun from a World War II movie.

They were, however, far enough away that they were at best barely heard in the palace. What was much more obvious was the effect of a hundred one-pound lead bullets on the hard-packed earth of the field. It wasn't smoke. It was pulverized earth, but it billowed in the air above the field.

Cleopatra pointed dramatically at the field visible from the window, and Olympias followed her pointing hand, just in time to see the field billow up. Olympias wasn't the only one watching. Many of her guards were, as well.

When Cleopatra turned and walked out of the palace, surrounded by her bodyguards, no one tried to stop them.

Queen of the Sea, *off Amphipolis*
May 22

Aristotle Edfu of Alexandria muttered darkly as the *Queen of the Sea* left the harbor. He had been about to seal a deal to buy five tons of Greek wool, and word of the conflict between Cleopatra and Olympias and the early departure of the *Queen* spoiled the deal. It was not a big trade, but a few tons of wool delivered in Rome or Carthage might well have paid for the trip. Now they were making a short stop back at Izmir, then back to Alexandria. He didn't have anything to sell in Alexandria. Almost all of his stock had been bought there and how was he ever going to show his father that he was up to the job if they kept going back to Alexandria? Well, at least he had the contracts from Tyre and Rhodes for shipments of wheat and linen. He turned back to the Hoypoloi Lounge and ordered a beer.

Cleopatra wasn't any better pleased than Aristotle. She'd been hoping to get Olympias' support for Eumenes, and even more she had been hoping to get Olympias to rescind the order to have Philip killed. "Well, at least we have your order to Eumenes and his generals that you don't want Philip or Eurydice harmed."

"Do you think he will obey it?" Marie Easley asked. "He didn't seem pleased by it."

"Eumenes will obey it," Roxane said. "I am less certain of his generals. Having Philip and Eurydice gives Antigonus too much legitimacy."

"Do you really think your healers can help Philip?" Cleopatra asked.

"I have no idea," Marie admitted. "It sounds like a spectrum disorder and from what Strom Borman has told me after looking at his squiggles, he does have some mathematical ability. So it's not likely that he's clinically defective. From your descriptions, the real question is whether he's *Temple Grandin* or *Rainman*."

Having seen both movies—though she understood the language in neither—Cleopatra nodded.

Mugla
May 22

"We go to Athens," Eurydice told Trajan.

"Why?"

"Because the *Queen of the Sea* is going to be there and they let Roxane leave the ship."

"After blowing a big hole in a mountain and threatening another if she didn't come back," Trajan said.

But by now Eurydice was good at reading the man. He didn't really believe his protests. "You know that Evgenij went ashore and I got word from her that she is safe. I believe her."

"Just because she is safe doesn't mean you will be."

"You're just arguing to be arguing. You don't believe that." Still, he had a point. Whether he believed it or not, it could be that the ship people had taken Roxane's side and that she and Philip would be executed as soon as they went aboard. The fact that the *Queen of the Sea* was making port in Amphipolis suggested just that. "No, I don't think so. I..." Eurydice stopped in surprise at the realization. "I trust Roxane. I don't think she will murder me if she has another safe choice."

Trajan snorted.

"We go to Athens. We need a galley. Can your men row?"

Trajan considered. There were one hundred twenty-eight men, plus their wives and servants. Also as many children, though it had been a bad winter. A little over three hundred altogether, perhaps a hundred of whom were slaves of one sort or another. War captives, usually. "What about the ship people rules?"

"Sell your slaves in Athens, or free them and see if they are loyal."

"What will you do?"

Eurydice had two maids, and Philip had four sitters, who were as much guards in case he went into a rage as servants. "I will free them all when we get to Athens and offer them jobs.

"Find us a galley."

"We'll need two for the numbers we have, and crews to do most of the rowing."

"Two, then. And, Trajan, when we get to Athens and I can tall' to Roxane, I will be able to pay you and the men more."

Trajan tilted his head and watched while Eurydice got more

and more nervous. Then he snorted and turned away. Eurydice hoped that she would be able to pay them more once she got to Roxane, but that was only a hope.

Trajan looked at Elysia, his wife in all but name. His woman for the last thirty years. "She's going to try it."

"I told you she would," Elysia said. "She can't stay under Antigonus' thumb. It's against her nature. In another month she will be making speeches against him and he'll have her killed."

"Probably pay us to do it," Trajan said, with some real regret. "She wants to go to Athens."

"That's crazy. They'll just grab her and sell her to the highest bidder."

"She says the ship people will be in Athens. And with them there, the Athenians won't try anything."

"Well, I'm not giving up Octavia."

"Eurydice says to either free them and hire them, or sell them in Athens before we go aboard the ship."

"I've had Octavia for years. You don't think they're serious, do you?"

"Yes, strangely enough, I do. I got a letter from Evgenij. He said..."

"I know what he said. You told me when you got the letter. You don't think he was exaggerating? You can't get anything done without slaves."

Trajan shook his head. "No, I don't. Soft as the ship people are, they will kill to enforce their rules against slavery." If it had been Macedonians, they would have killed all those involved in the piracy attempt. But that didn't change the basic calculation. Insane as it was, the ship people would kill over preventing slavery.

Finally, the real question came.

"Are you going to do it?"

Until that moment, Trajan hadn't been sure. Surprisingly, the decision didn't rest that much on Eurydice or Philip, or even Alexander the Great. It really came down to Antigonus. Trajan had always respected Antigonus as a general, but in the past few months, he had gotten a better look at what was behind One-eye's eye patch.

Antigonus One-eye would indeed betray the Silver Shields, just like he had in that other history. He would betray anyone in his attempt at the throne. He was getting ready to kill Eurydice and Philip. Antigonus would have killed Alexander if he had thought he could get away with it.

All of that played a part in Trajan's decision, but it wasn't the controlling part. The real deciding factor was that he no longer thought Antigonus would win. "Yes. We will take our chances with Eurydice and Philip. We may die, either way, but I would rather bet on the girl than Antigonus."

He got up and went to tell the others.

Karanos hit the slave again, almost casually. It was what he did when he was angry or frustrated. He hit his slaves, his wife, his children, his concubines. It was his business and no one else's. That, in a way, was why he was frustrated right now. Karanos was a commander of sixty-four, only one step lower in rank than Trajan, and one of those briefed on the plans. He hit the slave again. Then, with an effort, he stopped himself. If he was going to have to sell his slaves in Athens, he needed to let the bruises heal to get the best price.

In a number of ways, Karanos was the quintessential Greek hoplite. He was brave in battle and disciplined. And he had damn little respect for anyone.

With his ire mostly sated for the moment, he kicked the slave and started giving orders. "Pack for a sea voyage. We will be taking everything, but keep it quiet."

The slave, Hermagoras, did as he was told. He hated Karanos, had hated him for years. But it was a very subdued hatred, a hatred that was tempered by the fact that Karanos had killed more than one slave in Hermagoras' presence, and by the fact that Hermagoras was a battle captive. While still a slave, battle captive was a significantly higher status than being two-footed livestock. He knew his business and between him and Karanos' other two slaves, and Karanos' wife and daughter, they got everything packed away.

Then Hermagoras sneaked away for a couple of hours to talk. Daphne was a slave of Evander, the other commander of sixty-four. And a much nicer man.

"Did you hear?" Daphne asked.

"The packing? Yes. Karanos is angry about something."

"No. I mean where we're going. I heard Elysia talking to the mistress about it. We're going to the ship people."

"Why would that make Karanos angry?"

"The ship people don't allow slavery."

Hermagoras had heard that, but he didn't believe it. He snorted in derision and Daphne stood up.

"Wait. I'm sorry. But you must realize—"

"I heard the mistress talking to Trajan's wife, I tell you. They are going to Athens and there they are going to free us so that they can get on the ship." Daphne stopped abruptly and Hermagoras got a bad feeling in his belly.

"What else, Daphne?"

Daphne looked to the left, then to the right...anywhere but at Hermagoras. He reached out, gently took her chin in his hand, and forced her to face him. "What else?"

"Elysia...well, she said that once we got to Athens, they would have to decide whether to free us or sell us. My mistress said that she would free us because she would rather see us dead than owned by some Athenian farmer with pretensions of philosophy."

Now Hermagoras' stomach felt like lead, heavy and painful. And it wasn't fear of Karanos killing him that made it feel that way. It was the thought that Karanos wouldn't kill him. Instead, he would sell him, make him *andrapodon,* livestock in the form of a man. Hermagoras was *dmōs,* a war captive, someone who if the gods had frowned upon, at least at one time had been a warrior. To be made into livestock was more than could be borne. But Hermagoras remembered a time when the thought of being a war captive was more than could be borne. He remembered that time dimly, for he had been a war captive for many years.

Hermagoras had never heard of the white antebellum man from the southern United States who had proclaimed "I'd rather be dead than be a slave on one of these big plantations." But if time were to twist in such a way that he could face that man, he would laugh in his face and spit on his shoes. For Hermagoras had learned the hard way what it was to be a slave, and in a cold dread part of his heart he knew that he would fail, again, to kill himself to escape this further dishonor. Hermagoras hated himself for that knowledge, but he would have despised that self-righteous moron from the antebellum south.

Mugla
May 24

"We need to move, Trajan," Elysia said. "We can't keep the preparations a secret for long."

"I know. But we have to time this right," Trajan said. "I don't know what will happen to us if we get to Athens and the ship people aren't there. You know what the Athenians did to that bastard Harpalus, who stole all the money from Alexander."

"Well, it won't be any worse than what Antigonus will do to us if he finds out before we are gone. Hades, let them lock us up. They'll spend so much time arguing about it that the ship people will get there and—"

"That's right and what? We don't know what the ship people will do about Eurydice. Even if they insist that the Athenians turn her over, what makes you think they will rescue us?"

It was a good question, but it was already too late.

"No," Hermagoras muttered as he drank another mug of wine. "I won't do it. This time I'll fall on my fucking sword." But he knew he was lying. For one thing, he didn't have a sword any longer.

"Can't be that bad," said Hippolochus. Hippolochus was a slave of Antigonus, taken many years ago in a fight between Athens and Philip II. He had worked his way up in the household to a fairly comfortable position. He could read and write and was a scribe for Antigonus, and a tutor—when he couldn't avoid the duty—for Antigonus' son, Demetrius.

"They're going to sell me."

"To whom? One of the local fishermen have an especially good catch?"

Hermagoras looked blearily over at Hippolochus, made a rude gesture, and said, "Worse. Athenians!" Then, realizing what he'd said, Hermagoras clamped his mouth shut on the already escaped words.

Hippolochus was staring at him, and Hermagoras—though still drunk—now realized he was drunk and said nothing. Then, made brave by the wine, he committed a sort of suicide. He couldn't fall on his sword, but if he told the little snitch what was going on, Karanos would kill him. That had to be better than being the slave of an Athenian.

Hippolochus listened to the drunken sot and tried to decide. He had been a slave for years and he was fairly comfortable. But he wanted to see Athens again. He wanted to stand in the Parthenon, offering gifts to Demetria. If he held back and let them get away, Antigonus might well follow them. On the other hand, if he told now, he would be rewarded.

It was after midnight before Hippolochus had a plan. He would wait, but he would have a good excuse for waiting. He would investigate and discover all he could about the Silver Shields' betrayal, and tell Antigonus that he was trying to find out what was planned rather than just bringing him vague rumors. The only thing that really worried him was that someone else might catch on and tell Antigonus before he did.

CHAPTER 23

Mugla

"I have a boat," Trajan told Eurydice, "but I will need one of those bracelets as a surety."

"A galley?" Eurydice asked, confused. There was no galley in the harbor.

"No. A grain shipper. The *Demetria*."

"They'll catch us at sea."

"Not if they don't know where we're going," Trajan said. "Besides, it's out of Crete, and it has the new sailing rig and the compass and sextant that the ship people are selling."

"What's a sextant?"

"I don't know, but the captain says it will let him tell precisely how far north he is. And make a good guess at how far west. It means he won't have to hug the coast. In fact, the only reason he came here was to sell grain to the army."

"When?"

"Tonight. An hour after midnight. Something about the tides."

Amerias saw that arrogant snot Trajan leave the queen's tent and was curious. So he followed him. Trajan went around to the tents of the Silver Shields, and where he went activity followed. In all but two tents.

Something was going on. Amerias didn't know what it was, but it didn't bode well.

Once the commander of Philip's bodyguard was done with

301

the tents, he headed down to the wharves. Amerias followed quietly at a distance. It was almost not enough distance. Twice he was almost seen by other Shields as they too filtered down to the docks. After the second time, he knew. Or he would have known, if there had been a galley in the harbor. But there wasn't. There was just a sailing ship, a round-bottomed grain ship that was of no use at all in war.

Amerias was nervous enough by now to want to see what was in the tents that hadn't become active after Trajan passed. He made his way back to the Shields' part of the camp. It was like a ghost town. All the tents were there, but no one was home. He found one of the tents he was looking for, and slipped in. He stumbled over something small in the door of the tent, and pulled back the flap to get some light. There wasn't much. It was after midnight. Most of the lamps were out, and while the moon was up, it was a cloudy night.

But there was a little light. Enough to make out the leg of a child, maybe three or four years old. Pale white skin and black rivulets in the moonlight.

It was blood, and it was from the throat of the child. A throat that was opened to the bone with a single stroke. The work of an expert. It was a little girl, Amerias thought. And he smelled blood, and piss, and shit. People had died in this tent. Not just the little girl. Probably everyone.

He turned and made his way to the house in the fishing village that Antigonus had taken for his own.

Hippolochus heard the pounding and went to check. "You had better have—"

The Macedonian, a member of the Companion Cavalry who were unwilling to serve under Eumenes and too poor to go home, hit him. Hard, across the mouth.

"Fetch the general!" Amerias shouted.

Hippolochus was still getting up when Antigonus came in to the front room. "Never mind, Hippo. Amerias has fetched me himself. Now, why are you disturbing my sleep?"

"It's the Silver Shields. They are doing something."

"Doing what?" Antigonus asked, but he had been looking at his fallen slave when Amerias spoke. He saw the change in expression. "And what do you know about it, Hippo?"

"I don't *know* anything, Satrap. That's why I hadn't reported. But there were rumors that they were interested in Athens. Nothing solid. Barely more than mist in the morning."

Amerias held up a bloody hand. "This is solid, General. This is from a little girl whose whole family was murdered to keep them quiet."

"Where are they?"

"The harbor."

"That makes no sense. There are no galleys in the harbor."

"The *Demetria*," Hippolochus said.

"What about the grain ship?"

"It has the new sail rigging and the new floating compass," Hippolochus said.

"Why didn't..."

"I just thought of it this minute, Satrap."

Demetria
May 25

"Cast off the ropes," Samus, the master of the *Demetria* whispered, and the word was passed. The ropes were cast off. He tapped his brother and first mate on the shoulders, then gestured to the main sail.

His brother nodded and went to help loose the sail. The wind was from the northeast and light, very light. The docks were facing east and west, and by angling his sail about forty degrees, he could get some forward motion. It took practice, and the crew was still new at the technique, so it was taking a lot more time than he liked. The surprising thing was that the angled sail produced more motion than if the wind was behind them. He had flatly not believed that when he read about the rigging, but it was true.

Noise came from the village, and a grizzled man in worn and dirty armor was suddenly next to him.

"You just handle your boat. We'll handle them." Trajan hooked a thumb contemptuously at the village.

Now, for the first time, Samus believed that this was one of the famed Silver Shields. Really believed it. He swallowed against a suddenly dry throat and nodded. He couldn't get the words out.

☆   ☆   ☆

Trajan was amused, or he would be later. For right now, he was too scared to be amused. But it was an old fear, familiar as his sandal, and in its way as comforting as his woman. The fear was proof he was alive. He signaled Karanos. "You take your boys and hold the railing. Evander, I want a roof of shields over the whole deck. We don't have to kill the stupid horse boys, just hold them off while the wind carries us away. They can't get at our flanks, not unless they have taught those horses to run on water."

The women and the slaves were sent below deck to share space with the grain. Except Eurydice, who insisted on staying above deck...and if Eurydice was putting herself at risk, Philip III wasn't going to hide.

Oh gods! Trajan thought. *I don't believe it. Buggering Antigonus is leading the charge.*

It was true, though. The giant one-eyed man in his gilded armor was at the head of the cavalry force that was riding to the pier.

What? Trajan thought, then he realized why Karanos was using the long spear. Silver Shields were cross-trained and double-equipped. They had both the short ten-foot spears, and the long twenty-foot spears. In fact, their spears were both. You could pull off the back ten-foot segment and have a ten-foot spear or you could use both segments and have a twenty-foot spear. The fact that they could use the weapon either way, as well as their shields and swords, was a part of what made them elite troops.

What had first shocked Trajan was that Karanos had his men using the full twenty-foot version of their spears. It made sense, though. There it was. Karanos ordered them "half left face" and the Shields shifted their position. Then, just as the horses were getting close, the men lowered their spears.

And the fucking boat shifted. They were big heavy spears and they had a large momentum. With that much weight sent out over the side, the ship angled over. Not much. The deck didn't lower more than a foot or so, and that not suddenly. But these were ground troops, not sailors. They weren't expecting it. Four men lost their footing and were forced to let go of their spears or go over the side. And the whole forest of spear tips shifted and waved about.

Antigonus saw that shifting forest of spear points and thought he saw his chance. The Shields didn't shift like that. They held those massive double-length spears steady as rocks. He didn't know what it meant, not in any conscious thought-out way, but it felt like the famous Silver Shields had broken. He charged, leading his men.

But the Shields had not broken. Just momentarily lost their footing. By the time his horse reached the spear points, they were ready—if not exactly steady.

It is a truism that it is not the horses' war. And, like most truisms, there is some truth there. But also, like most truisms, it's an oversimplification. The horse doesn't know what the fight is about. But it generally knows that there is a fight, and its rider is on its side. A horse, a good horse, will run itself to death for its rider. It will also—sometimes at least—run onto pikes at its rider's command.

Sometimes.

This was one of those times. Through a combination of trust in its rider, its blood being up, and the fact that it didn't have anywhere else to go, Antigonus One-eye's horse tried to leap over the pikes and into the boat.

It tried.

But it didn't make it.

Antigonus' horse rose, and Pausanias lifted his spear to match the motion. It was a tremendous feat of strength, especially for a sixty-two-year-old man. But Pausanias had been manipulating that double-length spear for forty years, and he barely grunted as he jerked it up. He grunted only a little more as the just-over-a-ton of horse and rider impaled itself on the spear point. The spear went back and its base wedged against a hatch. It bent and as heavy and strong as the wood of that spear was, it wasn't that strong.

It broke.

But not until almost all of the horse and rider's forward momentum was used up.

Horse and rider went down.

Almost straight down, between pier and ship.

And for the second time in a conflict with Eurydice, Antigonus One-eye took a bath.

Eurydice stared, and was still staring when Philip laughed and exclaimed: "Interrupted arc!"

"Is the salt going to be good for your gold-plated armor?" Eurydice shouted at Antigonus.

Then the arrows started coming. Sheets and sheets of arrows, fired from shore, over the heads of the cavalry milling around on the pier. Most of the arrows, but by no means all, were being stopped by the shields held up as umbrellas against the deadly rain.

All this took only moments. Less than half a minute since they saw Antigonus riding down the pier. The ship was still no more than a spear-length from the pier, and less than fifty yards from the shore.

On that shore, Cassander sat his horse and ordered the horse archers to fire on the ship. It wasn't as glorious and legend-producing as Antigonus' charge, but it was proving a lot more effective.

Well...a little more effective. The ship was still moving away from the pier, and the sails were already rigged. For the people on the ship it was just "hunker down and let the wind do the work."

Cassander was shouting something, then someone was riding back to the village.

For a few minutes, nothing much happened. The ship made fifty yards, then a hundred, and it was getting hard for the archers' bows to reach. But a ship, especially a grain ship, makes a turtle seem fleet of foot. The *Demetria* was barely making one knot. A cripple could catch them...if he could crawl on the water.

Antigonus had been fished out by the time the first fire arrow was shot at the *Demetria*. By then they were almost out of range. Only four fire arrows out of at least a hundred that were shot reached the *Demetria*, and only one reached the sail. A quick bucket of salt water did for that.

"Get me dry clothes," Antigonus said with quiet menace, and his slaves ran to obey. "And bring me Hippo."

When Hippolochus arrived, at about the same time as the clothes, Antigonus waved the clothes away and asked, "Where are they going?"

There was something in the general's voice that reminded Hippolochus just how dangerous his master could be. Antigonus One-eye was a man of flamboyant gestures, but he hadn't lost that eye playing dice. He had lost it in a battle. Right now the very lack of flamboyance made clear the killer beneath.

"They went to Athens. They will attempt to meet the *Queen of the Sea* there and go aboard her."

Antigonus turned to Cassander. "Find me a galley."
Cassander nodded and left the room.

Demetria, *a mile from Mugla port*

"Well, we can't go back now," Trajan said.

"Did you want to?" Eurydice asked.

Trajan pulled an arrow from the deck of the *Demetria* and tossed it over the side into the sea. "I don't know. Back in Babylon, it wasn't just that Roxane was a foreigner, you know. The babe hadn't been born yet, and the heir should be at least a babe. It might have been a girl. But a lot of it was just that too much had changed too fast. We followed Philip and we followed Alexander, but we're Macedonians. Even the new ones who aren't Macedonians by birth had the same traditions. As much as we loved Alexander, he pushed us about to the breaking point before he died.

"After he died, there was no one left we would take that from. And Perdiccas was saying 'just wait while the generals decide, wait to see if the babe is a boy.' We were tired of waiting and an idiot was better than no one."

"Philip is not an idiot."

Trajan looked at the teenaged girl, and at the bearded thirty-year-old man who followed her around like a lost puppy. He shrugged. "If you say so, Queen Eurydice. Doesn't matter anyway. We chose Philip because we were tired of being pushed. That was all, really. We were just tired. Now we're off to meet these new people who are stranger than Persians. All I'm saying is be careful. Don't push us too far."

CHAPTER 24

Mugla
May 25

Cassander told the bookkeeper to gather funds for the hiring of "one, no, two, two galleys to come here and pick up part of the army, then go to Athens."

The clerk, unhappy, but having heard Antigonus' orders, disbursed the money. Cassander then gathered a dozen or so close companions and rode from the camp. They were gone before dawn, and had even informed Antigonus of Cassander's plans. Go overland to Marmaris, and if they couldn't hire a galley there, hire a small boat to take them to Rhodes and hire one there.

All through the trip, Cassander considered. He had sat here over the winter, living off the scraps of Antigonus' table, while Olympias pretended to be queen of Macedonia. Well, there might be a queen of Macedonia, either Roxane or Eurydice, but Olympias wasn't and never would be again. It was time to get home and put his house in order.

The sun was rising as Cassander reached Marmaris, and the morning light showed him his future. There was a galley. Not a trireme, just two rows of oars, sixty oarsmen, and barely room for a company of men. They would make good time on the trip across the Aegean Sea and back to Macedonia.

Royal Lounge, Queen of the Sea, Alexandria Harbor
May 25

"I would have been fine, Captain," Captain Adrian Scott said, shaking his head. "Atum had everything ready, and Ptolemy was downright cordial." He picked up his beer and sipped.

"I know, Adrian. No doubt I'm being a mother hen, but we were going to need to refuel before we headed back to Trinidad anyway. So if the schedule was going to get tweaked, might as well do it sooner rather than later."

The waiter brought over their orders. Adrian's burger and fries, and Lars' roast lamb with mashed potatoes and peas.

"Well, aside from wheat and barley, I'm going to be mostly deadheading back to Trinidad. Atum has a fuel dump and he's paying cash up front for our whole stock."

"Why?"

"Because Ptolemy is not an idiot," said a new voice.

Lars Floden looked up to see a Greek woman out of history, and one apparently with a sense of humor, for Cleopatra was wearing a twenty-first century costume version of pharaonic dress. In spite of which, she looked nothing like Elizabeth Taylor. It was almost enough to make Lars forgive her interruption of a private conversation. Lars didn't like rudeness, but he had been a cruise ship captain for over a decade and while he noted a lack of manners in the passengers, he never made a public issue of it. Besides, according to Marie, this woman had grown up with Ptolemy and the rest of them. So he simply asked, "How do you mean? Would you like to join us?" He waved to a waiter and signaled for another chair.

"He's working on steam engines," Cleopatra said, after sitting. "In fact, if there is a satrap or king anywhere from the Pillars of Hercules to the Indian coast who isn't working on steam engines, they will soon be deposed. They are better than elephants."

"Yes, I guess they are," Adrian said, looking at the woman with interest. "Steam engines rarely panic."

"But they occasionally blow up," Lars said. "Steam was a technology in an advanced state in our time, it's true. But just Wiki and Britannica articles on steam power don't provide enough information about how steam works to make it a safe technology for this time."

"Wine," Cleopatra said to the waiter, "and lamb kabobs." She turned back to Lars. "Why are you concerned, Captain?" Cleopatra sounded truly interested, even through Lars' still poor Greek.

"I would like to say it was strictly out of human decency, and that is a large part of it. But, honestly, I have to be concerned that we will get the blame when some idiot tries to build a steam engine from a badly drawn picture and kills himself."

"Oh, some 'idiot' already has," Cleopatra said. "Quite a number of them, actually. People have been working on steam engines from the time you left for the other side of the world last year. There have been deaths in Alexandria, Tyre, and Rhodes. Eumenes hadn't had anyone die yet when we left, but he had several scalded philosophers. I haven't heard anything but rumors from the Italian states, and Carthage is being very closed mouth about their projects and where they are getting their information. Believe me, Captain, they are working on it."

"That reminds me, Captain," said Adrian. "I got close enough to Formentera to have a look, and there were a bunch of ships tied up to the Port Berry docks."

"The Carthaginians," Cleopatra said.

"Do they really sacrifice babies?" Adrian asked.

Cleopatra's mouth twisted in a half-smile. "Only on special occasions. Mostly, it's lambs and calves like everyone else. I am not fond of the Carthaginians, but if I am being honest, the reason I don't like them has less to do with their religion than with their attitude toward royalty. They have royalty, but their . . . gentry, I guess you'd call it, has gotten above itself. Worse than Athenians in some ways."

"Well," Lars said, "we will be visiting both places in the next few days, and we already have passengers from both."

He turned back to Adrian. "When will you be through with the loading?"

"It's going to take them a while to fill their amphorae with oil. Probably two weeks. I can start loading the grains while they're doing that, but even the *Reliance* is an order of magnitude bigger than anything they have. And that's with us playing container ship."

"What's a container ship?" Cleopatra asked.

"They were common in the twenty-first century. You had a standard-sized container—think of it as a very big crate, except made of steel instead of wood—that was stackable. You would load the container, then stack it on the ship," Adrian explained. "The *Reliance* is a fuel collier, and not designed to carry cargo, but we worked out a way of tying down wooden containers on *Barge 14*'s deck and we gave Atum the dimensions and structural elements needed to make a standard wooden container. They are smaller than the ones we had back in our time and we can't carry as many, but it lets the *Reliance* double as a cargo hauler when her bunkers are empty. Or mostly empty."

"What about livestock?" Lars asked.

"No, Captain, you're not getting out of that. It will take us twice as long to cross the Atlantic as you. That's twice the fodder, twice the mucking out and—most important—twice the chance of storm or disease killing off the livestock. Twice the opportunity for broken legs. And the *Queen* is a much bigger ship, so more able to handle heavy weather. If we hit an Atlantic storm, anything not tied down is going to be thrown against the wall."

"What's wrong, Captain?" Cleopatra asked.

"The *Queen of the Sea* is designed to be a cruise ship. A floating center for entertainment. In the eight months since The Event, we have converted it into a university and factory. The floating university doesn't bother me. It's close enough to the original intent that it might even be considered a step up. The floating factory... I am less happy with."

He sighed heavily, trying to figure out how to explain. "The *Queen* was such a beautiful ship, inside and out. Brand new too. Everything as perfect as it could be. And now we're transporting cows and donkeys and pigs and chickens...."

Lars picked up his knife and sliced a bite of lamb. With the knife, he placed a bit of the mint jelly on the meat, then ate, as Cleopatra watched curiously.

Lars noticed when Cleopatra's gaze moved to Adrian, who was picking up his hamburger to eat. "Something wrong, Cleopatra?"

"It was pointed out to me that the 'table manners' of many of our people are considered, ah, less than pleasant by some of the ship people. I've been trying to figure out what exactly 'table manners' are. You're eating with your fork in your left hand, and the tines are pointed downward. Most of the ship people use their right hand for the fork. Adrian isn't using a fork at all. So which is the correct method?"

"I'm from Europe. Scandinavia, north of here. The custom where I grew up was to use the left hand for the fork. In America, it's to use the right hand." Lars switched hands and demonstrated the American manner. "Adrian's eating a hamburger, which is designed to be eaten by hand. There is a great deal of acceptable variation, but we mostly find it offensive if people speak while their mouths are full or chew with their lips open. It is a reflection of our customs in regard to sanitation. Food should not be seen after it enters the mouth."

"Burping is considered polite in some cultures," Adrian said with a grin.

Lars gave him a stern look. "Not in this one."

"I was just trying to help clarify matters, Captain."

"You were just trying to cause trouble, you mean."

Cleopatra laughed.

"We were talking about how long until you were ready to sail," Lars said.

"Two weeks, sir," Adrian said. "Possibly three."

"Darn. I'm not sure we can push the schedule that far," Lars said. Most of the sentence had been in Greek, both out of deference to their guest and for practice, but 'darn' had been in English.

"And what is the distinction between 'darn' and 'damn'?" Cleopatra asked. "I have heard both terms used."

Lars blushed a little, but on Lars' face a little was all it took. And he saw Adrian grinning at him.

"Wipe that grin off your face, Adrian." He faced Cleopatra. "I am perhaps a bit stuffy in my use of language. Part of my job as a cruise ship captain involved an over-careful choice of words to avoid giving offense."

"Don't worry about it, Cleopatra," Adrian said. "I can't think of anything more silly than worrying about darn and damn."

"No, Adrian, you're wrong. At times like these, people tend to cling even more to their beliefs and be more easily offended by their breach." He explained about darn and damn, and taking the Lord's name in vain, and suddenly Cleopatra was laughing.

That led to a discussion about what taking the name of a god—any god—in vain actually meant in this time, and the whys behind the prohibition that neither Lars or Adrian knew.

All in all, it proved to be an interesting and far-ranging discussion.

Piraeus, port of Athens
May 28

"I don't see the giant ship of the ship people," Trajan said as he leaned against the railing on the grain ship.

"I hope they haven't left," Eurydice said worriedly.

"You see it?"

"I wouldn't worry," offered the ship's captain. "Ships are often delayed. Do you think that Polyperchon will issue his proclamation of liberation for the Greek city states like he did in that other history?"

"He can't," Eurydice said. "He hasn't been named regent of the empire. He is only the deputy commander of Macedonia, left there when Antipater left on his mission to steal the crown."

The captain got a pained expression on his face and Trajan laughed. Eurydice's version of Antipater's goals was unkind.

"Besides, Polyperchon's proclamation was a desperation move in his war against Cassander, and in this history Cassander is still with Antigonus. The only people who might have a right to issue such a proclamation are Philip and Alexander IV, and that means me and Roxane."

"Which is why I'm worried about the lack of the *Queen of the Sea*," Trajan said. "The local government's likely to want, to demand, such a proclamation from you."

"Phocion won't." The captain snorted. Phocion was the Athenian general who had been left in command of Athens when Antipater had imposed his peace. "Neither will the present citizens of Athens."

"The garrison commander, Xander—that is, Alexander, son of Polyperchon—is not going to be happy to see you. He was appointed with Olympias' approval and he's liable to want to arrest you," Trajan said. "I want you and Philip to stay on the ship until we have a chance to see what the situation is."

Eurydice looked rebellious, but after a moment nodded. "For now."

Two hours later, the *Demetria* pulled in to the docks. Trajan, with a squad of Silver Shields, went to see the dock master and announce their presence. Another two squads set up on the docks at either end of the ship, to make sure no one interfered.

Forty minutes later, Trajan returned with a contingent of white-robed Athenians led by an old man in a simple tunic.

"You have brought the Macedonian wars down on us again," the old man said.

"Phocion?" Eurydice asked.

The old man gave her only a brief, sharp nod in response. Apparently he was even stingy with words.

"The wars are coming whether I bring them or not," Eurydice said. "They bubble and boil here in Athens all on their own. It's only the local Macedonian garrison that keeps the lid on."

"The garrison commander will have to arrest you. Olympias has ordered your execution."

"Has Polyperchon endorsed that order?" Trajan asked. "The garrison commander is his son and last I heard, he was satrap of Macedonia, not the witch." Trajan was referring to the fact that Olympias was considered an expert with poisons and magic. The Greek word he used didn't carry all the negative connotations that "witch" does in English, but it still wasn't a particularly nice thing to call someone.

"It doesn't matter what Polyperchon has endorsed. His son Xander will try to arrest you anyway, to give to Olympias or to use as justification for Polyperchon to attempt the regency, and the mob will go crazy."

Athenian politics had been blown wide open by the arrival of the *Queen of the Sea* and, especially, by the death of Antipater. Antipater had dissolved Athenian democracy, replacing it with a government of only the wealthy, with Phocion in charge.

The lower classes, who had been citizens of Athens until Antipater's forced restructuring of the city states' government, wanted their citizenship back. The upper classes were dithering, arguing that while if it were up to them they would gladly return citizenship to all of Athens' former citizens, they couldn't risk it. Macedonia was still there and so was the garrison on the harbor island.

"It's too soon to try to repeal Antipater's decrees, but the mob won't listen to reason."

"I repealed Antipater," Eurydice said. "I can repeal his decrees if I determine I should."

"Any attempt to go back to the way things used to be is premature. Do you want Athens going up in flames?" Phocion asked. "You and Philip are potential hostages for both sides."

"Not a good idea," Trajan said, and Phocion looked at him.

Phocion had twenty years on Trajan and both had extensive experience in war. Slowly, Phocion nodded. "I agree. But don't expect the same from Polyperchon's boy."

Xander, son of Polyperchon, was almost as upset by the arrival of Eurydice and Philip as Phocion was. He didn't need this. He had a smallish garrison, and the Athenian mob was getting more restive every day. Meanwhile, Antipater was dead and his father's hold on power was slipping away.

On the other hand, there was an opportunity here. The Silver Shields were a bunch of old men who were living off their reputation. And if he captured Eurydice and turned her over to his father, Polyperchon would be able to make a strong bid for regent of the empire.

He stood for a time on Munychia, looking down the hill at Athens, then turned to his second. "Turn out the garrison. We're going to fetch the bastard and his strumpet." He laughed at that. "What use, after all, does an idiot like Philip have for a woman?"

Agnonides was listening to the rehearsals of a play to be performed in the forum when someone brought him news that there were Silver Shields on the docks. The play was a new tragedy that wouldn't have made the grade in that other history, and after listening to half the play Agnonides was not at all convinced that it would survive in this history either.

His first response to the news was panic, fear that his arguments against the Macedonians had brought retribution. But, no. The Shields were mostly with Eumenes, and Eumenes was busy in Asia. "What are Silver Shields doing in Athens?"

"I don't know. I just got word a bunch of them were on a grain ship."

"Go find out."

After the man left, Agnonides turned back to the play, but it held even less interest for him now. Soon enough he stood up. When he did the action stopped and the producer of the play came over to see what was wrong.

"No, no, it's a marvelous play. You're another Euripides," Agnonides lied easily. "It's politics. I fear my duty to Athens calls me away." It was a good excuse to get out of this travesty of a tragedy.

By the time Agnonides reached the street, some of his associates showed up telling him that Xander was calling out the garrison. Then his man from the docks reported back. "Phocion and half his toadies are headed to the docks with Silver Shields. It's all over the place. King Philip III is on that grain ship with his wife Eurydice and a company of Silver Shields."

"We need to get there. Nikator, get to our people and get them ready. It could be that they are going to do a sweep for dissenters. We might have to run."

"But what if it's not? What if she's just shown up?"

"Then Xander will probably grab her for his papa."

"Wouldn't it be better if we got her? She could repeal Antipater's peace and restore the citizenry to their rights," Nikator insisted.

"In either case, we are going to need our people ready. Now get to it."

Nikator went.

Agnonides sent another messenger to warn his wife to be ready, then he made his way to the harbor.

"The *Queen of the Sea* went back to Alexandria to get resupplied by that other ship, the *Reliance*," Phocion was explaining. "Though how they knew it had arrived I have no—"

"Roxane wrote me about that," Eurydice interrupted. "They have something called radio that uses fluctuations in the aether to send messages."

Phocion looked doubtful, and Eurydice didn't blame him. She was doubtful herself and it was only, oddly enough, trust in Roxane that had made her take this risk. But she did trust Roxane. And she found that she missed Alexander the Great's pretty mouse of a wife. She shrugged. "I haven't seen it either, but I trust Roxane."

At which point Phocion looked even more doubtful.

"Wait until the *Queen of the Sea* gets here, and if you still don't believe, you can try something. Just let me get far away first."

Phocion's mouth twitched into something that might have been mistaken for a smile. "Well enough. But until it gets here, we Athenians can't defend you from the garrison. And however a battle goes, it seems unlikely it will go well for Athens." His expression, if anything, was more sour than usual.

So it stood while the garrison formed up and the mob gathered. The Silver Shields, warned by the delegation of what was going on, moved everyone else off the docks around the *Demetria* and prepared for whatever was coming. The dock was a wooden pier that stretched out a hundred yards from shore. It was twenty feet wide and wagons carrying bags of grain often used it as a roadway. Two of those wagons were converted into a barricade, and when the garrison got there, they faced a gap that would have made Thermopylae seem a wide highway.

Trajan stepped out from the wagons to see a red-faced Xander, and he felt like laughing. He was also angry, and used to speaking pretty bluntly to Eurydice. This pampered puppy of Polyperchon's didn't impress him at all. "What? You expected us to roll over on our bellies and make it easy for you? We'll just wait here till the *Queen of the Sea* arrives."

"What are you going to eat?"

Trajan stopped, stared, then bellowed, "We're on a grain ship, you idiot! What the fuck do you think we're going to eat?"

The peace talks didn't go well after that. Or last long.

"Bows ready!" Xander shouted, and Trajan hurried back behind the overturned wagons.

That's when the bows started raining arrows. It was a slow rain. The garrison had a thousand men and only two hundred were archers. There were six hundred infantry and two hundred cavalry, and they were all stopped dead by the barricade. The only way around it was to get a boat and row it over to the docks behind the barricade and attack from there. But that too would provide the Shields an opportunity to position themselves for maximum defense.

For a few minutes, it was a stalemate. The garrison fired arrows, then stopped as it became clear they weren't doing much damage. Then everyone waited.

Everyone...except the mob.

Agnonides watched the scene on the docks with a sort of terrified glee. He could start the revolution right here and right now, but the danger had never been the garrison. As long as they were in the citadel on Munychia, they would have been safe and hard to attack.

But the real threat, the threat that let the garrison exert power over all Athens, was the rest of the Macedonian empire and its eastern conquests. It wasn't Antipater who had stopped the League of Greek States before. Antipater had been forced back, holed up in his little fort until he was rescued by Craterus and the eastern army.

Now Antipater and Craterus were both dead. Eumenes, Ptolemy, Antigonus and the rest were all busy fighting against each other. He could start up the Lamian war again, and maybe win. But they had thought they could win when Alexander died too and they had been wrong. That possibility was why he was terrified.

But the glory of leading Athens to liberty... that was why he acted.

"Attack them!" Agnonides said, pointing at the garrison crowded around the pier. "Attack!" he yelled.

Citizens of Athens went through two years of military training. Every citizen of Athens. For many of the mob, that training was years or decades past. But for many, it was fresh. There were veterans of the Lamian war in that crowd, veterans with something to prove.

They were, for the most part, armed. And they hit the garrison troops from behind. But the truth was, they were a mob... not an army. And if the garrison weren't Silver Shields, they were veterans of Alexander's army, and they were in formation, armed and armored.

It was a stalemate.

The garrison couldn't get out of the trap their commander had put them in, but the mob couldn't break them either. On the other side, the Silver Shields were holed up behind overturned wagons, and if the garrison ignored them, the Shields could come out and bugger them good.

Eurydice had watched the whole battle from beginning to the present, sitting in a cabin of the grain ship. She saw the Shields stop the garrison and the garrison stop the mob, and the whole thing come to a frustrated end, as no one could move.

And then she saw it. It all fit together, her training as a little girl, her experience with the army on the way to Triparadisus, the fight at the bridge and Antigonus One-eye sitting his horse in his armor, trying to force the bridge with sheer presence. And she knew what to do.

She was up and out of the cabin before anyone could react. She leaped from the *Demetria* to the dock in a single bound and ran for the overturned carts.

Trajan was running the battle and the sergeant he left to watch her was not expecting anything. He was still on the boat when she got to the wagons. "Lift me up!" she shouted. "Lift me up!"

Trajan turned and cynicism warred with something he had long thought dead. This was Alexander, made new in the form of a young girl. Alexander going over the wall. And this time he would be protected. Trajan started giving orders then, and in only moments Eurydice was standing on an overturned wagon shouting to the soldiers of the garrison to put up their arms.

She was surrounded by a forest of shields as the Silver Shields left themselves exposed to keep her protected. But with all those shields, she couldn't be seen. She pushed them out of the way, and shouted again.

There it was. The painting, the statue of glory. Nike herself with the shields spreading like wings to reveal her.

The whole battle came to a stop. All three forces, staring at the seventeen-year-old hatchet-faced girl.

"Put up your arms and stop while we settle this!" She pointed imperiously. "Xander, son of Polyperchon, come to me. Phocion, you too, or whoever is in charge of—" Eurydice managed, barely, to stop herself before she called it a mob. "In charge of that force behind the garrison. Join me here, for I am the regent for my husband and I hold the reins of Alexander's empire."

CHAPTER 25

Demetria, *Piraeus dock*
May 28

The sun was setting over Athens as Phocion, Agnonides, Xander and Eurydice sat down on a hatch cover on the *Demetria* and decided the fate of Athens. Or tried to. Having brought the battle to a halt and declared herself queen of the empire, Eurydice didn't know what to do to settle the rather complex issues involved.

Part of the problem was simply that Alexander the Great and Antipater were not king and loyal retainer. Alexander the king had never trusted Antipater, who had been his father Philip II's general, not his. He had been planning to execute the old bastard at the time of his unexpected death. That meant that the commands that Antipater had issued in regard to the Greek states were often in conflict with what Alexander the Great had wanted. After Alexander's death, Antipater's handling of the Lamian war was probably not what Alexander would have done. In fact, as Phocion explained, "It was fear of what Antipater might do without Alexander to rein him in that led to the rebellion in the first place."

"How would you know, you old fool? You were opposed to the revolution from the beginning," Agnonides said.

"Because it was a bad idea, you young idiot. It left us with a garrison of Macedonian troops sitting on Munychia hill and our democracy restructured."

"Yes, restructured so that you're in charge."

"That wasn't my idea. It was Antipater's."

321

"Why?" Eurydice asked.

"Because he felt that it was the poorer citizens of Athens who had pushed for the rebellion," Xander said. "He was right, too. Agnonides here can get the mob to do almost anything. Though they usually end up regretting it later."

"Athens is not Macedonia's helot and never will be!" Agnonides proclaimed in ringing tones, which sort of proved Xander's point to Eurydice's mind.

She remembered something in the book they had received. Philip doted on the thing. Something about the Greeks not knowing how to run an empire, that the knowledge of how to run a nation had been developed later. "We need to talk to Marie Easley."

"Who is Marie Easley?" Xander asked, sounding confused.

"Haven't you read the butterfly book? It says on the cover page 'A description of the prior history and the probable effects of the *Queen of the Sea*'s arrival by Marie Easley.' Marie Easley is the scholar of that time who came with the *Queen of the Sea*. Roxane wrote me about her."

"And what can she tell us?" asked Agnonides, suspiciously.

"I don't know. But the ship people know a great deal more than we do about building, making, and medicine. Isn't it likely that they know something of politics as well? We don't have to actually do what they say, but it might be useful for us to hear it before we make any final or irrevocable decisions."

Mostly what Eurydice wanted was to buy some time so that tempers could cool. "I suggest that things like trials for treason against Athens, Macedonia or the treaty be put off until the ship arrives and we have a chance to talk to the ship people."

That produced even more argument from everyone, especially Xander, who still wanted to arrest her and force her to declare his father regent of the empire. Eventually, everyone ran out of energy, and since no one was willing to give ground on any of the complex issues of state, they put them off until the *Queen of the Sea* arrived.

Queen of the Sea, *Piraeus, port of Athens* June 9

After staying two weeks in Alexandria, the *Queen* resumed its schedule, heading for Athens. On arrival, they found the city waiting for their pronouncements on government.

Lars Floden watched the ship's boat head in to pick up the delegation, which included Polyperchon, whom they had missed on their stop at Amphipolis. He'd apparently been visiting Aegae, the historical capital of Macedonia. Lars suspected it was because he didn't want to meet the ship people, but Polyperchon had to respond to what Eurydice had done here in Athens. The extra time the *Queen* had spent in Alexandria meant that Polyperchon had the time to get here.

Lars was looking forward to meeting the young firebrand who was married to Philip III. The boat was getting close. Lars got up and headed to the Royal Lounge. Never before The Event had its name rung so true as it did nowadays.

"Welcome to the *Queen of the Sea*," Lars said when the delegation arrived. They filled all the elevators near the boarding area. Philip and Eurydice required one to themselves because Philip didn't like being too close to people. But now that they were in the lounge, Philip was the one who was handling the ship best. The rest were gawking at the LED lights, the screens, large glass windows, the leather chairs with rollers, and the hard plastic tables. But Philip, while examining everything with undisguised curiosity, wasn't at all concerned or overwhelmed.

"Take your seats please and we can get started," Lars said.

There were place cards arranged around the oval table. Pencils and tablets of paper as well. There was some confusion as Phocion and Agnonides realized they were seated next to each other.

Marie Easley was seated at one end of the table, with Roxane on her right and Eurydice on her left. Alexander IV was next to Roxane in a high chair and Philip was next to Eurydice. The Athenians were on Eurydice's side of the table and the Macedonians were on Roxane's. At the other end, Lars took his seat and Staff Captain Dahl took his, along with Jane Carruthers.

Lars Floden found himself wishing that President Allen Wiley were here.

He waved at Marie. She nodded and started to speak. "I have looked over the treaty by which the League of Greek States was formed. It is binding on all the Greek states, and places the head of government firmly in the hands of the Argead dynasty. However, it doesn't authorize the actions that Antipater took at the end of the Lamian war. The garrison should be removed from Athens."

"That garrison was placed in response to Athens and the rest of their allies breaching the oath," Polyperchon said. "Antipater was the deputy hegemon of the league. He had full authority to punish the oath breakers. When and whether to remove them is a decision for the government of Macedonia."

Thereby, Lars thought, *proving that his freeing of the Greek states was a political move in that other history.*

"He had the right to make them stop," Marie said. "He didn't have a right to overturn their government. In fact, the very same oath forbade him from doing so."

"Ha! So we are not bound by Antipater's ruling," Agnonides crowed.

Lars noted that the always dour Phocion was looking even more sour than usual.

"Have a care," Marie said. "Just because I say it, that doesn't mean that the generals will abide by it. Even if they do, you could set in motion your own execution. In the history that led to my world, you managed to get Phocion executed. After you got the mob to condemn Phocion, they regretted it and condemned you." Then she gave a small shrug, dismissing the fate of both Phocion and Agnonides as matters of little import. "But that is not truly the problem. Between them, Philip II and Alexander the Great carved out an empire, but they didn't develop the techniques to administer it."

"That was why Alexander was adopting Persian customs," Roxane said. "He knew that the Greek customs were not suited for empire."

Polyperchon and Agnonides both expressed derision at that. Then looked at each other in consternation.

So it went. They broke some hours later and while Agnonides went to the casino and the rest of the delegates went to their own pursuits, Roxane and Marie Easley took Eurydice and Philip to visit the ship's doctor.

Dr. Laura Miles was still alive and almost shocked to be so. The locals in Trinidad knew of a plant that thinned the blood. It was considered a poison and it had some unfortunate side effects, but it was working, so far, to keep Laura from dying. She'd read everything she could find on autism spectrum disorders and their treatments. Partly that was just a good doctor, concerned about the welfare of an expected patient, but in large part it was a politically motivated move. She knew perfectly well that if they managed to help Philip, they would have proven the efficacy of their treatments to this part of the world.

"The famous treatment," she explained, "was developed by Temple Grandin, who herself suffered from spectrum disorders. And it's only a treatment, not a cure. It seems there are two kinds of touches, soft touch and more firm touches..."

Laura made sure she was talking to Philip, who didn't look at her, but everywhere else in the room. Knowing that was one of the symptoms that was sometimes present in spectrum disorder patients, she didn't take offense or assume that because he wasn't looking at her he wasn't paying attention. She was especially heartened that he jerked his head in understanding when she talked about the kinds of touch.

Laura showed him the rig they had set up. "You control it by use of the rope. You can pull it tight or open it up." She demonstrated by using the rope, and again got that jerky nod not looking at her.

Philip climbed in, pulled the rope hard, and held it. He stayed that way for a while. After about twenty seconds, which— surprising as it may seem—is a good long while when you stand around and watch nothing much happening, he said, "It helps."

He got out of the device and Eurydice reached out. Philip flinched away.

"It won't happen all at once, girl," Laura said in very broken Greek. "Give it time. There are drugs we may be able to use to reduce his anxiety, and that may help. But it's going to take a while."

Marie Easley and Roxane, Eurydice, Phocion, Polyperchon and Agnonides first worked out a temporary settlement for the city of Athens. The garrison would stay, for now at least. At the same time Athens' original constitution would be restored and the citizens who had lost their franchise would have it returned to them. However, they agreed that any death sentences the assembly decreed would need to be endorsed by the garrison commander, Xander, son of Polyperchon, before taking effect.

Having settled that, and having both regents, Cleopatra, and Polyperchon all handy, they set out to draft a proposal for a constitutional convention to establish a constitution for Alexander the Great's empire. Questions like who to invite, where to hold

it, what would be required for it to be binding on the participants, whether it would be binding on parts of the empire that
failed to participate. They determined that it would—or people
would—avoid being bound by not attending. How many of the
participants would have to agree for it to go into effect. Whether
to require the presence of the actual satraps and kings or just
their representatives. They decided that just the representatives
would be enough, but the satraps would be welcome.

Meanwhile, Philip had fallen into the computers of the *Queen
of the Sea* like Alice down the rabbit hole, and showed little desire
to return to the real world. The scholars of Athens boarded the
Queen and started their course work in everything from perspec-
tive drawing to electrical engineering. There was, in fact, a quite
useful course in basket weaving.

Queen of the Sea, *Athens Harbor at Piraeus*
June 15

The cameras clicked as Roxane signed the document and three-
year-old Alexander IV used his seal to squash the hot wax onto
the proclamation. Then they clicked again as Eurydice signed.
After that Philip signed, and like Alexander IV, stamped the
wax with his seal. Both seals had been produced on the *Queen*
in its machine shop, and each represented half of Alexander the
Great's signet. Which was why Alexander IV had been first to
squash the wax. Philip could be trusted to put his seal in the
right place. The three-year-old couldn't.

It made an impressive ceremony, and Cleopatra got in on
the act by signing as witness and adding her own seal to the
proceeding. Then they had to go through it over a dozen times,
for each satrap in the empire would receive his own individually
signed proclamation.

By the time they were done both kings were feeling more
than a little cranky. Alexander IV had decided to give his seal
to his sometime-friend and sometime-antagonist Dorothy Miller.
Serve the poopy head right if she had to do this too.

Having issued their decrees, the co-queens graciously said
personal goodbyes to all the members of the conference, who
went back to Athens.

☆   ☆   ☆

From Athens to Sicily, two stops on the island, one for the Greek part, one for the Carthaginian part. Then what would become Salerno, Naples, then Ostia, the port of Rome. In Ostia, they waited a day for the consuls, Papirius Cursor II and Q. Publilius Philo III, to agree on who to send to the ship. Apparently the consuls were not great friends.

They also picked up several more scholars. Rome in this time wasn't the barbarian village the Greeks liked to think it was, but neither was it the Rome of Caesar and Marc Anthony. The Coliseum was four centuries away, and the senate of Rome was still mostly a city council, if of a good-sized city.

From Rome they went to Carthage and finally found something closer to civilization, at least the sort of civilization that the ship people were used to. Carthage was a city that included and even encouraged technological innovation, at least within limits. Making money was at the heart of Carthage's culture.

At least, large parts of the culture of Carthage were focused on practical matters. But the religious practice of child sacrifice as an appeasement to the gods was not, it turned out, just a slander by the Greeks and Romans who didn't like Carthage. It was an exaggeration and distortion. The Carthaginians believed that a family that lost a child was blessed by the gods in recompense. That belief had morphed into an actual trade, where the city or individuals would sacrifice a child in order to buy the favor of the gods.

"A bit like sending a big donation to a televangelist," commented Jane Carruthers, but there was a lurking horror under the humor.

They took on passengers at every stop, and by the time they reached the Pillars of Hercules, the passenger section of the *Queen of the Sea* was at capacity. At its new, lesser, capacity anyway.

The extra time spent in Athens meant that the *Reliance* was farther ahead of the *Queen* than they had planned on. It would reach Trinidad two or three days ahead of the *Queen*.

CHAPTER 26

Reliance, *Entering Boca Grande*
July 2

"Skipper, we are getting something from Fort Plymouth."

Adrian Scott swam out of sleep gradually, kicking and screaming, holding on to Morpheus. He had been up for the last twenty hours, managing the *Reliance* through the south edge of a hurricane, and he had just gotten to bed maybe three seconds ago. "What time is it?"

"It's dawn, Skipper. You've had four hours and you need to get up. There's trouble in Fort Plymouth."

"What sort of trouble, Dan?"

Dan Neely was the *Reliance*'s radio man and chief electrician. And the truth was, he knew the *Reliance* a lot better than Adrian did. He had been the chief electrician under Captain Joe Kugan. He owned a pretty decent estate in the New U.S. too. He'd bought it with his money from the sale of the *Reliance* to the colony, and had a deal with the Banner family to run it for him for a share of the take. If he lived another ten years or so, Dan was going to be able to retire a wealthy man.

"Wild injuns, Skipper. Wild injuns."

"Dan, I'm not in the mood."

"Neither am I, Skipper. The bastards have my ranch and Brad may be dead."

"What?" He was wide awake now. "Right. I'm up. What do they want us to do?"

"Mostly be warned. President Wiley had scouts out and word is he got most of our people into the fort."

"What about Brad?"

"He was trying to get his herd of those over-sized turkeys in. At least that's what the radio guy at Fort Plymouth said."

It took about fifteen minutes to get the rest of it, and to get some primitive cocoa into Adrian. It was a gritty drink, but it did the job.

Several of the ship people, especially Gerlinde Kettl and Torger Sundal, were lobbying to get the *Queen* to go around the horn to Ethiopia and acquire coffee, and Ptolemy had already sent an expedition up the Red Sea to the same end. Partly that was because Ptolemy had quickly developed a taste for coffee when he was introduced to cappuccinos. But mostly it was because he was looking for anything he could find to get and keep the ship people on his side. Meanwhile they had unsweetened cocoa, and Adrian had discovered that cocoa was as bitter as the worst Joe that ever melted a spoon.

"What have you got, Dan?" Adrian asked as he sipped and grimaced.

"They are warning us to stay out at sea and keep watch."

"Got that part. What's going on though?"

"Couple of things. The Tupky and the other tribes on the river are slavers. Word about slavery being illegal in the New U.S. got out before we even headed back to Europe."

Adrian nodded. There had been a few runaways in Fort Plymouth.

"Well, put that together with all the stuff we can make and the river tribes were getting pissed and greedy all at once. After we left, they figured that this was their chance and decided to put a stop to the abolitionists and get a bunch of useful slaves at the same time. Then they figured on retreating upriver out of reach of the *Queen*."

"How do you know all that."

"Lacula." Dan Neely shrugged. "Maybe we just got lucky. Or maybe Lacula was on the island because he wasn't happy with the folks back home in the first place. But he is more ship people than the ship people nowadays. He's converted. He's a Mormon now."

Adrian laughed. "I wonder how Wiley is taking that?"

Fort Plymouth, Trinidad

Allen Wiley had rather more important things to worry about than Lacula's religious conversion. He ducked as a flight of arrows was fired from the edge of the jungle. Fort Plymouth was away from the beach and though it had a cleared space around it, the river people had better bows than they were expecting. He was having to deal with iron arrowheads. The Venezuelan river tribes already had limited copper smelting capability, but didn't have a fully developed smelting industry especially on this side of the Andes. That left copper as rare—or almost as rare—as gold or silver.

The addition of the ship people and knowledge of ores and how to recognize them had blown the already cracked door to metals wide open. And the river tribes, already familiar with kilns for vitrifying clay, had the infrastructure to step through the opening. They also had a religious conviction that possession of iron arrowheads would allow them to defeat the ship people.

Retired Master Sergeant Leo Holland, Jr.—now Colonel Leo Holland of the New America Army—ducked down beside the President.

"Damn it, Leo, when are you going to do something about this?"

"As soon as you get me some more gunpowder, Mister President." The production of black powder was not amazingly complicated, but it was time and labor intensive. It was also not something you wanted to do in town. So the powder mill had been located well outside of Fort Plymouth. Also, the government had other priorities, roads through the jungle, plows, wagons, and wagon wheels, all the things that you just had to have to build a relatively advanced culture in the wilderness.

"I have already admitted that we should have given the military a higher priority, but do you want to do without the hospital or the computer center?"

"No, sir. But we don't have enough powder to shoot randomly into the jungle every time a bunch of them shoots arrows at us."

"It's been weeks!"

"Yes. Weeks where something like fifteen thousand river people have failed to take a city of less than six thousand, including our natives. We're doing well, Mr. President. It may not seem that way, but we are."

Allen knew he was right. The river people were more hierarchical than the island tribes. They had a priest class, and a royal class. They had armies and ranks, but they weren't set up for sieges. They didn't have much in the way of a logistics system and most of their battles were open field engagements or jungle hunts.

"What about the *Reliance*?" Leo asked. News of the arrival of the supply ship had hit the radio room shortly before dawn.

"I've ordered them to stay out. They don't have the height of the *Queen* and their steam cannons are considerably less powerful."

Leo snorted, but Allen wasn't in any hurry to risk the *Reliance* somewhere it could be swarmed over. "Look, I know that they would be a great help. But the *Reliance* has a draft of less than fifteen feet. The *Queen* has a forty-foot draft. The *Reliance* can go up the Orinoco River a ways, but the *Queen* can't follow it."

"It could, since this is the rainy season."

"And that's what I want the *Reliance* for, Colonel. Once this fight is over, we are going to have to send a punishment expedition up the Orinoco or this is going to happen every time the ships leave. We have to make it clear to the locals that attacking us is a bad idea."

"Floden isn't going to like that."

"You might be surprised. He may be a European liberal, but he's not blind. And he does understand that you have to defend yourself."

Leo shrugged doubtfully. "So what are you having the *Reliance* do?"

"Disrupt their supply train," Allen said with a grin.

Reliance, *Gulf of Paria*
July 3

"I see one, Skipper," Frederick Napier said.

"Well, sink it, Fred," Adrian said.

There were a mass of double canoes in the Gulf of Paria, but they were spread out. The *Reliance* had spent the last several hours going back and forth in the gulf, looking. They were long canoes, in the forty-feet range, and they were carrying supplies to the attacking river people. Mostly corn and yams of one sort or another.

"Right, Skipper." Fred swung the barrel of the steam cannon around and pulled the trigger.

The one-pound lead rounds went out and ripped through the crew of the supply boat, and Adrian felt a little sick. More than a little, actually, but he knew it had to be done. If Fort Plymouth was to be relieved, then the supply lines from the river people had to be cut. One of the canoes started sinking and the rowers were dumped into the water.

"Put out the ropes," Adrian said. They already had a collection of damp river people locked up between containers.

"I hope the *Queen* gets here soon," said Dan Neely.

"I hope the river people get the message," Adrian said.

Trinidad, four miles from Fort Plymouth
July 3

Jokalsa heard the report and knew that his world was ending. The ship people had strong magic. They had known that almost from the beginning.

But the ship people also denied the gods their due. It was suitable to feed slaves to the gods, but whether they were fed slaves or kings—the gods had to be fed. If the gods were not fed, the world would end. The gods would take back their life, all of it. So the tribes of the river had known for centuries.

Then the ship people came and upset the order of the world. The slaves had started running away to the coast and to the island they now called Trinidad. And the new tools had also offered great wealth. It had been too tempting.

So an alliance had been formed, an unheard of alliance of all five of the main river tribes. A plan was made and spies were sent out. The plan was good. Attack while the great ships were away and capture the ship people. Then, take them upriver and use the flood season to move them away from the body of the river. When the ships returned, their colony would be gone and the ships would not know where. Meanwhile, the five tribes would gather all the slaves and sacrifices they needed and the knowledge of the ship people as well.

It had started well enough. The tribes had captured a few of the ship people and a lot of the islanders. But then everything had stopped at the mud walls of Fort Plymouth. They had those crossbows and the cannon. A mass charge ended as soon as the cannons fired. And now the ships were back and it was still the flood season. The river was high and the ship people were in their fort, ready to tell the god-queen's ship where they were. Then the people of the river would die and the gods would not be fed and the world would end.

There was no point in fighting anymore. Nor was there any point in running away.

Jokalsa nodded slowly, a tear running down his cheek. Then he gave orders. First, there would be a royal sacrifice. "Tell the priests they will take my heart to appease the gods. And when that is done, the army will attack Fort Plymouth. Everyone."

It took several hours to prepare, but Jokalsa was ready by midnight. He drank the drugged drink and lay back on the makeshift altar with great and royal dignity.

Fort Plymouth
July 4

The sun was just coming up when the natives charged. All of them, it seemed like. All along the jungle edge, they came pouring out, wearing feathered headdresses and gold medallions, and not much else. With iron-pointed spears and painted faces and bodies, they came.

It was a general attack and all you could hear was the native screams and the cannons firing. The cannons ripped holes in the attackers' ranks, but they came on.

It was crazy. Every canister of grape shot was killing dozens.

But they came on.

Leo had been in the first Iraq war, and he had seen overwhelming force. What he had never seen were people attacking overwhelming force, madly, without any regard for their own lives. He was now deeply thankful that he had persuaded Wiley and Captain Floden to let him make breech-loading cannons. If they'd been using muzzle-loaders, he wasn't sure they'd have had a good enough rate of fire to withstand an insane charge like this.

In spite of the cannons and the crossbows, the attackers got to the walls, anyway. But that was it. The walls of Fort Plymouth were eighteen feet tall, and made of adobe and wood. The attackers couldn't pass them by standing on someone's shoulders. That needed a ladder, and the natives didn't have enough ladders. Not nearly enough. The defenders pushed the ladders away, or just shot the attackers as they climbed.

It was over an hour later when the attackers finally broke. They had taken horrible casualties. Though no one would ever know for sure how many had participated in the attack, there were almost three thousand native corpses when they got around to counting them and several hundred more who would die soon from their injuries.

Queen of the Sea, Trinidad
July 8

"Why?" Captain Floden asked yet again.

This was a meeting on the *Queen of the Sea* with all the interested parties. President Allen Wiley, Congresswoman Anna Vignola, Congressman Lacula, Queen Roxane, Queen Eurydice, Philip III, Cleopatra, Captain Floden, Captain Adrian Scott, and Marie Easley. Dag was there as one of Alexander IV's bodyguards, a title and rank that meant something very different in the third century BCE than it had in the twenty-first century. Alexander the Great's bodyguards—and Philip II's—had been effectively the king's privy council. Ministers without portfolio, or often enough, ministers with portfolio. Dag hadn't realized that when Roxane appointed him. Realization happened gradually over the ensuing months. He had also come to realize that it was an astute political move. Roxane had tied the ship people to her son, by the standards of the Macedonians. Dag looked around the Royal Lounge, at the assembled notables, and realized this was the ship people council, the ones who would decide if the ship people were to go to war and against whom.

"Because they were dead anyway," Lacula said.

"But..."

"They knew they were dead if the gods were not fed. *Knew it.* Not believed it. Knew it the same way you know the sun is going to come up tomorrow. And if they didn't win, their wives and children were dead with them. What did they have to lose?"

"What about you?" Dag asked.

"Why do you think I'm a Mormon?" Lacula said. "The old gods will destroy the world, but the new god, the god of Jesus and Joseph Smith, he will stop them."

Which made as much sense as any other religion Dag had ever heard of. Dag had been raised Lutheran, but not very Lutheran, and at this point he was a committed agnostic. Something had moved the *Queen of the Sea* from the twenty-first century to the here and now, and he didn't think it was an accident any more than the skipper did. That, to Dag's mind, pretty much blew "just happened" out of the water. But, whether it was an all-powerful god or a committee of little green men, Dag didn't have a clue.

All he did know was that he was never going to charge a fortified position with spears and not enough ladders because someone told him the gods required it.

Captain Floden looked at Lacula and finally nodded. "Mr. President, are you still determined that the *Reliance* should go up the Orinoco?"

"Yes, Admiral, I am. I want it packed to the deck heads with troops too, and towing a fleet of canoes to deliver those troops. One good demonstration, or year after year of pinprick raids, until one of them catches us unprepared and everyone in Fort Plymouth dies for our restraint."

"Adrian?"

Adrian looked a little sick, but said, "He's right, Skipper."

Floden looked over at Dag and Roxane, at Eurydice, Philip, and Cleopatra. And everyone was in agreement. Marie Easley was looking very grim indeed, but she too nodded. The locals weren't even hesitant.

"You have to prove your strength," Eurydice said. "Not just the strength in your arms, but the strength in your heart, or you can never make peace."

"What about fuel?" Floden asked, and Dag nodded. The *Reliance* had sold its whole load to Ptolemy. The Queen's tanks, when full up, would take them to Europe and back, but not with that much fuel left over. If they were going to be going around the Med, picking up delegates to the convention, they were going to need extra fuel.

"That's a problem, Skipper," Adrian said. "It's not the transit time that worries me, even going slow to make sure we have the depth we need. It's all the stops as we drop off troops and burn out villages."

"Do we..." Dag started, then stopped. Roxane was looking at him. So were Eurydice, Cleopatra and, especially, Lacula. Yes, they had to burn out the villages. Just proving they could wasn't going to convince the locals that they had the will to do it.

"I would recommend that the *Queen* stay here and help with the rebuilding. Also, the university students and other passengers can be familiarized with the local products. That way the *Queen* will remain available in case there are difficulties." Marie looked at Captain Floden. "Lars, about the radios? What about range limitations?"

"We can use the shortwave transmitters and atmospheric bounce, and mostly stay in contact. But shortwave is iffy. Atmospheric conditions can prevent its working. I think an hourly commo check, situation and location report. If we go twelve hours without a commo check, the *Queen* will go after them. But once they get upriver, it's going to take us almost a full day—maybe even a day and a half, depending on how far upriver they are and how fast the current in the Orinoco River is."

"Skipper," said Adrian, "for my peace of mind make it six missed checks and you come get us. Maybe it will turn out that it was just bad weather, but all it will really mean is the passengers get a cruise up the Orinoco."

Captain Floden nodded, and the decision was made.

Queen of the Sea, *Trinidad*
July 15

Epicurus watched the reciprocating steam engine operate. It wasn't hooked up to a boiler, but to an air pump. Even so, the mechanics were clear enough.

Hamilcar grinned over at Epicurus, his oiled curly black beard shining in the artificial lights of the lab. Hamilcar had been picked up at Carthage and was a member of the upper end of their trading class. "A useful device, I grant, but not nearly so flexible as a slave."

Epicurus found himself smiling back. Partly it was because he realized that Hamilcar was just teasing him. Not that the Carthaginian didn't mean what he was saying, but he was open at least to the possibility he might be wrong. Hamilcar was what the ship people would call amoral, and what a Carthaginian called practical. No, that wasn't entirely true. Hamilcar had a religious respect for contracts. What he didn't have was any belief in innate good or innate evil.

Epicurus, along with reading all of his own works that had survived and the commentaries on them, was finding the whole issue of philosophy more complicated than he had thought. But he liked Hamilcar because he wasn't what Mike Watson called a "superior sumbitch," as so many of the Greek philosophers were, justifying slavery as necessary to allow the better people the time to dedicate to the public good and social duties.

"I still say that Oscar Wilde's quote precludes slavery. 'Selfishness is not living as one wishes to live, it is asking others to live as one wishes to live.'"

"Then you should not indulge in slavery. But doesn't the same quote preclude you from requiring my agreement? In any event, as a Carthaginian I prefer Wilde's remark that anyone who lives within their means suffers from a lack of imagination."

Epicurus shot him the finger, a gesture he had learned on the *Queen of the Sea* and Hamilcar laughed.

Like the gesture, the language they were using came from the ship people also. They called it "English," although Epicurus had been told by the woman scholar Marie Easley that by now the language had so many new loan words and grammatical changes that it was definitely a new dialect and she wouldn't be surprised if in a century or two it became a brand new language of its own.

The university at sea was proving a very interesting place. There were Latins, Carthaginians, Greeks of all sorts, Egyptians, Jews and Canaanites, none of them in a position to impose their will on the others. And the issue of slavery had become a main focus of the debate. In response to the ship people's abhorrence of slavery, many of the locals—people from this time—had taken the opposing view and started justifying slavery as a natural and just institution. And they were good at their justifications, good enough to reduce some of the ship people to gibbering fury. Especially when they did basically what Hamilcar had just done and used the ship people's justifications of capitalism as justification for slavery. The notion that the better, more capable, people would rise to the top of such a system also implied that the worse, less capable people should be allowed to sink to the bottom into "that state of servitude that their natures assign them to."

Across the lab, Julius Crassus looked at the raining crystals of casein in a chemical experiment and saw a future of wealth, only dimmed a little by the fact that this knowledge wasn't exclusively his. He had enough influence that he could probably get an exclusive grant to make the stuff, at least in that part of Italy that Rome controlled. All he had to worry about was the damn Carthaginians and their ships. Julius Crassus was uninterested in the debate over slavery, save that he wasn't going to give up his.

"Yes, it does happen, but not nearly as often as you seem..." Hamilcar paused to let the noise of the strike roll over them. They were in the Hoypoloi Lounge and the two lane bowling alley was occupied. "...to think."

"Once is too often," Moses Wilson said.

"Of course, it is. Which is why you refused to send the *Reliance* on a punitive expedition to kill children on the Orinoco River. Oh, but wait! You *did* send the expedition, and you personally were cheering when they left."

They were talking about the practice of child sacrifice, which Hamilcar didn't like either. But the self-righteousness of the ship people could, as they would say, "get under your skin."

"It's not the same," Moses insisted.

"No, it's not. The gods require it of us. You're doing it on your own. For mere political gain."

Moses sputtered a moment but said, "God doesn't require human sacrifice."

"Maybe not in the twenty-first century that you came from. And even then it's more that he doesn't require them directly than that he doesn't require them. Considering the people killed in his name according to your histories—" Hamilcar pulled himself back from what Marie Easley called debate mode and held up a hand. "I don't approve of the practice myself, and as I tried to say before, it's not nearly as common as you seem to think. It started out as a way of making it easier for the parents of children who died naturally to cope, saying the gods blessed a family that lost a child. But we are a merchant people and somehow it changed. If the gods bless the family when they take a child, how much more will they bless a family and how much wider will the blessing spread if the family willingly gives up the child?

"And when a drought or a plague or a war happens, well, people get desperate and require greater sacrifices of their neighbors. Most of the time it isn't child sacrifice. It's children that the gods have chosen to take early and so they are cremated and put in urns in the playground of the dead. That's a poor translation, but it's a type of cemetery for children to reflect a special sort of heaven for the children. Ice cream and candy and never a bellyache. The actual sacrificing only happens when there is something dire going on," Hamilcar insisted.

That was mostly true, though some of the great houses adopted slave children and sacrificed them to get extra blessings. But Hamilcar decided not to mention that part, though he didn't doubt some of the Greeks would point it out.

So it went. Not just across the lab, but across the ship, as students of the *Queen of the Sea* university learned to make plastics and laws, steam engines and plays, math and science, theology, English, Greek, and Phoenician . . . the list went on.

Reliance, *Gulf of Paria*
August 11

Adrian looked at Fort Plymouth with eyes considerably older and colder than they had been just weeks earlier. Also, filled with a profound gratitude to be back among at least nominally civilized people. The things he had seen on both sides of the punitive expedition up the Orinoco River would be giving him nightmares for a long time, probably the rest of his life.

The *Queen of the Sea* blew its air horn in welcome. And the *Reliance*, now a warship in truth, fired a blank cannon round in response.

"Message from the *Queen*, Captain," said Pierre Minuet. Pierre was one of the retired military who had volunteered to go on the expedition, and was now the radio operator because he had broken his right arm a week into the mission. "They say that since we're here, they are heading out, and they will see us in Alexandria."

CHAPTER 27

Queen of the Sea, *Straits of Gibraltar*
August 18

The passengers were having a party. It was a tradition of the ship. Each time they passed the Pillars of Hercules, they had a party. The type of party varied with the passengers and off-duty crew involved, but there were ship people traditions about crossing the equator or the international date line or passing through the Pillars of Hercules. Since The Event, the *Queen* hadn't done the equator or the date line, but this would be their fourth time through the straits. They deserved a party.

Allison Gouch showed Captain Floden the bottle, which was a piece of theater because Lars Floden was by preference a beer man, not a wine snob. "Whatever you think, Allison."

"Oh, bring him a beer," Marie Easley said. "No reason to put on the act on my account. On the other hand, what have you got?"

"It's a passable Persian wine we picked up in Alexandria last trip," Allison said. "A bit of a fruity tone and a little smoke."

Marie Easley was a wine snob. Connoisseur, she would call it. Lars smiled at the way the scholar was fitting in with the crew. Then he looked at her, and his smile warmed. The respect he had felt for her from the outset had developed into something more since, although neither he nor Marie was ready to come to any conclusions yet as to exactly what that "something more" would wind up being. For a certainty, though, it was nice not to wake up alone every morning.

He turned his thoughts back to business. "What is the political situation likely to be?"

"I'm not sure. The women do play a significant role in the politics, but almost nothing of them—with the exception of Olympias, Roxane, and Eurydice—is recorded. Even Philip's mother, Philinna, isn't recorded beyond her name. Nor any of the wives of Antipater. Their influence, though often behind the scenes, is powerful. At least two of the wars of the successors are, from what Roxane and Cleopatra tell me, at least in part caused by cat fights between the wives and/or girlfriends of the successors in question."

"Which ones?" Lars asked curiously.

"Cassander and Polyperchon. Cassander's sister, Nicaea, hated Polyperchon's wife with a passion. Something from when Nicaea was a girl. So when, in that other history, Antipater gave the regency to Polyperchon, it's a safe bet—according to Cleo—that Nicaea would have encouraged Cassander to rebel."

"I thought it was just because he's a conniving little creep." Lars Floden had lived and worked among Americans for decades now, and their expressions were insidious.

"Well, he is. At least according to Eurydice and Roxane. But Cleopatra isn't as convinced. Cassander was Antipater's aide and assistant, and did most of the day-to-day parts of Antipater's job. What he isn't, is personally courageous. And the Macedonians, even more than the rest of the locals, put personal courage—or perhaps personal viciousness—as their top virtue. That's why Dag impressed them so much. When he tossed that grenade to Kleitos, he demonstrated not just personal courage, but a willingness to kill that impressed the Macedonians a lot."

Lars shook his head. "I can follow that logic—my ancestry raising its atavistic head, I suppose—but only with difficulty."

Marie gave his forearm an affectionate little squeeze. "We're doing rather well, I think. Much better than I would have projected in the days right after The Event. Any semblance of a democratic and egalitarian society is still a mist in the future, but we have accomplished two critical things."

"And what are they, as you see them?"

"First, we're playing a big role in keeping Alexander's empire from shattering into pieces. That makes a difference, Lars, it really does. Not only does it mean the chaos and bloodshed isn't what it would have been without us, but it also means that any social and cultural advances we foster get spread rapidly."

He nodded. "Yes, I can see that. And I suppose the second critical accomplishment you would point to is that by turning the *Queen* into the world's greatest university we are driving those advances forward."

She smiled widely. "Oh, but it's not just a university, Lars! The *Queen* is also the world's greatest safe house—no, let's call it the world's greatest time-out for over-aged and way-too-powerful children. That's possibly the greatest role we're playing in keeping the empire intact. Whenever one of the major players feels too threatened, they can come on board and relax instead of lashing out at their enemies."

Captain Floden laughed, then. "In other words, I'm still a cruise ship captain. Making people whose heads and wallets are too big feel that they're properly appreciated."

"Well...Yes. Except these people spill blood when they don't feel appreciated, instead of cutting the tip."

Dag leaned over and kissed Roxane. She kissed him back while Alexander IV watched. Dag might have had a bit too much to drink, but this had been coming since the first time he saw her. Roxane kissed him back vigorously, which surprised him.

"Why are you kissing Mommy?" The king didn't sound upset, just curious.

"I just wanted to," Dag said.

"I think it's time for you to go to bed," Roxane said to her son.

"No. Don't want to." There was a short, considering pause, like the king was marshaling his arguments. "It's a party."

Alexander pointed at someone who was poking at the food on a table she could barely reach, and made what he obviously considered the clinching argument. "Her mommy isn't making Dorothy go to bed and she's not even a princess."

Dag laughed. He couldn't help it. Which got him a glare from Roxane. "There will be time," he offered. "Let's let him watch the fireworks."

The *Queen* had fireworks again, a side effect of the New America armaments industry. Also useful, in the captain's opinion, to impress the locals.

At the request of the Carthaginians, the first stop this trip was to be Formentera Island, where they were assured the locals had repaired the docks. That was just under four hundred miles from the Straits of Gibraltar. The *Queen* would be arriving there tomorrow afternoon.

"Plenty of time," Dag said again, and hugged Roxane to him.

In another part of the ship, Philip III of Macedonia managed, with great difficulty, to put an arm around his teenaged wife. She stiffened for a moment then leaned into him, which almost made him pull back.

Touching still wasn't something he was comfortable with, but it was something he knew he had to learn to do. And in a strange way, it was something he wanted, even though it terrified him. He had always wanted it, even when he was a child, but he had been unable to stand being touched. Unable to trust the feelings it engendered.

"It's still hard for me, Eurydice, but I am learning."

"I know, Philip," Eurydice agreed. "You are getting better." She hugged him back, hard. That was another thing that they had learned since the ship people came. It was the soft, gentle touch that made him twitch away, not the strong touch.

Eurydice hugged Philip and wondered if he would ever be ready for the more intimate contact that true marriage required. But this was one issue—perhaps the only issue—over which she was prepared to be patient and bide her time.

All over the ship, people danced, and talked, and hugged, and more. The *Queen of the Sea* was the safest place on Earth, as well as by far the most luxurious. Besides, the scholars who had boarded in the Mediterranean were almost home, and the new students who had boarded in New America were eager to see Europe.

Queen of the Sea, *Formentera Island* *August 19*

The docks were in surprisingly good shape, but it was still with everyone on high alert that the *Queen of the Sea* pulled up to those docks. Docks offered greater convenience, but that convenience was dangerous. For, if the passengers could walk off the ship, an invader could walk on.

Captain Floden saw that the dock was empty, save for one man in the dress of a Carthaginian noble. Multicolored robes, and oiled and curled beard and hair. Sandals, and all held together by gold or at least gilded chain. Not the heavy chains of imprisonment, but the sort of chains that back in the twenty-first century would have been a woman's necklace.

Mosicar was standing on the dock and looked up at the ship. And up, and up, and up. As the monster got closer, it seemed to curl over him. Mosicar had no way of knowing it, but the boarding portal that would open to the dock was on the third deck. The deck he could see people walking on was deck seven, and the ship extended up beyond that. Way up beyond that. It was a castle, and taller than any castle he had ever seen, floating on the water. And those idiots in Alexandria had tried to seize this ship. Mosicar had always known that Greeks were crazy, but this was beyond lunacy. It was all he could do to stand his ground and wait.

The ship moved up and stopped, not quite touching the dock, and a portal bigger than a barn door opened. A ramp extended from it to hang a little above the dock and a group of men in strange clothing leaped to the dock. Ignoring Mosicar, they ran along the dock to catch a massive rope they were tossed by those aboard. Another party was standing at the portal, and though Mosicar didn't know the person, one of that party was wearing Carthaginian attire.

The unknown Carthaginian waved and shouted: "The crew will have the ship tied up in a few minutes! We'll come ashore then! Do you have the supplies?"

"Warehouses full of them!" Mosicar shouted back.

It was true. Mosicar had taken his gleanings to Carthage and gotten there while word of the *Queen of the Sea*'s arrival in Alexandria was still fresh. That news had meant that he had gotten amazingly good prices for the gleanings, and that had gotten him an interview with the *suffets*, the annually appointed judges of Carthage. There were two of them, like the Roman consuls, and they were, together, the administrative head of Carthage. It was a dangerous time in the life of a small, provincial land owner. But Mosicar had survived and managed to keep possession, and even partial ownership, of the docks. By the time the cruise ship was to reach Carthage on its second trip to the Mediterranean, Mosicar was back home, with the task of rebuilding and restoring the docks.

It had been a tremendous effort and tremendous expense, more than he had, even with the high prices that his gleanings brought. He was in debt now, and if the ship people proved unreasonable, he was ruined. If that happened, he would be a slave, his children sold to be sacrificed.

He waited, with hope and trepidation, as the ramp finally lowered to the concrete dock.

Hamilcar looked at the provincial and hid a grin. The fellow was as overdressed as a teenager at his first dance. In Carthage, young men were expected to make a public show of the prominence of their family when they entered the social scene in preparation for their marriage. Almost all of what the ship people called real property was legally held by the women. It was the product of that land that came to the men to be traded on ships all over the Mediterranean and north Atlantic, the profits of which were then reinvested in the property of their families back home. The young men were dressed in their finest in the hopes of making a good match.

It was also not the best strategy, not with the ship people. Hamilcar knew the situation. The ownership of the docks was in question, and Carthage was sure to come down on the side of the ship people, not on that of the provincial. Carthage needed to be on the good side of the *Queen of the Sea* because almost all of Carthage's area of influence was under the *Queen*'s guns. Nor to mention that the *Queen* could simply ram and sink any other ship—or entire fleet, for that matter—that it chose to, unless that ship got to shallow waters. And it would have to do it *quickly*. As huge as it was, the *Queen* was also much faster than any ship of the time.

Port Berry, Formentera Island
August 19

The storefront was much as he remembered it, Dag thought as he, Roxane, Alexander and a small contingent of Silver Shields wandered through the shops. The products in the storefront were markedly different, however. There were woolens from Italy and Spain, up to what would be France and even Germany. Also animal hides from Europe and Africa. Amber in silver necklaces and bracelets. But not an iPod to be seen.

Still, the locals seemed to have learned something. They had a set of copper wires hooked up to lights. No power but it was clear that they had managed to figure out that a circuit had to be insulated. It was impressive. If they could figure that out from the bits left behind what could they do with books on steam power and electrical generation?

There were cowboy hats. More than there had been. These people must have been making them. Also bowlers and fedoras. The designs must have been from examples they found here, but the bright purple color suggested they were locally made.

Roxane took one look at the purple cowboy hat and had to have it. It was one of the most expensive hats in the shop, of course, and it had a hat band of gold links. Negotiations commenced and Dag was lost in minutes. The shopkeeper spoke some Greek, but mostly Phoenician, and Roxane, though more comfortable in Greek, could speak Phoenician, so they switched to that language in less than a minute, and the translation app couldn't keep up. Dag hoped that the skipper and Eleanor were doing better than he was.

Eleanor Kinney looked at the pallets full of stuff and made notes on her pad. She was very careful with the pad. Over a dozen of the electrical pads had been broken or lost since The Event, and now they were all signed out and signed back in with a fulsome amount of paperwork. They were incredibly useful, and completely irreplaceable. Anne Keener predicted that it would be at least twenty years before they could produce integrated circuits of the sort needed to make a slate-style computer, probably longer.

She made a quick note on the pad, looked at the prices they had paid for the same goods in Alexandria last time, and determined that it was a good deal, but not a great one. "We'll give you four silver talents for the beans and no more."

Mosicar winced but Eleanor didn't buy it. He was good, but she had dealt with better since The Event and was learning the skills of reading merchants. All in all, the island of Formentera was looking to be decent competition for Alexandria, but not quite up to its standards. For now it was more convenient. Goods could be loaded directly onto the ship but that would be changing soon. Alexandria had already been building a pier on their last visit, and so were Rhodes and Carthage.

"Some restocking can be done here, but if you want regular visits what you need to do is build a hotel," Eleanor told Mosicar.

"A hotel?"

"Yes. A resort hotel where people can spend time in luxury," Eleanor explained. "I know about the entertainment industry. Granted, you won't have nearly the numbers that we did back in the twenty-first, but there are wealthy people. And they will come to a resort if they can do so safely and in comfort."

They talked about making Formentera into a resort and a regular stop on the *Queen*'s route. Before The Event, the *Queen* had been a cruise ship—not a means of transportation, but a ship that for the most part loaded its passengers, took them around the Caribbean, and returned them to the same port. Now it was the fastest, most comfortable, and most secure means of getting to any place it went. That meant many of its passengers were going to be boarding, not to vacation, but to get from Point A to Point B. But it also meant that any stop the *Queen* made was guaranteed to be a place that was regularly visited by the wealthiest one percent of Europe's elite. Formentera didn't have enough local industry to support regular visits by the *Queen*. If the ship was going to stop here, there had to be something to stop for. And to Eleanor, that meant a resort.

Port Berry, Formentera Island
August 22

Bisha watched the *Queen of the Sea* sail away with mixed feelings. Her husband, Mosicar, had come out of the negotiations with Captain Floden much better than they had feared. In essence, Captain Floden had ceded rights to Port Berry, that little bit of land that the gods had deposited on their little island, to them. All he asked for was permanent docking rights.

That was the good news. The bad news was that unless there was more investment within the next few years, the *Queen* would stop docking here.

The worse news was that the ship people didn't like slavery. In fact, they didn't like slavery so much that they had insisted—as a condition of the grant—that the part of the island that came with the ship people be free land. There wasn't any way for them to enforce it, not directly. They didn't leave anyone here for that. But they had insisted that it be written into the contract. For the people of Carthage, the contract was the basis for all law. Even religion was based on contracts between the supplicant and the gods. Not that the gods ever actually promised success. They would promise aid, but not victory.

And just because there wasn't a direct way to enforce it, that didn't mean they couldn't. All they had to do to hurt the island badly was stop coming.

Ostia Antica, mouth of the Tiber River
August 23

Titus Venturis Calvinus sat at an inn and drank sour wine. But not so sour as his situation. A tribune came in to the inn and Titus waved him over. "Have some wine, Appius." Appius Claudius Caecus had been with him at the battle of Caudine Forks, and had to walk under the yoke like the rest of them.

"The ship is here, General."

"It is?" Titus stood, swayed, and caught the wooden beam of the inn to steady himself. That was more from the wine than shock, but there was a fair amount of shock in there. Rome had sent him to be an observer of the convention to be held on the ship. But Titus knew full well that it was mostly to get him away from Rome after his disgrace.

"It is, General, and as big as we were told."

"Well, let's go see if there is really to be a convention."

At the dock there was a large sign in Latin, Greek, Egyptian, and Phoenician.

Slavery is illegal on the Queen of the Sea. *Any slave who boards the ship is thence and forever more a free person.*

Titus and Appius were each followed by two personal servants, and all of the servants could read. Titus went over to the crew of the small ship that was tied up to the dock and complained.

The crewman explained crudely that if it had been up to him, they wouldn't warn people, just free the slaves as they arrived.

Titus and Appius looked at each other and went back to the inn to discuss matters. Appius solved the problem by freeing his slaves right there in the inn. Titus, not nearly so profligate, arranged to have his servants sent back to Rome.

The metal door closed and the little room rose, then the door opened and Titus, followed by Appius, approached a young man who stood behind a counter.

"We are Rome's observers to the convention."

"That's fine, sir. We welcome your arrival, but there is the matter of the passage and accommodations. The *Queen of the Sea* is happy to host the convention, but delegates and observers, everyone, must pay their own passage."

There followed a list of accommodations and prices. An interior room with no windows was one price, a room with a balcony was another, and so on. Titus tried to bargain, but the clerk wasn't having it. However, they did show pictures of the various staterooms. Rome sent him, but he would be paying out of his own funds, and the prices were outrageous, so he got a single room that he would share with Appius. Appius then got a room for his servants.

Titus just shook his head. Appius was from a wealthy family. His father, Gaius Claudius Crassus, had been dictator seventeen years earlier. Dictator was a post that the senate of Rome awarded to a single individual during an emergency. It had incredible power, but the appointment only lasted half a year. To be appointed dictator meant you had both the trust and the respect of Rome's senate, and it only happened to the most successful of Romans.

Neapolis
August 24

Gaius Pontius left his slaves in Neapolis, and so did Laomedon. When they reached the counter, Gaius Pontius registered as the observer from the Samnites and Laomedon registered as the satrap of Syria.

The Egyptian man who was acting as translator for Anna Lang, the desk clerk, called Marie Easley, who called Roxane, and Roxane called Eurydice. After a brief consultation that didn't include Thaïs, they determined that—at least nominally—they would accept his registration.

Thaïs wasn't pleased when she heard.

Queen of the Sea, *en route to Sicily*
August 24

"Well, if it isn't the Roman general," Gaius Pontius said as he walked along the line picking up a plate of nut tarts from the buffet, "Titus of the Yoke."

Titus looked up and his hand—seemingly of its own accord—went for his belt knife. The ship's crew had taken the swords of the passengers and were holding them safely locked away.

"The Samnites," Appius said calmly, not even looking at the Samnite general, "have good soldiers and effective generals, but exceedingly poor politicians. That, General, is why they ceased to exist in that other history save as a minor province of Rome."

Titus saw Pontius stiffen and managed a smile. He looked over at Appius. "Well said, Tribune."

Now Appius did look at Gaius Pontius. "Come, General, join us. Let us discuss the effect of doing an enemy a small hurt."

"A small hurt?" Gaius Pontius asked.

"The army you sent under the yoke is still there, still intact, and having been humiliated, has every reason to want vengeance. Compare that to the queens who are regents for Alexander's heirs. And the *Queen of the Sea*, herself. They stop at ports all around the Mediterranean, and at each they pick up delegates and observers. That is what is taking so long. Captain Floden is waiting for the observers to be rounded up. He will do the same at Sicily, I don't doubt, and at Carthage. Thus, every nation will feel that they were represented and listened to."

It proved to be true.

In Sicily they picked up Agathocles of Syracuse—probably because the oligarchs wanted to get rid of him and his trouble-making.

The *Queen* didn't pick up an observer from the Carthage-owned part of Sicily because their next stop was Carthage itself.

Queen of the Sea, *off Carthage*
September 4

Hamilcar looked over at Capot Barca and grinned. Then he tossed the dice down the craps table.

"Four's the point," the croupier, Faith Marie Essence Jordan, informed them, and used her hook to pull the dice in.

Capot was a member in good standing of the up-and-coming Barca family. Hamilcar suspected that the Barca family was the same Barca family that in that other history would produce the famous Hannibal, who, through his victories, would prove such a disaster for Carthage. In the here and now, Capot was the observer sent by Carthage to watch while Roxane and Eurydice worked out the constitution for the new Macedonian-Persian Empire Alexander had formed and the generals seemed to want to tear apart.

"So what do you think of craps, Capot?"

Capot grinned back. "I like it when I'm winning. Not so much when I lose. What do you think of the queens?"

Hamilcar picked up the dice, shook them and rolled again.

"Nine," Faith Marie said, grinning. "No winner."

"I've only spoken to them a little," Hamilcar said. "Roxane...you know the stories about her having Alexander's other wives killed?"

Capot nodded.

"I find them quite believable. I don't know that it happened, and Roxane denies that she had anything to do with it. Blames it all on Perdiccas, and that might well be true. But if she had felt the need she would have done it. Practical as a priest of Ba'al, that one."

Hamilcar rolled again and got a five.

"And Eurydice?"

"All fire and passion. But she listens to Roxane, Cleopatra, and especially Marie Easley. That's the one you really should be watching. The woman knows more than even the gods ought to know."

Hamilcar picked up the dice and threw. A three and a four.

"Seven," said Faith, and raked in the bets.

Hamilcar stepped away from the table and Capot followed. The *Queen of the Sea*'s casino was doing a brisk business. People won and lost as they always had, but here it was done in comfort,

with flashing lights, and waiters with distilled liquors and entic-
ing foods added to the feeling of wealth and luxury.

Capot waved a waitress over. "Bring me a plate of crab puffs."

"And I would like an Egyptian Lightning, please," Hamilcar
said. Egyptian Lightning started with the rich, brown Egyptian
beer. The alcohol was distilled out, then about half the water was
distilled out as well. Finally, alcohol was put back in, to the point
that the liquor was about a hundred proof. It was a thoroughly
artificial drink with much of the rich flavor of Egyptian beer,
but a lot more kick.

"I don't know how you can drink that stuff."

"It's an acquired taste," Hamilcar said in Phoenician and added,
"And remember that the servers here are not slaves but..." He
paused, looking for the right word, the English word. Employees
didn't really translate. "...contractors, perhaps craftsmen, with
their craft being the serving of food and drink. It is polite among
the ship people to say please and thank you without much regard
to station."

Hamilcar pointed at a somewhat quieter nook in the casino
and they sat down.

"Is it important?" Capot asked.

"Yes. Not every time, but often enough. And any time you slip,
it's possible that either the person you're talking to or someone
listening will take offense."

"What does it matter if a servant takes offense?"

"The croupier at the craps table is Faith Marie Essence Jordan.
She is the granddaughter of Gary Jordan, who was what they call
a gentleman host before The Event. But he also has a bachelor's
degree in English composition, and in cooperation with one of
the Greek playwrights is translating the works of someone named
William Shakespeare into Greek. Faith was a croupier before The
Event, and is now both a croupier and a student of engineering at
the *Queen of the Sea* University, with what they call a minor in
business. In five years, you may be trying to hire her to redesign
your rope factory with ship people machines. Do you want the
cost of the insult with five years of interest added to her bill?"

"I'll hire someone else."

"Will there be someone else?" Hamilcar asked. "And if there
is, will they have the level of understanding of ship people technology that Faith, who was born in that other time, will have?

Besides, Amanda Miller, the representative of President Wiley, will be taking careful note of it every time you fail to show what they call proper courtesy."

Capot didn't respond immediately and Hamilcar waited while he worked it out. "Just how important is Amanda Miller? Remember I only boarded at Carthage. I have never been to New America, and anyway, they are across the Atlantic. What influence can they truly have on affairs on this side of the world?"

"Steamboats." Just the one word was enough. Steam as a power source had hit the world of this time with a clang that could be heard from the Tin Isles to India. Every artificer was trying it and some of them were starting to succeed. Or at least, starting to look like they would succeed. Besides, Capot had already seen the example steam engine that was on display in the mezzanine where the Help Desk was situated. Most of the local passengers were entranced for a while by the device, and it was a big reason that Hamilcar had enrolled in the university.

"Can they build them?"

"They *are* building them. There were a dozen or more passengers that had an interest in steam, and they have the Wiki and the Britannica and the engineers who studied the history of shipboard engineering as part of their studies. There are working steam engines in Fort Plymouth as we speak. They don't have the ships to put them in, not yet. But that will change."

By the time Hamilcar finished, Capot was pale. "That could spell the end of Carthage. Our hope was that there was only one *Queen of the Sea* and she couldn't be everywhere. Even with the *Reliance*, there were only two. But if they can build them, make..."

"They can't. Not of the size of the *Queen* or even the *Reliance*. They can build ships, smaller and made of wood, but still with steam engines and better hulls and rudders. But so can we. I will be able to design a steam engine when next I see Carthage. I probably could now, though I am afraid that our smiths are not up to making the boilers safe."

It was a wide-ranging discussion, and it lasted for hours. But, by the time they were done, Hamilcar thought—or at least hoped—that Carthage's observer to the constitutional convention realized that he should pay attention to Amanda Miller and that the ship people, even the ones on the other side of the world, would have a real influence on the world.

CHAPTER 28

Alexandria
September 6

Ptolemy looked out at the great ship and wondered what was coming. The politics since the *Queen of the Sea* left in June were complicated. Antigonus One-eye had retreated south and east, but gained the support of several eastern satraps, and was building a strong army. Eumenes was training his army and rebuilding his territory after Antigonus' raids. Polyperchon was nominally satrap of Macedonia, but Olympias was criticizing every move he made. The Greek states were quiet, based on the almost-promise of either independence or membership in a coalition of Greek states where they would have a real say. Everyone was waiting for the conference to establish a constitution.

Ptolemy looked over at Eudemus. "Have you found any more about constitutions?"

"Not really. The ship people mean basically what we mean by *Athenaion Politeia*, but there are differences. Their constitution is less a description than instructions, and has the power of law."

"Perhaps Thaïs will know."

"It's entirely possible, Satrap. I look forward to speaking with her."

"Not nearly so much as I do." Ptolemy smiled at the thought, then frowned. "I guess I should talk to Cleopatra as well."

"It would be wise, considering your plans."

By now Ptolemy had shared his plan to eventually split Egypt

355

off and make his own kingdom of North Africa, perhaps including Carthage, with Eudemus. It was sort of an open secret, anyway. Everyone knew by now what happened in that other history after Alexander's heirs—real and imagined—died. But all the generals, even Cassander, were busy insisting to anyone who would listen that they were loyal as long as there were heirs to be loyal to. And Heracles was busy insisting to anyone who would listen that he was no relation to Alexander and didn't want to be.

"Are you going to send a delegate?"

"I have to or declare myself traitor," Ptolemy said. "I think it will probably be you, though if I had my choice I would send Thaïs."

"She might well be the best choice. The ship people seem to be even more radical than the Egyptians in regard to letting women involve themselves in politics."

"And yet the captain of the *Queen of the Sea* is a man. The president of the New America is a man, the captain of the *Reliance* is a man. Women can have jobs, and important ones, but they can't be kings," Ptolemy said.

"It's a small group. For all we know the captains of most of their ships are women," Eudemus said, but Ptolemy could tell he didn't mean it.

"Papa, they have flying machines!" Eirene yelled. "And I know how to make them! Well, almost."

She came charging onto the terrace, with her mother Thaïs closely behind. Eirene was eight and full of enthusiasm but this was more than Ptolemy expected even from her.

"How do they work?" Eudemus asked before Ptolemy could speak. The satrap of Egypt looked at his librarian in surprise bordering on shock.

"It's airflow. Bernoulli's law."

"Who is bernewly and how did he gain the power to legislate flight?" Ptolemy asked before Eudemus could interrupt again.

"That's what Lagus said. But it's not that kind of law. He didn't make it. He *discovered* it. It's a natural law," Eirene said, her voice not so loud.

"Is that what the constitutional convention is for? To discover laws?"

"No," said Thaïs, "though I think some of the ship people think the Constitution of the United States is made up of natural laws. And even more, something they call their Declaration of Independence. A document that seems to be the attempt of their first kings to claim that their revolt was legal." She reached him and gave him a peck on the cheek, but there was a bit more reserve in that gesture than Ptolemy had been expecting, and it made him a little nervous.

Still he turned and put an arm around her, and led the way into the palace. "Are Roxane and Eurydice still afraid to come ashore? I had at least expected Cleopatra to be with you." Apparently that wasn't the right thing to say, because Thaïs stiffened in his arm. Could it be because of the possibility that he might have to marry Cleopatra? No. That didn't make sense. Thaïs knew the rules. She had lived with them as long as he had.

Then she relaxed a little and murmured, "We'll talk about it later."

Later arrived.

The sun was setting, the children were in their rooms with their books and games, and Thaïs took a chair across the table from Ptolemy. "Laomedon is on the *Queen of the Sea*, claiming to be the satrap of Syria. His argument is that the satrapies are not the property of the satraps, but the property of the empire and one of them cannot be conquered by the satrap of another without that satrap being in rebellion against the crown. So far, Roxane and Eurydice haven't ruled on the issue."

"That little weasel." Ptolemy stood up and paced to the window. "It didn't stop him from taking my money. Are they really listen— No, of course they are. If I can't take Syria without their say so, they gain a great deal of direct power over the empire." He went back to his chair and sat. "What else?"

Thaïs nodded. "Cleopatra won't come ashore unless she first receives strong assurances that she will be allowed to leave again. Also, the offer of marriage is retracted."

That was bad news. A political alliance with Cleopatra would have possibly given him enough legitimacy to go for the regency. "Why? And who has she decided to marry?" If she chose Eumenes, she would effectively give him the regency. That had to be prevented at any cost. If she chose Cassander, she would legitimize him and put him back in the game. And Cassander was dangerous. He was smarter than most people gave him credit for.

An effective planner and skilled strategist. If he lacked personal courage, he didn't shrink from hard decisions.

"She hasn't decided to marry anyone, but she is leaning toward a ship person named Sean Newton."

"Who? A ship person? But they don't have royalty, do they? I mean, none of their leaders came with the ships. Except perhaps Wiley."

"The ship people don't have the respect for royalty that is common in the world. They talk about royalty and their ship is named *Queen of the Sea*, but they are all republicans like the Athenians or the Romans. Well, some of them call themselves democrats and they argue with the republicans about things that make no sense. Don't ask me what the difference is. But whether they call themselves republicans or democrats they don't even have the level of respect for lesser ranks that is common in Athens or Carthage. They say everyone is equal before the law."

"Even slaves?" Ptolemy started to say, then realized the ban on slavery meant no slaves. "So who is this ship person?"

"He was a manager of a grocery store and on vacation. He is now a professor of business management at the *Queen of the Sea* University."

"Why would she choose such a man?"

"Because she has a choice. On the *Queen*, she is safe and she can, to an extent, exercise political influence by influencing Roxane and Eurydice, and by commands, decrees, and instructions. By marrying Sean, she would remove herself as a prize and become safer from the machinations of the generals and her mother."

"Well, at least it's not Eumenes or Cassander."

"What is Cassander doing?"

Pella, Macedonia
September 6

Cassander stepped out from behind the wall hanging and said, "Hello, Aristide."

Polyperchon's aide went pale, then shouted for the guards. The guards continued to stand their posts, paying no attention at all to the puffed-up Greek mercenary. Cassander was a Macedonian of noble birth. Besides, he had paid them well and they could expect more.

Cassander gestured and two guards came over to take Aristide into custody. It would be a short imprisonment. They would kill him as soon as they got somewhere private.

Pella was the true capital, where Philip II had ruled, and from which Cassander's father, Antipater, had administered Macedonia. It was also where his family's money was kept. Cassander went to the dais, stepped up, walked to the throne, and sat. He had been a long time getting here. Years serving his father, and months sneaking around the back country of Macedonia, pulling together all the young conservatives who had never approved of Alexander's adventures in Persia and didn't respect Polyperchon.

But he had done it. He had his army now. It was small and still in need of training, but it was enough, with Polyperchon sending most of his army to support Eumenes against Antigonus. Roxane was too busy with the empire to worry about Macedonia, just like that maniac Alexander had been. Stupid bitch.

He waved over a guard and had his generals called in. It was time to take back Macedonia, for it was the core of the empire.

Where Macedonia led, the rest would follow, soon or late.

Amphipolis, Macedonia
September 8

"What are you still doing here?" Olympias demanded.

Polyperchon closed his eyes. He had never understood how a voice could be so harsh and so dulcet all at once. "I am satrap of Macedonia, and where else should I be?"

"With the army in Anatolia. Roxane ordered you to support the clerk."

"I sent an army to support the clerk." Polyperchon snorted a laugh. Olympias and he didn't agree about much, but neither of them thought much of Philip II's clerk. Not as a general anyway. They had both known Eumenes when he was a teenager, and the fact that his father was nothing but a wagoner was well known to them both. A man like Eumenes could be trusted and be of great value to the dynasty, but he should never be placed above a noble.

"You leave noble Macedonians and allied clans under the command of a carter's son?"

"No. Your daughter-in-law places them under the carter's

son," Polyperchon said. "I was just obeying the orders of the wife of Alexander. It was your son, Olympias, who made Eumenes a general, not me."

"Alexander, chosen of Zeus."

Polyperchon looked away and rolled his eyes. He knew about the cult that both Philip and Olympias were members of, and he knew Olympias had powers. But her visions and ramblings could get wearing at times.

"Word has reached us from Italy. The *Queen of the Sea* is back. So you can ask Roxane why she appointed Eumenes *strategos* of the Empire."

Queen of the Sea, *Ashdod*
September 11

"They are insane," Rabbi Benyamin Abrahamson said. "Half the Pharisees insist that Abraham actually sacrificed his son."

Dag nodded politely as he escorted the rabbi and the reverend to the elevators. This wasn't news. They had gotten regular reports over the radio.

The religious émigrés were still in Ashdod. They had made a couple of trips to visit the Second Temple, but had been refused entrance by the priestly class of this prerabbinic version of Judaism. The Jews of this time mostly believed that each nation had its own god or gods. Their interpretation of the commandment *Thou shalt have no other god before me* was that it clearly signified that other gods existed but that they were inferior to the god of the Jews.

It followed that the Jews thought *they* were better than the other nations also. They had apparently paid scant respect to Rabbi Abrahamson, and none at all to Reverend Terrence Hewell. In fact, if it hadn't been for Ptolemy's guards, Hewell would have been stoned for heresy, because he insisted that the messiah was coming on a specific date and he knew when it was.

"Do you want to come back aboard the *Queen*?" Dag asked.

"No," Hewell insisted. "God requires this of us. It is clearer to me than ever that we must prepare the way for Jesus. The crucifixion cannot be allowed to happen again."

Rabbi Abrahamson was rolling his eyes, but not where Hewell could see it. With an effort, Dag schooled his expression to polite enquiry. Then he turned to Rabbi Abrahamson and asked, "And you, Rabbi?"

"No. I need to understand what these people believe, as disgusting as I find much of it. There is something altogether too reminiscent of Nazism in their beliefs for my peace of mind."

"Jews as the master race?" Dag asked, surprised.

"Apparently."

"Well, if it is, it's certainly not unique to them. Some of the tribes in Venezuela were busy trying to sacrifice our people to their gods and had a very similar attitude."

"It's a universal condition that only Jesus put an end to!" Hewell proclaimed.

Dag got them to the conference room and made his escape. He had a date with a queen. Dag grinned. He had called Roxane a dowager queen once, and she had looked confused. Then, after she talked with Marie Easley, she hadn't spoken to him for a day and a half. It wasn't the specific meaning that she objected to, as the meaning was all true. It was the connotations, the image of a sixty-year-old walking with a cane, that she didn't like.

Queen of the Sea, *Izmir*
September 15

From Ashdod to Tyre, where they picked up delegates and observers, then to Rhodes where they got more observers, and Arrhidaeus as Antigonus One-eye's delegate. Then to Izmir, where Eumenes was waiting, along with a wet nurse and his infant son.

He bowed to both queens, but to Roxane first. "So, Your Majesties, do you want me here or commanding in the field?"

It was Cleopatra who answered with a question. "Do you have someone you can leave in command?"

"Well, Attalus might do. He's Macedonian and of noble blood. Frankly, my generals would be more comfortable with him than with me. Besides, I don't think we want him on the same ship as Arrhidaeus."

"No, probably not," agreed Roxane. "But Cleopatra could be your representative."

Eumenes looked at Cleopatra. "What have you decided for my satrapy?"

"Nothing specific to your satrapy, Eumenes. That's not what

we are doing. We are designing a structure for a government that recognizes local sovereignty in some ways, but where military and international relations are controlled by the central government. Your satrapy, and Ptolemy's, as well as the others, and the Greek states, and even the allied kingdoms, would become part of the same structure."

"I don't see how such a system could possibly work."

"Then come along, if you can trust Attalus not to attempt to usurp the crown while you are with us."

"It's not his usurping that worries me. It's his impatience. He is likely to rush into a battle with Antigonus, and Antigonus has been doing an excellent job of rebuilding his support among the eastern satraps."

"Then leave him firm instructions," Eurydice said. "Philip and I will co-sign them."

"Have you decided you trust me then, Eurydice?" Eumenes asked.

"Not entirely. But I am safe enough on the *Queen*, and Philip is getting better every day."

"What?"

"They have treatments for Philip's condition," Roxane explained. "It's not a cure, but they help."

There was more discussion, but it was decided that Eumenes would be the delegate for his satrapies. He would delegate command of the army and administration of his satrapies to others.

Queen of the Sea, *Athens port at Piraeus*
September 20

"The meeting of the Constitutional Convention of the United Satrapies and States of the Empire will come to order," Cleopatra said into the microphone. She spoke in Attic Greek, not Macedonian, as had become the custom of Macedonia's upper classes. But it was a version of Greek that was rapidly becoming modified—or adulterated, some insisted—by the addition of a multitude of English loan words. More than half the words in the sentence she'd just spoken, for instance, were either completely new or had a different connotation than they had in Attic Greek.

Much like the language they had all agreed to use, a compromise had been worked out. Cleopatra would start the convention and open it up to nominations for president of the convention. Though they were more trusting of one another than they had been, neither Roxane nor Eurydice was willing to cede any advantage to the other. And president of the convention was a real advantage.

People looked around and mostly quieted, but a few continued to talk, either because they weren't paying attention or as a snub. There were thirty-eight satrapies in Alexander's empire, and that was including several of the Greek states as part of a single satrapy.

At the same time, some of the satraps held more than one satrapy. Eumenes was satrap of Cappadocia, Paphlagonia, Greater Phrygia, Pamphylia and Lycia, the last three of which had been assigned to Antigonus at the Partition at Babylon.

Antigonus had sent Arrhidaeus as his representative to the convention, and was claiming the same satrapies on the basis of the Partition at Babylon, the outlawing of Eumenes by the army, and the documents that Eurydice had signed while in his custody.

Ptolemy was represented by Thaïs and was claiming two votes as satrap of Egypt and Syria, but Laomedon was there too, claiming that a satrap could not be yielded or sold, but was issued by the authority of the crown.

That was an argument that Roxane and Eurydice were inclined to accept, though even in Persia it was an iffy argument by the time Alexander arrived.

Aside from the delegates, there were over a hundred observers from nations and cities, as well as students at the university. Cleopatra opened the convention to nominations.

Laomedon rose and nominated himself.

Thaïs jumped to her feet. "Laomedon is not a true delegate," she protested. "He sold his satrapy. Even if, in the fullness of time, this convention decides that he can't do that and that the sale is invalid, all that means is he abandoned his satrapy without authorization, and as such still has no place here."

"I had no choice. The histories show that if I had failed to accede to Ptolemy's demands, he would have sent in his army and taken the satrapy anyway."

"You took his money," Thaïs insisted.

Cleopatra pounded her gavel. When there was a bit of quiet, she looked around the hall and saw a hand raised. "Yes, Shirley. Did you have a suggestion?"

"Have you determined that you have to be a delegate to be nominated as president of the convention?"

"Well, I just assumed..." Cleopatra stopped. "No, that hasn't been determined."

"In that case, go ahead and put his name in nomination and table the issue of whether he is a delegate or an observer."

Cleopatra nodded and then said, "Laomedon has been nominated. Is there a second?"

More delay, as Robert's Rules of Order were explained. Then Arrhidaeus stood and seconded Laomedon's nomination, but he didn't sit down once he had finished. Instead, he nominated himself as president of the convention and sat down, giving Laomedon a pointed look.

So it went. None of the delegates knew the ship people rules for discussion and debate, much less voting. The convention was as much a school of political science as a constitutional convention.

At the end of the day's meeting, the delegates and observers went their separate ways to enjoy the accommodations aboard the *Queen of the Sea.*

Polyperchon's delegate, Kostadin, was one of Philip II's retainers, all of seventy years old and not convinced that the convention was legal. He went to the spa on the recommendation of Epicurus, where he got a massage on the table next to Sogdiana's satrap, also named Philip but nicknamed Shorty.

"This is a waste of time, you know, Shorty?"

"Considering that in the other history Peithon had me put to death, I think I would prefer a less violent future."

Kostadin snorted, then groaned as the masseuse worked on a tense muscle group.

Olympias had sent her own delegate, Nikifor, a priest of Dionysus, who had a satchel full of mushrooms and other things that encouraged spirit dreaming. They were taken away when he boarded, with promises that they would be returned and stored in the pharmacy, which led him to the ship's pharmacy, where he got into a discussion of the various uses of drugs to heal as well as to contact and commune with the gods and release inspiration.

☆　　　☆　　　☆

Peucestas sent Amyntas, his younger brother, as representative of Persia, so Alexander IV's third bodyguard finally got to meet him. The little boy saluted with an upraised toy sword, then went off to play. Amyntas talked a little with Roxane, then went to the Cattle Baron restaurant, where he was served tuna steak with sweet potatoes. There he talked with Jahan, a Persian sent by Tlepolemus to represent Carmania, and Cassander's brother, Alexarchus.

"Which satrapy do you represent, Alexarchus?"

"Macedonia," Alexarchus said. "Not that it matters. The collapse of the empire was inevitable in that other history, and it's inevitable in this one. It was only Alexander's personal charisma that held it together as long as it lasted. Look at what happened at Triparadisus. This is too much land spread over too much distance with too many people to be one nation."

"Then what are you doing here?"

"I'm here to see the ship. What else? Besides, my brother wants someone here to make his claim on the kingdom of Macedonia made clear. Oh, and to make his loyalty to the crown clear, as well," Alexarchus added as an afterthought.

Queen of the Sea, *Athens port at Piraeus*
September 27

"Those who are not delegates fall into two categories," Roxane said. "Pseudo-delegates. That's people like Cassander's little brother and Laomedon. Or like your other vote."

"What?" asked Thaïs.

"Well, you're the delegate from Egypt. That much is clear. But whether you're the delegate from Syria as well, that's another question. It might be you, or it might be Laomedon, or it might be that someone else will be appointed satrap of Syria. After all, Ptolemy did fail to get permission from Alexander IV, Philip III, or their regents before he took an additional satrapy for himself."

"That would be Peithon and Arrhidaeus," Thaïs said. "They were the regents selected after Perdiccas was killed."

"No," Eurydice said. "That would be me and Roxane. The appointment of Peithon and Arrhidaeus wasn't legal."

"That's the sort of thing that a Greek demagogue can spend years arguing about, or a Macedonian army will settle in the field," Thaïs said. Then she held up a hand to keep Eurydice from interrupting. "All I'm saying is you don't want to push Ptolemy until he is forced to use the army. You might be able to get him to accept that he's not supposed to do it again once the constitution is in place, but to go back and undo it? As the ship people say, that won't fly." She turned back to Roxane. "What's the other category?"

"Observers, like the ones from Carthage and Rome."

"And the difference between the two categories? I mean, why did you point out the two categories?"

"Because the observers won't get a vote on anything. They can observe and make comments, but since they don't play a role in the empire, they don't get to vote on what's in the constitution."

"Like Capot's proposed amendment to the war powers section, making attacks against Carthage illegal."

"It doesn't make them illegal. It just requires us to get Carthage's consent before any attack."

"Actually, that's what I'm afraid of if we let the observers vote. We have enough trouble with the delegates wanting to put in special provisions to benefit them or the satraps they represent. But Capot's smart. He's trying to get support for his amendment from the other observers. Trading a rule against us attacking Rome for Rome's vote."

"The problem is that they are going to be angry if we prevent them from voting," Eurydice said. "We should have settled the issue of who has a vote first."

"I'm not so sure," Roxane said. "The way we are doing it keeps them engaged in the process. And the more involved they are, the more likely they are to support the eventual document."

"Not after we take away their vote," Cleopatra said.

"Even then, if we do it right," Roxane said. "We need to thank them for their input and make it clear that we are listening to them, but also make it clear that the constitution will be made by us, for us. At the same time, we are going to need to regularize the voting status of the pseudo-delegates. When we have two delegates from the same place, or when the delegate we have is from a satrap that we haven't endorsed, we need to determine if those delegates get a vote."

Through the window they could hear the Silver Shields drilling out on the pool deck of the *Queen*.

"That still leaves the Greek states like Athens, Rhodes, Thrace," Thaïs pointed out. "As for we pseudo-delegates, I think we should get a vote." She stopped and considered. "I watched that movie about the founding of their nation with Marie the other day. *1776*? Have you seen it?"

Cleopatra shook her head, as did Eurydice, but Roxane nodded. "Horrible music."

"I sort of liked it," Thaïs said, "but what I am remembering is that at one crucial part, Franklin asked that the delegation be polled."

"Which one was Franklin? The tall redhead?"

"No. The short fat one."

"Who cares? What's your point?"

"I think that when there is more than one delegate from a satrap, we should treat the group of them as a single vote. So, for instance, I would be the delegate from Egypt, and Laomedon and I together would be the delegation from Syria."

"And what if you disagreed?" Eurydice asked.

"Then our vote would not count. But if a delegation has three or more delegates, the majority would determine the vote of the delegation."

"And the Greek states that are all in the satrapy of Greece?"

"The same, at least for this convention," Thaïs said then added, "It's a compromise, but it might keep us from needing that—" She gestured out the window at the drilling Silver Shields.

Eumenes watched the Silver Shields with their spring-steel crossbows. It was impressive. They moved forward behind their shields in a line four ranks deep. One rank would shoot, then the next rank would move past them while they were cocking and reloading. The second rank would shoot, then the next, until by the time the other three ranks had shot their bolts, the first rank would be reloaded and ready to move forward again. The deck of the *Queen of the Sea* was large enough for drill, but only limited drill. Just enough to let these veterans of many battles know how to integrate the new weapons.

He walked over to Dag Jakobsen. "How would they do on a long march?"

The big Gaul smiled at him with even, white teeth, and said, "Not as well as they would have before they came aboard the *Queen*.

Don't get me wrong. They are probably in better overall health than they have been in years. But there isn't room to do forced march practice and there isn't much need, either. These are becoming marines, and shipborne marines at that. It's unlikely that they will need to go very far to get to battle."

"Where would I learn about your techniques for moving armies?"

Dag gave him a sharp look. "What's up?"

"A courier just in from Cappadocia. Antigonus has taken Babylon. Attalus proposes to go take it back."

"Why haven't you relieved him?"

"Two reasons. First, it would take the queens acting together as regent to remove Attalus from command, but the second reason is more important. He has the support of most of my generals. They want to prove that they can win without the presumptuous wagoner's son. And I'm not there, so they would just ignore any orders I sent, even if they were cosigned by the queens-regent."

"What do you think will happen?"

"I'm not sure. Craterus was Alexander's best general, but after him...Ptolemy or Antigonus might be the best. Attalus is mostly competent, but he lacks Antigonus' presence."

They were talking using a combination of Greek and the translation app. Eumenes was an educated man, but not yet conversant in ship people English. "Presence" was one of those words that they had to go to the app for, and the app showed "style" and "savoir faire" as synonyms.

Later, Dag passed along to Evgenij the conversation he'd had with Eumenes concerning the Silver Shields' capabilities on a long march.

The veteran chuckled. "I have no intention of finding out. Nor does any Silver Shield on this ship. We like it here. It's the best assignment we've ever had. We even get along well with you."

Dag studied him for a moment, very seriously. "You have no regrets? Misgivings?"

Evgenij chuckled again. There was even less humor in the sound than there had been before. "Such a diplomat! What you're really wondering is whether we still pose a security risk to the ship."

"Well...Yes, I suppose so. Do you?"

"Doesn't it seem stupid for you to ask me that question? If I wasn't trustworthy, I'd lie to you anyway."

"Yes, but you won't." Now it was Dag's turn to chuckle. "Which I suppose answers my own question. But I'm still...call it curious, if you will."

Evgenij shrugged. "Why would we? We've gained as much wealth—no, more—as we'd have had if we'd kept our slaves. You don't need slaves anyway, on the ship, and even barely when we operate in Trinidad. You pay well and we're able to get land on Trinidad, for when we finally retire. Except for the ones who keep gambling it away in the casino. But there're only two of them. So why take the risk? Stupid."

Spotting a movement in the lounge, he nodded toward a trio who had just entered. "Very stupid, when you have that one on your leash. Any time I hear some idiot—none of whom are Silver Shields, not anymore—talk about how soft the ship people are, I remind them that the ship people have their own harpy. Who is more deadly than any monster of legend."

His eyes followed the trio as they passed through the lounge into a corridor beyond. Elise Beaulieu was in the center of the trio. Her two companions were members of the security force, both of them also ship people. All three carried pistols on their hips.

After the shooting on the bridge, Captain Floden had appointed Beaulieu as her own independent security force. She would always be accompanied by two guards—also armed—and neither of them would ever, under any circumstances, be a Silver Shield. He sometimes referred to the practice as his French insurance policy.

"We are not stupid, Dag," Evgenij said softly. "And...to be honest, as time goes by I find myself even agreeing with you most of the time. Well. Half the time. But the other half is well paid, so it doesn't matter."

And he chuckled yet again. There was even quite a bit of good humor in the sound this time.

CHAPTER 29

Babylon
September 28

Antigonus One-eye looked over the walls of Babylon in a much improved frame of mind. This day could not get better. The roof gardens of the city were in fruit and there were grapes, berries, and fall flowers, as well as vegetables and spices growing on the roofs of buildings all through the city.

Antigonus didn't know it, but a ship person seeing the famed Hanging Gardens of Babylon would have been reminded more than anything of an article on box gardening from the *Mother Earth News* magazine or some similar publication. Started by Nebuchadnezzar centuries ago, the custom had grown. Most of the roofs of buildings in Babylon, from the royal palace to a tannery, had boxes or pots of plants on the roofs. It kept the city cooler and the air pleasant. Not so much over the tanneries, but in general. Even the famed walls of Babylon had potted plants, and Antigonus could smell the mixed aromas of flowers and spices. They buoyed his spirits, but not nearly so much as the reinforcements he had received from many of the eastern satraps. That, and the treasury he had managed to seize intact.

Antigonus took a deep breath of the fragrant air and turned as he heard the shout of a palace messenger.

The messenger, having gotten his attention, ran up to him and, panting, handed him a note.

Antigonus read the note.

Attalus with force of ten thousand approaching along Euphrates River. Six thousand foot, three thousand horse, and a thousand auxiliaries. He is some five days travel from the walls of Babylon.

Antigonus had been wrong. The day could get better. He crumpled the note and strode along the walls with a grin on his face. Not that there was any rush. Five days was plenty of time to make things ready for his guests. They wouldn't be staying long, after all.

Menander and Leonnatus were waiting for Antigonus when he reached the palace.

"What are we going to do?" Menander asked.

For just an eyeblink Antigonus was stopped by the worry in Menander's tone. Then he laughed out loud. "We are going to rip Attalus and his army to shreds. That's what we are going to do. And by the time those spoiled girls and their Thrachian lapdog Eumenes are finished writing up their document, they will look up to see they have no empire left for it to govern."

Leonnatus joined in the laughter and after a moment so did Menander.

Queen of the Sea, *Athens port at Piraeus* September 28

"Miss Kinney, how long are we going to delay for this conference?" Aristotle Edfu asked.

"What's the problem, Aristotle?"

"I have goods to deliver in Rome and Constantinople and I need to acquire latex from New America. This delay is costing me money and I am not the only one."

"The problem is the *Reliance*. It was delayed in New America. The punitive raid had some unsuspected consequences that didn't come up until after we were on our way."

"What consequences?" By his tone, Aristotle wasn't happy to be hearing about it now.

"Nothing dire. In fact, just the opposite. After the raid, two of the other tribes on Trinidad asked to join New America."

"I heard about that."

"But it wasn't just them. A set of the coastal tribes from Venezuela have also offered tentative feelers about joining New America. President Wiley is using the *Reliance* to go along the coast, picking up delegations."

"Ah, I understand. The *Reliance* is delayed, and the *Queen* will use more fuel moving than we do just sitting here."

"That, and we don't want to show up in Alexandria with empty tanks and have to deal with your father and Ptolemy to buy fuel oil."

"I'm certain we can work something out with my father, Miss Kinney." Then, seeing her expression, he asked, "Is there anything you can do to get the *Reliance* headed this way? We need to make a circuit of the Med if nothing else, to let the observers report back to their respective states."

"There is the radio system."

"Not every city has a radio station," Aristotle muttered, and it was true.

"I'll see what I can do, Aristotle. But the convention is important."

"Yes, I know. What is the latest news? I haven't been attending the meetings."

"I don't see why imperial law should supersede satrapy law," Laomedon complained. Thaïs and several other delegates slapped their hands on their tables in support.

Marie Easley raised a hand before Eurydice could say something rude. Eurydice was a persuasive speaker, but she lacked anything remotely like patience in dealing with anyone except Philip III.

Phocion, the president of the convention, called on Marie with almost indecent haste. Not because he was fond of Marie Easley. He wasn't. He considered her to be much too smart to be a proper woman. But he knew from experience that Eurydice would likely ignore him if he called on one of the men instead of her.

"We need a universal structure of rules, else the conflicts between the satraps will lead to wars between them and the empire will tear itself apart. Besides..." Marie paused and looked around the room. "...this convention derives its authority from the queens-regent. That gives them effective veto power."

Roxane lifted a hand demurely, while Eurydice stabbed at the ceiling with her whole arm.

Phocion called on Roxane.

"Eurydice and I will not endorse or accept a constitution that is designed to fail." She looked over at the table that held Thaïs and Laomedon. "So, when a law made by the imperial council is in conflict with a law passed within a single satrapy—or even all the satrapies—the law of the imperial council will take precedence. We will not yield on that."

"And we," Laomedon shouted without waiting to be called on, "will not be dictated to like spoiled children! We must have a say in the laws that govern us!"

More table pounding. Laomedon was proving much more effective as a politician than he ever had been as a general.

"Captain, when can we get underway again?" Eleanor Kinney asked. "Aristotle buttonholed me this morning, and he wasn't the first."

"The *Reliance* is on its way, so we will be making the Mediterranean circuit starting in the morning," Captain Floden informed her. "Albrecht Niebaum called us from Ostia complaining over the delay, and he also informed me that Stalia, what was going to end up as Genoa in our history, has requested a radio. So we will be going all the way up the Italian coast, then around to Formentera, and back along the North African coast."

"How are the delegates taking the news?"

"Quite well. Though I suspect that sightseeing will cause delays in their deliberations."

Ostia
September 30

Rome was eighteen miles up the Tiber River. There was no Coliseum to look at, nor were most of the roads or aqueducts in existence. It was the center of an empire, but an itty-bitty one. There would be no tours of Rome. But the *Queen* did pick up twenty passengers, members of the senatorial and equestrian class. And Titus Venturis Calvinus got to make an in-person report to the present consuls of Rome, who came down to Ostia to see the *Queen*.

After introducing the consuls to sweet potato pie, chocolate, and yerba mate, Titus learned that Attalus was attacking Babylon.

They had gotten it over the radio located at Ostia, which was managed by Albrecht Niebaum.

Babylon
September 30

Attalus looked at the walls of Babylon, so close he could almost touch them and as far as the moon. Just as they had come in sight of Babylon his scout had reported a large force of cavalry on the Tigris River, just the other side of Babylon. Four thousand, if his scouts were right. And that spelled disaster for Attalus.

He could turn around and retreat back up the Euphrates, but to do so was to grant Antigonus One-eye the victory without cost. To announce to his own army that he had wasted their time and strength in a fool's quest. That would strengthen Antigonus and destroy Attalus.

Babylon was a rectangle of a city that was built on both sides of the Euphrates River, with triple walls behind wide moats. Attalus had expected Antigonus to come out to meet him—or, to huddle in the city. And he had plans for both contingencies. He would have used his infantry to pin Antigonus in the open field when he came out. And if Antigonus hid behind the walls, Attalus would put the city under siege and have old One-eye trapped, leaving the royal forces free to restore order throughout Alexander's realm.

What Attalus hadn't expected was this. He couldn't besiege Babylon without being harried by the cavalry, and he couldn't catch the cavalry with his infantry. He didn't have enough cavalry to face Antigonus. If he let it get separated from his infantry, he would invite defeat in detail.

Polemon rode up. "What now, Attalus?"

Attalus wanted to punch the arrogant bastard, but he didn't. "We take Nuchar across from the King's Gate. We'll camp there and build defenses against the cavalry."

"Then what?"

With sudden inspiration, Attalus said, "We send out some patrols and find some boats."

It took several days, during which cavalry skirmishes determined that the cavalry contingents of the two forces were about equal on a man-for-man basis. But Antigonus' army had more cavalry. Without the infantry to hide behind, Attalus' cavalry would be defeated. Not easily and not without inflicting heavy losses on Antigonus' cavalry, but defeated.

Babylon
October 5

Attalus boarded the boat with his bodyguards. There weren't enough of the boats to hold his entire infantry force. Most of them would be making a diversion against the King's Gate. But as soon as the sun went down, Attalus and five hundred picked infantry were going to float downriver and hit the western part of the city from the river.

One of the many things that Attalus should have realized—but didn't—was that Antigonus had spies in his forces.

Antigonus, too, waited for the sun to go down.

Josif looked at his commander. "Should . . ."

Antigonus was shaking his head. "No. Not until we see the signal. I want them fully engaged."

They waited. Waited as the infantry made a diversion against the King's Gate. Waited as Menander moved the infantry in the west half of the city to the walls, just as Attalus would expect.

There was a flash in the distance, a fire covered and uncovered . . . once . . . twice . . . thrice.

"They have pushed off the boats."

"Another few minutes, Josif. Let them think they are winning for a little longer."

"I'm more worried about Menander thinking they're winning," Josif muttered, and Antigonus laughed. He had not warned Menander about the enemy's diversionary attack against the walls, or—especially—about the boats. Partly that was because he wanted Menander reacting as he would do if it was real, but it was mostly because he didn't want Menander talking and word leaking back to Attalus' forces. A decisive victory here, and he might well be strong enough to declare his independence, even if the kings were still alive.

Leonnatus chugged the wine and grabbed the girl. And it was a girl, perhaps sixteen, perhaps less. But he wasn't interested in talking politics with her. He nuzzled her neck and squeezed her breast, then jerked away as a guard pounded on the door frame. "What?" he roared. "And it had better be important."

"The enemy is attacking the King's Gate."

"So what? Why tell me? That's Menander's part of the city."

The boats floated through the gloomy night and no one noticed the demonstration against the King's Gate had done an admirable job of fixing the enemy's attention away from the Euphrates.

"Mount up!" Antigonus roared.

The call was repeated and in less than a minute five thousand cavalry were mounted and ready to ride. They started slow. These weren't the heavy cavalry of later centuries, but they were still armored men on horseback. They would hit the infantry like a hammer unless the infantry was ready, with its *sarissa* pointed in the right direction. Right now, most of that infantry was standing on the banks of the moat around Babylon, making noise and doing an admirable job of keeping the attention of the city's defenders.

They weren't expecting Antigonus to be ready for this or to move this fast.

"At the trot."

The cavalry moved out.

Attalus looked up at the shout. They had been spotted. That was no real surprise. If anything, Attalus was surprised that they had gotten this close. They were less than a hundred yards from the walls.

The walls along the Euphrates were not high or strong. They couldn't be. The river was festooned with docks to bring in food and raw materials, and to take out finished goods and fertilizer.

"Move!" Attalus shouted.

And they moved.

Up to then, they had been drifting with the current, using their paddles just enough to keep them near the center of the river. Now they rowed like their lives depended on it.

Menander was on the walls, watching Attalus' infantry try to get into position to stop Antigonus' cavalry. He was considering a sally in support of Antigonus, but he didn't have any cavalry.

Antigonus had taken it all. He was, as it happened, less than a hundred feet from the King's Gate, and all the way across the western city from the river.

A runner had been sent to inform Menander of the attack on the river, but in the dark it was taking him more time than it should have, and the noise from outside the wall masked anything Menander might have heard from the river.

So Menander watched the shadows and torches across the moat.

It took Polemon a few vital minutes to understand the intent of the distant shouts. He turned in the saddle and peered into the night. But Polemon didn't have great night vision and at first he didn't recognize the darker mass moving along the ground.

By the time he did understand, it was too late.

He tried. He gave the right orders to re-form the infantry to face the cavalry. But it was too late.

A phalanx of Greek hoplites doesn't turn quickly, and *sarissa*-carrying Macedonian infantry makes snails seem agile.

Polemon's infantry were in the middle of the evolution when Antigonus led his cavalry into their flank.

Bolstered by the Silver Shields, the infantry did a decent job. They held together and took losses. Heavy losses. But they managed to hold the cavalry for several minutes. Polemon was right with them, leading by example. He fell too, but not for several minutes. And the hand he fell to was Antigonus' own.

Even as Polemon was dying, Attalus won the docks of the west side of Babylon, and his five hundred men were inside the city with only light casualties. They quickly moved west to secure the Samas Gate from the rear, but there was no one outside in a position to exploit the breach. For most of the night, the battle raged.

Attalus ordered some of his men to steal horses and try to contact the forces outside. The battle raged on, men fighting and dying in the dark, mostly not knowing who was who, except increasingly those on horseback were assumed to be Antigonus' men and those on foot Attalus'.

That was close enough to true. By late in the night, most of Attalus' cavalry had either run off or retreated into the city by way of the Samas Gate.

☆   ☆   ☆

The morning light showed Attalus in control of Babylon west of the Euphrates. There was still fighting in Attalus' part of the city, but he held the walls and had enough men in the city to continue to hold them. Almost all of Attalus' army that had made it to the Samas Gate were cavalry. His infantry had been shattered, and those not killed were captured.

The morning light also showed that Antigonus was in control of Attalus' army's baggage train.

Both generals had led from the front, but Attalus' position had prevented him from seeing or responding to Antigonus' attack. And Antigonus, even knowing it was coming, had failed to counter Attalus' capture of the west side of Babylon.

In the next few years, this battle would be taught in the ship people's war college as an example of why leading from the front is a bad idea.

Babylon
October 6

Antigonus rode up to the King's Gate only to hear a shout from the walls. "We've read the butterfly book!"

"So have I!" Antigonus roared back. "It doesn't matter, I have your baggage train! I have your women and your daughters! I even have your food!"

"There's plenty of food in Babylon, and we have half the city! And we have your women too, you old bastard!"

That was true. Antigonus' baggage train had been placed in Babylon for safety, but much of it—at least the common soldiers' part of it—was in the west, the poorer side of the city. Antigonus' own wife and family were in the eastern part. He could murder their women or give them to his men, but the confusion of the night battle had left both armies savaged. Attalus' worse than his, but his cavalry had taken a beating too. He wasn't in a position to exploit the weakness of Attalus' army, especially since a good chunk of Attalus' cavalry had escaped into Babylon late in the battle. Attalus had over two thousand men in the western part of Babylon, which gave him more men than Menander had.

More importantly, he had to do something . . . or did he? He had cavalry, more of it than Attalus did. He had captured most of Attalus' infantry. He could operate and contain Attalus. Again

Antigonus was tempted to make a demonstration—kill off the prisoners, sell their wives and concubines to the slavers. But he knew that with the damn butterfly book it would be trumpeted to the world as betrayal, not just punishment of undisciplined troops.

He turned to one of his officers and started giving orders. He would offer the captured infantry a choice. Join him or be made slaves. He still wouldn't be able to trust them, but he could use them here in Babylon to guard Attalus in his prison.

Yes. Turn the west side of Babylon into Attalus' prison, put guards around it, and let them stew. He doubted that Attalus would do nearly so well as Eumenes did in that other history. Meanwhile, Antigonus would take most of his army west.

Queen of the Sea, *in the Mediterranean*
October 11

Joshua Varner was the first to get the news. He was babysitting the forward communications array. They didn't have satellites anymore, and he was working on converting his sat links to something more useful in the third century before Christ.

Attalus attacks Babylon.

The report went on to describe the battle in terms that were more suited to hyperbole than to proper reporting. He sent back asking for clarification, but the radio station at Tyre didn't have any more. It was a dispatch delivered by a dispatch rider, and the rider himself hadn't been anywhere near the battle. He was the fifth rider on the route and didn't know any more than he had already reported.

The report was read in the convention hall, the room where the constitutional convention was meeting.

Slowly, Thaïs rose to her feet and just stood there. The room was in an uproar, people blaming Arrhidaeus, others blaming Eumenes, some even blaming Ptolemy, who was neither on the ship nor anywhere near the battle. They blamed baby Alexander for being a baby, and his father for being dead. They blamed Philip for being an idiot, and Eurydice for failing to kill Antigonus One-eye. They would, if any of them had thought of it, no doubt blame the moon for being full or the stars for being bright in the night sky.

And through it all, Thaïs just stood there.

Finally, gradually, there was quiet.

And then Thaïs said, "I'm tired." She paused, took a deep breath, expanding her already reasonably expansive chest, and looked around the chamber. "I am not speaking for Ptolemy in this. Just for myself. I knew Alexander the Great, and I knew his dream. I have seen the wars to make that dream real, and the wars that followed his death, and I am tired of the killing.

"We need a government. We need something to get the generals under control. We need to stop the wars. In that other history, the ship people history, these wars continued for another century. And by the time it was done, there was little left of Alexander's dream. And Macedonia, all the Greek states, were easy meat for the Romans. Even Egypt fell to Rome. Carthage was destroyed, sown with salt.

"We need another way. We need to find an agreement that we can live with."

It was a moving speech and spoken with all the skill Thaïs had learned as a hetaera and all the real passion she felt on the matter.

It left the room quiet and contemplative.

She sat down and it was a few minutes before the arguing started up again. And when it did start back up, there was, it seemed, a greater willingness to find a compromise. They made real progress that day and the next, and managed to set aside the lawmaking to focus on the structure of how the laws would be made.

By October 25th, they had a tentative constitution. It wasn't anything that the ship people approved of. It had little in the way of democracy and while it didn't enshrine slavery, it didn't forbid it either. It didn't even specify where the government of the empire would meet, leaving that up to the representatives to sort out. But it did have a system for making laws and creating money, both of which would be respected throughout the empire. It provided a structure for a government that would be able to make laws, declare and fight wars. Try cases in a system of courts. And do all the things that governments by rights do.

Eumenes looked out at the Mediterranean Sea. The constitution was written and pursuant to it, the queens-regent had appointed him *strategos* to the empire, under civilian oversight, with a budget and, at least in theory, an army. He had learned something of the ship people's ways of war.

Now it was simply a question of whether he could put those lessons into practice before the empire collapsed.

CHAPTER 30

Amphipolis, Macedonia
October 25

Cassander rode over the hill and looked out at the valley leading to Amphipolis and smiled with satisfaction. The sons of the great houses had followed Alexander, many to their deaths. But other sons had stayed home to secure the kingdom and serve their fathers. It was those sons who had rallied to his side. He looked to the hilltop where the lookout would be stationed as the first of his army crested the hill.

"Oh, crap!" The lookout just stared for a moment as the rising sun lit the rank upon rank of soldiers marching on Amphipolis. Then he turned and started shouting.

Amphipolis was a port. In fact, it was Alexander's main naval base in Macedonia, from which he had launched his campaign into Persia. It had a modern port—at least by third-century BCE standards—and lookout posts on the surrounding hills. It was also thoroughly tied into the network of signal fires and dispatch riders that tied Alexander's empire together. Even though it didn't have one of the ship people radio stations, it still had good communications with the rest of the empire.

That army could not be there. Amphipolis would have gotten the news.

☆　　☆　　☆

Word reached the palace at Amphipolis, where Olympias had been running things since Polyperchon had taken half the army off to defend Abdera.

"How did they get here?" Polyperchon's general demanded, sounding querulous to Olympias, who had just gotten the news and come straight here.

Olympias laughed. "Did it never occur to you that Cassander knows where the signal fires are as well as you do? He knows where the dispatch riders get their remounts too. He was in charge of setting up the remount stations for his father." With great drama, Olympias raised her eyes and hands to the sky. "Oh, my son, why did you have to take all the competent officers off to Persia and leave me with dolts?"

"We have been getting reports all along! He can't have cut our communications."

"No, he didn't cut the communications links. He corrupted them. That's why Cassander seemed to be massing his forces everywhere but here. And why Polyperchon has run off to Thrace with half my army."

Tactical surprise on a hilltop fort was the next best thing to impossible to achieve. But strategic surprise ... that could be achieved with skill and subterfuge.

Cassander, the black-hearted murderer, had both. Olympias didn't need more than five minutes to examine the massing army from vantage point of the palace tower to realize that Alexander's favorite city in Macedonia was going to fall. The question was what to do about it.

Of one thing she was determined. Her son's city would not be given to his murderer.

Amphipolis, Macedonia
October 27

The walls were holding for now, but it wouldn't be all that long before they fell. Olympias poured the ergot extract into the amphora of wine and mixed it. Then she took two gallons of distilled wine, and added it to the amphora as well. It was the wine she would give to her household slaves as she freed them.

Once it was mixed, she went to the door and called in two

of her slaves to carry the amphora, and then she called everyone together.

"I will not give you to Cassander, so you must either die or be freed. Those who would be made free, come and drink this wine. And with the wine, take your liberty."

Then she watched as most of her slaves came up and took the wine. She made sure that each drank the full draft. There were only three who had decided to die rather than be freed, and it was those three she would take with her down to the docks. The rest would have strange and exciting dreams before they were freed from life.

"Burn with your liberty, my children, and burn the town as well." She turned, sweeping her cloak, and slipped from the dais. It would seem almost as though she had disappeared.

It would take a while, and they would raise quite a fuss before the potion took them. The noise and the fires would help mask her escape.

Cassander noted the smoke from the city. Then, as the sun faded in the west, he could see the fires. "What has she done?"

"Olympias?" asked his brother.

"Yes. See the fires?" Cassander considered, but not for long. "We have to get into the city now."

"It's night, or it will be in minutes. Certainly before we can organize an assault."

"There's no choice. Order the men to form up."

It was, as it happened, precisely the wrong move. Olympias hadn't been able to poison the whole garrison, just her own household, and they would have been suppressed by the garrison soon enough. But with Cassander massing his army just outside the walls, the garrison couldn't be spared to fight the fires or restrain the drugged-out followers of Dionysus.

Four figures crept out onto the docks and made their way to the trireme that waited for them.

CHAPTER 31

Queen of the Sea, *Athens port at Piraeus*
November 2

The phone rang and Dag felt Roxane's elbow in his chest as she scrambled up. "Ouch. It's just the room phone." He reached over and answered it. "Hello?"

Roxane, meanwhile, pulled up the covers as if whoever was calling could see.

"Dag? Is Her Nibs there?" asked Doug Warren.

"What's up, Doug?"

"We have a ship coming in. It's a galley, one of those big ass ones with three rows of oars, and it's headed this way under full sail."

"Right. But I'm not on wa— Wait. Why do you want Roxane?"

"Hell, Dag, I don't know. Heraldry on the flags it's flying. Marie Easley said we should warn Roxane. She's talking to Cleopatra."

"Look, Doug, could you route the video to channel fifty-two?" The ship had its own video network, and that included dedicated channels that could show movies or direct feeds from cameras on the ship. Channel fifty-two was a normally empty channel that was used as needed.

Dag grabbed the remote, turned on the flat-screen TV across from the bed, and switched to channel fifty-two. He could see the ship. "Doug, you want to zoom in on the sail so we can see the heraldry?"

Roxane stared at the screen and dropped the covers.

When Dag managed to look at her face, the look on it drove all thoughts of warm embraces from his mind. "What is it?"

"Ahura Mazda! It's my mother-in-law."

"Doug, zoom in on the people standing in the bow." Dag peered more closely at the image on the screen. "That's funny, she doesn't *look* like Angelina Jolie."

"And I don't look much like Rosario Dawson and Alexander certainly didn't look like Colin Farrell! So what? That whole movie was ridiculous. Oliver Stone is—was—will be—whatever—an idiot."

The *Queen* had an extensive collection of movie recordings. By now, Roxane had watched many of them. Certainly more than Eurydice, though not as many as Philip.

Roxane, widow of Alexander the Great and now in a relationship whose nature was still undetermined with a certain Norwegian Environmental Compliance Officer, glared at the image on the screen.

"Don't let her on board," she commanded.

Dag made a face. "We can't do that, and you know it. If we start refusing sanctuary aboard the *Queen* to prominent political figures, everything will start unraveling. A good part of the reason the Convention voted to establish the USSE even though most of the delegates were skeptical it will work is because they figure if worse comes to worst they can always take refuge here."

Roxane glared at him. "She is the most evil witch in the world. She'll poison us all."

"Oh, that hardly seems likely."

Elsewhere on the ship, Alexander IV, co-ruler in name if not yet in reality of the newly established United Satrapies and States of the Empire, came to a momentous decision.

"You can be my first wife," he solemnly informed Dorothy Miller.

The imperial bride-to-be looked up from her coloring book. With equal solemnity, she pondered the proposition.

"Okay," she said. "But you have to promise never to call me 'poopy head' again. And I get to pick the ice cream flavors."

"That's not fair!" the emperor protested.

Solemnly, Dorothy pondered that proposition as well.

"Okay," she said. "You can pick them on Monday and Tuesday."

"Poopy head!"

CAST OF CHARACTERS

Abrahamson, Benyamin—Rabbi, passenger on the *Queen of the Sea*

Ahmose—Foreman for Atum Edfu

Alcetas—Officer under Eumenes, brother-in-law of Attalus

Alexander IV—Son of Alexander the Great and Roxane

Antigonus ("One-eye")—Satrap

Antipater—General for Philip II and Alexander

Argaeus of Macedonia—One of Roxane's Silver Shields

Arrhidaeus—General for Alexander the Great

Artonis—Persian wife of Eumenes

Attalus—Satrap

Atum Edfu—Merchant of Alexandria

Beaulieu, Elise—First Officer, Navigation, *Queen of the Sea*

Carruthers, Jane—Hotel manager, *Queen of the sea*

Cassander—Eldest son of Antipater

Clarke, Romi—Crewman on the *Queen of the Sea*

Cleisthenes—Merchant in Triparadisus

Cleopatra—Sister of Alexander the Great

Crates of Olynthus—Designer of the sewers of Alexandria

Dahl, Anders—Staff Captain (Executive officer), *Queen of the Sea*

Dinocrates of Rhodes—Chief Architect of Alexandria

Easley, Josette—Passenger on the *Queen of the Sea*; Marie Easley's daughter

Easley, Marie—Historian; passenger on the *Queen of the Sea*

Epicurus of Samos—Greek philosopher

Eumenes—General of Alexander; loyal to the royal family

Eurydice—Wife of Philip III

Evgenij—One of Roxane's Silver Shields

Floden, Lars—Captain of the *Queen of the Sea*

Gorgias of Thrace—One of Ptolemy's generals

Hewell, Lawrence—Baptist minister; passenger on the *Queen of the Sea*

Ithobaal—Captain of a galley out of Tyre

Jakobsen, Dag—Environmental Compliance Officer, *Queen of the Sea*

Jones, Jason—Passenger on the *Queen of the Sea*

Josephus—Hellenized Jew, guard captain of Atum Edfu

Karanos—Silver Shield; Eurydice's bodyguard

Katsaros, Panos—Crewman on the *Queen of the Sea*

Kinney, Eleanor—Chief Purser, *Queen of the Sea*

Kleitos—Commander of Roxane's personal guard

Koinos—One of Roxane's Silver Shields

Kugan, Joe—Captain of the *Reliance*

Lacula—Trader from up the Orinoco river

Lang, Daniel—Chief Security Officer, *Queen of the Sea*

Laomedon—Satrap of Syria

Lateef—Atum Edfu's wife

Menander—Satrap

Menes—Greek soldier

Metello—Carthaginian commander of naval units under
    Attalus; effectively an admiral

Miles, Laura—Chief Medical Officer, *Queen of the sea*

Miller, Amanda—Aide to Congressman Al Wiley

Mosicar—Carthaginian minor nobility, husband of the owner
    of the better part of Formentera Island

Nedelko—Commander of the Greek forces in Tyre

Olympias—Mother of Alexander the Great

Pascual, Bayani—Crewman on the *Queen of the Sea*

Peithon—Satrap

Philip III—Half-brother of Alexander the Great; husband of
    Eurydice

Philippe—Crewman on the *Queen of the Sea*

Plistarch—Son of Antipater

Polemon—Officer under Eumenes

Polyperchon—Satrap of Macedonia

Ptolemy—Satrap of Egypt

Roxane—Widow of Alexander the Great; mother of Alexander IV

Scott, Adrian—Second officer, Navigation, *Queen of the Sea*

Seiver, Keith—Crewman on the *Reliance*

Seleucus—Satrap of Babylon

Sonnenleiter, Jon—Assistant Engineer, *Queen of the Sea*

Thaïs—Hetaera; mother of Ptolemy's children

Trajan—Commander of Roxane's Silver Shields

Tyrimmas—One of Roxane's Silver Shields

Warren, Douglas—Apprentice Deck Officer, *Queen of the Sea*

Wiley, Allen ("Al")—Congressman from Utah

Yaseen, Ali—Crewman on the *Queen of the Sea*